SONG OF IRELAND

Forge Books by Juilene Osborne-McKnight

Daughter of Ireland

I Am of Irelaunde

Bright Sword of Ireland

Song of Ireland

SONG OF IRELAND

JUILENE OSBORNE-MCKNIGHT

A TOM DOHERTY ASSOCIATES BOOK
NEW YORK

SONG OF IRELAND

Map by Jonathan Bennett

A Forge Book
Published by Tom Doherty Associates, LLC
175 Fifth Avenue
New York, NY 10010

www.tor.com

Forge® is a registered trademark of Tom Doherty Associates, LLC.

Library of Congress Cataloging-in-Publication Data

Osborne-McKnight, Juilene.
    Song of Ireland / Juilene Osborne-McKnight.—1st ed.
       p. cm.
    "A Tom Doherty Associates Book."
    ISBN 0-765-31243-3
    EAN 978-0-765-31243-3
      1. Mythology, Celtic—Fiction.   2. Celts—Ireland—Fiction.   3. Fairies—Fiction.   4. Ireland—
Fiction.   I. Title.

PS3565.S455S66 2006
813'.6-dc22

                                  2005044637

First Edition: May 2006

Printed in the United States of America

0 9 8 7 6 5 4 3 2 1

This one is for Ireland, for the gift of story.

I have wandered through the ring forts at Kenmare Bay,
passed through the dolmens on the Burren,
stood in the singing wind at Tara,
pondered the ancient moon maps at Knowth.
Because Amergin gave dwelling places to the others,
magic still remains in Ireland, shimmering in the world.
May it never leave you on a wind of change.

ACKNOWLEDGMENTS

First, I would like to thank Father Caoimhin O'Neill, Father Conn O'-Maoldhomhnaigh, Dr. James Heaney, Ms. Cheri Conlon, and all of St. Patrick's Carlow College, Ireland, for reading to me in Irish, for singing to me in Irish, for hiking us to the tops of the mountains and taking us to the fairy mounds and the monasteries, for dancing, for the singing pubs, for Jameson's with red lemonade, for looking just like himself, a throwback, for adding such a layer to my life that both the book and I were reimbued with magic. Also, to Michael Norris, who got us to the ring fort on Kenmare Bay, and to Dr. Ellie Wymard of Carlow University in Pittsburgh, the Great Organizer, who is the person I would like to be when I grow up.

At Tor/Forge, I would like to thank Claire Eddy, the best editorial eye in the business, and Deborah Wood for all of her help and organizational assistance. At Curtis Brown, ongoing thanks to Maureen Walters, Dave Barbor, and Josie Schoel.

I would also like to thank my students at DeSales University, who see it all fresh, and make me laugh out loud.

Mostly I would like to thank my family and friends, who never abandon me, even though I dwell for most of each year in another time, in another language, in another world, with people who are just as real as me, but who never ever go with me to book signings, offer to do the dishes, take me out for coffee milkshakes, or pretend to be interested in hearing the stories just one more time.

Ah, now, just one more time.

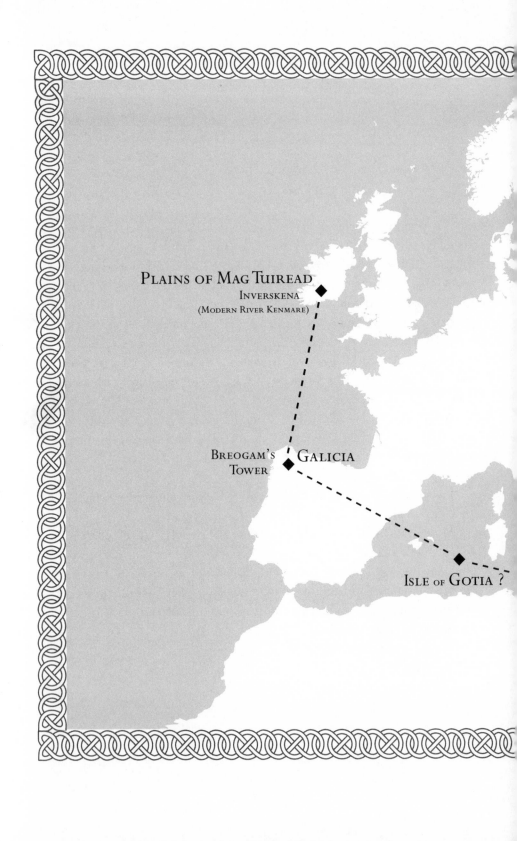

PLAINS OF MAG TUIREAD
INVERSKENA
(MODERN RIVER KENMARE)

BREOGAM'S GALICIA
TOWER

ISLE OF GOTIA ?

The Journey of the Milesians

Isle of Irena ?

Egypt

GLOSSARY AND PRONUNCIATIONS

A DANU CHARACTER AND PLACE-NAME GLOSSARY

Airmid (Air vid) Daughter of Dian Cecht in the ancient Celtic myths. He was so angry over her restoration of Nuada's arm that, in the myths, he destroyed her herb gardens, which would have healed all the illnesses of the world.

Bres (Bresh) half Fomorian, half Danu king, called "the Beautiful" for his physical appearance. One of the original traitors in Irish mythology.

Dagda (as spelled) Called the "good god" in later versions of the myth, "good" meaning provider. In many versions of the myth, Dagda is a giant who drags a huge club behind him and possesses a giant cauldron sunk into the earth and constantly replenished with food so that the Danu will never go hungry.

Danu (Da noo) This is the tribe of the goddess Danu. They are also called the **Danaan** of the **Tuatha de Danaan** (Too a ha day dan an), or the tribe of the Danaan. They became both the panoply of gods in ancient Celtic Ireland and the **sidhe** (shee), or "others," who are also called the "little people."

Dian Cecht (Deean Kecht) Original physician of the Danu, he killed his son Miach and destroyed the herb garden of his daughter Airmid in his anger over their restoration of Nuada's biological arm.

Fir Bolg (as spelled) One of the five original races of Ireland, supposedly a Stone Age hunter-gatherer people who were the ancestors of Connachtsmen.

Fomor (Fovor) Also Fomorians. Supposedly these dark and terrifying sea raiders had their stronghold on an island off the coast of Ireland called Tor Mor (Great Rock) or Tober Mor. No one knows who they were.

Lugh (Loo) Lugh is the son of the Sun, the all-powerful male god figure of the Danaan myths. His origins are unclear; some versions of the myth have him as the son of the Dagda, others of a half-human, half-Danaan liaison. **Lamfhada** (Lam fa da) is his "Long-Arm" designator, evidently from his skill with a spear. **Ildanach** (Ill da nok) is his "All-Craftsman" appellation, from the myth in which he wins over the Danaan by being good at everything.

Mag Tuiread (Moy Teera) Three battles take place on the Plains of Mag Tuiread, and a variety of places in Ireland claim themselves as the location. (See "Historical and Mythological Background"). Wherever these battles took place, there must have been multiple monoliths and sarsen circles there, because the name means Many Towers.

Miach (mee ak) Son of Dian Cecht and a physician himself, he restores Nuada's biological arm. Some versions of the myths say that his father killed him because he was jealous of his son's higher medical skills.

Morrigu (Mor ee goo) The Morrigu is a triad, a form that seemed to be essential to the ancient Celtic myths. Each of the three sisters of this triad performs a specific function.

>   **Macha** (Ma ha) is the shape-shifter and evidently the intellect of the triad.

>   **Banbh** (Ban ev) is the carrion crow. She encourages war so that she can feed on the dead from the battlefield.

>   **Nemhain** (Nev in or Ne whain) She is the sower of chaos and panic.

Nuada Argetlamh (Noo a da Ar get lav) First "king" of the Danu, his arm was hacked off in battle with the Fir Bolg, replaced by a Silver Arm, and restored as a biological arm in time for the battle with the Fomor in which Nuada was killed.

The Three Sisters In the ancient myths, pre–Milesian Ireland was ruled over by triads, first three men—Mac Cuill, Mac Cecht, and Mac Grene—and then three sisters—**Banba** (as spelled), **Fodla** (as spelled), and **Eriu** (air ee oo). The sisters encounter the sons of Mil; Eriu predicts that they will rule in Ireland forever, the sons of Mil name the island Eire in honor of her.

A GALAECI CHARACTER AND PLACE-NAME GLOSSARY

An Scail (an skel) While it means the Shadow or the Ghost, An Scail represents the druidic presence among the ancient Celts. Druids were highly learned professorial characters who kept the history, knowledge, and theology of the tribes. Many sources say that druids existed at three levels: those who were essentially priests, those who were what we would term professors, and those who served as poets or bards, keeping, telling, and passing the history of the tribes from one generation to another. At any of these levels, druids could be considered **ollamh** (ol lam) or master. Once the Milesians were settled in Ireland, poets possessed particularly high status, second only to that of the king.

Breogam (broc em) The ancestor of the sons of Mil, who built the first lighthouse on the seacoast of Galicia in Spain. Although a Roman tower stands in this location now, Breogam was supposedly the founder of the Celtic city of Brigantia, that is now called La Coruña, on the northwest coast of Spain.

Galaeci/Galicia The Galaeci were a tribe, clan, or collection of clans in northwestern Celtic Spain, around 500 BC. That region, known today as Galicia, is still Celtic in its topography, archaeology, climate, and mind-set.

Inisfail (as spelled) The Galaeci name for Ireland; they translate it as Isle of Destiny. In actual translation from the Irish it means something like Island of Getting or Finding.

Ith (as spelled) In the legends, Ith is the brother (or uncle) of Mil, who serves as the scouting party for the Milesians on the first trip to Ireland.

Skena (skee na) Supposedly the first wife of Amergin; she drowned en route to Ireland.

Sons of Mil Mil is variously known as Milesios, Mile Easpain, and Golamh (his original Galician Celtic name). He was married first to Seang, with whom he had two sons, and later to Scota, daughter of the pharaoh of Egypt, with whom he had five to seven sons. These legendary travelers are the Jason and the Argonauts of Celtic mythology. Some versions of the legend list them as nine sons, some as seven.

> **Amergin** (A ver geen) Probably originally spelled Amhairghin. The most famous of the sons of Mil, he was bard, poet, or **ollamh** (master). To be ollamh (ol lam) in a Celtic tribe was to be

13

master of the word. Such a person had tremendous power in the tribe and could rule on matters of war and battle. There are hundreds of translations of his poems, of which we have two or possibly three, depending on the translations.

Airioch Feabhruadh (Air ee ok Fev roo ahd) Mentioned in some of the versions of the myth as being one of the two sons of Mil by his first wife, Seang of Scythia.

Bile (Beel ya) In some of the myths listed as a son of Mil, in others, variously, as Mil's brother, uncle, father, or grandfather.

Colpa (as spelled).

Eber Donn (Ever Don) Son of Mil by his first wife, Seang of Scythia.

Eber Finn (Ever Fin) In the legends, went to war against his brother Eremon because his wife wanted Eremon's land.

Eremon (Air e mon) First king of Ireland, who supposedly began the construction of the Hill of Tara, although, in terms of artifacts, the hill probably dates to about 95 BC.

Ir (eer).

GAELIC TERMINOLOGY

Aither (a her) father.

An Corr (as spelled) Also called the **corrguinecht** (cor gwee nect), it means the "crane-wounding." Evidently it is some kind of martial art in which the warrior stands on a single leg and then launches forward.

Buiochas le cruthú (bwee e has le croo hoo) Blessed be Creation.

Ceolas (kee yol as) Music maker or song maker.

Coracle (as spelled) A round boat made of hide stretched on a wickerwork frame. Extremely difficult to maneuver because it is round.

Curragh (cur a) Long hide boats still used in Ireland today.

Eistigi (esh te gi) The command form of Listen!

Erbe ndruad (as spelled) A druid fence. Once pronounced by a poet, this imaginary fence could not be crossed, even in battle.

Fanacht le solas (as spelled) Wait upon the light. Ancient Celtic myth is replete with references to the light, sometimes as in the Sun, sometimes in a much larger concept that seems to signify the All-Good or the All-Knowing or the Source.

Fidchell (fid kell) Ancient Celtic chess.

Fulacht fiadh (foo lact fee ahd) A pit lined with hot stones in which the ancient Celts cooked both meat and fish. Remnants of these pits have been found in many Celtic locations, including Ireland.

Gaeilge (gale ge) There are six Gaelic languages: Irish, Scots, and Manx, called q-Goidelic and believed to be the older form of Gaelic; and Welsh, Cornish, and Breton, called p-Goidelic, or Brythonic Gaelic and believed to be a later alteration of the language. There was, of course, an original Proto-Celtic language, and many scholars now see links between that language and Proto–Indo-European or Italic, the precursor to Latin. Other scholars claim links between Celtic and ancient Hindu-Sanskrit.

Gaimred (gaiv roo) Cold season, November 1 to May 1.

Gaita (ga ta or guy ta) Spanish bagpipes. Listen to Carlos Nunez.

Gutruatri (goo troo a tree) A Milesian Celtic druid who is a singer of praise to God.

Keltoi (kel toy) This is the Greek name for the ancient Celts. The Romans called them the **Gauls** or the **Gaels.**

Lughnasa (loo na sa) The Celtic summer festival, which took place on August 1. A celebration of the warm season, of crops being in the ground, of life in general. This festival may actually have been named for Lugh.

Maither (ma her) mother.

Mo ghra (mow graw) my beloved.

Na biodh eagla ort (Na viod egla ort) Be not afraid.

Ogham (om) The Ancient Celtic stick language. It consists of a horizontal or vertical bar over which sticks are incised in various combinations. Evidently, it was a language used primarily by initiates, i.e., druids.

Ollamh (ol lam) master. Used to refer to a variety of druids, also physicians, judges, and lawyers who had achieved the top of their profession.

Samhain (sau win) The evening of October 31, the turning from the warm part of the year to the cold season. This was considered the beginning of the New Year and was an extremely dangerous time in the Celtic world because, the Celts believed, the doorway between this world and the otherworld is very thin on this night. Samhain eventually became All Hallows' Eve or Halloween.

Samhradh (sau roo) The warm season, May 1 to November 1. Summer.

Tir Nan Og (teer na nog) Variously called Mag Mell, the Island of the Ever Young, the Country of the Young, and in later myths, Avalon. This concept pervades the Celtic world; ships of light will carry the departing soul into the west, where he will be young and happy in a place of feasting and music, until he is ready to return, or is asked to return.

pROLOGUE

Near the water's edge, where the sea had thrown up round, speckled stones, Eriu halted. Behind her, her sisters stopped, Banba at her right shoulder, Fodla at her left. Mist from the sea dusted through the air, fell in crystalline drops on Eriu's long copper curls, lighted like flickering gems on the black thickness of Banba's hair, vanished into the white-gold mane of Fodla. Eriu sighed. The stones, the mist, the long green sweep to the sea. How she would miss it all. She sighed again, a long, deep exhalation. Nothing would stop what was to come.

"I will look for them now," she said to her sisters.

Without even turning, she felt them close in behind her, form the perfect triangle, heard the soft reedy chant that issued from deep in their throats.

Eriu held her arms before her, formed her fingers in the triangle, symbol for the Journey. Next, she raised both hands with fingers spread, for the children of Maker in infinite variety. Finally, she placed her hands upright and palm to palm, then interlaced the fingers, turning her hands in opposite directions to symbolize the Braid.

"Mother," she whispered, "clear my sight that I may see, clear my mind that I may understand, clear my spirit that I may choose wisely for my people."

She closed her eyes, placed her palms together parallel to the ground, then thrust them forward like the prow of a ship. She followed their line in her mind, out, out, over the waters and south.

Nothing.

Not even the vision of the coastline of the great continent came to mind. She drew her hands back in, repeated her gesture, tried again.

Still nothing.

Eriu opened her eyes.

"What do you see?" asked Banba, impatient as always.

"Nothing."

"But how can that be? You saw them when Ith first came among us."

"I do not know. I thought that I saw them once again, after Ith departed from us, but now their ships are obscured in mist. Now I cannot see anything at all."

"Well, what on the Green Orb is wrong with you? Your vision never fails you! The Danu rely upon it. Upon you."

"Banba, when Ith came among us more than a year ago, I had not used my Journey vision for more than five hundred years. How should we know if it fails me or not? Ith promised us that he would try to persuade them not to return once he understood clearly who we were and from whence we came; I took him to be a man of his word. I sent his people the message of his return with its veiled warning. Why would I need my Journey vision for a people who promised us that they would not return? That is why I asked you to help me. Perhaps I only imagined a returning fleet, or dreamed it, an anomaly of vision that has seen nothing but the sea for centuries of their time. Perhaps there are no ships on the water, or, if there are, it is a fleet of some other country, going somewhere else and not to the Green Isle after all."

She sighed and sat down hard on the bank. Oh, if only that could be true.

From behind her Fodla spoke in her voice like soft wind.

"There is another possibility, Sisters."

Eriu turned toward her sisters, who now sat opposite her, forming a triangle. Fodla was, as always, the voice of quiet reason.

"The Council recommended that all of us adopt the Metaphor again, as we did with Ith and the brothers. And so we have. Perhaps the Metaphor prevents the vision from congealing, because in it, we are not our true selves."

Banba shook her head impatiently. "For Danu's sake, Fodla. We have used the Metaphor for five centuries when we have approached the Fir Bolg who dwell here in the western bogs. Have we ever frightened the Fir

Bolg? And they are known for being easily frightened. The bogs in which they dwell may well describe their entire thought process. Has the Metaphor ever prevented us from interacting with them?"

"You do not hear me, Banba," said Fodla quietly. "I do not say that the Metaphor is a bad choice. All who dwell on the Green Orb would be frightened by our true appearance. And the Fir Bolg are known for being easily frightened. But we have never attempted vision in the Metaphor. Perhaps it blocks our ability to see."

Eriu nodded. "I think Fodla is wise. How can we look out into the future if we are not who we are?"

Banba shook her head emphatically. "We dare not abandon it. The Council has said that we must all practice the Metaphor until we can keep it in place, until no slipping occurs. These who come will be travelers, the clan of Ith. Unlike the Fir Bolg, they will have gone beyond the bogs. These new travelers may be more sophisticated. They may well know the Greeks!"

Fodla laughed. "Admit it, Sister. You find the Greek Metaphor beautiful. You like to look like a tall Greek woman with sweeping hair. You liked the one who came among us who looked like a Greek. Airioch Feabhruadh. Speak the Truth. You like the appearance of the humans."

Banba snorted, but she cast a sidelong smile at Fodla. "They are beautiful, these creatures, with their long limbs and their thick hair and their eyes like interior rainbows."

"You are beautiful too, Sister, just as you are."

"Fodla, you love the humans too. I have seen your gentle care of the Fir Bolg."

"They are like little children, so trusting, their sweet gratitude for the smallest binding of wounds, the simplest medicaments for their children. How do they see us, do you suppose?"

"As gods," said Eriu.

Banba and Fodla gasped as one.

"I mean no sacrilege, Sisters. This is how they speak of us. We are the gods of the place. Illyn has told me this."

"Then Danu forgive us," said Fodla. "For there is only one Weaver of the Braid."

"But how would we explain that to children such as these? These are not the Greeks."

"Ah," said Banba. "You see, Fodla. Eriu loved the Greeks as well."

"I did love them," Eriu said, lifting her chin. "How well their spirits contended citizenship, the nature of the state, the purpose of man, the choices of good and evil. Their minds turned on all the great questions, and so often they came right to the core of the argument. They were minds of great sophistication, spirits of great striving. And we could not have chosen a better place than the Greek Isles for our first dwelling place when we arrived here on the Green Orb."

"And yet when the Metaphor slipped and some of the Greeks saw us as we truly are, all their sophistication left them. They were as terrified as these Fir Bolg would be," said Banba.

"Illyn says that the Fir Bolg might be less terrified to see us true. She makes a good point that the Greeks were so sophisticated that they had an expectation for the behavior of the world. Our appearance violated that expectation. Hence their terror. But the Fir Bolg think in small bursts and dwell in darkness and superstition. Our true appearance might be less frightening to them."

"And what of these new ones who come?" asked Fodla.

"I know not," Eriu answered. "I saw ships. Greek biremes. Accompanied by cargo ships. Hired ships for traveling great distances. I did not see those who manned them. Nor those who visited us before."

"Still, we raise interesting questions Sisters," Banba interrupted. "Where shall we tell them we are from? Metaphor or no, our appearance here, the apparent sophistication of our civilization, will surprise them."

"We shall say we are from Greece," said Fodla.

Eriu nodded. "It is not untrue, after all. It was the most recent stop on our journey. And the Metaphor emulates the people of that country."

"And what of those like Illyn? How shall we explain them?" Banba raised her fingers, one at a time. "First these were human. Then we altered their braiding. Now they are Hybrids. No human in all the history of the Green Orb could comprehend such a thing."

Fodla shook her head. "Banba, what would you have had us do? When the Fir Bolg left their cripples and their sickling infants on the hills to die, should we have walked past them in the darkness, shrugged our shoulders? All life is of the Braid, and our physicians have the knowledge to make them well and whole. Sometimes that required rebraiding. The Hybrids who resulted are a joy among us."

"And what of our own Raveners? How shall we explain them?"

"Their darkness came within them, surely," said Fodla. "As it will undoubtedly come with the Invaders. Perhaps they will understand our Raveners best of all."

Eriu sighed. "Sisters, you debate well, and as always I thank you for your clear articulation. But we will not answer all of these questions today."

Banba and Fodla grew silent, knowing that Eriu was about to choose.

"I think that perhaps Fodla was right. It is the Metaphor which stops the vision. To see well and truly we must stand before Maker as she made us."

No argument ensued. The sisters simply stood together and turned toward the sea, forming again the triangle with Eriu at its prow.

"Sisters, remove the Metaphor," Eriu commanded softly.

As one, the three sisters touched the luminous crystal triangles with their twining spiral vines, that dangled as pendants around their necks.

There was a flashing snap of blue light. The air around the threesome congealed and grew viscous. Tiny sparkles of light and color coalesced and then dispersed. Standing on the shore were three beings who could never be mistaken for human. Their slender bodies did not look strong enough to support the weight of their large heads, of their huge oval eyes colored the deep blue-gray of the sea. Their warm golden skin was luminous, as if an aura of soft blue and gold light, constantly changing and sparkling, surrounded their little frames. Their ears folded back and up in a shape like the feathers of a bird's wing. Soft tufts of silver hair grew from each sharp triangle of bone. Around their skulls, a cloudy cap of silver-white curls seemed to catch the light in blue and gold, no more substantial than a mist upon the sea. Their mouths were their most human feature, for their lips were full and rosy and seemed curved into a permanent expression of joy. An observer might have guessed at gender, but their own people would have known them as female by their long, slender hands and delicate fingers, by the soft feathering at their ears.

From Banba and Fodla issued the deep sustained sound of the chant, the base note for Vision. Again, Eriu made the signs, Triangle, Children, Braid. Again she placed her palms parallel to the ground and sent them before her like the prow of a ship. Over the water. South and south.

And there! Seven great ships with sails unfurled. Greek biremes with the forward square sails. Cargo ships. Not hugging the coast as the non-seafaring people did but dipping and heaving, fearless in the open sea.

Destination, she must find destination.

Ith had said that they would not return; she had known him to be a man of honor. So who were these approaching travelers?

With her hands she navigated, deck to deck. Huge men, more than six feet tall. Long, braided hair. Bearded and laughing. Shouting to each other. Weapons at their belts. Women, tall and broad of shoulder, their braided hair festooned with bells. How lovely the sound in the wind! And on their backs, great swords, tall and broad. Swords down the backs of the women! No, these were not the Greeks, these loud and massive voyagers. Nor were these like the simple Fir Bolg who dwelled in the stony boglands of the Green Island. These were warrior people. Eriu shuddered. Warrior people. Against her people, who had not made war for five hundred years. Who had put away Nuada's Silver Arm. She searched among the voyagers. Was Ith among them? Or Airioch, who had made her so wary with his wandering and his watchful eyes? Was there anywhere a sign that her Green Isle was their destination? What made her think it so?

Again she navigated her hands, back to the last large ship of the fleet. Seated in the stern, a huge man, unbearded, dark hair spilling behind him in the wind. Alone. Upon him the mark of the outsider, the dreamer. Before him a map. Crudely drawn and raw, but clearly marked. The starting point on the peninsula in the south, the long coast, the island to their east, the Green Isle.

Eriu closed her eyes. There was no mistaking the map. Would her people die? Where would they go? Would any choose for war, call for the use of Nuada's Silver Arm? O Weaver of Worlds! The children of the Braid should not make war! So great grew her terror that it began to affect the chant of her sisters. It raced among the ships; some of the sailors, always superstitious, looked behind them or shaded their eyes at the sea ahead. Eriu drew a deep breath. She must not make them aware; they must not sense the presence of the Danu here on the Green Isle. Her people must have time to prepare.

Eriu opened her eyes. The one with the map was looking in her direction.

No!

She pulled her hands back, began the slow withdrawal of the vision.

He stood, stepped forward. His dark eyes fastened on her own.

By the Danu!

This one could see her. And not in Metaphor. He kept his eyes locked to hers. He lifted the map, pointed to the Green Isle. He was waiting for her to nod, to confirm, to tell him that yes, they were here, waiting. Her heart beat so fast that it felt as if it would burst out of her chest wall.

Another man approached across the deck of the ship.

"Amergin! What are you staring at now?"

It was Airioch Feabhruadh, he who had come with Ith! Then this was Amergin, the nephew Ith had spoken of with such obvious love.

Amergin broke gaze with her. "Staring?"

"We need you to watch the sea, look for the coastline, interpret the map. This is not the time for one of your strange fugues. There will be plenty of time for that on the Green Isle."

Amergin nodded.

Eriu blessed the Danu for the distraction. She withdrew her hands, navigated backward toward safety, toward the sweet ground beneath her feet. She brought her palms in against her chest, cradled them in a gesture of thanks to Maker, closed her eyes, and dropped to the ground.

"Resume the Metaphor," Banba commanded.

"Sister, she cannot. She trembles and is weak as a child." Fodla rushed to cradle Eriu in her arms. "Hush now, hush."

Banba knelt next to them. "Tell us what you saw. Now."

"There are seven ships. Airioch Feabhruadh is with them. The nephew of Ith."

"He who tried to enter our cities?"

"The very one."

"Was Ith among them?" asked Fodla.

"I did not see him."

"Then surely we are doomed," said Banba.

"Doomed I cannot say, but surely we must consider it an invasion force. They are garbed as warriors."

Eriu fell silent; her eyes were thoughtful and clouded.

"There is more," said Fodla.

"There is," said Eriu, "but I do not know what to make of it."

"Tell us, and we will bring the wisdom of three upon it."

"There was one who saw me."

"Saw you? In vision? Not possible," said Banba.

"Yet it was so, Sisters. It was Amergin, he of whom Ith so often spoke."

"He saw you this way, without Metaphor?"

"So he did, and that was the strangest thing of all. He looked directly into my eyes. He saw me true and he did not look away."

PART ONE

AM GA'ETH
TAR NA BHFARRAIGE

I AM THE
WIND ON THE SEA

I am the stag of seven tines ...
I am a flood on the plain ...
I am a wind on deep water ...
I am a tear from the sun ...
I am a hawk on a cliff ...
I am the fairest of flowers ...
I am the god who fires the mind ...
I am the spear of battle ...
I am the lake of the salmon ...
I am a hill where poets walk ...
I am a wild boar ...
I am the roar of the sea ...
Who but i knows the secrets of the dolmen?

THE SONG OF AMERGIN

1

My father was ever a wanderer. Even in my earliest, unformed memories of him, he is always standing on some parapet or framed in the embrasure of a tower of Egypt. Even now, I see his cloak blowing back in the wind, his gaze fixed west and north, the long thickness of his chestnut mane twisting against the bunched cloak as he pondered the distance. I can hear the dry rattle of the palm fronds and feel the constant friction of the wind-borne sand of Egypt, gritty against my skin.

Though I was my father's fifth son of two wives, with more still to brood in my mother's womb cradle, it was with me that he shared his vision of a magical journey. He would hold me up to the window, close his eyes to the breeze.

"Inisfail," he would say. "The Isle of Destiny. I smell her on the breeze, lad. I see her in my dreams."

"How do you know of her?"

"She is in the legends of my people. The people of Galicia. Inisfail, the Isle where dwell the Magic People. They say that he who finds her will be gifted with their magic. But in all my wanderings, I have never found her."

Usually, his dreams of Inisfail were the sure sign that soon we would be wandering again, so that by the time I reached my fifteenth year, I had been already to Rhatokis on our north coast, to the Greek democracy more than once, and even to the newly minted republic of Rome, though my father was not of any of those countries.

My father had begun his life as Golamh, son of Bile, the great chief of the Galaeci. Our tribe dwelled in the town of Brigantia in the far west of

Spain, in the region called Galicia for the people of our tribe. My father had described it to me as a soft and rainy country, itself green. I must admit that when the sands of Egypt blew against the sky, I often longed for Galicia, though perhaps it was only my father's love of the place and my worshipful love of him. The tales said that our people had wandered there to the edge of the sea centuries before. Perhaps our ancestors too were searching for the Isle of Destiny, but knew not how to find it when they reached the edge of the water.

For them, my grandfather, Breogam, had built the tall, slender broch that stood by the sea and placed into it the Eternal Flame. My father referred to it always as Breogam's Light Tower. Though my father had grown up in Galicia, even my elder brothers had never seen the place at all, though truly we had all caught the wandering disease.

For my older brothers Eber Finn and Eremon, it took the form of land longing.

"When I have my own parcel," Eber Finn would say, and Eremon would chime in, "I will fill it with grazing cattle as far as the eye can see."

For my eldest brother, Eber Donn, the sickness took the form of acquisition. What he needed or what he wanted he took, be it women or wine, land or weapons. To be truthful, women seemed to sense the hunger in him and rushed to fill it. By the time I had a mere eight years, he was possessed of three handsome wives whom he pleasured together and separately, much to the envious jesting of Eber Finn and Eremon, who possessed only one wife each.

Eber Donn was the son of my father's first wife, the long departed Seang, daughter of the king of Scythia. There my father had first taken service when he was a young man. So powerful a soldier was he, so vital to the king, that he became known as Mile Easpain, Soldier of Spain, and he captained the armies of that country.

But when Seang died in the birthing of my second brother, Airioch Feabhruadh, the king of Scythia was racked with grief and took against my father for the womb-death of his daughter. My father fled to Egypt and there took service with the army of the Pharaoh Mesuti Ra. There, he met my mother Scota, daughter of Pharaoh. Though my mother was a strong and beautiful woman, she was no woman of Egypt. Mesuti Ra, my grandfather, began his life as Cambysis of Persia. Never satisfied with single conquest, Cambysis resigned his position as king of Babylon to invade and conquer Egypt and to name himself after the sun god Ra. He died before my birth, leaving my father to serve his cousin Darius, ruler of Persia and Egypt.

Though my mother seemed always to be bearing, as fertile as the delta of the Nile, she was ever a warrior woman and so beautiful. Her hair was glossy and dark, her skin smooth, her black eyes huge, and her body strong. From her, my father had first Eber Finn, then Eremon, then me. One brother died soon after his birth when I had but six years. When I had ten years, she gave birth to my little brother Bile in the dark hours of the night. Though she had women aplenty to assist her, she rose and washed both herself and the babe and suckled him. Before she slept, she handed him not to her women, but to me. In the dark of the night, rocking my baby brother, something fierce and loving arose in me for the first time. In the morning, she dressed them both, slung Bile into a hip bag, and went about the business of the day. My father called her fearsome strong, and that was so. For me, I longed for the babe all day, and though I was only ten, felt sick with shame that a man should be so besotted of a child. I knew that my warrior brothers and even my father would pay him no mind until he could fight, until he could take to horse and ride.

In me, the wandering sickness had taken a stranger form than in my brothers, a great, vast longing that would not be satisfied by land or palaces or having. I eschewed them all. Sometimes I felt that the things of this world could all pass away, but I would still be present, my eyes looking, my ears listening.

So I looked in the eyes of everyone I met, seeking something, I knew not what. A port? A tower and a light? Magical people on a fabled isle? Perhaps it was simply belonging I sought, for I knew myself to be different, surely, from my brothers. I could not have said myself what I sought. I became a watcher of humanity. I knew that I made people fearful, that the directness of my probative gaze made them squirm. Among our people, some came to believe that I could read them, could see the tale inside. Since many of them had secrets they wished to hide, many avoided me. They should not have worried; what I looked for I found in no one. Though I tried to train myself away from staring, I could not, and eventually it came to pass that I did indeed find myself reading their stories, their jealousies

29

and hopes, their aggravations, in the tilt of a head, in the woman their eyes followed, in the cross of the arms, in the sighs or laughter which coalesced around them. There was no magic to it, only the wisdom that one who watches and listens accrues.

Even my own brothers, though they would clap me on the shoulder or grasp my forearm in the soldiers' way, would not look at my eyes. Only little Bile saw to the core of me, and by the time I was twelve he was my constant companion, swinging up into my arms, laughing aloud when he met my eyes, placing his chubby hands against my cheeks.

So, in my awkwardness, I became like the sponges that the Greek sailors would bring us from the sea. I listened to the words that everyone spoke around me, learned the languages of Greeks and Phoenicians, of Romans and Egyptians, badgered my father and mother for the languages of their homelands. I collected people through their stories and their behaviors and told myself the tales of their travels. In the stories, I belonged.

At last my father must have realized my strangeness, and in my twelfth year he put me into the bardic training with his brother Ith, the druid, who was a teacher and a gutruatri, a singer of praise to God.

Ith taught me how to drift on the pool of silence, how to dwell in the great stillness that permitted me to hear, to reflect, to sink into deep knowing. From him too I learned the language of our homeland and all its tales and poems. It was Ith who gave me my first and most beloved clarsach, the harp I called Ceolas, the Song, and Ith who taught me the mournful gaita, the bagpipe of our people.

Still, in all my training, I never once saw what I sought, never once met the eyes of anyone who reflected either my music or my stillness back to me. Only my little brother Bile seemed to me to be tethered to my soul by an invisible rope. I came to think of myself as dwelling in the great alone; only the poems and the tales filled the well of my longing. So I took to the bardic life as the wind takes to the sea, pouring out stories until the stories became my coin; all demanded them of me; all took delight in them despite my seeming strangeness.

And then I began to have the dream. I was standing at the prow of a ship, a Greek bireme, laden with cargo. I looked out to the north. It was as if I sped across the water then, my own body a sail. There in the sea rose a blue and green land, the rain misting across it, high cliffs spilling to the sea. I looked into the eyes of something, someone, I know not what. They were ovoid and huge, gray as the water, deep as the sea. I saw nothing else but the eyes. A voice said, "Poet, we of the Braid have been expecting you," but it was no voice, no language that I knew. Still, it centered me, like the polestar the sailors follow.

And then I would awake, words threading and weaving in my head for weeks, composing in the darkness, trying to capture the voice and the place of the dream, trying to move the poem into the deep stream of memory. At last, with much trying and rewording, I captured it, the elusive country my father had spoken of so often. My song would be my gift to him. I had thought that would be the end of it then, that my mind would move to other subjects, begin to compose new tellings, as it had always done before. I was wrong.

It was the month when the light grows short and we were sailing on the Nile, on one of my father's rare holidays from duty. The green fields stretched away from the broad, flat river, and the sunlight splintered the water into stars. I was in my fifteenth year then. My brothers, all but Bile, had been left behind for this trip, all of them being men about their business, so I would not be subjected to their constant jibes about their strange brother, dreaming words into the world. I was glad of that, for on this day, I would give my father the gift of the poem of Inisfail. Bile wandered the boat on his sturdy five-year-old legs, occasionally stopping to smile sweetly when I played some song that he particularly loved, placing his chubby hands on my knees.

I remember that the breeze danced across the deck as I tuned up Ceolas. Strangely, the wind smelled like rain. And I began to sing.

CEOLAS SINGS OF INISFAIL
Green is my longing, Inisfail
Isle of Destiny, northern diadem.
Why do you call to me?
How shall I sing them,
sloe-eyed creatures at your shore?
Do you await me, Inisfail?
Country of my dreams;
I am Amergin, son of Mil,
warrior, wanderer.

Dream of the father now become
the harpsong of the son.
Inisfail, land of mystery,
Sing to me.

I got no further. My father stood abruptly in the boat. He stared into the sky. I followed his gaze.

The sun had begun to darken, a wedge of it obscured by a crescent of darkness.

My mother screamed aloud. She rushed for Bile, pressed his head against her shoulder. He began to cry in terror.

"Do not look at it!" she cried. "Do not look! I have heard tales of this; to see the darkness will make you blind."

We dropped to the deck of the boat, curled in upon ourselves. My father wrapped his body around my mother and Bile. Our sailman began to weep aloud and to call up Ra, the sun god, to deliver us. He released the tiller and fell to the deck, repeatedly touching his head to the boards. Our little boat slewed wildly, the wind filling the sails, no hand on the tiller.

I leaped to the tiller and trimmed the sail, but I took my mother's advice and kept my eyes on the deck. Darkness came across it like a shadow; my heart filled with dread. For a few moments, I sailed on what seemed to me the river of death, no light, no color, and then a wedge of color reappeared upon the water.

"Look!" I cried. "The light returns!"

My father looked up; he rose and glanced into the sky, albeit obliquely.

"We will journey," he said to my mother. "We will leave Egypt."

She did not hesitate, nor did she argue.

Though she barely crested five feet and though she was heavy with bearing yet again, I remember that she stood and tilted her chin, all the way to my father's six-foot height.

"To Inisfail?" she asked, and her voice was soft with something that sounded like wonder. I remember thinking that the idea was not new to her, not strange or unwanted.

But my father shook his head.

"No. First we go home. Across the mountains to Galicia. First we must gather the clans."

The light returned to its full strength, dancing across the water. My father nodded in certainty.

"Amergin has sung us to it. Did you say north, boy?"

I nodded.

"How do you know this?"

"It is what I dreamed. It is what Ceolas permitted me to sing."

He shook his head. "North. All these years. North. I thought that I would find them in the Internal Sea." He seemed to muse for a moment, then shook his head. "Perhaps that is why my grandfather built the tower. I have been a fool then. All the while it was before me." He shrugged, then nodded. "The sun was the sign. We go first to Galicia. From there we sail north. Amergin has sung it." He clapped me on the shoulder.

Bile must have sensed the adventure. He ran between Scota and Mil, and when they paid him no mind, he dashed to me and lifted up his arms. I scooped him up.

Father turned toward our oarsman.

"Make to the shore, Aknet," he called. "We must prepare our horses and our wagons."

Perhaps I should have been afraid at all that we were leaving, afraid of the loss of all that I had known. But I was not. Instead I felt a surge of joy as visceral as light.

Perhaps at last I would find the place that I could belong.

2

"Why does our brother Airioch's shadow grow large?" asked Bile.

I looked up from where I was working with my uncle Ith, memorizing star maps. Far below, my brother Airioch was climbing the hill toward us, his cloak billowing around him in the island wind.

"It is large because he is so tall." I turned to my uncle Ith. "See where he comes. Perhaps he brings news that we will depart again."

My uncle looked toward the approaching figure of my half brother. His face, which had been rapt on the star maps, shuttered a little and seemed to grow cautious. He sucked in at the sides of his cheeks.

"Perhaps," he answered.

We were on the isle of Gotia, in the second year of our journey.

Though we had traveled on Greek cargo ships, though we were burdened with horses and wagons, with women and squalling children and shamefaced soldiers who were green with the sickness of the sea, the two years of our journey had for me the feel of great wandering, an epic of the Galaeci.

CEOLAS WANDERS
Who dwelled here
on the isles of the Inner Sea
among the stone pillars
in the shimmering temples?
It was the ancient ones,

the keepers of the white city
beneath the sea.

I plucked gently at Ceolas and considered the journey. In truth, it should not have taken us two years to cross the great sea that the Romans call the Internum Mare, the Inner Sea. My father scornfully called it the Little Water and kept telling us to prepare ourselves for the great Atlantic Sea, but we had no comparison. To us it was sea enough and more.

Fortunately for the stomachs of the soldiers, our journey was broken up by Scota's pregnancies.

We stopped first at the island of Irena near Thrace so that my mother could give birth to my brother Ir. There we set up camp and lived in our circled wagons with their curved tops; though they were minuscule compared to the palaces of Egypt, we were happy. At night by the fires, I sang the stories of our journey, and all of my brothers and their wives would call out the additions to the tales.

Little Bile would stay beside me, and one night he surprised all of us by taking up the harmony and singing with me in counterpart. From that night forward, my brothers' wives would have none but that he should sing with me, and he flourished happily under the attention of all the women.

We took to sea again when six weeks' time had passed, but before long my mother was with child again and sick of a morning, so we spent the whole of her pregnancy on the isle of Gotia, where my brother Colpa was born.

We were nearing Spain by then and isles grew greener, their stands of forest thicker. This filled my uncle Ith with joy, for as all the Keltoi well know, forests are the sacred places of the gods. There on Gotia, at the crest of a great hill, my uncle had found a sort of temple made of circled stones and surrounded by great cedar trees. He pronounced it to be one of the sacred circles of our Old Ones, the StarWise Druii. In the center of that ancient circle he had set up our traveling pole of oak with its carvings of birds and leaping deer, of animals that those of us who had been born in Egypt and Scythia had never seen.

Daily Uncle Ith and I began the mornings there, his arms outstretched in prayer, a look of sublime joy on his face as he tilted his visage upward with the rising light. There he began to train me in star maps and the movement of light across the pairs of stones, in the families of the gods, in more stories of our tribe. I could see in him the great joy of anticipation, the gladness that he would soon be home.

Little Bile accompanied us to the stone-and-cedar circle, my mother being occupied with Ir and with the suckling of her newest babe. To distract Bile and his seven years while we worked on our lessons, Uncle Ith had given him Egyptian parchment, with a little collection of paints and pots. He had become an artist of some little skill, capturing ships and sails, birds, and even the faces of our clan.

Now my uncle Ith looked up at the approaching form of Airioch and then down at the drawing by my little brother. Though Bile had well captured Airioch's tall, rangy form, the golden hair that fell constantly forward over his eyes, Airioch's form was surrounded by a smudgy nimbus of gray.

"This is what he does," I whispered to Ith. "His humans . . . billow, in various colors. Their edges are never sharp."

"Hmm." Ith looked down the hill at the approaching form of Airioch. "Bile," he said, sharply.

My little brother looked up at him.

"What mean you with the shadow of Airioch? I see his shadow before him on the ground, long and thin, the morning sun behind him."

Bile smiled happily. "Not his sun-shadow, Wise One. His other shadow. The one that comes from his body. It grows larger than once it was."

Ith regarded Bile seriously. "Can you describe it to me?"

"It is not the same as yours."

"As mine?"

"Yours is gold, like firelight." Bile smiled in delight.

"So. So. And gold is a color that you favor?"

"I favor you because of it. You are always warm."

"That we all know well enough," I interjected.

"Hush!" Ith held his hand up toward me. He was entirely focused on Bile. "And your brother Amergin here?"

"Oh, his is blue and green and sometimes silver. Like the sea or the bending trees in wind or rain." He smiled up at me. "Your shadow is most beautiful, Brother. When I see it, I feel . . ." He tapered off, looking off into the distance. "Forever."

"What does this mean?"

Bile shrugged. He returned to his drawings, Ith and me forgotten.

I looked toward my uncle; Ith was staring down the hill at Airioch, who would be upon us momentarily. I regarded his face, felt surprise course through me.

"You like him not! He is my brother, your nephew. He is clan!"

"Clan is all of creation!" Ith snapped. "Have you not been listening to my teachings?"

"Do not avoid me, Uncle. You are my teacher. You have taught me to question all of creation, all of life."

Ith looked at me directly. "What do you know of this brother of Scythia?"

"But little. He is the son of my father's first wife. She died in his birthing. He is more than twenty years older than I." I shrugged. "I know little else; like my father he is a soldier. He pays me no mind. What do you know?"

Ith looked at Bile, at his little drawings. "This little one sees well; we will begin to train him in his drawings."

"That is no answer."

"Men choose their destinies, Amergin; remember this. A man's character is his destiny. We are not born to our character; we choose it with each small action of each day, accruing light or darkness to us, putting light or darkness into the world. That is my answer. Now Airioch is upon us." I watched as my uncle composed his face, smoothing out his features, dropping into a practiced smile. It was the first time that I had ever seen anything duplicitous in my uncle. Surely my own astonishment must have made me slack-jawed.

"Welcome, Airioch, son of Mil. What news do you bring us?"

Airioch made a formal inclination of his head and shoulders. The golden brown hair dropped across his eyes, as always. He regarded all three of us.

"Well, brother Amergin. You seem surprised to see me."

I felt a flush begin to rise in my cheeks.

"I am indeed surprised, Brother. Though not by you. For Uncle has just told me that the star maps change their faces in the southern part of the world. So he has learned from the Phoenicians and the Greeks."

Why had I lied?

"Is that so?" Airioch asked, his voice utterly uninterested. "Well, our uncle has much knowledge. But I bring news. Your mother is well and walking, her newest spawn fit now to travel. Our father says to set aside your studies and prepare. We will journey within the week."

He turned, his cloak swirling around him. He began to lope down the hill, his stride tipping left and right for the angle of descent. We three were silent. When he had gone far enough away, Bile drew a deep breath and exhaled.

I turned to my uncle.

"I would know," I said.

He pointed at the top of Bile's head and pressed his finger to his lips. Later.

"We have much to do," said Ith.

Bile looked up and smiled at us both. He held up his little drawing. He had begun to sketch a ship in full sail.

3

Most of the stories of my life I have learned from my uncle Ith, who had learned the great tradition of the seanchaie of the Keltoi and knew how to keep even a great crowd rapt with his telling.

Once, though, when I was young, my mother told me a story.

We had gone to Rhatokis on the great Internal Sea. I loved the sea, the wash of the waves against the rocks, the smell of far traveling places, and I told my mother that we should move our household here beside the sea.

"Oh no, my dreaming boy," Scota replied. "You do not wish to live by the sea. She can rise and overwhelm the land with no warning at all."

"Not so, for see the gentleness of these waves upon the shore."

My mother smiled.

"When I was much upon the age that you are now, my father, your grandfather, told me a tale." Here she turned to look at me. "I wish that you had known your grandfather. He was an emperor in Persia, where we come from in the long ago."

"I remember well," I said, more anxious to hear the tale than to speak of him. In truth, he had been dead before my birth and I thought of him not at all.

"Good," said my mother, smiling. "I should not wish him to be forgotten." She wrapped an arm around my shoulders—even then, I remember, my head was nearly level with her own—and pointed out across the water. "My father said that long, long ago, the gods grew tired of the ways of men, so tired that they created a great flood. The seas rose up and overwhelmed the world." She pointed at the vast body of water before us.

"This sea itself stretched across all the lands around us, they say. My father swore that there are ancient cities drowned beneath the sea. The rage of the gods was so great that all of humanity was destroyed."

Though I had not yet begun my training with Uncle Ith, I fancied myself a budding philosopher, so I applied my child's logic to the tale.

"This cannot be," I said. "For surely if the gods destroyed all humans, you and I would not be here."

"Ah, my little Greek," said my mother, ruffling my hair. "But the story goes that one of the gods had grown fond of these human creations. That god chose a man named Atra-hasis, who was wise and soft of speech. To him, the god gave the warning of the waters. He told him to build a great ship and to put in it his own family and two of every creature on the earth. Thus did they ride out the flood of the world, and thus, slowly, was mankind restored. For his work in saving all the creatures of the world, Atra-hasis was rewarded with immortality."

"What god would destroy its own creation?" I demanded.

"I am not a philosopher like you, Amergin," she answered, smiling, "but it seems to me that if the gods indeed created humans, they created also trees and earth, river and sea, and even the great crocodiles of the Nile. Surely mankind is the most difficult of the creations of the gods, for do not the Egyptians call us the tears of Ra? Why should the gods protect mankind above all their other creations, for surely they must be proud of all that they created?"

I remembered thinking about her answer for days afterward, turning it over in my head, seeking out the idea of what the gods themselves might hold sacred. Or disposable.

And I thought of that story again as we fought to load our wagons and our wretched, balking horses onto our Greek cargo ship for the final leg of our journey to Spain. Immortality did not seem gift enough for Atra-hasis, if this was what he had to endure with all of the creatures of the world. The horses kicked and snorted, their eyes wild, their ears drawn back. They stamped their hooves among the wagons and pulled on their leads as we tried to drag them to the cargo holds.

Oh, you gods! Why did I not see then what would befall? Where were my powers of observation when the horses shifted their weight in fear? Had I known what was to come, I would have stayed on the island of Gotia forever, never again to think of Inisfail.

We made landfall well enough, our ships coming into a quiet harbor on the far eastern coast of Spain. Our mother disembarked with the two babies and her waiting women. We brothers and our retainers stayed on board to move the horses and the wagons.

We managed to get the kicking, snorting beasts onto the deck, but from that point chaos reined.

I saw my brother Airioch sidling among the horses, looking busy enough, but doing nothing to hold them. My uncle Ith called out to him, "You know they like you not, Nephew. Go ashore and there await the wagons!"

I saw the look that Airioch returned, full of disdain. Who was he to take direction from our uncle, never mind a druid? He moved among the horses swiftly and they snorted back from him. I saw my brothers Eber Donn and Eremon try to calm the beasts, blowing into their nostrils and talking softly. But just when the horses began to calm, the boat shifted on the incoming tide. One of the wagons was standing at the head of the gangway, awaiting the horses to draw it to shore. With a creak, it began to plunge down the gangway, then to tilt toward the water. This spooked the horses further. Three who were not tethered reared up in fear, then plunged toward the selfsame gangway, manes tossing and eyes wild. They divided around the wildly tilting wagon the way the crowds parted for the pharaoh of Egypt. Two careened to its port side, thundered down the gangway beside the wagon. One veered stupidly to the side nearest the edge. He slipped and dropped over the side, rear legs landing in the water, forelegs hammering a terrified staccato rhythm on the boards as he tried to drag himself back up to safety. Other horses witnessing the scene began to buck and scream, to tear their harnesses loose from the hands who held them. A wild parade of hooves and manes pushed against the shifting wagon as all cascaded toward the docks.

And standing just below the onrush, his mouth agape, his eyes wide, was Bile.

I knew then what would come.

"Bile," I screamed. "Bile!" But by then it was too late.

The stampede roared over him like a tide. I watched in horror as he was trapped beneath them, hooves and wagon wheels, flopping like a whitened fish out of its element against the shore. Finally his cloak caught in the rear wheel spoke of the wagon. The wagon thumped over him, then rolled him up in his cloak like a shroud, like a mummy of the Egyptians, tipped to its side, and fell.

Strangely, because the cloak had caught the outside edge of the wheel, the wagon did not fall on Bile. Rather, it pulled him up into the air, onto the surface of the wheel, and, still spinning, wound in his cloak like a shroud, he circled endlessly as the assembled company grew still.

I heard my mother's wail split the silence at the same time that some fool began to scream. I saw my uncle Ith approach me and say something, but I could not hear his words for the caterwauling of the fool. His hands came up suddenly beside my face and he clapped me on both sides of the head. The screaming stopped.

I launched myself toward Bile in the selfsame moment that I realized the screaming had been my own.

I halted the wheel and examined him.

The cloak had wrapped itself tight around my little brother, and his face had a grayish cast. I pulled my close dagger from its sheath and began to slice away at the plaid. Immediately, his face regained some color, but it began to swell and distort, like the face of a bloated fish. He coughed and sputtered.

One of his legs was bent and broken in several places. Though his body was tightly wound in the cloak, blood had begun to seep through the fabric. I placed my hand at the side of his neck, where the heartsounds are strong, but could not find the rhythm.

"Physicians!" I cried, looking around wildly.

I saw my weeping mother straighten, hope moving over her face. In the tongue of Egypt she called for the healers who had accompanied us, but Skena, the meiga, a midwife healer of my father's people, reached us first.

She was young, only some five years my senior, and her knowledge would be for the birthing of babies and of elixirs and tisanes for cough or wounds. I could see the panic in my mother's eyes.

"Where is Mehmet?" my mother demanded, searching the crowd for the surgeon of Egypt who journeyed with us.

"In the hold," Skena replied, "caring for those who did not voyage well. Fear not, Scota; I will hold your child's life as mine until he comes." She moved toward Bile.

"Send for Mehmet!" my mother cried commandingly, pointing to her household staff. "Tell him Scota, daughter of Pharaoh, commands him. Now!"

They scurried to do her bidding while Skena bent above my brother. She turned to me and spoke softly.

"Cut him away from the wheel, Amergin. We will lift him to the ground."

I did as she bid me and together we laid him gently behind the tumbled wagon. At Skena's command, I cut away his cloak and peeled it back from him, thinking all the while of the death bandages of Egypt. My screaming had given way to silence, and I could not speak at all. When we had cut away all of the strips of cloak, I looked upon a sight the likes of which I have never seen in my life.

My baby brother's body was a pulpy mess, bruised and bloody. His leg was broken in three places and his face was swollen and bruised. One of his eyes had disappeared into the pulpy mass of flesh that was his face. And oh, his arm! His right arm dangled just below the elbow, from a single bloody thread, the forearm and hand hanging loose into the air. Blood gushed everywhere.

To her credit, Skena was efficient and quick. She grabbed strips of the bloody cloak and tied them just above his elbow, stopping only to command me.

"Break me a spoke of the wagon, Amergin. Now twist it tight until all the bleeding stops. Now raise his little legs. Higher. Good. The blood must go to his heart and his brain."

Mehmet arrived accompanied by my father, who had stayed behind to see to the unloading.

"What has happened?" my father demanded. "Will it hold up the journey long? We have been delayed enough!" He pushed around the cluster of my brothers and their wives. When he saw Bile, he fell silent.

Mehmet knelt beside Skena, his white tunic shrouding my brother. Skena bent her head before him.

"The leg and arm are beyond my skill, Physician. And the rest." She gestured at her own head.

Gently Mehmet examined my brother with his long, thin hands. Then he turned his full gaze on Skena, his huge dark eyes with their kohl rings taking her in. "You have saved his life, Meiga," he said. He turned to my mother. "Her speed and skill have let your son live to fight the day. Now we must work to bring him through the night."

He turned back to Skena. "You will assist me. Who else?"

She pointed at me. "Amergin will do well for his brother."

Mehmet nodded. He scanned the crowd until he saw my uncle Ith. When their eyes met, Mehmet raised his two bloody hands and held them up at either side of his head. Ith came immediately among us and knelt. He held his own hands at either side of Bile's head and began to chant. I will remember his words all of my days.

"Eistigi, eistigi," he began.

"Hear me, hear me.
Here is the soul of Bile
Do not hide it from us
O Maker of the world
Return his spirit to us
Full of song.
Here is the body of Bile
Our brother and our child
Do not return it to earth, O Maker
Give us the skill to heal
Come you now to Bile
O come you now
O come you now."

Over and over he chanted, and while he sang, Mehmet worked. He instructed our men to build a tent over us. They did so, attaching canvas to the wagons and shoving poles into the ground. At the edge of the tent he requested fire and water and sent his apprentices to find a cold stream with fresh water.

The hours of day passed into night. Ith chanted, his face a mask of worry, while Mehmet and Skena wrapped my brother's head again and again in cold compresses, set the leg against strips of polished wood, cleaned and washed the wounds. All the while Bile uttered no protest, made no sound.

"Why does he not protest at the pain?" I asked once. "Surely, we wound him with our ministrations."

Mehmet shook his head, his hands never stopping. "His head was injured, whether by wagon or horses we know not. You see how swollen it is?"

I nodded.

"To protect the spirit encased there, all around it has swollen like a pillow. The mind itself, so fragile in its casing, has retreated, to allow the healing to occur."

I shook my head, not understanding.

"His spirit travels," said my uncle Ith. "It departs so that the healing of the body will not affect the spirit."

Mehmet nodded at this explanation, evidently finding it satisfactory.

I took the nod to bode well. "So he will return to us as he was before."

Mehmet sighed and leaned back on his heels.

"We cannot know that yet. The brain inside its casing of skull is fragile and soft." He cast around for a comparison. "You have been to the sea and seen the jellyfish that sometimes wash up on the shore."

I nodded.

"Just so the human mind. Smash or dent a piece of the brain and other systems in the body may not work."

"Such as?"

He shrugged. "I have seen those who could not walk, though their limbs were whole. I have seen those who could not talk or feed."

"And Bile?"

"We will not know for a time. Perhaps for some time." He sighed. "And there is yet more sorrowful news." He gestured at the dangling thread of arm. "This arm must go. I have no skill to patch so torn and shredded a limb."

I suppose something in me must have known the conclusion of it all. The arm dangled shriveled and useless from its thread, but the idea revulsed and terrified. My gorge rose, and I rushed from the tent and vomited. Not all the blood of the day had brought me to this, until the thought of my brother, crippled and maimed, all his life reduced to the awkward stares and muttered sorrow of the tribe.

My love for him and my terror welled up in me and I curled myself against the ground and let out a single sob. Then I rose, knowing that my little brother would need my strength.

Mil and Scota were waiting outside the tent, surrounded by the ebb and flow of my brothers and their wives, by endless cups of wine and murmured words of hope and sympathy. My mother cradled the newest babe in her arms, as if she could sustain her hope in the holding.

They regarded me as I wiped my mouth on the fold of my cloak. Their bodies had gone rigid and still.

"What is it?" my mother whispered.

"The arm must come off. It cannot be saved."

She made no sound, pressing her hand against her mouth, but my father rose and swept into the darkness.

"It would be better if he had died!" he called aloud as he vanished.

And though I wanted to hate him for the saying, I could not. I had thought the thought myself and was ashamed.

CEOLAS PRAYS FOR BILE

Take my arm, this poet's arm.
I offer it as payment, gift
for the arm of Bile,
child of sweetness,
best of all brothers.
Take my life, the poet's life.
I offer it as payment, gift,
against the life of Bile,
child of sweetness.
For if he is gone,
surely there can be
no more song
no more song.

4

The sickness of a loved one is itself like a sea; we lose ourselves upon it, we ride its tides and currents like a ship, adrift on hope and sorrow.

The hours of Bile's recovery grew to days. We placed him on a raised sleeping platform and covered him with the finest linens of Egypt. Twice he rose and broke in fevers. My mother's servants fanned him during the day with huge straw fronds, and my mother herself once bathed his forehead and his wrists with cool water. My father did not visit him at all. Mehmet changed the dressings on his arm and put poultices against the wounded stump, all the while sharing with Skena the medical skills of Egypt. Three times a day, Ith chanted for my brother, and through all of it Bile did not move. He uttered no sound; beneath his eyelids, his eyes did not move as those of a proper dreamer should.

Mehmet insisted that my brother's stillness was a blessing.

"Let him be," he warned. "While he journeys, as you of the Keltoi call it, he feels no pain, nor fear. His body has time to heal itself, free of his own fight against it."

Each night I slept beside him, stretching my body against the ground. Each morning, Skena arrived to awaken me, to spell me that I might bathe and eat. After a week, she no longer needed to touch me, for deep in my dreams I would smell the perfume of her long auburn hair as it cascaded toward me. I began to awaken each morning to those silken strands as they brushed my forearm, tickled the back of my hand. I began to feel that I needed them, as one who has wandered in the desert needs water.

On the eighth day of my brother's journey, I returned to the tent after my morning rituals. Skena's back was toward me and she did not hear my approach.

"Ah, little Bile," I heard her say. Her voice was cheerful and singsong. "When the leg is healed up well, we shall set Amergin to teaching you to ride and to fight with that strong left arm. How wonderful you will be, the left-handed warrior of the tribe!"

Joy leaped up in me! My brother was awake. Bile had returned to us!

I shouldered in beside Skena and looked down at his little form. Nothing had changed. My brother lay still and silent, a one-armed sarcophagus. I turned on Skena, bewildered.

"Why do you speak to him thus?"

For answer, she placed her fingers on her lips and led me outside the silken tent. Her hand never released mine. She answered in a soft whisper.

"Just because he travels does not mean that he cannot hear us. Your uncle Ith will tell you this as well. The journeyer moves above the world, swift as wind. We cannot let him become confused about his dwelling, for during this time, his spirit dwells wide in the world. So we speak to him. We remind him of the dwelling of the body. We call him back to us."

A sense of wonder overtook me.

"You love my brother," I said.

Skena's eyes met mine.

"Of course I love him, Amergin. I am his healer; a healer mends the spirit as well as the body. The truest healers pour out their love with their skill; we healers of the Keltoi know this to be true."

And that was the moment that I fell in love with Skena. Deeply. Irrevocably. The difference was clear to me immediately. My brothers fell for their women for beauty or sensuality or warrior skills or wit. I had fallen in love with Skena's spirit. Now I saw her whole, the silken skeins of her hair, the wide gray eyes, each soft motion of her slender hands; all were the mirrors of that great and generous spirit. My heart was overwhelmed with gratitude that she, of all the Galaeci, should be my little brother's healer, for in that moment, I was certain that only she, among all humans, could return him to us. I was awestruck.

Of course I did not tell her. I was a stripling lad of seventeen summers, and though seventeen is the year of manhood among the Galaeci, she had five years upon me and was a healer's apprentice. She thought of me in the same way she thought of Bile. I was a boy. But in her reflection, I knew the man that I wanted to become.

Heeding her words, I began each night to sit beside Bile's bed on a small camp stool. I would hold his good hand in my own, stroking at the long fingers, and while I did, I would tell him stories. I told him of our grandfather's people, the warriors of Persia, and of the Galaeci, the history of our father's tribe. I spun him wondrous stories of Inisfail, the Isle of Destiny, of the wide-eyed and magical people of that island, of hidden waterfalls and forests of fairy ferns. Of course I knew nothing of the place, but I invented, drawing out the stories of our father from childhood, spinning upon the fanciful tales of Greek and Roman sailors and soldiers. But as I spun them I came to believe them, came to think of Inisfail as the green and magical land of my own invention.

Finally there came a night when I thought that perhaps our little traveler might enjoy Ceolas. I tuned her to sweet perfection and began to sing. The song was a long and complex one, another story of the journey to Inisfail, and I closed my eyes and began to sing Bile on the journey with me. I was some way into the song when I noticed that a soft, harmonious humming accompanied me. Thinking that perhaps Skena had joined me in the tent, I opened my eyes. I was alone!

I looked around and behind me and finally down at my little brother. His eyes were wide open and his mouth was slightly pursed as he hummed along with me!

CEOLAS SINGS JOY
Here you are returned to us
Bile my brother,
child of my heart
journeyer returned.
What stories you will tell us,
what far countries you will draw.
Here is our joy at your return
that these strings quiver to hear you.

I did not dare stop. I wanted to set Ceolas down, to call aloud to Skena and Ith and Mehmet, to send for my mother, but I could not. I feared that if I stopped, Bile would disappear again, would fold back down into his travels and disappear forever. So I kept on singing, Ceolas thrumming beneath me, my own harp quivering with so much joy at the return of my little brother that my legs trembled beneath her. On and on we went. I sang of the journey on the sea and Bile hummed the tune. I took us to the far green island and Bile hummed the tune.

At last, outside in the darkness, Skena must have awakened from her rest, must have realized that my evening song had gone on far too long. She came into the tent softly, her hair undone and tousled, her white sleeping gown billowing around her in the torchlight. I could see her long-limbed shape beneath its diaphanous folds.

She looked at me, a query, and then followed my eyes to Bile. She started back, then dropped to her knees beside him. Gently, gently, she kissed his little cheeks, his forehead.

"Welcome back, my little traveler," she whispered. He watched her with his great eyes and kept humming.

Skena stood and came before me. She lifted my chin in her hand. "How great a spirit you have, Amergin, that you have called him back from his journeys. How magical is your song."

She dropped her hand and the place burned.

"I shall call the others."

She swept from the tent, and I turned back to my little brother. His eyes watched me, huge and luminous, and I knew that he had learned much on his journeys. I was filled with anticipation to hear the stories he would tell.

5

In three days' time, Bile made rapid progress. Mehmet and Skena assisted him to sit up, and he took some soup and drank cool water from a cup. My mother came in to cool his brow and hands with her own hands again and to elevate Skena to the position of Healer of the Household, an honor that Skena accepted with her head bowed humbly. Her only response was, "I thank you that I shall be able to spend more time with my boys." Here she gestured at both Bile and me, and though I was glad to be included in her regard, I felt deflated to know that she did indeed think of me as a boy.

Even my father swept into the tent; although he blustered and cried out a welcome, he would not look at Bile's arm.

By the evening of the third day Bile was sitting up on his own, propped against pillows. My uncle Ith came and held Bile's remaining hand and sang a chant of thanks for his return while Bile hummed softly in accompaniment.

Bile did not ask about the arm, nor venture any words on any subject. He watched the company with wide luminous eyes that seemed to me now much older than his seven years.

I wanted desperately to hear him speak, to learn the wisdoms of his journey, to see if he remembered aught of the accident. But Mehmet cautioned me against conversation.

"Let his mind and his speech return as they will," he said. "Remember the fragility we spoke of? The mind must heal slowly, as it will."

So I contented myself with singing for my brother and listening to his sweet accompaniment. Indeed, his spirit, which had always seemed to me to be made of sweetness, seemed now large with joy.

He smiled when our brothers swept in and out, looked upon our father and mother with both pity and love, laid his hand in Skena's whenever she arrived.

That was the scene that Airioch encountered when at last he made an appearance by Bile's bed.

Skena was kneeling by our brother's side, her left hand enfolding his remaining little hand. Her auburn hair was unpinned; it tumbled forward over her shoulders and spilled like water into the folds of the blue tunic she was wearing. Her feet were bare, as they always were in the tent. She was talking to Bile softly as she bathed his face in cool water. I sat behind them, Ceolas in my lap.

Airioch paid little attention to Bile and none to me. Beyond his perfunctory welcome back to our little brother, all of his attention was focused on Skena.

"So . . . ," he said. "This is the exquisite creature who has been elevated to Healer of the Household. It is no wonder my brothers never leave this tent." Here he looked significantly at Bile and then winked at me, as though we were little children, privileged to be made part of his jest.

Skena came to her feet before him and bowed her head, but she was silent.

"I like a silent woman," Airioch said, smiling. He boldly reached out a hand and lifted her chin. When her face came up, I could see that her eyes were blazing, whether with anger or fear, I knew not. I stepped up beside her and drew my arm around her. She did not resist, instead folding herself into my shoulder in a way that she had never done.

"This is Skena, she who has healed our brother."

Airioch regarded me in surprise, as if, for the first time, he had heard speech from a tree. Then he lifted her arm and pressed his lips to the back of her hand. It was a courtly Galaeci custom, nothing more, but something about the way his lips lingered on her hand turned my stomach in its hasp.

I knew not what to do. My hand itched toward my dagger, my mind reminding me that this was my brother, son of my father, a warrior of more than thirty-five years.

We were saved by Bile. He began to gabble, to make noises that sounded like speech trapped below water. "Agghh, arrww, waahn, ah waahn."

All three of us relaxed our postures and turned toward him, Skena dropping immediately to her knees beside him.

Bile turned the huge luminous eyes on Airioch. He kept voicing, the inarticulate sounds of cattle or yard fowl issuing from his mouth. His eyes never left Airioch's face. Airioch regarded him for a moment and spoke, his tone surprised.

"I did not know that the accident had made him both fool and cripple. He were best to stay mute. Does our father know this?"

The anger that flooded me was white-hot and dangerous. "He would be neither dumb nor crippled had you not stirred the horses on the day of disembarking."

Airioch turned his full regard on me then, scrutinizing me as one would a new species of bug. "Think you so, little poet brother?" He turned. His cloak swirled in a dark arc around him. "Well, our father shall hear of it."

"Shall hear of what?" Our father himself stormed into the tent, wafting in the smell of horses and warm metal. In a single glance he took in Bile and the kneeling Skena, my angry stance and Airioch's intention. It was when he looked on Airioch's face that I saw something I had not expected to see: my father's face shuttered, just as my uncle Ith's had done; it grew wary, hidden, closed. I could not have been more surprised if serpents had risen, speaking, from the sea.

"What shall I hear?" he said again, his tone testy.

"It is nothing," said Airioch, sulky as a child. "Or nothing that you shall not know soon enough."

He swept from the tent.

"Never mind," said Mil, his hand waving Airioch away. "I come with good news. Now that Bile is back among us, we make ready the wagons and strike the camp. We will journey in three days' time."

Skena came to her feet, her eyes wide, one hand upraised. I saw that she would plead for waiting, to allow her little patient time to heal. But I looked beyond her to Bile. He made no sound at all, but when he met my eyes, he winked!

JUILENE OSBORNE-McKNIGHT

I spoke before Skena could say anything. "We will be ready," I said. "Bile is anxious to go!"

I did not miss the look that Skena turned on me, nor relish the wrath that would follow the look.

6

She dragged me outside the tent and out of Bile's earshot, eyes blazing with anger. "He cannot travel yet. He has returned to us from his journeys only three days past! Are you daft to tell your father he can go?"

"Bile is ready to go."

"Bile is a child. By the gods, you also are a just a boy! I am arguing with children."

I could see the speckled heat of her anger against her neck. I feared making her angrier still if I could not stop my gaze from returning again and again to the red pattern on the white skin.

She followed the path of my eyes. "What do you regard?"

"Your anger blotches your skin. I fear that you would not be good at secrets."

She tried to look at her own neck, abandoned the effort. She sighed. "I sometimes think that Mil and his sons are too good with secrets. Give me instead a man who speaks his mind."

"I like it not that Airioch approaches you so. There is my mind."

She looked at me in surprise. "Should I fear him, Amergin?"

I squirmed. "I know not," I said. "He is not for you. Be cautious of him, Skena."

I sounded like the lame and foolish child she thought me. She sighed.

"You see. You speak no more clearly than the rest. Your father will not look at his broken child, your brother threatens to tell him—what? That his little son no longer speaks? What does he hope from such a pearl of wisdom? That your father will send Bile away? I do not understand you sons of Mil."

"We are a family of brothers, men all. When have you known men to speak themselves clearly, Skena? Is that not why so many judges of the Galaeci are female? And as for Bile, you must not mistake his speech for his mind itself! The leg is healing and we can do nothing for the arm. But my brother Bile is there inside that broken, speechless body!" I grabbed her upper arms. "Do I speak clearly enough for you there?"

She looked down at my hands upon her arms. "Oh my," she said softly, and I saw the red speckling begin again across her throat. I dropped my hands.

"I am sorry. Healer, accept my apology. I did not mean to hurt you or to frighten you."

"You did not," she said, softly, but she would not meet my eyes.

"Please, Skena. Do not be angry with me. I could not bear that. Nor your disappointment."

For answer, she simply turned her back on me and headed back toward the tent. Oh, I could have kicked myself for a gangling fool. I did not know whether to follow her like a dog or to turn and run away in shame. She solved the problem for me.

"Come, Amergin," she called over her shoulder. "We have three days to prepare your brother for the rigors of travel."

CEOLAS SINGS OF JEALOUSY AND DESIRE
Even in her anger I desire her,
the sweet whiteness of her skin,
the lightning of her eye,
her spirit like great water.
Rigid am I; quivering with desire,
my own anger turned against my brother,
against his ways with women,
his winning ways, his courtly ways,
his ways that I despise.

I suppose that they thought we three the most disposable of the tribe, but no matter. We were given our own wagon and no duties but to see to

Bile. By day, we sang silly songs and took turns propping him against us by the rear opening so that he could see the countryside unfold behind him. When we stopped to set up camp, we got him walking around the circle on a little wooden crutch that our mother's craftsmen had made; by a few weeks into the journey, he needed only a cane.

He did not speak of the arm, or speak at all. Each time he tried, the sounds came out as a series of animal utterances, unintelligible as human speech. Skena and I took to interpreting his vocal clues and learned that "Ah" meant yes. For no, he simply shook his head; for all other wants he took to gesturing, eventually creating a language with his hand and face that only Skena and I could read. We two knew instantly when he was hungry or ready to walk. Sometimes when we were camped, I brought him his papers and his chalk. Bile would mime to me the things he would wish to draw; I would steady his left hand in my own right hand and let him guide our sketching. The sketches became more complex as our journey progressed, and eventually he was capturing the mountains and rivers, the trees and campfires of our journey.

At night the three of us slept together in the wagon, Skena and I on sleeping platforms attached to the walls of the wagon, Bile between us on his little silken bed. I took to watching Skena as she slept, waiting for the moonlight to slip across her cheeks and illuminate the pale skin. I loved the way she shifted in her sleep and the soft noises that she made in her dreams.

One night as I was watching her I looked down to see Bile, eyes wide open, watching me from his little bed.

"I love her," I whispered.

"Ah." He nodded simply, as if he had known all along, and I wondered if she knew as well, if she was aware of my longing stares, if she suspected that the poems I wrote and sang on Ceolas were all for her. I felt a great fool, until Bile patted my hand gently with his own little hand. From the moment that he returned to us, I had felt that he was, after all, the older brother, an ancient spirit made wise by its journeys, and I took comfort in his approval.

But the next evening I returned to our wagon to the sound of my brother Airioch, making wry and pungent observations about our journey to gales of laughter from Skena. I had taken Bile to visit with Uncle Ith; the two of them were happily absorbed in Bile's drawings when I returned to the wagon. I will admit it honestly, I hoped to spend the evening there with Skena, helping her with the simple domesticities of the wagon, engaging in conversation as we worked. But instead, there was Airioch, propped on one arm.

I stopped outside the wagon and listened.

"So the horse reared up and caught my brother in the chin. You should have seen him then; his eyes wept like a girl!"

I could hear Skena's laugh in response and then a murmured comment I could not understand. For a moment I felt a flash of jealousy that my older brothers were riding to horse on the journey, while I rode the wagon like a child. Airioch spoke again.

"In truth I am not much better, Healer. All this jostling by horse and wagon makes the bones ache. That is why I have come."

I heard her murmur again, concern in the tone.

"It is this shoulder, and my rein arm; they ache. Do you have a poultice you could rub in for me?"

A pause.

"Here, allow me to remove my tunic."

I came around the corner of the wagon and launched up the steps like a cat. Airioch was stretched out on my sleeping platform, his boots grinding dust into the linens of my bed. He was shirtless and propped on one elbow, his long, muscled body gleaming in the lamplight of the wagon. Skena was busy rubbing one of her salves into the exposed shoulder and down his arm.

Rage pulsed through me as hot as coals. Jealousy. I wanted to stab his heart, to strike her down for her hands upon his skin.

Airioch did not stir when I entered. He looked up, lazy and satisfied, a big cat before the kill. "Little brother," he said. "Your good healer ministers to my aches. Already I feel better."

He took his large hand and closed it over hers where it worked on his shoulder.

"I thank you, Healer," he said. He brought the hand to his lips and kissed it, his eyes locked with hers. Something seemed to be working around her mouth, but she said nothing. Airioch stood, long and lean and shirtless.

"I shall return," he said, his voice fraught with significance.

Skena nodded, saying nothing; she caught her bottom lip between her teeth.

Airioch disappeared into the darkness. Skena dropped to her knees on the wagon floor, holding her stomach, absolutely silent.

My anger was replaced by fear and I dropped beside her and lifted her face in my hand. Tears were streaming down her face.

"Did he hurt you?"

She placed her finger on her lips, then drew my head down until my ear tickled against her lips.

"The salve," she whispered. "It was fire salve. To warm the muscles. He kissed my hand. His lips will burn for days."

Then she dropped to the floor and, stuffing her face into Bile's pillow, laughed until she had no wind left to her.

All my anger left me, but I did not tell her that the place where her lips had touched my ears burned too. And yes, for days.

All the way, in fact, to Galicia.

7

There! I had heard it again.

From my perch in the top of the tower I heard soft laughter.

For a fortnight now, when Bile had drifted off to sleep, I had climbed Breogam's Tower to look out over the moonlit sea, longing for the north, for Inisfail.

I did not know how soon my father would choose to depart, but for me it could not be soon enough.

Here in Galicia, I was a stranger.

I do not know what I had expected from my father's country. I had lived in Egypt, traveled in Greece and Rome. Perhaps I had expected the alabaster palaces of Greece with their white colonnades, or the billowing silks of the Nile River palaces with their white light.

Perhaps I had expected the worldliness of all those places, where all the citizens of the world contended together.

Galicia was none of those.

The countryside was rainy and green, swards of green hills down to the roiling sea. My kinsmen dressed in braichs, a kind of baggy belted trouser, and plaid cloaks, and dwelled in conical huts that reminded me of the slave huts of Egypt. They scattered brochs—huge stone towers with many levels—around the countryside and used them for both meeting places and storage holds for grain and supplies. Though their villages were well fortified, surrounded with circles of stone walls and laid out on a well-defined street system, they were not the great cities of Egypt and Greece. And though my kinsmen were prosperous, mining, herding cattle, farming the sea and the land and trading beautiful artwork to the Greeks, I missed the scrolls and libraries, the rich learning of Greece and Egypt—and was ashamed of myself for missing it. Here, the Galaeci spoke my father's tongue, but in a rapid and inflected way that he had evidently forgotten, so that all his teaching of us was for naught. We sounded like foreign fools, stumbling over the language of our ancestors.

Here in Galicia I was a stranger, but I wondered often if this was why my father had departed Galicia, the search for Inisfail an excuse merely, a ruse for venturing into the wider world. For surely my father's restless spirit was too large for this place, for the repetitive days and nights, for the clans who had all known each other for generations and who now excluded us from the small borders of their world.

Oh, they welcomed us well enough, my father's cousins exclaiming over the return of Mile Easpain, the great warrior of Scythia and Egypt, but we were strangers among them. In truth, I could understand their suspicion of us. We traveled with Egyptian servants and Roman plateware, Persian cousins and fine silk garments. Never mind that we traveled in the same curved wagons as our kinsmen; our horses were fine Greek warrior beasts; our wagons were swathed in silks. Our women and our physician wore kohl around their eyes. We brothers were not all of the same mother, the same clan, or even the same country. And then, of course, there was Bile.

They took great pains to avoid Bile, making small signs with their hands when they encountered him, but in truth, even my own father and my brothers avoided him as well. Only my mother visited him; Skena and I were his constant companions. Because of this, I too was exiled in their midst, and my heart grew hard at the treatment of my brother.

To fit in with the Galaeci, my little mother abandoned her Egyptian ways. She took to braiding her hair with bells, and she wore the tunic and leathers of the women of the Galaeci. She learned to fight with shortsword and dagger from one of their warrior teachers—all women—and began to speak the language of the Keltoi exclusively, to the frustration of my father and older brothers, who had taken pains to learn the tongues of Persia, Egypt, Greece, and, in Airioch's case, even Rome.

Our attendant strangeness had made me even more reclusive than I had been in Egypt.

And so I came to love this tower with its night fire encased in stone and its long views out to the heaving sea. Here Ceolas and I would sing, seated at the stone window, gazing out over the northern sea. Here my loneliness, my sense of belonging nowhere and to no one, grew, mitigated only by my time with Skena and Bile.

From far below me came the sound again, giggling and then the low murmur of a male voice. A man and woman then, coupling. Well who was I to disturb them at their play? My loins tightened up at the thought. What man of my people and eighteen years of age had never bedded a woman? I felt suddenly ashamed of my own inexperience. Suddenly the woman cried out, as if in pain. Her cry was followed by the sound of a slap.

I took the tower stairs two at a time. Outside in the darkness I made my way around the tower until I saw them. Airioch and a woman of the Galaeci. He was sitting on a patch of sand, leaning back against one of the great rocks which line the shore, and she was kneeling before him, riding him hard. Periodically he smacked her flank, and his teeth and tongue worked at her dark nipples, which were rigid with desire. Though I had never lain with a woman I felt my own manhood swell to bursting with need. I saw my brother arch against her, then sigh with satisfaction.

"Go," he said, smacking her flank again.

She moaned and leaned into him, evidently not finished with her plea-sure, but he set her off from him and pointed up the path.

"Go! I am finished."

She said something unintelligible and angry and strode away, pulling clothing over her head as she went.

My brother sat back and let the moonlight stream over him. He sighed with satisfaction. "Did you enjoy watching, little brother?"

The hot shame burned up into my face.

"Come out here."

I stepped into the clearing, my eyes downcast. "I heard her scream and I thought that someone was hurting her," I mumbled. "I did not mean to intrude."

"You did not intrude. I knew that you were in the tower and I knew that you would hear us. Did it give you pleasure?" He stared hard at my braichs. "I see that it did not and I am sorry. I would have called her back to share her with you. It greatly enhanced my pleasure that you were watching."

"Enhanced?"

"Of course. To know that you were watching me perform. I would have liked to watch you take her. You have never had a woman, have you?"

I said nothing, not sure if I burned with my own lack or at his offer to share.

"Too much time with our baby brother, I suppose."

"I love Bile," I said defensively.

"Obvious enough," he said. "But he is not much draw for women. But for that glorious red woman, the healer. Oh, I do so like women."

"You seemed to like this one well enough."

He grinned at me. "She was willing. In truth, I like them all."

"You have bedded many?" I was ashamed of wanting to know.

"Hundreds. All shapes and sizes and ages. Boys as well. Does that shock you?"

"I know it is the Greek and Roman way."

"Very good, for that is where I learned my habits. You know little about me, Brother. I spent much time in Greece and Rome. There are many ways to pleasure, and I have tried them all. Galicia offers me new delicacies from the table, and a man should take his pleasures where he will."

"What of her pleasure?" I found that I truly wanted to know.

He opened his eyes and regarded me coolly. "Ah, I hear the makings of a connoisseur. A woman can be pleasured. They are slow creatures, though, and it is only worth the effort if there is something to be gained."

"To be gained?"

He smiled. "Yes. For example, once when I was soldiering in Greece there was a woman—much older than I, but married to a wrinkled ancient Greek near twice her age. I knew that if I could pleasure her, she would give me anything. So I took my time and did it well." Here, he flicked his tongue at me. "And more than once so that she was besotted. And then I began to ask for things. Fine tunics and gold and a deed of land. All of these she gave. And when I had them and more, I asked for her handmaids to join us, and then her houseboys, and at last I could sate myself with her and with any person or thing of her household. I was sorry to be posted away from that little treasure trove." He shook his head.

I thought for a while about what he had said. "Does our father—cavort—as you do?"

"Our father seems to have eyes only for Scota. And she for him. Even

Eber Donn seems to have all that he can do to pleasure his three wives. But perhaps that is all that his paltry tool can do. You see what gifts I have been given." He stroked himself once or twice and looked with affection at the huge shaft. "My soldier. Always at attention. And I like the games of seduction; I like best to win them."

He leaned back against the rock in the moonlight, sighing with satisfaction, content in his naked splendor. As I looked at him there, I realized that he looked like a statue of the Greeks, and then I knew, suddenly and certainly, why my father's face shuttered each time he saw this brother. I tried to turn toward the sea to hide the knowledge, so that he would not see it in my face, but it was too late.

"You are thinking," he said, "that I was sired by a Greek. Do not fear to say it; I believe it to be so. Much better that than the little Gael you call your father."

"My father has given you a home, has treated you as his own son."

He inclined his head. "Well, he has given me a home, that much is so."

"What of Skena?" I blurted out suddenly.

"Oh, I would love to bed that one. All that auburn hair and those eyes. And I think she is a virgin, although . . ." He fixed me with a stare. "Have you bedded her, little brother?" His tone was teasing. He met my eyes directly. "No, of course you have not. Well, then, fresh fruit. Though it would be much work to win her." He sighed again. "All this talk of mating matters. I am ready again. I must go look among the willing. I did enjoy this conversation, little brother. It was, I think, our first as men."

He pulled on his braichs and sauntered off into the moonlight.

I remained on the beach, deeply troubled, rigid with desire and shame, fearful that I would be just like him, not sure if it was a source of fear or of pride.

CEOLAS SINGS DESIRE
I burn.
In the dark of the night I burn.
Rigid with longing, I burn.
Red woman, cailin rua,
I am on fire for you.

I sought out my uncle Ith. Since we had returned to Galicia he had taken to living among his fellow druids in the oak groves and the small stone dwellings that perched like mushrooms on the ground among the great oaks. Of all of us, he was most content among his brother and sister druids.

I found him seated in a circle of sages, the wind lifting the sleeves of their white robes, all of them conversing on the nature of the soul.

I stood at the fringe of the grove, waiting in silence, but he called to me, "Come sit among us, Nephew."

Again I felt a fool. Twice in the same week to be caught out as I lurked near the activities of my elders. I felt like a gawky, stripling boy of no experience, loud and awkward. I vowed at least to learn to move as the forest cat moves, silent on the ground.

I came in among them. For two days, since my conversation with Airioch, I had been feeling confused and ashamed, half of me filled with longing; but now, in this oak grove, my curiosity lifted me out of my miasma.

Here was the brother-sisterhood of the druii, the wisest elders of the Galaeci. All my life my uncle Ith had spoken of them. I studied their faces.

The oldest of their company was a woman of indeterminate age, older than my uncle. Her hair, though thick with gray, cascaded around her shoulders in long waves of alternating dark and silver. Her eyes were luminous and deep, of some strange color that moved between gray and silver, so that the orbs seemed to catch and hold the light. I found myself staring at her, and she returned my look with such intensity that I could not look away.

"Brothers and sisters," she said. Her voice, though soft, was commanding. "Our little brother needs the company of his uncle. Shall we depart?"

They seemed almost to vanish then, like blowing leaves of snow, their white robes billowing toward the trunks of the huge trees, fading into the forest and gone.

Uncle Ith gestured to me. "Come sit, lad; it is obvious that you are troubled."

I sat before him, unsure of how to begin, nearly squirming with shame.

"You wish to speak to me about a matter of the body." Uncle Ith spoke kindly and without preamble.

"How do you know?"

"It is a subject that preoccupies the young and fills them with confusion. Your body shouts confusion, so I have concluded a mating matter."

"I watched Airioch at the mating," I blurted. "I did not mean to, but I thought that he was hurting her." I raised my hand at the look on Uncle Ith's face. "He was not, but I watched them. Airioch knew that I was watching, so he called me out."

"He was angry?"

"No. He was . . . pleased. He said that it . . . that I . . . that he . . . enjoyed it more for knowing I was watching. He said that women are difficult to pleasure. He said that he would like to bed Skena. He said that he was sired by a Greek. . . ." I trailed off and lifted my hands helplessly.

Uncle Ith sighed. "Well, it's all a bit much at once, isn't it?"

"Yes." In Uncle Ith's presence, I no longer felt like a stupid child. "I am overwhelmed, I guess. I need help to sort it out."

"As do we all. Let's begin with the Greek."

"Is it true?"

"It may be. Surely Airioch does not resemble either your father or his mother. It is why your father kept him."

"I don't understand."

"Seang was the daughter of the king of Scythia. She died giving birth to Airioch. This turned the king's wrath against your father."

"All of this I know."

"Well consider further, then. If Airioch were to have remained in Scythia when your father departed and if he were to have grown up there, eventually the day would have come when the king also would have seen the Greek in Airioch. Where would his rage for the loss of his daughter have turned then?"

"Oh, you gods! So my father protected him even if Airioch is not his own."

"He did."

"This is a most noble act on the part of my father."

"Your father is a most noble and honorable warrior. I would say this of him even if he were not my brother."

"But his treatment of Bile?"

"To move in the world is difficult. To move in the world with no speech and one arm and the fear and strangeness of those who encounter you is nigh to impossible. Your father weeps for Bile, and it hurts him to the core to see his little child so maimed. He has told me more than once that he is proud and grateful for your care of Bile."

"He has said this of me?"

"He has."

I turned this over in my mind, felt a gladness of heart in knowing it. "But then why does not he himself spend more time with Bile?"

"He feels responsible."

"Why should he?"

"Because the wagons and the horses were his charge."

"But not his fault. It was Airioch who disturbed them."

"You cannot blame Airioch for Bile's misfortune. Airioch riles the horses by virtue of what they sense in him, but he bore no ill will toward your little brother."

"Does Airioch bear ill will toward me?"

"Perhaps. Perhaps he only craves your woman."

"He has said that he would like to bed her. She is not my woman." I ached to say that she was.

"What if I told you that what will pass between you and Skena goes far beyond bedding?"

I hung my head. In his usual subtle way, Uncle Ith had seen straight to the heart of my shame.

"I would also like to bed her." I mumbled it out.

"Of course you would."

I looked up in surprise. "Then how am I different from Airioch?"

"We of the Galaeci and, in fact, all of the Keltoi believe that woman is the mother of the world."

I nodded. This was obvious to anyone who saw the world.

"Therefore, if woman is mother of the world, we men must treat her with respect. We must honor her, learn from her, heed her counsel, and yes, mate with her, but always with her consent and desire."

"Airioch had the consent of the woman with whom he mated."

Even as untried as I was, I knew that clearly enough.

"And did he respect that consent?"

"Well, he . . ." I squirmed under Uncle Ith's direct gaze. "He did not pleasure her."

"He pleasured himself?"

"Yes."

"So he did not respect her."

"So the mating is always good if it is done with mutual respect and pleasure and consent."

"Yes."

"Now I see, Uncle. And thank you." I started to rise.

He held up his palm. "As of yet, you see nothing. Airioch is a man of many desires. He sates most of them. A man who accrues to himself all of the things of this world cannot lighten himself of their burden unless he gives something away."

"This I do not understand."

Ith sighed. "Here is what we druii know. We are not of this world. Not really. We are here and gone and then return again. But what is true of us is this spirit that moves between the worlds." He placed his hands on either side of my head, surrounding my soul. "The things of this world have weight. They tie us to this world. They do not allow the spirit to travel well and lightly. And a man like Airioch, a man who sates so many desires, weights himself down with a kind of darkness, a heaviness of spirit. That is the darkness that Bile sees around him, the darkness of so much accrual, of so many choices for the self and not the other."

"Is this the nature of evil, then?"

"No. Evil occurs when the darkness begins to spill off onto others, when the bearer of darkness chooses to do harm to sate his own desires. It is a process of small choices, little decisions that grow larger over time."

"Is Airioch a servant of darkness?"

"Right now he is a servant of the self. We do not know the way that he will choose, so we are cautious."

"We?"

"Your father and I. We watch him."

"I would not like him to choose for Skena."

"Then do not let him do so."

"I am a lad of eighteen years; he is a warrior of some thirty-five years. And Skena is five years my senior."

"Have you not listened to me?" Ith's voice was angry. I started back, for he had never been angry with me before.

"You are a spirit, as ageless and timeless as I. The body is young, but the spirit is old and wise. You have before you a great gift, a gift that is given to few on Earth."

"I wish to be wise," I said. "Teach me."

"You have before you the gift of anam cara, the gift of the beloved soul. It is the gift that travels through time, through lifetimes, through distance and age and death. Very few ever receive it, Amergin; too many pass it by or throw it away. But I see in you a man capable of wisdom, a man capable of knowing the Light. Do not let that slip from you for foolishness or youth."

"You speak of love as if you know."

"You have met my beloved."

I gasped aloud. "The woman with the silver eyes."

"An Scail. The Shadow."

"You were parted from her for forty years!"

"Yes," he said simply. "And no. Your father needed my counsel. His family needed their druid. She and I agreed that I must go. Love . . . travels. It sustains. It endures. Be wise, Amergin, for few are offered so priceless a gift."

8

CEOLAS SINGS OF ANAM CARA
The longing of my body
is the longing of my soul.
Selfsame the desires,
that all of your mysteries
will open to me.
I will treasure them
as spirit gifts
dwell in you complete,
belonging.

S kena, come walking with me."
It had taken but little time after I talked with Uncle Ith to decide, to know that my soul had chosen for Skena and would move to win her despite our ages.

Over Skena's shoulder, Bile met my eyes. He must have sensed my new urgency, for his eyes widened.

Skena's back was to me, her fingers firmly placed on either side of his little cheeks. For all the weeks of Skena's working, Bile could utter no more than "Ah" and a sound that resembled "New, new, new," like the mewling of a kitten.

It seemed to me that we were better to leave him be, to let him express himself with his eyes and his humming tunes and, best of all, with his drawings, which grew more complex and expressive as he learned to manipulate his chalks with his left hand.

Now he nodded at me enthusiastically and pointed to his chalks and papyri.

"Do you wish to draw?" Skena asked, beginning to gather his materials.

"Ah," he answered, pointing toward the door.

She shook her head, not comprehending. He snatched a papyrus and made a rapid-fire sketch of a tower.

"Oh, you wish to go to the tower?"

He shook his head, frustration specifying every gesture.

I smiled at her gently. "He wishes for you to go to the tower with me so that he can have some time to draw alone."

"Oh!" Skena clapped her hand over her mouth. "I am frustrating you, little brother! I am so sorry."

His eyes filled with laughter and he held out his good arm. She dropped toward him and he threw the arm around her neck and kissed her cheek gently.

I felt an odd surge of envy that she would embrace him so freely, immediately felt ashamed of myself for so selfish a thought.

"New," he said, and pointed at the door.

"Go?" I asked. Bile nodded with delight, well pleased with both of us for finally understanding our lessons. When I looked back at him he was bent above his drawings, already absorbed in the detail.

Skena threaded her arm through mine and we walked across the edge of the cattle pasturage to the forest that lined the crest of the hill. From deep inside the trees, we could hear the soft rhythm of the sea. I loved this moment, the moment when I would emerge from the trees to the insistent pounding of the surf, when the soft hint of the forest became the urgent tumble of the shore. From all my years in Egypt, I was unused to the deep green of the forest giving way to the sea, and the walk had a magical aspect, more so that she was beside me, her arm resting in mine.

I thought of Airioch and drew my other hand over her fingers, entwining them with mine. She did not remove them, let them remain in the braidwork they made.

We threaded our way to the top of the tower, me bounding the stairs, she puffing a little and stopping to place her hand over her heart, then swatting me playfully.

"You are a warrior and young, Amergin. Go more gently for an old lady."

"No old lady you, nor warrior I," I protested. "Only a man of songs and dreams. From here I can see them."

"From the tower?" she asked. "All the way to Inisfail?"

We had reached the tower platform with its wide embrasures overlooking the sea, its central fire banked and untended until darkness.

I did not look out to sea, but kept my back to the wall, regarding her. I did not take my eyes from hers.

"No," I said. "Not from the tower. From here."

For a moment she looked confused. Then her face suffused with color and she lowered her head, hid behind the waterfall of auburn hair.

"Skena," I whispered. "I dream of you in the darkness and the day."

What happened next I shall not forget. Though I grow old and foolish, though I journey to the Country of the Young, it shall remain in my memory like an ember, like the light that burns forever in that tower by the sea.

Skena stepped forward until her face was tipped up inches from mine.

"Then awaken, dreamer," she said, softly. And in that moment I knew that she, too, had chosen for me.

My arms were around her so swiftly that even I was surprised. I moaned aloud when my lips covered hers. She whimpered, a soft, girlish sound that made my legs feel weak beneath me. I found that I needed to feel my hands on her skin, her skin against mine. She helped me with the fumbling and I drew her down upon me, the curtain of her auburn hair dropping over our kisses and our sighs. And then there was the rhythm of the waves and the rhythm that we made, one heartbeat at the center of the world.

When at last we had crossed our own vast sea, she raised up on her elbow beside me, her hair curling over the curve of an impossibly white breast, her legs still entwined with mine.

"Amergin," she whispered softly, "I shall remember this day with joy for all of the days of my life."

"Remember?" I said, bewildered. "Shall we not wish this day again and yet again? Oh, sweet my love, you sound as though you will part from me."

Her eyes filled with tears. "Your brother Airioch will speak for my hand; I fear that it will come at the Beltaine feis."

"You fear it?"

Her face had tightened until her eyes seemed to fill the orb. She nodded.

"You are a woman of the Galaeci. Say him nay."

"If I say him nay, I will wound his pride. He will see to it that Bile is removed from my keeping."

"But this would be beyond all cruelty—to both you and Bile."

"See him clearly, Amergin."

I thought about what my uncle Ith had said and of Airioch himself. Would he speak for her hand to win her? Would it be to best me, his young half brother? Would it be just a play in his game of seduction?

"But why would he speak for you? He knows you not at all."

She said nothing. And then I understood.

"Because he could not have you any other way."

She nodded. "Your brother is twelve years my senior; most of the women of the Galaeci are married. He does not have as wide a pool to choose from as once he did, and I am . . . I was . . . untried . . . until to-day. He thinks of me as a prize to be won." Her neck speckled with color. I brushed my fingers across the blushing whiteness, felt desire rise in me again. I cupped my hand around the back of her head, leaned toward her. She pressed her fingers gently against my lips. She spoke softly. "Amergin, I cannot be removed from Bile. I love him as if he were my child."

"He cannot remove you if you are wife to another."

She shook her head, the auburn hair skimming across the milky skin so that I could feel my desire ignite my body again.

"Oh no. No. I could not ask that of you, though I have thought it often."

"You have thought it?"

She nodded, her face a mask of shame. "But such a thought was selfish of me. You are poet and bard, apprenticed. The time will come when your tribe will rely upon your judgment, when you may be required to journey as your uncle Ith did. Besides, you are a young man. I have more than five years upon you. You have never married, nor had another love. You deserve to be a young man, to explore all the worlds before you."

"You are saying that you would want me? As husband?"

She silenced. Looked away.

"Look at my eyes."

She looked up, locking her eyes with mine.

"Tell me that you look into the eyes of a boy," I commanded.

"I look into the eyes of him that I have loved for so long," she whispered, fear welling up in the words.

"You love me?" Joy surged through me then, unlike any that I had felt before in my life.

"Of course," she said softly. "I have loved you from the first moment that I saw you tune your harp for your brother."

"I thought that you would not love me because I am too young."

"And I thought the same because I am too old."

"See what fools our thoughts have made of us."

She lifted a shoulder, said nothing. When her eyes met mine, they shone with water.

"I shall speak for you at tonight's meal if you will have me," I said softly. "Now. Before anyone else can speak."

She hesitated for a moment only, and then her eyes lit with determined radiance. "Then, I will have you, beloved."

I lifted my hand tentatively to her breast. "Do you wish me to love you again?" I whispered.

She raised to me a face of complete joy and trust. "I am your Ceolas," she whispered.

For the rest of that afternoon, we sang in a language that would be ours and ours alone for all of time.

9

The time has come for the sons of Mil to depart for Inisfail! All of the Galaeci are welcome to accompany us. This will be the journey of our destiny!"

The clans gathered around the fire erupted in a babble of voices.

Why my father had chosen this feast, this night of all nights, to announce our departure, I knew not. Some inner mechanism of his longing, some sundial, seemed to tell him that the hour was upon us. Selfishly, I was glad that I had spoken for Skena at the start of the evening, and that my request had been accepted with a nod and my mother's quick "Of course, dear." Even Airioch had raised his fist to me in the soldier's sign of victory and grinned his most suggestive grin.

Perhaps I should not have been surprised; our care of Bile had made us inseparable. Perhaps the clans already saw us as a mated pair. The knowledge of it filled me with quiet joy. I kept turning toward her where she sat with Bile on her lap, certain that I had imagined it all. Each time she looked back at me, her face was suffused with love. Bile even winked at me once, as though he had always known it.

For a moment it struck me that all along, I had been wishing for our journey to Inisfail, and now that it had come, I no longer needed to go. My Inisfail was wherever Skena and Bile were; the journey of my life would be made with them.

Though my father, too, had decided on his journey, his announcement among the clans had not produced the result that he desired. Women shouted that they would not part from their homelands; some of the Galaeci warriors called my father crazy.

"You have wandered far from us, Mile Easpain," one cried. "You are more Greek or Roman than Galaeci. They are the wanderers of the world. We are the clans of Galicia and here we shall remain."

My father looked stunned, never mind that he had never served in either Greece or Rome. He had just discovered the sad truth that he was a stranger among his own people. My heart moved in sympathy.

Now my mother stood and moved into the firelight. She made an imposing figure with her sturdy little body clad in warrior leathers, her long black hair cascading down past her waist, her eyes ringed for the occasion with the precious kohl of Egypt. I wondered if she knew how strange her little darkness seemed among her husband's huge clansmen or if she felt that she had truly become one of them. She answered my questions immediately.

"I am none of your clan!" she cried. "I am daughter of pharaoh of Egypt, king of Persia. Yet all of my life with my warrior husband, I have heard of the great deeds of the Galaeci, of your fearless, nomadic spirit. I have journeyed far in your wagons to reach you here, and I have chosen to become one of you for the journey. Where is your wandering spirit now?"

"The wife of Mil speaks well," cried one of the clan mothers. "I and my clan will journey!"

"Nay," cried another. "You will divide the clans; how shall we stay related when the sea separates our children one from the other?"

It seemed to me that all of the arguments made sense. Though I was poet by training and knew that my words would hold weight, I kept silent, knowing myself also for young. Perhaps too there was some selfishness in me, for here in the firelight with Skena and Bile, I had no wish to test the whims of the great heaving sea beyond Breogam's Tower. For the first time in my life, I was full of belonging and needed no journey to explore what was here within my grasp.

Into the void around the fire came An Scail, the Shadow. She wore her long white robes, embroidered with gold and silver, enhanced with little bells at hem and cuff. At her neck was a lunula of hammered gold in the shape of the crescent moon. Her long white hair cascaded behind her, at one with her robe. Though she was most ancient, I had the fleeting thought that it was obvious to me why my uncle Ith had loved her alone through all the years of his exile.

An Scail circled the fire once, those odd silver eyes catching the firelight, mesmerizing the company. Silence fell down upon us like the sea fog.

When only the crackling of the logs could be heard, she spoke, so softly that all the company leaned in to hear her.

"My brothers and sisters. Hear me well, for my wisdom is old. Here at the edge of the sea we have dwelled for more than a hundred years. Here did our ancestor Breogam build the great stone lighthouse and command that it cleave the night's darkness with fire. Here did we first hear the tales of Inisfail.

"Who among you has not climbed those stony stairs and looked out to the north? Who among you has not whispered, 'Inisfail, I will come to you, Isle of Destiny'?"

The crowd shifted and murmured, for surely it was ritual among them.

"In Mile Easpain, that ancient journey is more than ritual. It is an imperative."

I knew what she meant. For my father, this journey was his polestar, the fixed constant of his wandering life, the final place of his journey.

"Still," she continued, "the best journeyer is the wise journeyer. And we of the Galaeci would be wise before we send our children to the sea."

Again, nods and murmurs.

"So we of the Druii offer to you our services as emissaries. From among us Ith, brother of Mil, will take to the sea with two of our own druii. Together, they will petition the Greeks for passage. They will journey to Inisfail and return to us with the wisdom of the place.

"Mile Easpain, will you allow us to choose from among the company three warriors who will best serve us on the journey?"

I do not know if my father had been aware of their plan. If he had not, none of the company could have known it from his response, for he stood among the druids as if the idea had been known to him all along.

"I salute my brother and his companions, bravest of our wisdom keepers. I will abide by the knowledge they return. To them the choice of fellow journeyers from among my sons and the clans of the Galaeci."

I knew him well enough to see the look of hope upon his face, his wish to journey to Inisfail, but I knew with certainty that it was me my uncle Ith would choose. The impending separation from Skena and Bile sat in my stomach like a stone. Had she not said to me only yesterday when she was cradled in my arms that I would be called upon to travel. She turned toward me now, her face pale in the firelight, her eyes large.

Ith came forward with two young druids by his side. He embraced my father, clapping him on both shoulders, clasping arms from elbow to hand.

"I shall be the faithful ears and eyes for our people," Uncle Ith cried. "The safety of our journey shall be my sacred trust. I shall return to you the knowledge of my going and my coming home. I choose as my warrior companion"—here I drew myself up and let out a long, ragged breath— "Airioch Feabhruadh, son of Mile Easpain."

The shock on my father's face was mirrored only by the shock in my own heart. I barely heard as the second druid chose his own brother, a man of the clans that I did not know, and the third my own elder brother Eber Donn.

10

"Why not me? Why not my father? Not Airioch! Uncle Ith, I plead with you to change your mind."

In the low conical hut amid the towering pines, Uncle Ith was packing his hide bag for the journey. Behind him I saw An Scail wrap a long crescent of wood incised with markings in a tanned and waterproof hide. She slipped it into his bag.

She saw me watching and smiled. "We are the Oak People," she said. "It bears our sacred name."

"How could you let him do this?" I asked, my anger making my respect for her slip.

"Let? One does not let fate, Amergin. Fate is; to be his brother's eyes and ears has been Ith's fate for all his life. Your father is an impetuous man, a strong warrior who acts first and thinks second. Your uncle is his wisdom; they are two halves of one being. I do not 'let,' I accept."

"But why Airioch?" I turned back to Ith. "He will not serve you. Airioch serves himself. This you know."

"It will serve my purpose to have him with me."

"What purpose could that be?"

"The purpose is you, boy," said An Scail. Her voiced sounded frayed, irritable.

"Me?"

"Can you see nothing?" Her silver eyes challenged me from across the dwelling.

Uncle Ith sighed. "Sweeting," he said softly. "Did we not agree?"

"We did," she answered. But her voice broke on the saying.

Uncle Ith smiled. "All life is duality, Amergin. Learn this well. Action is followed by reflection. Journey is followed by remembrance. Learning is followed by teaching. You have a new family; Bile needs your strong arms, and Skena your love and protection."

"My own selfishness has told me this. But you will need me on the journey. I can protect you. I can sing the truth of what we see."

"This I know to be true, but I need other things from you. You are a poet in training. That position will bear much responsibility to the clan; a poet must be well schooled and wise. I will not live forever, lad. You must follow me. I do have a mission to ask of you, and I ask that you perform it well."

"Ask anything of me and I will give it. This you know."

He looked at me long then, and his eyes filled with unshed water.

"I know it well," he said softly. "You are the son of my heart. In our journeys together, I have taught you all that I know. But there is one whose knowledge is deeper and older than mine. I would have you learn from her before this journey begins."

I knew he spoke of An Scail; I am ashamed to say that the knowledge made my stomach curl with fear.

"While I am gone, I wish you to study with her. You must learn the deep knowledge, the workings of the universe. You must study every day. Will you promise me that?"

For my uncle I swallowed my fear for him and my pride. I spoke humbly to An Scail. "If you will have me, Wise Teacher, I will prove an apt pupil."

Her face registered surprise.

"Do you see?" asked Ith. "There is wisdom here beyond his years."

"I do see," she said softly. "I thought that he would argue."

"Then let me argue Airioch," I said. "Any other of my brothers would be a wiser choice."

"Which is why our apprentice has chosen Eber Donn," said An Scail. "He is your father's twin, an impulsive warrior, but loyal as the trees."

I saw then that they had planned it carefully: my warrior brother and two men not of our clan, all but Airioch loyal to Uncle Ith.

"O you gods. You take him away because you fear what trouble he might cause. For my father. For me. For Skena and Bile."

Ith acknowledged the truth of my words with a single nod. "But also, a man like Airioch has a singular eye. Because he sees what will benefit him, he sees what will benefit the tribe. You will have much to do here, Amergin. Your father must prepare all of his clan for this great journey, their goods and their gear. You must prepare their spirits."

"I will do as you have asked," I said.

"This I have known from the first," said Uncle Ith. He exchanged a long look with An Scail, full of unspoken sorrow for their impending separation.

CEOLAS SINGS OF CHANGE
Even the wind sings change.
The very seasons
wear it as a cloak.
All souls journey into the West
and all return.
Do not fear change, my kinsmen.
Stand strong before it.
For it will come upon us
whether we will it, or no.

We came down to the sea, to the inlet where the Greeks had anchored the bireme that would take our scouting party north. I clasped Uncle Ith hard by his arms and did all that I could not to weep like a stripling child. Bile did weep, the "Ah, ah" sounds ripping me to the heart.

"Return to us safely," I whispered.

He put me back at arm's length. "I am never gone from you, lad. Never. Learn well from An Scail."

My father approached, and he and Ith bent heads together in whispered conversation as I had seen them do since childhood, then clasped each to the other. I realized suddenly and for perhaps the first time that my father loved Ith as I did.

I clasped arms with Airioch in the soldier's way. "Care for him," I urged him. "He is old and more frail than he seems." I would not release him until he answered.

"Why, what else would I do for our uncle?" Airioch replied lightly. "And you care well for her." He pointed at Skena. "Ride once or twice for me; I should have liked it well." He grinned his most wolfish grin and bounded toward the ship. "Come, Uncle," he cried. "The sea waits for no man, druid or no!"

I saw Uncle Ith place his hand against An Scail's cheek. I saw her tip the silvery eyes toward his own. I do not know what words passed between them, but I saw her nod once.

And then they were gone, the square sail of the bireme dipping and rising as it led them out to sea, away to the north. To Inisfail.

11

The full moon crested the horizon, luminous and orange, its resident rabbit tilted forward toward the bowl of the sea. I made my way through the forest softly, rolling inward from the sides of my feet, making no sound at all, just as An Scail had taught me to do.

My heart hammered like a bodhran as I shifted through the dark trees. Samhain.

Tonight I would stand among the druids as they ushered out the old year and chanted in the new. There in the sacred oak grove, I would stand in the Sacred White Circle for the first time. More than six months had passed since my uncle and my brothers departed on the sea. Tonight we would know what message Ith had sent us from across the sea.

Had I known what studying with An Scail would entail, I might not have agreed so readily to Uncle Ith's request to be her student. Hours of standing first on one leg, then the other, my arms encircled, in a move that An Scail called An Corr, the Heron, were followed by the study of star charts drawn on the forest floor, each with its own story.

"We believe," An Scail said softly, "that there are Star People out there, for would the Creator waste so vast a sky as this?"

Each morning there was warrior study. The druids of the martial arts taught me to run in the forest in absolute silence, even to still my breathing to the breath of the leaves. I could throw a spear and hit the smallest target, leap into the air and twist down, stabbing sword in hand.

I memorized hundreds of poems and songs, the entire history of the Galaeci and of the greater Keltoi who wandered across the world. I learned the cycles of the earth and the cycles of the people, we whose souls go across the water and then return again and yet again. I learned that the Creator of the world is a maker of superfluous abundance.

"We must acknowledge that abundance with both solemnity and joy," An Scail taught me. "It is a gift worthy of the gratitude of the Galaeci."

And then at last, after many months, the Dreaming—three days of fasting without food or water, alone in the far forest on a high cliff overlooking the sea.

But no vision came.

On the third night the moon had been full and white, a knowing eye in a sky spangled with stars. I was seated in the Sacred Circle, staring out at the sea. I felt drowsy and cold, almost empty, a vessel awaiting water. I looked out at the geese-wing path the moonlight made on the water. At the apex of the V was an island, a small stone outcropping that the Galaeci knew to be deserted but for cormorants and water seals.

Suddenly I saw a white light followed by a strange blue ovoid. Moments later, a flame flared up at its crest, sending red sparks toward the night sky.

I did not dream it. I know well enough that to deprive the body of food and water is to open the door to vision. We Keltoi have practiced such rituals for centuries. This was fire, real and red and warm, like the hill-to-hill signal fires of Samhain Eve. It was followed soon after by a flash in the sky, a sudden whiteness followed by blue light, something shimmering, viscous like a waterfall, through which I could see the attenuated stars. Then darkness. The fire had been extinguished. The night sky was as it had been: moon and pinprick stars.

I remember that I tried to rise but my body, folded so long into its waiting position, would not come up with me. My legs had fallen asleep. I crawled from the circle and threw myself on my back, massaging the blood back into the limbs. When at last they stopped tingling, I rose and ran through the midnight forest all the way to the hut of An Scail.

"Coracle or curragh, it does not matter. If I have to swim, I will go. Someone was on that island. Something is there!"

An Scail held up her hand.

"I believe you, Amergin. This is the strength of vision, that the veil between this world and the next separates, and we see what is there. You have had a powerful vision, a parting of the veil. You are most fortunate."

"No. Honored Teacher, there is a quality of vision that was not present at that moment. No vision came to me in the Dreaming. I sat hungry and tired, my legs asleep, and nothing came. And then I saw fire on the Isle of Seals. Real fire."

She tipped her head, and the strange silvery blue eyes regarded me. At last she spoke. "We will need the largest of the curraghs and several men to row. The water between here and the stone is rough."

"We?"

"Do you think that a good teacher would let her pupil go alone?"

And so we went, the ancient woman, her student, the rowers who would not venture from the boat, who turned it beetle-backed upon the rocky shore and made the sign against the evil while we scrabbled our way to the crest of the treeless rock, at the last, me dragging and pulling a weary An Scail up the stony scree.

We were not disappointed. There at the crest, wrapped carefully in its waterproof hide, was Uncle Ith's curved oaken stick. Between us, An Scail and I turned it all ways, face up and face down, toward the light and toward the shadow. She ran her hands over it delicately again and again. It was precisely the stick that he had taken with him. It said exactly what it had said when Uncle Ith departed—"The Oak People"—carefully incised in ogham letters on its face. It was alone, wrapped in hide, at the top of a hill on a deserted island. And that was all. Nothing more.

For a long time we sat there at the crest of the hill, amazement rendering us silent. At last I ventured what we both were thinking.

"How did it come here? And why? And if it says what last we saw, what message more?" I also feared for Uncle Ith's safety, though I did not say so to my teacher.

"Ith is well," she said simply, having read the question in my mien or perhaps in my heart of hearts. I no longer questioned the well of her knowledge, which was ancient and most deep.

"And of the message?"

"I try to think as Ith thinks. Samhain approaches. He will know that we are strongest then, that the druii in the Sacred Circle speak directly to the gods themselves. It is then that he will speak to us. He must want you among us, boy, to have sent the message at this very time." She nodded.

"You will stand with us in the Sacred Circle. We must prepare your lunula and your robes."

And so the orange moon rising into white by slow degrees, my heart beating beneath the soft wool of my new robes, the small golden circlets of the male druii clicking at the hem of my robe as I nervously shifted side to side. While other druids had been sent to the village to perform the Samhain rituals there, this was the circle of High Druids, the most ancient and wisest among the priesthood. I felt humbled and more than a little afraid to be among them, and my legs trembled. Each druid was flanked by two tall oaks so that we formed a perfect forest circle, the dark oaks, the druii in their white cloaks tinted orange, awaiting full moonrise.

On the neck of each was a lunula, a huge hammered crescent of gold or silver that represented the moon, the Keeper of Time. As the moon rose higher and whitened in its arc, the lunula reflected her face, so that a dark crescent winked and flickered between each oak.

I stilled myself, inhaled the breath of the forest—oak leaves and pine needles, mint and onion, fecund life, wet with promise. Here was the smell of abundance, the pungent odor of forever. Awe caught at my breath.

Just at that moment, the moon approached zenith. The drum began, one of the acolytes beating on the bodhran in deep, measured tones. Another drum answered from the far side of the circle. Back and forth the drums spoke.

We began to chant with them, the deep thrumming of the male druii counterparted with the light voices of our sisters.

"Give thanks to Creation.
Buiochas le cruthú.

Oh, be not afraid.
Na' bi'odh eagla ort.

Give thanks to Creation.
Buiochas le cruthú.

Wait upon the Light.
Fanacht le Solas."

Back and forth we chanted as the moon crested. Now An Scail approached the eldest of the druii, a lighted pine-pitch torch in her hand. I saw her ancient brother limned in firelight as she tipped the torch toward his own. It caught and flared with a whooshing sound. One by one she moved among us; one by one the torches lighted. As they did, I could see clearly each druid, white-haired and dark, male and female, standing small between the ancient, towering trees, a pail of water by each priestly side as precaution for protecting the wise old oaks, who bore our prayers skyward.

"Buiochas le cruthú," An Scail whispered to each acolyte, who whispered in repeat as the torches lighted. She reached me last, her torch tipping forward to ignite mine. "Buiochas le cruthú," she whispered, and I repeated the chant. Suddenly, her ancient hand reached out, and I felt her delicate fingers on my cheek.

"Ah, wondrous, Amergin," she whispered. "Most wondrous. You weep at the presence of the Sacred. Here in the Sacred White Circle, you are truly blessed among us, for Creation has made its full Wonder known to you and you have wept for the Presence of God."

I bowed my head in awe.

Silence moved around the circle then. Drums and chanting stopped. A wind picked up and whispered through the forest top. Far beyond the grove I could hear the wash and drum of the sea. Our torches burned and tiny sparks ascended toward the stars. We were silent for a long time, until the moon passed zenith and began its retreat to the horizon.

An Scail led us in procession out of the Sacred Circle to the Druid Broch, a stone tower just beyond the trees. There we extinguished our torches and sat in a circle around the lodge fire, the sacredness of the moment still holding us in silence.

At last, An Scail stepped forward with Uncle Ith's oak curve in her hand.

"We have received a message from our brother Ith," she said, "who has journeyed for many months to Inisfail. We ask the gods for wisdom that we might unlock that message on this most sacred night.

"Amergin." She beckoned in my direction.

I stepped to the center of the circle and took the proffered curve in hand.

I tipped it toward the firelight, first the plain side, then the side with its ogham incisings. There, among the stick words, was something new, something that had not been there when An Scail and I rowed out to sea. It looked like a triangle, slightly raised from the wood. Deep in its surface were spirals, twined together as vines.

"Here, Honored Teacher," I said, handing the curve toward her.

"Tell us what you see," she commanded.

"I see a raised shape, three-sided, like the pyramids of Egypt." It crossed my mind that perhaps the druii did not know the pyramids, but they said nothing, and I remembered that their wisdom was old and well traveled.

"And it was not there when first we found the ogham stick?"

"It was not."

"Stand before the fire then and press upon the shape."

I turned and faced the fire. I pressed the little shape with my thumb. There was a slicing of the air, sharp and white. It mimicked what I had seen from the vision circle. For a moment, the fire looked viscous behind the white light, slow and gleaming like a waterfall. Then, suddenly, there was a woman, most beautiful. She stood encased in blue light at the center of the flame; it seemed she stood upon the flames themselves. Her hair was copper, long, curling in wave after wave. Her skin was milky white. Only her eyes seemed somehow unlike ours, huge, almond-shaped orbs, blue and gray as the wild sea beneath the cliffs. Though she looked at us directly, I had the strange impression that she did not see us at all.

"I send greetings to An Scail, the Shadow, and to Amergin, son of Mil, from Ith of the Sacred Circle. He dwells among us here in . . . Inisfail and is well." Her voice was mellifluous and low.

There was a pause; the form of the woman dipped and seemed to shrink; it crackled out of shape and then re-formed itself. Her voice began again as though it echoed, as though it came from a deep well.

"I am Eriu of the Three Sisters."

Behind her, two other forms shifted into place, female, though they seemed shadowy and insubstantial, as if they stood in a place of little light.

"These are my sisters Banba and Fodla. We are of the Tribe of the Danu, the Children of the Braid.

"Ith has been among us and has told us of the desire of the Galaeci to journey to Inisfail. We are not a warrior race, though, like you, we are journeyers. We have spoken of Ith. Of us, Ith alone will tell you. You must trust the story he brings you. He has treated us with honor. We return him to you with honor. May he come safely back to you."

The woman sputtered like a candle in wind. Her form seemed to shrink and thin until it looked like a single blue flame. With a popping sound, she vanished.

I stared at the place where she had been. I pressed the little triangle with my thumb again but no form emerged. I stared down at the little pyramid shape on Ith's oak crescent.

"Honored Teacher," I whispered. "The pyramid is fading."

"She has said what she came to say," said An Scail. "Obviously, she expects we of the druii to remember her warning."

"Warning?"

"We will be welcome only as long as we come in peace."

"She must already have met Airioch," I muttered, unthinking. One or two of the druids hid their mouths behind their hands.

An Scail did not reply. She seemed deep in thought.

"You and Skena will move with Bile into Breogam's Tower," she said suddenly. "We must begin the watch for Ith's return. We will be most curious to hear of the Journey of these Children of the Braid, for something went unsaid. I will go to speak to your father."

One of the druids spoke from the circle. "Will you need my arm, Honored One? It is a night of much strangeness."

"Amergin will accompany me," she said. "I thank you. I will fetch my cloak."

When she left the room for her lodge, the druid approached me. "Support her well, younger brother. The Samhain Circle wearies her vision, and we fear that her Sight will be much taxed by the events of the evening."

"The torches trouble her eyes?" I asked. "Or was it the message from the ogham wand?"

"Neither," said the druid, his head tilted sideways. He seemed to be eyeing me in surprise. "It is her vision that is taxed. An Scail is blind."

*   *   *

I held to her hard in the dark forest, all my months of study, all my pride in my hard-won knowledge, shaken to the core. How had I not known? All this time; the strangeness of the silvery owl eyes. Why had I not seen?

An Scail sensed the difference in the way I guided her. "They have told you that I am blind, have they not?"

"I should have seen . . . should have known."

"And how?"

"I don't know. You asked me to describe the oak crescent. On the hill, you kept running your hands over it. I don't know." I shook my head helplessly.

"I could have seen it perfectly well myself, Amergin. I asked you to describe it for the group."

"How would you have seen it?"

"With my hands. I hear more than you hear. My hands can see more than most people see with their eyes. I can smell and identify the way our wolfhounds do."

"So you have always been blind?"

"No. My sight left me more than ten years ago. I could actually see the first eye go milky in my mirror, but even before then I knew that my vision was departing when I could not see the stars."

I stopped suddenly on the path, struck by a thought so sad that it took my breath from me. "Oh, An Scail. You could not see Ith when he returned."

She was silent for a long moment and her hand patted my supporting arm gently. "I see why Ith loves you so, Amergin. You think with the soul of the poet. You speak with your compassion. But do not trouble yourself. I have seen Ith's face with my hands, but perhaps I have been given a gift, for my mind's eye sees him as he was when he departed with your father so long ago, young and strong with his hawk nose and his long dark hair."

I thought of my uncle now, the thin ring of white hair, the bald pate. I said nothing at all.

After a moment, An Scail chuckled gently.

"You are becoming a wise man, Amergin. But now we must go to your father. There will be many preparations, and first among them, we must keep the tower light at full fire. Now be careful, for there is a great root here on the path and it will trip us both."

"How do you know that?" I asked in awe.

An Scail laughed aloud. "Because it was here yesterday. And last week. And the year before."

12

Scota had us seated in family groups around the fire: Eber Donn's three wives and their children, all crying and babbling incessantly; Eber Finn and Eremon and their clans, quieter by virtue of fewer wives; Skena and Bile; Ir and Colpa.

An Scail and me she had seated in the position of honor at the front of the room, a place which made me very uncomfortable surrounded by my elder brothers and their families.

Scota's servants moved among us with warm mead. They served the traditional meal of the new year, wild boar and haunch of deer steamed in fulacht fiadh, the wood- and stone-lined cooking pits that made the meat so tender that it fell from the bone; a rich seaweed soup heated in leather bags by hot stones; and a salty seaweed laver bread. Finally, they brought sticky, delicious honey-cakes, all designed to fuel us for the cold and dark half of the year—the Gaimred—that we had entered at the turning of last night's moon.

When the feast was finished my father stood before the company. In his blunt and soldierly way, he went directly to the heart of the matter.

"What does it mean?" He turned his attention to An Scail and to me with a look that was as trusting as Bile's face when he regarded Skena. For the first time, I realized that my father was a man completely composed of action, a man who acted and reacted to everything with no wavering— sudden decision, complete movement. I realized that it was no real wonder that he had wandered the world, made his decision to return to Galicia based upon the darkening of the sun. It was as though a wind shifted inside him and he turned in the way that it blew. I realized that his ability to act quickly was probably what made him so masterful a soldier that emperors and pharaohs trusted his actions. I also realized that I was cut from completely different cloth.

An Scail stood before the company; I knew that she sensed my diffidence, my awkwardness before the whole assemblage of my clan, and I was grateful to her for assuming the burden of telling.

Mothers hushed the children; by degrees, the central chamber of the dwelling grew quiet.

"We have had a message," she said; "Ith returns to us."

My father shouted aloud. "This is well!" he cried. "Lads, we must begin the preparations. The ships. The horses. Which of the clans will accompany us?"

An Scail held up her hand. "There is more." Her tone was ominous, quiet.

Even my father sat instantly.

"The island . . . Inisfail . . . is already occupied."

"That will not impede us," said my father, cheerful and sure of himself.

"It may," said An Scail. "I hear in them some difference from us. Their voices sound . . . reedy, somehow . . . like the bone flutes of the cattle herders."

I looked up in surprise. She was right. I had not noticed the sound, because I had been so occupied with their appearance, with the strange vessel for the message. An Scail turned her attention to me.

"Amergin," she said quietly. "You must tell your clan what you have seen."

I stood and cleared my throat, bringing Ceolas up with me. I had begun the tale on that night when I had seen the flash of light on the Isle of Seals. All day my mind had been composing it further: the moonlight among the oaks, the druids, the little triangle on the oaken curve, the beauty of the woman in the blue sphere of light, her sisters, the warning, the message that Ith had been treated with honor. I chanted it to them, Ceolas moving warm beneath my fingers, and when I was done, there was silence.

CEOLAS SINGS OF STRANGENESS

How has she sprung from the oak wand
her gray eyes upon us,
her very presence in the room
but not among us?
On this night of moonlight
our wisdom keepers see her, hear her,
though she be worlds away.
Who is the woman in the oak wand,
she who returns our uncle to us,
who sends her message to Seal Isle,
wings it to us in a flash of light?
Return, Uncle, for we would know
the origin of strangeness,
the tale of these,
who travel in the wood.

At last, it was my brother Eber Finn who broke the silence. "What should we do, Amergin?" he asked.

I felt a strange lightness spin through me, a kind of giddy surprise, followed by a weight that settled on my shoulders like a heavy woolen cloak. I cleared my throat.

"An Scail has asked that Skena and I move into the tower. She requests that we keep the tower fires burning high that Ith and our brothers can see their way home. Beyond that, I think that we should wait. The woman Eriu said that Ith alone would bring us the knowledge of her people, of their journey. We must hear that knowledge before we decide to journey to Inisfail."

"This is wise," said Scota. "Mil, I think that we should do as our son has suggested."

My father nodded. "Thank you for your wisdom, Amergin," he said. He came to where I was standing and clapped me on the shoulder. "Good man."

"Amergin?"

"Mmm?"

I came up from a deep slumber, to the long threads of her hair fanned across my chest, to her lips tickling the side of my ear. I turned toward her, as I did each morning, traced my hand along the sweet curve of her cheek, the soft whiteness of her breast. I loved the sound of her breath catching at my smallest touch.

"The night watch has left the tower and Bile has descended to fetch the breakfast. We have a little time."

"Ah, really? Time for what? What do you suggest, red woman?"

She laughed and swatted at me. "I suggest that you love me."

"You suggest that every morning."

Her face flushed. "I am emboldened, then, because you take my suggestion every morning."

I rolled up then and over her, bracing myself on my arms. She stroked them gently, her hands sliding down from my shoulders.

"I must be easily suggestible."

"Well, you are a poet after all. The smallest words suggest large purpose." She smiled, veiled her eyes. I watched the delicate lashes fan against her cheeks.

"Large purpose is it, love? Who is the poet now?"

She laughed and pushed against me, but her back was already arching.

We had moved into Breogam's Tower, Skena and Bile and I. And though I had but nineteen years, I was at last fully a man. Wisdom singer for the clan. Husband to Skena. Father for all purposes to Bile. Skena and I kept the fire in the lightkeeper's room just above our own chamber burning so high that our room below was warm, even though it was winter. On the nights when the watch was mine, she kept me company, humming along to my harpsongs, sometimes joining me at the window, our arms twined around each other, our faces illumined by the light from the sea, our watch punctuated by small kisses and sweet sighs until at last we could bear it no more and wrapped ourselves together for the briefest of couplings before resuming the watch.

On nights when others of the tribe took the watch, we slept folded together in our chamber below. Though it was furnished simply with a sleeping platform wide enough for two, a smaller platform for Bile, a table, and four curved Roman chairs that some long ago Galaeci had acquired in a trade, for me that chamber in the tower was and will remain forever the room of complete abundance.

Even when we were apart, tending to the business of the clan or to

Bile, we remained tethered to each other by an invisible thread of shared knowledge.

As for Bile, he ran up and down the tower stairs like the mountain goats of Greece, climbing and descending so many times a day that his legs grew strong and tireless.

He took to playing with our baby brother Ir, who had upon him now four years. This made Bile, with his own nine years, the big brother. No matter to Ir that Bile possessed only one arm and could speak only three sounds. To Ir, Bile was an object of worship. For his part, Bile was tirelessly patient in helping the baby to run and to learn to draw. In Ir's adoring gaze, Bile grew confident and happy. When Ir began to imitate Bile's speech, articulating his own wants as "Ah, ah, ah," Bile stopped vocalizing entirely and taught Ir his own system of gestures and signs. Somehow, Bile's strong body, his silence, and his obvious care for his brother made him much less terrifying to the clan, and I noticed that one or two of them began to learn his signs and to return his conversations with their own hands.

For me, when I did not watch for Ith's return, I studied with An Scail. I wrote songs for Ceolas and played my gaita at the window while I kept the watch for Ith. The songs became beloved of the Galaeci. In the evenings, Bile and I would sing them by the fire, and in his humming accompaniment, the people ceased to fear Bile. By firelight they would call for us by name and Skena would push us forward, whispering, "Sing well, my boys."

I had loved my Skena so often, by day and by night, by the fire in the lightkeeper's room, on the end of the rocky shore, that when she told me that her courses no longer came, it seemed to me inevitable perfection. So much great love could only serve to produce another being, to call back a spirit from the Country of the Young. I began to sing to the womb-child on my harp, and when the moon was full, I sang my praises to Creation with a heart more full than all its whiteness.

CEOLAS SINGS A LULLABY
Come to us, returning child.
Here is the hand of your mother,
she who rocks the womb-cradle,
softly, softly, little one, beloved one,

here is your beautiful mother.
Here is the song of your father
that you might know his voice,
the love he will bear you always.
Come, little journeyer,
swiftly among us.
Grateful our hearts
that we are chosen.
Great the love between us
who will keep you safe from harm.

And at last the morning came when I was standing at one of the windows of the tower looking down at the village spread below us and it came to me that I no longer wanted to leave Galicia, that somehow this place and its people had become home. And soon I would have to leave them.

Too soon, for our idyll lasted for only two full turnings of the moon.

We began the month that bore my brother Airioch's name with a wild storm at sea. Not for the first time, my father fretted that Ith had chosen to return on winter seas. On the sixth morning of that month, when Bile and I were keeping watch at the window, we saw Ith's ship undulating toward the harbor.

I sounded the alarm on the long curved war horn that hung by the tower window for just this purpose and raced for the shore, hand in hand with Skena, Bile and Ir behind us.

By the time I reached the curved bay, the ship was coming into harbor and my father and mother and half of the clan of the Galaeci were assembling.

My father grinned when he saw me and slapped me on the shoulder. "Inisfail, lad. At last, I see our destiny!"

So it was to my father's face that I first looked when they carried my uncle Ith down the gangplank on a litter, Eber Donn and Airioch beside him.

My father ran toward them. The bearers lowered the litter to the ground and we pushed in toward my uncle.

The Ith who returned to us was not the uncle who had left us. Drool coursed from one side of his mouth, and like our brother Bile, Ith had to him no speech. His arm on that same side was useless and flopped about like a fish. Only his one eye seemed to hold any awareness of his surroundings, and it swung wildly from side to side as if it searched for someone or something.

Our father dropped to his knees beside him and gave out such a heartrending cry that I thought my own heart would break. Scota knelt behind him and put her hands against his shoulders. When she looked up to meet my eyes, her face bore a look of piteous supplication, as if she thought that someone, I or Skena, could somehow nurse Ith back to health as we had done with Bile.

I turned to Eber Donn. "He was injured on the sea journey?"

Eber Donn's face twisted with rage. "No. It is they who did this to him, the treacherous Danu, the Children of the Braid."

"The Danu? But they sent us greetings, said that they returned him to us with honor. They indicated that perhaps they would welcome us if we were people of peace."

"We will not give them peace. We will go among them and slaughter them for the treacherous, dangerous creatures that they are."

This Eber Donn shouted, raising his arm in the air and screaming it to the assembled Galaeci as if he bore aloft an imaginary sword.

"Hush!" I commanded. "You frighten our uncle Ith." And indeed, Uncle Ith was twisting on his pallet, mewling and wagging his head from side to side.

Eber Donn heeded my wisdom, pulled me aside. "Hear me, Brother. They are dangerous, duplicitous folk, these Danu. Their women are beautiful but strange. . . . Their eyes, I do not know. They possess magical powers beyond anything even our druii have seen. They seem to disappear and reappear in all hours and in all places with no signs of journey upon them. They are keepers of dark secrets. There are places on the island from which they warn us away, even taking to charging some of their most sacred doorways with lightning bolts. Can you imagine?"

Airioch had sidled over to us and now nodded his head vigorously. "It is true, Brother. I tried to penetrate one of their secret spaces!" He whispered it and then turned his back on the assembled company gathered around Ith.

"Why did you try to do so?"

"They keep treasure," he said. "Vast treasure. They wear ancient jewels and diadems."

I waved my hand at this. "I care not for treasure. Return to Ith. How was he injured?"

"I know not," said Eber Donn. "I was preparing our ships for departure. Ith had decided, he said, that we would not return to Inisfail."

"Why did he decide this?"

"I know not. He said that he would speak to our father of what he had learned. I will tell you that it suited me well enough, for I like them not; they keep impenetrable secrets. On the morning of departure, I went to his hut to fetch him and I found him thus."

Airioch broke in. "They were with him before departure. All of the evening before. The Sisters!" He spat the word. "Banba, Fodla, and Eriu. They did this; they cast some spell upon him."

I returned and leaned over my uncle Ith. Skena was bending to him, wiping the spittle from his cheeks.

"I do not see a spell here," I said. "We will send for Mehmet."

Mehmet, surgeon of Egypt, had become much valued among the Galaeci of all the region, traveling from village to village where his medical expertise could right many wrongs. Eber Donn dispatched a rider to find him.

We carried Ith to the village and made him comfortable in one of the conical dwellings. We placed him on soft furs and pillows, built up the fire. My father refused to leave his side. He wept and apologized over and over for sending him to Inisfail, and rubbed constantly at his own left arm, so agitated that I began to fear that he worsened Uncle Ith's condition.

The druids brought An Scail; her presence seemed to calm Ith greatly as she sat beside him and gently stroked his good hand.

When he was calm, Skena bathed him and fed him sweetened porridge and water.

At last Mehmet arrived and hurried into the dwelling. He examined Ith with care, then spoke directly to Ith himself.

"I have seen this before, old friend. You suffered a great shock, did you not?" Ith slowly closed and opened the one good eye.

"Should I take that to be yes?"

Again the blink.

Mehmet nodded. "Sometimes when the body is old and it suffers a great shock, the mind cannot sustain it. It closes all the pathways that it can. Was it accompanied by a blinding headache?"

Again the blink.

"Pain in the arm."

Blink.

"I *have* seen this before," Mehmet repeated. "But the mind is beyond the practice of medicine, as we have seen with Bile. I have seen the brain that dwells inside the skull. It is carved like a river, with streams and channels that flow in all directions. Sometimes I have seen its pathways reroute themselves. Other times, as with Bile, it is as if the mind has put a dam in its own river. I cannot tell you what your fate will be. Only time will tell that. I am sorry."

The mention of Bile seemed to awaken something in Ith. He began to gesticulate with his good hand, and at last I realized that he was speaking in Bile's finger language.

"Do you wish me to fetch him?"

Ith blinked.

I ran for our little brother, who came into the dwelling, his eyes wide with fright.

"Uncle Ith would speak, but his voice will not work. Only his hands work. Only you can speak to him now."

Bile drew himself up, and I was proud of the way his little body girded itself for the work.

Uncle Ith's hands began to work, and Bile turned to me. He made the sign for his papers and chalks. I ran all the way to the tower, took the stairs two at a time, clutched everything to me, and returned at a run.

Ith gestured to all of us but An Scail, Mil, and Bile that we should depart. Though I was wounded to be sent from the bedside of my beloved uncle, I complied, waiting outside the hut.

Half of an hour passed.

My father staggered from the hut, his eyes wide. He clutched his own arm and reeled against the wall of the hut in an agony of grief. He cried aloud. Sure that Uncle Ith had crossed, I ducked beneath the lintel. Ith was still alive, his eyes turned toward the door through which my father had departed, his face sorrowful. He gestured to me and I knelt beside him. He placed his hand on my head. He shook his own head gently.

"What has happened?"

"Bile has drawn something," said An Scail. "It has greatly upset your father."

I looked down at Bile's sketch. "But it is nothing. It is simply a sketch of lightning, a storm at sea perhaps. Or perhaps the lightning Airioch has spoken of."

Again Ith blinked.

"Is that it, Uncle? Airioch has told us that they guard their doorways with bolts of lightning."

My uncle became agitated again at that, moaning and thrashing from side to side.

"Leave us!" An Scail commanded. "Let me try to calm him."

From outside the hut I heard a piercing cry. I raced to the door. My mother was kneeling beside my father. He had collapsed in the dust; his skin was the color of the winter ground. He was dead. Ith followed before morning.

The sparks rose skyward from the headland.

We had built their biers side by side, lighted the torches beneath them at precisely the same moment. At their heads, we placed the urns that would contain their ashes.

An Scail had been given the honor of lighting the bier of Ith. As eldest, Eber Donn lighted my father's bier, and though he was a warrior, he could barely steady his hand for the strength of his weeping.

Eber Finn and Eremon stood side by side in silence, as much a pair as Ith and Mil had been in life. When the grief threatened to shake them, each fastened an arm over the shoulder of the other, and so they stood, a bulwark against sorrow.

Bile clung to Skena on one hand and held hard to Ir on the other. Someone of the tribe had taken Colpa from my mother. I knew not who quieted him.

Only An Scail seemed well, moving back and forth between the biers, chanting to the brothers, the red fire reflected in her lunula and in the sightless silver eyes.

In the darkness of the sacred moon, their spirits rose from their bodies and drifted toward the stars. I could see the path of the twin fires reflected in the sea far below.

My mother clung to me, barely able to stand alone, so shaken by sobs that I thought they would wrench apart her bones. From time to time, she would cry out, "Inisfail my love, Inisfail." I do not know if she mourned his failure to go to the place of his dreams or blamed the place for his passing. At last, when the fires had burned to nothing, she simply crumpled to the ground like ash. I liftted her up; it was the first time I ever realized how very small she was. I carried her back to her dwelling, and Skena brought a draught that at last allowed Scota to sleep.

Skena and I returned to our tower with Bile and Ir. She curled the children into her arms, until at last the three of them slept. I stood late and long at the tower window, watching away to the north, hollow with the loss of Ith and my father, feeling strangely orphaned in the world.

The night had gone well past the turning time when the breeze carried the sound of weeping, muffled, from the shore below.

I took the tower steps by rolling inward, soundless as the air.

He was curled up below the rocks, his head dropped onto his knees. He was wrapped in his cloak like a shroud; already, its neck was wet from the tears he had wept. He lifted his head and stared out to sea. It was Airioch.

For a moment, I considered departing, returning to my tower. But he was my brother. Or so my father had behaved. And so I came up soundlessly beside him and knelt upon the shore.

He must have sensed my presence. His head snapped up, swift and angry, his eyes wide. He regarded me for a moment and his expressions softened.

"Amergin," he said. "I thought that you were Eber Donn."

"And that angered you?"

He shrugged. "He is my brother. We are sometimes angry with each other."

"I am your brother as well."

Something about the statement brought fresh tears to his eyes; they spilled down his cheeks, silver in the moonlight.

"What have I said to bring you such sorrow?"

He shook his head. "You sounded, then, like Mil."

"Our father?" A wave of loss swept over me again to think him gone.

"Your father. But he never said so, Amergin. Never once. He must have known that I was not his own. Just look at me. But all my life he called me as his son. He treated me no differently than he did Eber Donn. Than he did any of you."

"And this has made you weep?"

"I was not grateful enough. I . . . Why do you think he died, Amergin?"

I sighed. "Sometimes I thought that he and Ith were two halves of the same soul. Mil the warrior and Ith the philosopher, Mil the man of action and Ith the thinker. Perhaps he did not know how to live without Ith."

"O you gods," said Airioch. The sound wrenched up from his soul. "Ith knew me for a bastard, Amergin."

"Ith would not have judged you for your mother's weakness."

"Ith watched me for weaknesses of my own."

It was true enough. I thought for a moment.

"All of us have watched you, Airioch. You keep your feelings close within. Until tonight, I thought you saw our father with disdain. You seem always to have some hidden purpose, some plan that is all your own. And your appetites are large."

My assessment seemed to agitate him. He shifted his position, punched his fist into his hands.

"O you gods," he said. "O you gods."

He turned toward me, his eyes meeting mine. I realized with a start that it was the first time that Airioch had ever looked me directly in the eyes.

"Ith loved you like a son," he said.

It was not what I had expected. The full loss of Ith hit me in the chest and I flattened back against the rock. A sob shook up from my core and I pressed my hand over my mouth that it might not carry to the tower and wake Skena, Bile, and Ir.

Airioch's eyes never left my face. I watched as some decision formed on his face. He nodded once.

"I am your brother, Amergin," he said. "Just as I am Eber Donn's. Know this. You have nothing to fear from me, ever. I am your brother."

He stood and looked out to sea, turned, and walked away. We did not see him for two fortnights.

CEOLAS WEEPS

We have lost a brace of fathers.
What cruelty is this O gods?
What whimsy, that you take from us
our wisdom and our strength
not separate, but together?
How shall we live

Without Ith, without Mil?
How shall we journey
In the hollow world
Without them?

On the night that Airioch Feabhruadh returned, my mother called a Council of the clans.

"I say that we shall go! The sons of Mil shall avenge him in Inisfail!" My mother stood among the assembled company, her dark eyes flashing. She was dressed not in mourning, but as a warrior of the Celts, in leather and war boots, her dagger at her belt, her shortsword at her side.

In the month since my father had died, Scota had mobilized her sorrow to such rage that she had brought my brothers with her, so that Eber Donn, who knew of Uncle Ith's wishes, shouted also for revenge.

Across the fire, my eyes met those of Skena and Bile. I stood among the company. I raised my hands.

Silence moved across the assembly like a wind; even my mother sat down in the circle. When had such a thing occurred? When had I become poet and bard, wisdom keeper and sage? I felt it not as a joy, but as a weighty burden with Ith and my father both gone.

I cleared my throat.

"People of the Galaeci. Let us reason past our grief. First we must consider history. All our lives we have thought of Inisfail as the place of destiny; our legends speak of it for ten generations past."

A general nod moved around the circle.

"Yet in any of those legends, did we hear of those who dwelled there?"

"A well-thought point, Amergin," An Scail called from the fireside.

"And our own brother Eber Donn has told us that Ith did not wish us to return among them. Speak, Eber Donn!"

My brother stood, shamefaced, but determined not to lie.

"It is so. Ith told me that he would recommend to our father that we not go among them."

"And did you not tell me that you liked his decision well and found them fearsome?"

"Fearsome, no! They are little people and would be no match for the sons of Mil and the clan of the Galaeci!" Again he was screaming and raising his arms as if he wielded an imaginary sword.

"Eber Donn!" I shouted above the noise of the crowd. "Speak without the theatrics of war! What did you say of them?"

"I said that they are dangerous and duplicitous, keepers of secrets. And is that not borne out by the deaths of Ith and Mil? Perhaps it was one of their own lightning bolts which killed our uncle. Ask Airioch."

I turned toward Airioch Feabhruadh. "Brother?"

Airioch stood among the company like a stranger, clearing his throat and shuffling from side to side. He would not meet my eyes. It seemed to me that he had not returned from Inisfail, nor from his month of wandering, the bold and insouciant Airioch of old. I wondered how much of that had to do with the Children of the Braid. Had he angered them somehow? Been frightened by them?

"Tell us what you learned on Inisfail," I commanded.

"I tried to enter one of their secret doorways," he said. His voice was soft. A wave of chatter passed across the company but I kept my eyes on Airioch. A crafty and calculating look passed across his face. Here at last was the Airioch of old.

"They are keepers of great treasure, these Danu. They guard it well; they charge their doors with bolts of lightning. I told this to Uncle Ith, but he was not much interested in worldly goods, as well we know."

His statement had precisely the effect he desired. My brothers Eremon and Eber Finn stood at once.

"More reason still to go!" shouted Eremon.

"I agree," cried Eber Finn. "Donn has told us that there is land and cattle pasturage aplenty. Now Airioch tells us of treasure. And all of this in the possession of a people who have killed our uncle and our father, he who wished forever to journey to Inisfail."

"Then we shall take him with us!" cried our mother. She lifted my father's urn, which she would not allow from her sight. She held it into the firelight. "The sons of Mil shall take their father to Inisfail!! And their uncle Ith as well."

And so it was decided.

I returned to the tower with Skena. I folded myself down into her

arms, and I allowed myself to weep like a lost child for my father, who
had never seen his dream; and for my uncle, who had seen it and had not
lived to tell the tale; and for myself, who had lost not one father but two,
and who had not been able to dissuade or protect his clansmen, though I
sensed great danger in the journey.

Eber Donn was dispatched to the south, to the people of the Arganthos,
who traded silver with the Greeks, there to trade tin and other goods for
the fleet that we would need to journey. In the end, we required only seven
ships, for many of the people of the Galaeci declined to accompany us,
based, I supposed, on the tales of Airioch and Eber Donn and on Ith's death,
for he had been beloved of the Galaeci. Frankly, I thought them wise.

We departed in the month of April, with a fair wind and sunny skies,
a fleet of three biremes and four cargo ships. Scota and our baby brother
Colpa sailed on the first ship, with my brother Eber Donn and his three
wives and children. They were followed by my brothers Eremon and Eber
Finn, each in his own ship with wives and children and retinue.

My own ship consisted of myself and Skena, now four months heavy
with our child, Bile, Ir, An Scail and the three druids who had chosen to
accompany her to Inisfail, and various of the Galaeci. Airioch Feabhruadh
commanded our ship, though many of the Galaeci who had chosen to accompany us seemed less than happy to have him as commander.

Most of the days of the journey were uneventful, though once I
thought that I saw her, the woman of the message, when I was seated with
my map across my knees. The vision slipped away when Airioch interrupted me with a reprimand.

The weather at that time of year was warm, and Skena and I slept each
night on the open deck, the clouds scudding across the moon, the great
veil of the cosmos throwing its diaphanous scarf across the night sky. My
love for her, my adoration, grew as the child in her belly grew, and somehow I felt that something of Ith and Mil would be returned to us with the
birth of our child.

Despite the deaths of my father and Ith, we were true Milesians, I
suppose, for a spirit of adventure overtook the company as we moved
north.

Skena and I whispered of it in the darkness.

"I wonder if we shall always be this way," she whispered, "the people of the Gaels, scattering ourselves before the wind, turning toward every curve in the road."

I had my arm wrapped around her and I whispered gently in her ear. "These are the only curves I wish to travel." I ran my hand gently over her swelling breasts and belly.

She giggled aloud. "Your babe will hear you," she whispered.

"Then she will know how much I love the mother who bears her."

"She, is it?"

"It is. And I think that she will be as beautiful as her mother with skeins of ruby hair."

"Such foolishness." She swatted at me, her eyes full of laughter.

"I am foolish for you," I answered, and she turned on her side toward me and pressed her lips to mine, making our little foolishness as vast as the stars sweeping by above the moonlit clouds.

We sighted land in the far distance on the day that tragedy struck. Oh, we were filled with high spirits! Even the sea-wise Greeks had caught some spirit of adventure from us and had taken to calling the island Inisfail. One of our Greek sailors had scurried up the rigging and cried the sighting aloud. I shaded my eyes and watched him from my position in the stern. "Three days hence," he called.

Excitement raced through the ship.

Far ahead, near the bow, Ir and Bile were dashing from railing to railing to see if they could spot their destination. Ir clambered up on the railing, in imitation of the sailor in the crow's nest. Skena was amidship and she called to him to climb down. I saw Ir's little body shifting forward like a seabird, too far forward on the railing. We ran for him, both of us at once. Skena was closer and reached him first. I saw her arms dart forward, saw her swipe at his little body where it tipped above the railing.

She had him! I saw her arms close tight around him. They would have been fine. But then the great ship plunged downward into the trough of a wave. I saw Skena lose her balance, tip forward at the prow.

I called her name aloud, ran toward them.

If only she had not been so heavy with child, her balance undone. If only we had begun the climb along the next crest! They would have been flung back to the deck. Instead, they were flung forward into the sea.

Her face turned toward me as they fell, on it a look of terror and sorrow.

By the time I reached the prow of the ship, both Ir and Skena were gone.

Behind me Bile began to wail his "Ah, ah, ah," and my own soul emptied into the sea and drowned.

PART TWO

CINIOCHA FÁIN

WANDERING TRIBES

NONE WILL KNOW US DARKLY SUNG

Am gaeth i m-muir
    is gaoth ar muir mé
Am tond trethan
    is tonn treathain na farraige
Am fuaim mara
    is glór na mara
Am torc ar gail
    is torc ar gail
Am he i l-lind
    is bradán i linn
Am loch i m-maig
    is loch i maigh
Am brí a ndai
    is briathair aindéithe

13

P eople of the Danu, we call this Council. May we seek wisdom in the Braid!"

The assembled Danu began to take their places, to move from the clusters of discussion in the room to the long, curving benches which lined the walls, their cushions and backs adorned with braiding in cobalt blue and red and emerald green.

The room was a soft blue-gray, the lighting muted so that it would not trouble the eyes of the Ancients. Curling all around the ceiling in purest silver and gold, inlaid with gems, was the unbroken symbol of her people, the woven knotwork that symbolized the Braid.

The acoustics in the chamber were perfect, the walls curved and arched and battened. Eriu would need only to speak in a normal voice. She sighed. The sound carried around the room. The people of the Danu began to silence themselves.

The Sisters stood before their assembled people in the Great Council Hall. Eriu stood at the prow and raised her arms high. She felt the hands of Banba and Fodla slip into hers. Not for the first time in her life, she experienced profound gratitude that she traveled through life in the company of these, her beloved sisters.

"We serve you as did the three brothers before us," said Banba. She referred to Mac Cuill, Mac Cecht, and Mac Grene, who had been the Triad of Brothers before them, and who had been also their three first husbands and teachers as the Sisters trained for their duties as Council Triad.

We serve you as Threeborn of One Mother," Fodla intoned, aware of their nearly miraculous status as triplet sisters.

"We serve you in the ancient Triad decreed by the Weaver of Worlds, she our mother, the Danu. Know in us that all of the creations of Danu are Mother, Child, and the Love that moves between them. See us now and know that you are seen and loved by the Maker of the Braid."

The room silenced, the people's upturned faces waiting. Eriu took a deep breath. She spoke.

"Now is the time to prepare, now when there is still a little time before the arrival of the Invaders. To remember is to prepare. Our own history will sustain us now; we will gather from it the wisdom to go forward. As we have done before." She paused.

"Speak to us of the Invaders," one of the people called out from the crowd.

Eriu nodded. "They come from the south, from a land they call Galicia in a country at the western edge of the Internum Mare." She paused, considered for a moment. Her people would know or remember the reference. It would need no explanation. "They call themselves the Galaeci. Of those who came with them, one was a priest, a druid called Ith. He was a man of great spirit and honor; when he learned of our doorways and saw our Hybrid children, he decided that his people would not return. Of this decision, he said that the Galaeci and the Danu would succeed only in frightening each other."

"And yet you say that they return? Where is honor?" one of the people called out.

Banba spoke. "To our great misfortune, he was not their only spokesman. With him were others of his priestly caste and three warriors. Of these, one was a massive, loud, and hairy being who tramped every field for miles and shouted about cattle and pasturage. The other was a tall and handsome Greek"—here the crowd chuckled, knowing Banba's preference for Greeks—"who was nonetheless far too curious. He asked many questions about our jewels and once tried to enter Tara through one of the portals."

A collective gasp went up from the company. Murmurs of "Fomor," "Just like the Fomor," ran through the room.

"How would you assess them?" asked one of the Ancients, her voice practical and competent. Her very tone seemed to quiet the room, to quell the impending panic.

Fodla stepped before the company. "From what we have been able to judge, they are brighter and more developed than Fir Bolg. Their civilization is complex; they have traveled well. Although we cannot yet know, they seem less brutal, less warlike than Fomor, but far more curious and perhaps as acquisitive. Obviously, they are stubborn or single-minded, as it seems they return against the advice of the wisdom keeper. If these who came here are an indicator, they are, as a race, quite large."

A collective murmur ran through the room.

"And so, what will they think of us?" asked one of the Danu.

Eriu sighed.

What would the Invaders think of them indeed, her diminutive race with its huge eyes and long fingers; what would the Invaders make of their nimbus of light, of their Ancients, of their Raveners?

Here, deep below the earth, in the great city of Tara beneath the great hill, it was not necessary to maintain the Metaphor. Eriu looked out over her people. The littlest children of the Danu dashed about laughing. Their laughter pierced Eriu's heart. Would they laugh again if they could not play on the surface, tumble in the long grasses, bathe in the lakes and waterfalls? How long could she and her people hide here below the surface? The subterranean cities were large and well supplied, but they were purposed to keep the surface pristine and green that all the people of the Danu might enjoy the upper world. And when they could no longer hide, where would they go? Worse, would they laugh again when they had heard the terrible story of the Journey of Exile?

The Ancients were already seated, their skin pale, almost gray, their eyes gone dark and cloudy. Some of them wore the dark lenses that covered their whole orb even here in the soft, subterranean chamber. They gestured slowly with their long, thin fingers. So few were left of the original Braided Ancients, these few who were not of the mixed race of Braided Danu who had married with the Penitents. Eriu herself was mixed, her eyes the soft blue-gray, her hair the curling silver that the Penitents had brought on the Journey. The day would come soon when there would be none of the First Journeyers, when all of the Danu would be those who had been born here on the Green Orb. The few remaining Ancients had lived for more than two millennia.

Some of the Hybrids moved among the Ancients, gentling, bringing libations. Among them she saw Illyn moving, directing. Her heart ached with love for this little daughter of the Bog People, the Fir Bolg.

Near the far wall, some of the Raveners were present, the black almonds of their eyes impenetrable as always. Even in Metaphor nothing could change those eyes, that darkness. Perhaps the Raveners were the inevitable result of the long-ago experiment that made them exiles. Or perhaps darkness simply found a way, as it always did, to sidle into the world. She wondered briefly if the coming Invaders were servants of the Braid or of the Unweaver. Perhaps they knew of neither. How should the Danu protect themselves?

"There is one more thing that you should see," said Eriu softly. The acoustics carried her voice around the room. The Danu stilled, looked up expectantly. From its velvet bag, Eriu took out the gift that Ith had given them. It was a wine cup in fine silver, its handles rendered as leaping stags. All around the rim of the cup was elaborate chasework, and endless series of braided knots.

"By the Braid!"

"O Danu, what does it mean?"

For the chasework on the cup and the braidwork at the ceiling of the room were nearly alike, an unending stream of ribbons and knots, complex, beautiful, eternal.

Before any of the people could render opinions on the meaning of the coincidence, one of the doors hidden in the wall made a soft swishing sound and opened. Morrigu entered. Around the room, the assembled company grew silent, then whispered their presence to each other.

The three sisters of Morrigu were clothed as always in unremitting black, their long slender fingers gesticulating as they talked, their black eyes deep and hungry. Eriu realized with a start that even when Morrigu had hidden herself in Metaphor, she could not hide the dark hunger of those eyes. Around their heads moved a cloudy nimbus of darkness. They formed themselves into a triangle, standing at the far end of the hall. Eriu felt Banba and Fodla move closer behind her, instantly moving into the protective triangle. Eriu held the cup behind her; before Morrigu could see it, Banba slid it into its velvet case, hid it under her skirts on the floor.

The triangle of the Braid faced the triangle of the Raveners, like the prows of two great ships. The room silenced. It had been five hundred years since last they had all gathered in this room for this purpose. For many children in the room it would be the first time that they had ever seen the Journey of Exile, the first time they had ever known themselves as Braided Children. Eriu ached for them at the knowledge. It was time to reopen the Journey of Exile.

The lights in the room dimmed to an ambient silver glow near the floor. To the left and right of Eriu, the walls grew viscous, like a waterfall made thick. Suddenly the room was filled with stars, a sky full of stars. They were not the stars that arched in the night sky over the Green Island.

Among the people, one or two of the Ancients cried out, as if they remembered these pathways, this night sky.

Eriu did not remember. Nor would her own parents have remembered. Not the sky, not the journey that had brought them through it.

The voice of the Teller issued through the walls. Not for the first time, Eriu wondered who he had been, his voice mellifluous and so sorrowful.

"This is the place you came from," he intoned. The stars blurred and swept through the arc of the sky, and they were on the Homeworld. The room filled with its sights and its smells—mint and water and something honey warm in a breeze. There were long green fields filled with flowers, huge trees, their limbs shifting from side to side in an emerald forest. By a great sea were cities of gleaming crystal and coral and turquoise, some of the shapes and colors mimicked even now in their own underground cities. Vehicles shaped like triangles of light moved through them in the air.

Eriu reflected that it seemed to be less bright there than here. The quality of the light seemed somehow softer, muted. She wondered if that was why the light so troubled the eyes of the Ancients, so that they always covered their eyes, wearing dark lenses over the whole eye. Another reason for their love of the Green Island, for it was often rainy here and soft. Eriu stifled another sigh, knowing that it would carry around the room.

"We were a learned people, as you can see. We had learned to preserve our world in pristine beauty. We educated our people. We had mastered the world of science and we bent its rules to our uses. All of these things we had learned over centuries. We believed that we had learned at last to value the ways of the Braid. We tried to emulate Her in all things. Our mistake was that we tried to take from her the power of Creation. Because we made many mistakes in the management of our world, many—no, most—of our people became infertile. Women were unable to bear. We tried to correct that problem with the best and brightest of our people."

The picture shifted again; it seemed to show some hall of science. Patients were receiving care. The Teller's voice resumed, weighty.

"We had become healers of great skill. The lame and the blind we healed, the paralytic and the diseased. We did this through PreBraiding and ReBraiding. Even now, we hope and believe that Danu, the Weaver, would be proud of us for the healing of her children. Among us now, even such healing as that has been banned. We take responsibility for that loss. In our great pride, we went beyond healing to try to usurp the right of Creation, the power of life and death. Over many generations of the Danu, you, the Children of the Braid, were created.

"You possessed intelligence and immense longevity, the power to heal your own diseases. But in the process of achieving that end, we destroyed hundreds"—his voice paused, wearied—"thousands of your people who were imperfect or deformed. Some of those imperfections were physical, some were mental. Some must surely have been imperfections of the spirit, but those we could not see. I fear that those creatures may be among you now."

Eriu thought of the Raveners, glanced toward the triangle of the Morrigu at the far side of the chamber. The ancient voice continued.

"We bear the weight of the murders of your people, for that is what we now know them to be. Even when, at last, we created you of the Braid, you were judged by the people of our world to be not of the Danu. You did not look as we looked, you lived much longer, your vast intelligence terrified our people. To keep you in control, you were granted no rights among us. You were placed in the holds, removed from the sight and thought of our people." Here the picture shifted to a kind of prison structure; though clean and well appointed, it was nonetheless an obvious camp surrounded by lightbolt-walls.

"Though they were few in number, your ancestors rose up. Who would blame them now? All creatures yearn toward freedom and respect. Your ancestors began the BraidRising.

"We had created a race of people who were self-healing, who would live to be most ancient, who were physically beautiful, intelligent beyond our own capacities, dangerous. We tried to repress, to exterminate, the very thing we had created.

"We are the authors of your exile. The result of the BraidRising was that you were granted freedom, but only in exile. From the four great cities of our world, we provisioned you for a distant journey. From Falias, they sent with you the Lia Fail, the Stones of History and Destiny. They speak to you now. From Gorias, they sent with you the Invincible Spear Arms so that you might protect yourselves. It is my hope that you have never had to use those weapons.

"Finias provisioned you with the Spear Ships in which you traveled. Murias provisioned you with food and the means to store and duplicate those stores. All shared in your provisions for all shared in the shame of what had been done to you.

"Here, in the time and place that you see now, we of science have been judged and found guilty. We have received the ultimate punishment for our pride. That punishment is death; we accept that judgment as fair for what was done to you.

"You, our brothers and sisters in the Braid, have been forced into exile by the very nature of your creation. To assist you on your journey, we have sent with you our own people, healers and lawgivers, wisdom keepers and historians, who have volunteered to accompany you into exile to right the wrongs that have been done you. They have called themselves the Penitents; they will live to right the wrong that has been done you."

The picture shifted now to her paternal ancestors, the solemn, tall Penitents with their copper skin and curling silver hair, their expressions of sorrowful solemnity. They were ranged up by the hundreds. She felt a surge of love for them, these ancient sacrificial people. How afraid they must have been! All had been dead for hundreds, thousands of years.

"With you we have sent the knowledge of the healing, of the PreBraiding and the ReBraiding. You may guard it or destroy it, but use it wisely. It must never fall into the wrong hands, for it could lead again to the knowledge of Braid creation. That knowledge will never again be used on this world.

"In the way of all creatures, time will pass and you of the Braid will marry and mate with those of the Penitents who accompany you. Some of you may well mate with the inhabitants of the worlds you will encounter.

You will form a new race. We cannot say what your attributes will be. Will you live forever or will you die? Will you be creatures of the light or servants of the dark? What we have set in motion, we will not see to fruition. But we ask that you retain the name Children of the Danu that our two races will be joined forever across the stars, that She, the Mother Weaver, will protect you. We offer this as our apology; we seek your forgiveness. We ask that you remember that within the Braid dwells the spirit of Creation; that spirit moves in all and every create thing. We send with you our profound shame that we did not remember such a thing before we usurped the powers of the Weaver."

Not for the first time, Eriu wondered about the Teller's people. How long had they lived? How wise had they become? Did they dwell out there still, among the far stars? Among her own people were none of them now, for all who had journeyed with them had died long, long ago. The Teller was right, though. There had been much intermarriage through the centuries, and now her own race was an admixture of Exiles and Penitents.

And now a new race would soon come into their midst.

Eriu sighed. It was the first time she had seen the history in hundreds of years, yet just as it had done the first time she viewed it, it had made her feel alien to herself and profoundly sad. She could hear soft weeping in the room and knew that it had had the same effect on some of her people. The Braided Ancients were silent, their eyes lowered, as if they were ashamed. The children in the room were silent.

Eriu moved to the front of the chamber. She lifted her hands. From behind her she felt the hands of Banba and Fodla close around hers.

"People of the Danu," she intoned, "braided we are unbreakable, braided all life is unbreakable, all one, all in the Braid." In the great room, her people linked hands, arm over arm, a physical representation of the Braid. She waited until all were linked.

"Shall we hear more?" She almost hoped that they would say her nay. It was a sad history; in her memory it terrified her still.

"We must!" An old and tremulous voice rose above the discussion. An Ancient couple arose from among the company and made their way toward the front.

Historians. The man a descendant of the Penitents, the woman one of the last of the living Ancient Creatures of the Braid.

Immediately, the Hybrids rushed to assist them, to raise them gently to the platform, to bring them chased stools with cushioned seats and soft backs, to attach the devices that would engage the Lia Fail. Not for the first time, Eriu blessed the Hybrids for the love and adoration they brought to the Ancients, for treating them as honored grandparents. When the Ancients were seated before the company, the woman spoke first, as was always the way of the Danu.

"Children, it may be that soon we will be exiled again. We must know our history to choose our future. Open the Walls of Wisdom!"

The walls of the room slid back to reveal a kind of museum. Suspended in midair were wavering, three-dimensional pictures, an island in the Internal Sea, the temples of the Greeks, the pyramids of Egypt, a city of lights encased in bubbles below the sea. In shimmering cases around the room were the gifts that the people had been given by those they had encountered, Egyptian necklaces of jade and gold, Greek diadems encrusted with jewels, beautiful chalices and dishes of chased silver and gold, finespun linens, musical instruments, gifts of gratitude for teaching and knowledge.

"When first we came to this place, we slid our ships into the sea. We built our cities below the water and there we hid for many years. The shame and terror of the BraidRising dwelt upon us still." She touched a button on the arm of her chair, and the Danu could see the city below the waters, its lights shimmering beneath the sea.

She stood, her mate rising to hold her on his arm. She was withered, her skin a dusty white, folded on itself in ridges and creases. Her eyes were rheumy gray, her head completely bald, her fingers overlong. She was tinier than Eriu and her sisters by almost a foot, standing only three feet off the ground. Her grandchildren must have towered over her. She continued.

"At last, however, some of our number ventured to the surface. They captured the images of those they encountered. They returned to us and learned to create Metaphor. The taught us to practice so that we could hold the image in place."

She touched the triangle at her neck with its braided vines. A rainbow shimmered within it. Suddenly she was more than five feet tall. Her black curly hair was swept back at the crown and cascaded in long ringlets down her back. Her eyes were dark and expressive. She wore a white gown, single-shouldered, attached to a necklet of gold. The children in the room laughed and applauded. Eriu wondered how many generations of children and grandchildren she had delighted with her multiple transformations.

She smiled. Pearly teeth glistened in a mouth that possessed none in its true form.

"With Metaphor we could travel. Some few of our people came north into the region of the world where we now dwell. Our own ancestors built a city on an island in the middle of the Internal Sea." Again she pressed a button. A city of curved white dwellings and huge gleaming columns arose on a mountainous island filled with light.

"We traveled among all of the people of that region, Egyptians, Greeks, Persians. We taught and we learned. We shared our skills for building and healing. Our island in the Internal Sea became known as a center for wisdom and learning. I fear that the Greeks began to think of us as gods. This filled us with terror, for those who perceived us as different had exiled us.

"But before the problem had time to grow, the Green Orb itself changed our circumstances."

She pressed a button on the arm again; a great volcano shimmered up in three dimensions, spewing hot red fire. The earth cracked apart. The people watched as the white-columned temples tumbled to the ground, as the island slipped beneath the sea. The ancient woman was silent, her eyes filled with sorrow. Her companion took up the tale.

"Many of our people were killed, both Ancients and Penitents. Our ancestors retreated to the sea. Those who remained, intermarried and gave birth to the new children of the Danu, the true ReBraid of our races. When enough time had passed, we searched for a new place where we could dwell. We remembered that some of our company had traveled to the north, and we decided to follow. We found the Green Isle. Imagine our joy when we found evidence of the Danu in the structures of the people, huge lunar circles, temples incised with the Braid of the Weaver. We found no evidence of our vanished brothers and sisters. We could find no sign that they had married with the people of the place. Did Metaphor fail them? Were they destroyed? We do not know.

"For a time we dwelled on the surface, but there came among us two great crises—the Fomorian sea raiders and the years of no summer. To be safe from those, we built our cities here"—he paused—"beneath the ground. Here we have dwelled for more than a thousand years. Now a new race will come among us, warlike and strong. It is time for the Danu to consider. Where shall we go?"

From the back of the room came three voices in succession, nasal and smoky, sure of their powers. It was the voice of Morrigu.

"We shall not go. We shall destroy the interlopers."

"We have the power. Did we not drive the Fomor back to the sea?"

"We shall unleash the power of the Silver Arms."

14

CEOLAS MOURNS
Forgive me, my beloved.
Oh, take me with you
into the dark sea, the cold sea,
that she may keep us both together.
I cannot live apart from you.
My heart is cold and dead.
My heart is a drowned vessel.

ush! Do you hear it?" Eriu pressed her hand against Banba's lips to still her sister's chatter, tilted her head toward the stone passageway that led to the surface.

The Sisters had secreted themselves in one of the wedge passages whose secret doors opened into the hidden city of Tara below. They were seated together in the circular chamber at the end of the long passage that descended into the earth. Together they had examined the chamber, made certain that none of their people were anywhere nearby. Particularly, they looked to see that the Morrigu had not followed them to the surface.

The command had been given that the people of the Danu were to remain below until they had decided what to do about the Invaders. The Sisters had violated their own order to enter the Chamber of Memory.

"Hear what?" Banba swatted the hand away. "Do you think they are among us already?"

Eriu shook her head. "I don't know. I thought I heard singing . . . or chanting . . . I don't know. It drifts in and out on the wind."

"I hear it too," said Fodla softly. "It is a most mournful sound, a cup full of sorrow."

Banba stilled at last and tipped her head.

Eriu shook her head again. "It is gone now. Finished. It made me want to weep."

"I think you are both imagining it," Banba snapped. "We have more important things to consider. Did you charge the doorway?" she added in a soft whisper.

"I did," said Eriu. "They have not yet come to shore, but if they do, their attempt to enter will bring them the same reward that Airioch Feabhruadh earned."

"Oh, if only we had not worn the jewels and diadems when first we met them!" said Fodla.

"We were trying to appear as Greeks," said Banba. "Their ships were Greek."

"Ith had no interest in jewels and gold!" said Eriu. "Even his interest in our crops and cattle pasturage faded to nothing when he learned from whence we truly came."

"But, Sister, Airioch Feabhruadh had much interest," said Banba. "As did the brother Eber Donn, though I think he too was more taken with the green fields and forests. And neither of them knows the dangers. There was too much here that called them back. Too much beckoned. Oh, we beckoned them." This last came out of her as a moan.

"What will become of our people?" Fodla whispered.

"Come now," said Eriu. "Do not give in to despair. We have lived long on the Green Orb and long on the Green Isle. We know that our ancestors did not have an easy way here in the beginning. Did we not lose Nuada Silver Arm in the war with the Fomor?"

"Do you remember aught of Nuada's Silver Arm?" Fodla asked.

"It was a thousand years ago." Banba shrugged. "We were children."

"I know that it was during the time when the Brothers presided over the Council. Mac Cuill, Mac Cecht, and Mac Grene," Eriu replied softly. "And the Morrigu said 'arms.' Plural."

"Well, there is only one way to know," said Banba.

Eriu nodded. "We will study our ancestors here in the Chamber of

Memory and reason how best we can defeat the newcomers. We are wisdom givers and gatherers. Throughout our history we have learned from those we encountered. We can reason our way out of this dilemma with our own history, Sisters."

"We should have studied our history earlier, Sisters," said Banba. "Why did the Brothers not teach us this when we were bonded to them?"

"You would not have studied it then," said Fodla. "You were too busy fondling your new husband to study. You would have paid no attention at all."

Banba grinned. "Oh yes, I remember it well. One of these dark chambers, a huge cozy chair, and a husband who had been bound to me for the sole purpose of teaching me everything. And besides, they had learned the history before us and did not seem much interested in passing that part of our heritage on."

"And the result is that we are deficient in history," said Fodla.

"Did you ask them to teach it to you?" Banba asked. Fodla shifted uncomfortably. Banba laughed aloud.

"Very well," said Eriu. "We were young and full of desire."

"You too? Our senior sister?" said Banba and Fodla in unison.

"The young should be full of desire," said Eriu. "And our bond husbands did not seem troubled that they had to them such young and . . . frolicsome . . . wives. I do not remember them calling us back to any of our lessons. When once I did ask to study the history, they simply shrugged me off and suggested a picnic instead. They were men, after all." She smiled at her sisters. "But now we are old and alone and our people are in danger." She sighed; the mood of all three sisters changed liked quicksilver. "Now we must learn the lessons and draw from them the answers. Our ancestors dealt with invaders. How did they protect the Danu? That is what we seek to know."

From deep inside her robe, she took a speckled stone the size of a hand.

Fodla gasped. "How did you get that? Is it the turnstone of the Lia Fail?"

"It is. I simply took it from its case in the room of the Walls of Wisdom." A single protrusion jutted from the great rock at the center of the room. She lowered the stone over the protrusion, placed her hand upon its jutting surface.

"Stop!"

A door slid open at the back of the chamber, seeming to open out of the unbroken stone wall. An Ancient entered, a tiny woman of only three feet, bald with gray skin and long, slender fingers.

All three sisters stood.

"Ancient!"

"Airmid, daughter of Dian Cecht!"

"We are honored that you have come among us, Great Physician."

"You will not be so pleased when I have spoken." The voice of the ancient woman was nasal, almost metallic, the words undergirded by a continuous soft, buzzing sound. "You must not use the Lia Fail."

"Ancient," said Eriu. "With respect, this is why the Lia Fail was sent with us, that we might accrue knowledge and disperse it, that we might learn from it the true way to go. We must immerse ourselves in Memory now. We no longer have husbands to carry that knowledge. We must learn from those who came before, those who forged truce and those who drove the Invaders away. We must choose the right way to go."

Airmid shook her head. "To experience the Lia Fail is to experience history as those before you lived it. It will be as if you are there, seeing, hearing, smelling what they encountered. That is why these chambers are . . . above the surface. They are a space between our world and their world, a place where history may be experienced out of its sequence of time."

Eriu nodded. "Then this is well. We will learn much."

"The experience will ask much from you. It will exhaust you, render you incapable of speech or movement for some time after you have returned."

"Very well, we will work independently then, each of us alone. The one who goes will teach the others."

"There is more." Airmid hesitated, then leaned her head back against the chair. "Have you never wondered why your husbands are no longer with you, why they did not live many millennia, as most of the Children of the Braid do, why they died younger than most?"

"They were much older than we, Ancient," said Banba. "We . . . assumed . . . oh, Mother, I begin to suspect what you will tell us."

Airmid nodded. "There is a price to pay for the access of memory. This is why the Brothers kept you from it. It is a price of time. We do not simply view the past; the Lia Fail allows us to relive it, to shift into that time with those people, to see as they saw, to know as they know. Such access requires a price. Such access changes us at the level of the Braid."

"And the price is a price of years," said Banba softly.

"It is. That is why the stone has remained under glass for all these years since the Brothers passed, why they asked me specifically to keep it from you."

"They protected us," said Fodla softly.

"How many years?" asked Eriu.

Airmid sighed. "I do not know. Oh, you will live long, surely, longer than the Fir Bolg, longer than these who come. But your lives will be shortened with this learning, with this traveling through time."

"We have no choice, Ancient. Invaders come to our shore. Our people require our wisdom. If that is the price, I will pay it." Eriu's hand rested on the speckled stone.

"No!" Banba raced forward, slapped her hand down upon Eriu's. Fodla followed, her eyes resting on those of each of her sisters. "We are a Triad. We live together and we die together. If there is a price, we pay it together," said Banba.

"Whatever it is," said Fodla softly.

Airmid stepped among them. She nodded. "I too have had just this dilemma, when my decision had upon it a cost too much to bear. Will you heed the wisdom of an old physician?"

"We will, Ancient," said Eriu softly.

"Then learn here in short bursts, in small snippets of time. Allow yourself recuperative time between the journeys. Think about what you have learned and how you may apply it to the Danu. In this way, you may minimize the damage, but hear me clearly. You will not stop it. Do you understand?"

"We do," said Eriu. "Leave us now that you may not also be affected."

The door in the rock shivered open, closed behind the Ancient.

Eriu pressed down upon the surface of the speckled green stone, twisted the stone to the right twice. A soft whirring sound arose from the great altar stone at the center of the chamber. All around the Sisters the walls shimmered and came to life. They were standing in a great forest, the trees towering above them like sentinels, a breeze moving the leaves. On the path before them were two men, still as paintings.

"Nuada Silver Arm!" Fodla exclaimed.

The little man with his cap of cloudy curls and his high curved ears was completely unaware of their presence, though the Sisters were standing on the path, the wind shifting their curls, the smell of the forest all around them. Beside Nuada was a much taller man, his features more like the dwellers of the Green Orb, his hair a deep red-gold.

"Bres the Beautiful. Why did our people not see his unlikeness to us from the first?" asked Banba. "He is as much like the Danu as these new arrivals."

"Because our people would have been the last to judge him by his appearance, that having been the standard by which we were judged. Among us was the safest place for his treachery."

"He was aptly named, wasn't he?" said Banba.

"How so?"

"The Beautiful. For is he not?"

Fodla chuckled softly. "You do like the look of these humans, Banba."

Banba shrugged. "I did not say that he was good. Only that he looked good."

"But look how small Nuada is; he cannot quite reach four feet."

"There had been less intermarriage then, Exiles to Penitents, and none yet with humans." They all looked at the two men side by side. "Well, almost none," Fodla amended.

"Sisters, shall I make the third turn?"

Banba and Fodla nodded solemnly.

Eriu twisted the speckled stone. The forest began to sigh and move. Before them, the two men ran softly along the path. The Sisters had stepped back in time a thousand years.

"Look where before us comes a man of the bags." The voice of Bres was sarcastic, nasal.

"You will treat him with respect, Bres. He is a man of the Braid, no matter his station." Though he was head and shoulders smaller than Bres, the voice of Nuada was commanding, confident. He walked toward the approaching stranger, held up his hand.

"Welcome, man of the Fir Bolg. We greet you as newcomers to the Green Isle. I am Nuada; my companion is Bres."

The man was taller than either of them, stocky and dark, his brows beetled together and heavy, his body covered with dark hair. He eyed them both, but the weight of his suspicion fell obviously on Bres.

"I am Sreng. I ask what you will demand of us. More corn? More cattle? The firstborn of our children?"

"Why would we want such thing?" Nuada's voice was puzzled.

"It is what the Fomor ask and more." He gestured toward Bres with his chin. "Are you not of them?"

"I am of the Danu," said Bres. "I do not know these Fomor."

"You will. They will ask the same of you. Your cattle, your women, your children. All in thirds. As if they think of thirds as fair." He snorted.

"They dwell here?"

"You really do not know?" asked the Fir Bolg. "Would that we did not. They are sea raiders from the north. But they maintain a stronghold just offshore on Tober Mor. A better location from which to fleece us naked, I suppose. They are a bottomless well of demands; the holds of their ships must be huge and hollow."

"This from a man who makes his boats of dirt bags." Bres spoke in heavy disdain.

"The leather of our bags is bog-tanned," Sreng said, his voice defensive. "Until you know the bog, do not ridicule its ways. The ships of our tribes do not sink."

"Tribes?"

"We are three clans, Fir Bolg, Fir Domnan, Fir Galioin. And you?"

"We are one. Children of the Danu. People of the Braid."

"Danu?"

"She is our Mother. Weaver of Worlds."

"How is it that you speak our language? I was told that you had come in cloud ships. I thought that we would not understand each other."

Nuada was silent. It would not do to mention the pulsing triangles beneath their tunics, rendering the languages intelligible. Nor would they speak of the cloud ships, those giant triangles, now carefully hidden in the lakes and under hollow hills. Even Bres did not know of them, his mother, Eri, having only returned to the tribe some years ago.

Nuada inclined his head politely. "We have learned your language that we might negotiate."

"Nego?" The Fir Bolg got lost in the word, stood staring.

"We come to you with a proposal for your people."

"Propose as you will." Sreng gave a shrug, as if the proposal were of no matter.

"We would share this green island with you. Your people would have the north and we the south."

"Why would we agree to such a thing?"

"We would provide three gifts: We have some skill at healing; that we would share with your people. We have some skill at defense; we would assist you in defending against these Fomor. Last, we have some skill with the land; we will assist you with provision."

"I shall take this to our people. Meet us tomorrow at the Plain of Mag Tuiread."

"This is not a place that we know."

"It is the Plain of Many Towers. There we will give answer." Sreng of the Fir Bolg turned and moved away into the forest, a lumbering, silent beast.

"How strangely he responds," Nuada said.

Bres smiled. "I did not know your Greeks, but I would venture to say he is not one of them."

"As different from them as night is from day."

Bres tapped the side of his head. "Very little up there, Nuada. Trust me. They will respond with force. That is what they know. He has looked at you. You are small and slight and weaponless. He will judge that you are defenseless as well."

The Chamber of Memory darkened; for a while the Sisters sat silent in the darkness.

At last Eriu sighed. "What have we learned, Sisters?"

"Bres was no fool," said Banba.

"No," said Eriu thoughtfully. "Perhaps in what we saw, there is wisdom for us."

"How so?" Fodla tilted her head toward her sisters.

"We agree that these new Invaders are warrior people?"

"They bristle with swords and daggers. It is the logical conclusion," said Banba.

"Then perhaps we should make a first show of force."

Fodla gasped.

"No, Sister, I do not mean to harm them. Only to show force, that they respect it and are wary. That they will think us many more in number than we are."

Fodla shook her head. "Force did not work for our ancestors. Do you not remember? Take us to the Plain of Mag Tuiread. Let us see."

"Perhaps we should wait a little," Banba said, her voice unsure.

"And if the Invaders come to shore while we are waiting?" asked Fodla.

Eriu nodded. She twisted the speckled stone.

15

Fog moved among the great megaliths on the plain.

"So this is what they meant by many towers," Nuada said. "These that were built by our ancestors."

"Or mimicked by these ponderous Fir Bolg? It is not likely, is it? Surely they must have seen our ancestors as gods," said Bres. He examined one of the great pairs of stones, then whispered, "Our ancestors, Nuada. See where they have left passage to the world below." He pointed at a raised triangle on the stone with its interlocked spiraling braids.

Bres was carrying a Scythian shortsword from the weapons horde deep below the earth. The piece was a museum piece, taken from the wall, but it suited his greater height. Nuada and his companions, diminutive men with caps of cloudy silver hair, carried replicas of Greek spears made shorter and lighter for their small size. They came up among the great stones, crossed under a lintel. Nuada raised his spear.

"I salute the Braid who binds us."

Bres snorted. "Your Braid won't bind you to these folks, I can tell you that with certainty." He gestured with the shortsword.

Ranged up on the plain were hundreds of Fir Bolg. They carried heavy broad spears. They were garbed in animal skins, the men covered with hair from their faces all the way to their feet. Many of them were toothless, heavy-lidded, and beetle-browed.

"Sreng!" called Nuada. "I return with our proposal." The sound bounced around the great circle of stones, echoed eerily between the lin-teled dolmens.

Sreng did not step forward from the crowd. There was a general shifting and moaning among the Fir Bolg. Behind him Nuada could hear the silver buzz of alarm as it passed among the Danu.

"Do they not remember you?" someone whispered in Danaan from behind Nuada.

"They seem not to wish to." Bres's voice was heavy with its usual sarcasm. "Or perhaps they are a race of folk whose memory lasts for less than a day; they do not look as if they could hold much, do they?"

His remarks brought a silver wave of laughter through the ranks of the Danu. As if the laughter were their signal, the Fir Bolg gave off a mighty roar and charged at the Danu.

What ensued next was almost impossible to follow, the cloudy curls of the Danu nearly obscured by the fog and by the hairy presence of the larger Fir Bolg. At times there was the sound of metal on stone, at times screams, though the watching Sisters could not have said from whom.

Suddenly there was a scream of rage and pain. The picture narrowed, rushed toward a dolmen, focused. Nuada. He stood with his head tilted back, an expression of agony on his delicate features. His right arm had vanished at the elbow. Blood was spurting everywhere in arterial streams.

One of the Fir Bolg raised the severed arm and lifted it high into the air. It dripped blood down into his hair and across his face. He shouted something in his guttural tongue. Behind him the Fir Bolg began to make an ululating sound, a warble that could only signal victory. Suddenly Bres was beside Nuada. He stripped off his cloak, wrapping it hard around the tiny leader.

"We go below!" he shouted.

"We cannot abandon our people!" Nuada screamed.

Bres yanked hard at the cloak, pulling Nuada with him into the dolmen space. His hand reached out to the rock and smacked it hard. There was a flash of white light, a shape like a blue ovoid that thinned and vanished. Where the two had stood, there was nothing.

On the Plain of Mag Tuiread the assembling Fir Bolg ceased their warbling. Many began to hold up their right hands, to make signs in the air, their eyes wide.

It was the opening the Danu required; they rushed among them with their sharp light swords. The screams of the Fir Bolg were now screams of pain.

Suddenly the snap of white light with its ensuing blue moved among two dolmens at the far side of the plain.

Bres and Nuada appeared between the standing stones. On his arm Nuada wore a silver appendage that resembled a hand on a long shining gauntlet of silver, covered with shimmering triangles and spirals of color. He held it forward; the silver fingers curled and unfurled. When they had reached full extension, one finger snapped forward an arc of blue light. A dozen Fir Bolg fell, stunned and wounded, to the ground.

The battle was over. Those Fir Bolg who were still of sound body, who were closest to the edge of the stone ring, ran for the forest, their high gabbling screams ringing behind them. Those who were wounded curled into themselves on the ground, clung each to the other. Hairy men sobbed and scrabbled backward on hands and knees as the Danu approached them.

Nuada stepped into the circle. He tapped the triangular crystal etched with twining vines at his neck. In its depths, a rainbow shimmered and coalesced.

"Hear me, men of the Fir Bolg," he called. "Fear us not. We will heal your wounds. Be still and unafraid."

Suddenly white light and blue ovoids snapped between every portal in the circle. The physicians appeared, the long white robes wafting in the breeze, their hands gloved, faces covered. They moved among the wounded, easing pain, their huge eyes assessing the wounds, slender fingers working. When the field surgery was organized, Nuada called again.

"Come before us three men, one each of the Fir Bolg, the Fir Domnan, and the Fir Galioin."

Sreng came forward then, accompanied by two companions.

Nuada said nothing for a moment, assessing the threesome.

Sreng bowed his head before Nuada. "You were so small, Nuada; I judged you weak. I did not know that we fought with gods."

"No gods, just men of the Danu, weary of exile."

A crafty look passed across Sreng's face.

"Then we will agree now to your proposal. We will divide the land with you north and south."

"It is too late for that, Sreng," said Nuada. He held up the silver arm. "You must now bargain for less, for you bargained falsely at the first."

Sreng was silent.

Nuada regarded the three men. "What is Sreng's territory?" he asked at last.

The second man spoke. "Sreng and his tribe bespeak Connacht. We call them the Tribe of the Bogs, for it is stony country and full of bog, though the fishing is good."

Nuada nodded. "Then that shall be the territory for all three of your tribes in perpetuity."

The three men eyed each other, their looks uneasy.

"You will have to learn to get along among your tribes," Nuada continued. Though it was easy enough to read their looks, even for the Sisters these many centuries later, the men of the Fir Bolg seemed surprised to be so easily read. The third chief, still silent, made a sign in the air.

"But this, we of the Danu, will promise you. We will not make war on you again as long as you keep to your territory, nor will we build our cities there. The hunting and the fishing will be yours. We will trouble none of your women, nor ask of you grain or children or cattle." Surprise ran over the faces of the three Fir Bolg chiefs, and they glanced at each other again. "Finally, when your children are sick or ailing, we will offer the services of our healers."

"Why would you do this for us, Nuada Silver Arm?" asked Sreng.

Nuada shifted his position, cradling the silver arm in his good hand. "You too are Children of the Braid," he said softly.

A long silence pervaded the chamber when the pictures had vanished. The Sisters were still. Fodla rested her head on the arm of her chair. At last Eriu stirred.

"And so he became forever known as Nuada Argetlamh," Eriu said. "Nuada Silver Arm."

"How noble he was and how wise," said Fodla.

"At last I have found my true love," Banba sighed.

At this all three sisters burst into laughter, hiding the sound behind their hands.

"When do you not find your true love?" hissed Fodla. "It is too bad that both of these have passed into the Braid."

At her statement, all three grew silent momentarily. Eriu sighed.

"There is no point in dreading what might befall us. We must think only of the safety of our people now. And we have learned much, Sisters."

"We have learned that Nuada tempered punishment with promise," said Fodla. "And that he required consequences for actions. There was a wise ruler indeed."

"And we have seen that Bres was a true friend and companion in arms," said Banba. "The histories have painted him as traitor."

"Well, whatever he later became, he saved the life of Nuada on that day. But I wonder at the arm," said Eriu.

"Wonder what? It looked to me as though the weapon operated on the same principal as Metaphor and Transport do, rearrangement of the molecules of matter, water, air." Fodla waved her hand in the air at her obvious and simple conclusion.

"That, yes, but what of history?" asked Eriu.

"Ah . . . I see what you mean." Banba closed her eyes. "The histories say that the physician Dian Cecht created the arm for Nuada after his had been lost in war. They say nothing of the arm being already created and ready."

"Precisely."

"And yet we have seen him using it on the Plain of Many Towers on that very day." Fodla shook her head. "How was it done?"

The Sisters fell into a long silence, curled into their chairs, deep in contemplation. Long moments passed. Then Eriu gasped.

"Sisters, hear me now. For our ancestors have given us the answer. They did not shift the molecules of matter, water, air. Not on that day. They shifted time!"

"By the Danu!" said Banba. "I see it too. They slowed it down."

"But how was it done?" Fodla shook her head.

"I know not, but I know that we must know. Somehow, in that timeshift is the answer to our problem."

"Then let us return to them," said Banba. "I welcome the task."

"You would," said Fodla.

"I think we must ask the Ancient. Airmid the Physician," said Eriu. "Perhaps she will know or remember."

Suddenly there was a soft, hissing sound in the wall and a door slid open. Illyn moved through, her slippered feet quiet on the stone floor. In her hand she held a tray filled with fruits and small crystal candies. Steam rose from three clay goblets bearing warm honeymead.

She set the tray on the surface of the rock.

"How did you know we were here?" Banba snapped the question at her. Illyn's eyes went wide.

"Have I done wrong? The Ancient wished for you to have libation. She said that it is time for you to rest from your labors."

"Banba." Eriu wheeled toward her sister. "You frighten our Daughter of the Braid."

Banba stood and threw her arms around the child. "I am sorry, truly. I am so sorry. I fear that the Morrigu will find us here. We try to prevent a war of the Silver Arm. Of course the Ancient knows that we are here. It was she who warned us. O Danu, I am babbling." She released the little girl, who stepped back immediately and hid her hand behind her back.

Eriu knew that she made her own people's ancient sign against the evil. Eriu sighed.

The child heard the sigh, pulled the hand forward from behind her back, guilt washing across her face. She twisted her hands together.

"No, child," said Eriu softly. "You need not hide it. These are troubled times; we are all filled with fear."

Illyn's huge dark eyes filled with tears. "They will not hurt my mother, will they?"

"The Morrigu or the Invaders?"

"I know that you will keep the Morrigu from her. But the Invaders. I think that they grow closer."

"Have you seen them?" Banba asked, her voice imperative. Tears sprung into the little girl's eyes.

"Sister!" said Fodla. "Surely the Chamber of Memory makes you more irritable than usual."

Banba hung her head.

Eriu sat and opened her arms. Illyn launched herself into the huge chair, snuggling up beside Eriu. She leaned her head on the little woman's shoulder. For a time, Eriu stroked Illyn's long, dark hair. She loved the silky feel of it between her fingers, remembered the days eight years ago when Illyn had first came among them, when Eriu had calmed her by washing and braiding and flowering the rich tresses. This child of the Fir

Bolg was the closest thing that Eriu had to a daughter, and she loved her as she would her own child.

"You have been on the surface, haven't you, sweeting?"

Guilt flashed across Illyn's face, but she nodded. "I was afraid for my mother. I thought that I would go to her, but when I got to the surface I thought that I heard music. It was sad and angry all at once and I grew afraid."

"Would you like to see your mother?" Eriu asked softly.

Illyn looked up, hope spreading across her features. "Will she know me?"

Eriu closed her eyes. They had let her return once, when she was eight years old. She had accompanied Illyn then, cloaked carefully in Metaphor. The child's mother would not come near her daughter, repeatedly making the sign against the evil in the air. At last Eriu led a weeping Illyn away. Only when they reached the edge of the village did the woman come dashing after them, slipping from tree to tree. Though she would not approach them, she called from hiding. "Woman of the Danu!"

"Eriu," she called back, thinking that a real name might calm the Fir Bolg woman. But the woman made no connection between Eriu and her name.

"Woman of the Danu! Do you keep my child safe inside her?"

"Inside Illyn?"

"Inside the girl that you call Illyn?"

Eriu understood then. The girl that the woman had left to die in the forest was not the girl that she saw now. That child of four years had had a clubfoot and a harelip. She had been mentally deficient and had possessed no speech. How could the woman recognize the fleet and beautiful Illyn with her quick speech and bright mind? So Eriu replied, "I do. I keep your child safe inside her. Illyn keeps her safe."

From behind the tree, she could hear the caught breath, the muffled sob.

"Then I thank you and I am in your debt."

Now Eriu stroked Illyn's hair. "I think," she said softly, "that she will see you as the bearer for Illyn, that she will believe that inside your beauty is the wounded child of the forest. She may not know you as Illyn, but she will revere you as keeper of Illyn."

Illyn sat up straight. "I do not wish to frighten her. That is how I will introduce myself. 'Keeper of Illyn,' so she will not be afraid."

Eriu felt the tears well up in her eyes. Not for the first time, she wondered if they had done the right thing in rescuing the abandoned children of the Fir Bolg, in using all of the skills of healing and ReBraiding to right them physically and mentally. Now they were children of no tribe, neither Fir Bolg nor Danu.

She felt Illyn's soft hands against her cheeks.

"We are the Children of the Braid, Eriu. Do not fear for us; we know that we belong among you and are loved."

"You are wiser than we are," said Banba. "I am sorry, little Braid sister, for my quick tongue today."

"How lucky we are that you are among us," said Fodla.

Eriu said nothing, used the sleeve of her gown to wipe away the copious tears that flowed from such large eyes.

"I will send three Danu with you, two warriors and one woman. All of them will go in Metaphor. You may take with you any other children who wish to see their tribe."

"You will not go with us?"

"No, we will watch by the sea while you are gone."

"You will look for the Invaders?"

Eriu nodded quietly.

"And may we warn the Fir Bolg of them?"

"I thought perhaps that was why you wished to go. Warn them, Illyn, but do not frighten them. The Invaders look for land or cattle or riches. Your people's country is stone and bog and far to the west and north. I do not think the newcomers will wish the harsh lands of the Fir Bolg. Only say that some are coming from the sea. And specify the south."

Illyn leaped to her feet, her twelve-year-old frame bursting with energy. "Lest they think the Fomorians have returned."

"Precisely," said Eriu.

It crossed her mind that the newcomers could prove to be as bad as the Fomor. Or worse.

16

b ow long did it take to make the Silver Arm?"

Airmid, daughter of Dian Cecht, the most ancient physician of their created race, was one of the original children of the Braided Ancients.

Although she had lived now for almost three millennia and looked every day of her years, even at this great age she was busy in her lab, her eye glued to some instrument, searching out the patterns below the lens.

She leaned back and regarded the threesome for a long moment and then smiled, a toothless upfolding of the lips that seemed so reminiscent of an infant smile that Eriu turned her head to hide the answering laughter.

"Why don't you ask what you really want to know, Sisters? And did you rest as I asked you to do?" No trace of the infant in the acerbic directness of the question.

"We rested and partook of——" Eriu began, but Banba cut her off.

"We want to know if they somehow shifted time to create the arm," Banba said, ever blunt. Eriu realized with a start that a thousand years hence, Banba would be this very woman, looking infantile and cherubic, with speech as caustic and direct as a spear.

The old woman set down her instruments. "Not precisely. Why do you ask this question?"

"In the Chamber of Memory, we saw Nuada lose the arm, saw him return on the same day in the same battle with the Silver Arm upon his own." Eriu shrugged. "Biology alone would tell us that such a thing could not be possible."

"It was not; he was badly maimed. Even with all of our skills, the arm would have required some time to heal. So Dagda moved him to an alternate leaf, and Bres with him."

"Dagda himself?"

"An alternate leaf?"

The old woman sighed. "It is strange how the story of my life has become the history of your generation."

"Well it was more than three thousand years ago," said Banba.

Eriu glared at her for letting her acerbic tongue run away.

"Not to me," said Airmid. "To me, it all seems as present as you three. They were a threesome, you know. The first Council Triad. That is how they were created by the Makers, as a Threeclone. Dagda, Dian Cecht, Nuada. Like your husbands, like you, but create, not a natural birth. We say that they are the first sons of Danu, because they were the first to be created from the Braid."

"I apologize, Ancient One," said Banba, her eyes shifting to Eriu's glare. "It just seems so strange to hear them spoken of that way, as if they were present and alive. Dagda is the Father of Our Freedom; it is a large title."

"It was large work. It was Dagda who organized the people in the camps, who created the three-pronged attack. My father, Dian Cecht, co-ordinated the medical care so that we could be renewed and healed. Dagda was the provider, the great engineer. He created the Silver Arms. A dozen of them. Nuada, my uncle, was the chief warrior and negotiator. How he wrangled from the Creators ships and Penitents and provisions I do not know to this day. I do know that the Creators wanted to destroy the arms. As weapons they had been too effective in the BraidRising. But Dagda negotiated for those that remained. He argued that we would need them to protect ourselves in the new world and that the ancient world would be safer with them gone." She smiled again. "You have heard the Teller say that Gorias provisioned us with Invincible Spear Arms?" The Sisters nodded. "Well they did not provision. They relinquished. They gave up the arms. They did it to get rid of us."

"You were born on the ancient world?" asked Banba, hearing the tone of deep bitterness in Airmid's voice.

"I was. I was a child, I and my brother Miach, two of the Firstborn of Joining, natural births resulting from mating between two Braideds. That alone terrified the Makers, that we could reproduce all on our own apart from science. They feared that we would multiply and take over the world, long-lived, self-healing, intelligent. They feared that they had created a master race who would enslave them. They were right, of course, to fear the arms." She shook her head.

"And how many of the arms still exist?"

"Three. We never used any of them until Nuada, but we lost almost all of them. Only three remain."

"We lost them to the humans?" asked Eriu, a note of alarm in her voice.

"No, thank the Danu. When the great volcano destroyed our island in the Internal Sea, the entire armory was lost. We can only hope that it tumbled to the bottom of the sea and will never be found by humans. One can imagine what they would do with such a weapon."

"And those that remained?"

"Three arms. My father had been keeping them in his BraidRoom, had been working to alter them so that they would slip on like a glove, so that each finger would articulate a different purpose. Only those three remained, and it was one of those that Nuada used."

"But as to the alternate leaf?" said Banba, direct and hurried.

Airmid grinned. "I like you, girl. You remind me of me."

Eriu laughed aloud. "She reminds me of you as well."

"Never mind," said Airmid. She patted Eriu's hand. "You are triad leader. You are supposed to be the diplomatic one. As Nuada was. They can't all be like us." She winked at Banba, who made a face at Eriu.

"Now. The alternate leaf. Fetch me that silver spear," she said. She pointed at a thin silver needle stuck upright in a base of gold. Near the base, a series of small, bright leaves of silver and gold fluttered in the constant breeze of the recycled air.

"It was supposed to be a replica of the spear used in the Fir Bolg war. I thought it a particularly stupid thing to commemorate, so I use it to incise reminder notes to myself," said Airmid.

At this all three sisters laughed aloud.

Airmid pulled all of the bright leaves with their hieroglyphic markings up and over the top of the spear, their little rips increasing in size as she did so.

"Very well. Pay attention, girls; you may ask questions when I'm finished. Most people think of time the way you see this spear, a long straight line with a defined beginning and a defined end. That is a simplistic and inaccurate view of time."

She took a blank silver leaf from her table. On it, in the stick-letter language of their ancient world, she wrote the words "City of the Danu." She slid this slip down over the spear. A little tear increased in size as she lowered the leaf onto the spear. Next she took a golden leaf. On it she wrote, "Plain of Mag Tuiread." She slipped it down over the spear and lined it up so that it was precisely over the first slip.

"This is how it happened, is it not? At precisely the same time that we physicians were below the earth preparing for the wounded, Nuada and Bres were above the ground engaged in battle."

"Obvious enough," said Fodla.

"Now I ask you to alter your thinking. Pretend for a moment that the spear is all of the universe, all of life, all of time. On successive leaves she wrote "BraidRising," "Star Journey," "Greece." She slipped these down over the spear and fanned them so that they looked like the petals of an exotic gold and silver flower.

"What if these things are occurring always, at all times?"

"Not possible," said Banba.

"Not possible if you are standing on a single petal. But what if you could jump from petal to petal?"

Eriu shook her head. "I do not understand."

Gently Airmid reached down and caught at the bottom petal, the one she had labeled "City of the Danu." She pulled it so that it was out of alignment with the slip labeled "Plain of Mag Tuiread," so that they intersected only at the triangle of their base.

"O Danu, the monoliths." Eriu gasped it out.

Airmid clapped her hands. "My good wise girl; I am most proud of you."

"Call me stupid," said Banba

"But we still do not see," Fodla echoed.

"It works thus," Eriu began, but Airmid held up her hand.

"They are Danu; let their own good minds work upon it."

Banba and Fodla circled the spear with its bright petals. At last they looked up.

"Each petal exists in its own time, separate from the others," Fodla said slowly.

"Yet each intersects at the base in a . . . O Danu, in a triangle." Banba sounded excited now.

"And so," Eriu continued, "the wedge-shaped passage graves, the stone circles, the pyramids, the triangles we wear at our necks, all of these are doorways, or reminders of doorways, passages between . . . between what?"

"The time in which we dwell," said Airmid, "and the time as it moves here on the Green Orb."

"Why are we not taught this? Why do we not train in this timeshift?"

Airmid shrugged her shoulders. "Would you train the wind? The stars? This is how the universe is made. We discovered so on our travels across the stars. There are places out there"—she waved her hand skyward—"passages, if you will, where time shrinks and we can jump through space and time. Do you see the little tears in the paper?" The Sisters nodded in unison.

"In those passages are entrances and exits to worlds and times aplenty. Accidental doorways, if you will. We came here through one doorway to the Green Orb. It took us a very long time to harness the secret of those passages and doors. For a time we thought that Metaphor might be suffi-cient to protect us, but when it became clear that our knowledge and longevity were at least as frightening to the creatures here as our appear-ance, we knew that we would have to find a way to protect ourselves. You know that some of our brothers and sisters journeyed here to the north and built the monoliths, but they vanished. We suspect that they were de-stroyed because the locals feared them. And so we built these cities; we ourselves think that they are beneath the ground, but they are not; they simply rest on a different leaf of time.

"So that we might not be so alone here on the Green Orb, we opened doorways—the passage graves, the standing stones. The dwellers on the planet believe that we have armed our entrances with lightning bolts. We ourselves speak of arming the doors, but in truth we do no such thing. In-stead we launch ourselves through miniature versions of the passages in space, time corridors, if you will. It is part of the reason we live so long. This petal of time in which we dwell grows slowly. Were you to live constantly among the surface folk, your life would be shortened. Just as it will be shortened by your use of the Chamber of Memory. You do not so much see our history there as reenter it. Through a tear in time. For that you will pay a price."

"We will live only as long as the humans do?" asked Banba in alarm. "They have to them only some forty of their years."

"No. No. Never so short as that. You are Braided; your biology is engineered for longevity. But shorter than now, yes."

"So . . ." Eriu moved one of the paper petals further out of alignment. "To protect our people, could we shift the timespread wider, move further out of alignment with the humans here? They would not see us or know us."

Airmid inclined her head. "Had we the knowledge, yes. We could do just that. But what we have here is the limit of what we know. We can shift in and out of times that are closely aligned. We cannot move time itself. And even then, even if we pulled the petals further out of alignment, we would be at risk at the doorways. If the invaders ever found their way through the doorways, they would find us still."

"So what you are saying is . . ." Eriu pondered for a moment. "To avoid them completely, we must close the doorways."

"Not just close, seal. Not just seal, destroy."

"And if we do, we will live all alone on this petal of time, while the humans live on theirs. There will be no contact between any of us and any of them again. Ever." Eriu's voice broke.

Airmid inclined her head. "It would be a terrible price," she said softly. "Just as there was a terrible price for the arm."

"For the Silver Arms?" asked Banba. "Where are they now? Have you hidden them?"

But Airmid's eyes had filled with tears. "Enough!" she said. She held up her hand. Then, with slow dignity, she simply left the chamber.

17

The Fir Bolg village in morning light looked worse than it had by torchlight and fire. The conical dwellings with their thatched roofs were small and squat; smoke drifted skyward through their central holes.

As the oldest Hybrid in their little group, Illyn spoke sharply to her companions. "Speak to them only in Fir Bolg! They will fear you if you address them in Danu. Do you hear me?"

The children nodded, their eyes wide.

"Do not speak of the cities or of the Danu. Do not tell them of our clothing or our food or our dwellings. All would frighten them. We are here to tell them that Invaders come from the southern sea. Reassure them that the Invaders are not Fomorians."

The children who had been allowed to make the journey were all close upon Illyn's age. The Danu had judged that children younger than nine years would not know what to say and what to keep. In truth, these children should be dead, or, if they had been kept, they would be the broken of the tribe, those who could not see or hear or speak or reason, those who had been left in the cold hills to die.

Illyn well knew that her people would perceive her as a changeling child. In truth, she was. Neither Fir Bolg nor Danu, neither human nor Braid. The Danu had been rescuing the Fir Bolg children for generations, long ago stealing healthy children away from the slave-hungry Fomorians, later rescuing the imperfect of the tribe.

In the beginning, the Fomor captives had simply returned to their tribes with fanciful tales of rescue by a race of golden-haired Fair Folk. But the Hybrids could never return. Some dwelled forever among the Danu. Others formed their own strange tribes on the Green Island, different by degrees from any humankind, and so considered strange. Illyn wondered briefly what choice she would make.

Beside her, her Danu companions untidied their hair, spread dirt on their faces and feet. They had chosen for Metaphor to look as much like the Fir Bolg as possible so as not to frighten them. Now they were attempting to look as if they had made a long overland journey, though they had simply stepped from a portal a half hour before dawn.

Illyn smiled. They were kind and careful to a fault, these Danu. She did not wish to disappoint them with the knowledge that their nuances of disguise would be lost on her people. She sighed. Sometimes she felt so lonely. A creature of no one and nowhere. An old, old mind in a young and ill-fitting body.

The village began to bustle.

"Come," said Illyn. "And remember your lessons."

They moved in among the villagers. The Fir Bolg were slow to react to the strangers among them. Then suddenly, buffeted by a wind of gutturals and shouts, the Danu were surrounded by Fir Bolg men, their heavy spears in hand. The men tilted their heads, assessing the group, trying to recognize those they could never recognize.

Illyn spoke.

"I am Keeper of Illyn, daughter of Degna. Call her to me." This she said in a voice that was at once commanding and kind.

Degna arrived between two warriors, her legs trembling with fear. She swallowed and nodded. "This is she; she keeps my Illyn safe inside her."

The warriors lowered the spears. "Why do you return to us?"

"These children are also keepers." Illyn gestured around her. "We live far south of here; it may be that we cannot return for a time; these . . . keepers would like to see their parents."

"Why will you not return?" Degna asked.

"We have seen raiders approaching from the sea."

A collective gasp arose from the Fir Bolg; they began to chatter in tones of fear.

"They are not Fomor," said Illyn, but her child's voice was lost in the deeper noise of the tribe. One of the Danu struck his spear on the ground. A spark of blue lightning shot from its point. The tribe stilled, moved back from the visitors and away.

"They are not Fomorians," said Illyn quietly.

"This you know?" asked Degna. She seemed to have gathered the courage to function as the speaker for the tribe. Illyn felt a little surge of pride.

"This we know."

"These that you dwell with." Degna gestured at the disguised Danu. Evidently she was not fooled by their Metaphor. "They are knowers of many things?"

"They know more things than you and I have ever known," said Illyn softly.

Degna nodded her head. "Long ago, they say, we went to war with them; they were Fair Folk. The stories say that they came among us from doorways in the stones."

Illyn said nothing at all.

"It is also said that long ago there was a great war with the Fomor. It is said that these folk defeated the Fomor and drove them to the northern sea. Is this true?"

One of the Danu spoke up. "It is true, woman of the Fir Bolg."

Degna cleared her throat. "Then we are in your debt not only for these keepers but for driving the dark ones from our shores. We will trust that you will do the same with these newcomers."

Degna looked around at her tribesmen as if making up her mind about something. Then she stepped forward. Gently, timorously, she drew Illyn into her embrace. A little gasp arose from the gathered Fir Bolg. While Illyn was in her embrace, Degna whispered in her ear. "That is why I left you there, between the stones wrapped in the warm pelts of wolves. I knew that they would find you there; I wished for them to take you among them. I could not bear it if you had been taken by the Fomor."

Illyn felt her eyes fill with tears. "For that I thank you . . . Maither," she whispered back.

"You will keep my Illyn safe?" Degna asked.

"Here, inside me." Illyn gestured at her heart.

"She was not . . . right," said Degna. "But she was mine. I did not want to give her away. She was not right."

"I know," said Illyn softly. "But she is now."

18

CEOLAS MOURNS
I am the sea for drowning
I am the dark night
I am a wave of sorrow
I am the cold, dark water
I weep more salt tears than the sea
I shall never cease weeping.

A strong wind moved across the headland and the full moon was threaded with clouds. The threesome stared out to sea, unencumbered by Metaphor. The moon slipped from behind its scarf; it made a silvery path along the water.

"I love this beautiful isle," Eriu sighed.

"Listen where they sing again," said Fodla softly.

"Some sorrow moves them," Eriu said thoughtfully. "Twice now we have heard their songs, and both were sad."

"Sorrow is what they deserve," said Banba. "They should have stayed in their homeplace."

"Banba! I do not wish ill on them; I wish only that change will not come. Though it always does."

"Sister, do not abandon hope. They may not be as the Fomor were," said Fodla.

"Or perhaps they will turn around and go back," said Banba. "Perhaps some sorrow has befallen them on the journey."

"Well then, let us look," said Eriu.

Eriu held her arms before her, formed her fingers: Journey, Children of the Braid, the Braid itself. She raised her hands, felt Banba and Fodla close hands around her own. She closed her eyes and drew a deep breath, opened them. She gazed out over the water in silence. Behind her Fodla and Banba chanted the deep sounds of vision.

The ships were within a day of landing. Eriu sped among them, searching for Ith. Under the moonlight on the deck of the last ship she found Amergin. He plucked at the strings of his harp. His face seemed hollowed out, empty. Dark bruised circles outlined his eyes. As before, he seemed to sense her once again. He looked up.

"Skena?" he whispered.

Eriu felt his pain wash over her. What tragedy had befallen these voyagers? This was not the Amergin of just a few days ago. Eriu filled with pity. She sighed aloud.

"You have seen them again?" asked Fodla.

"I have. Something terrible has befallen them."

"And still they progress toward us?"

Eriu nodded. "Unless they go down in the sea, they will make landfall within the next day or so," she said softly.

"And we are still unprepared," said Fodla.

"Well, we shall hope they go down in the sea," said Banba.

"Banba!" This time Eriu and Fodla spoke at once.

Banba waved her hand. "You know that we are all thinking it. Will they be warlike? What will they wish of us? Fear moves through the Danu like this light moves across the water. And to think that we invited them."

"We did not invite," said Fodla. "We sent the message that Ith asked us to send. We greeted them as we had greeted Greeks and Romans, Egyptians and Persians, with a message of peace and warning."

"Ith said that they would not come," said Eriu. "I took him to be a man of his word. And I can find him nowhere on the ships."

Banba shrugged. "He is an elder. Perhaps he is seasick below."

"Or perhaps there are warriors among them who overrode his word," said Banba softly.

"Then we, too, should be more warlike. Be fierce against them." The voice came from behind them, nasal and smoky.

The Sisters turned as one. Morrigu stood behind them, the three sisters cloaked in black, their gowns shifting and swaying in the sea wind, their huge black eyes reflecting the silver moonlight.

"Banbh, Nemhain, Macha." Eriu addressed them separately with a formal nod. "We of the Council Triad are willing to listen to your wisdom."

"Wisdom, is it?" said Macha. She smiled, her lips folding up into a rictus that looked almost painful. "When have any of the Danu considered us wise?"

Eriu resisted swallowing. She looked at them each in turn. Panic rose in her throat when she met the eyes of Nemhain, but she fought it back. Panic is what Nemhain engendered. Everywhere she went, she seemed able to draw upon any creature's worst fear, bring it to the surface, strengthen it until the poor victim gibbered in terror, made terrible decisions based upon that panic.

Panic was not what Eriu felt when she regarded Banbh; rather, she felt revulsion. It was rumored among her people that Banbh's favorite use of Metaphor was as carrion feeders, ravens and vultures, birds of darkness who fed on the blood of the fallen.

And then there was Macha, their primary sister. She was beautiful, although she in no way resembled the People of the Danu or the Penitents. She was taller even than her sisters. Her long black hair floated and shifted in the breeze, and her dark almond-shaped eyes gave away nothing, reflected everything. Eriu could see herself in them now, small and pale, her cap of cloudy curls ruffling in the wind, her eyes wide and startled.

Macha was the mistress of Metaphor. Even now, Eriu did not know if she looked upon the real creature or some image Macha wished her to see. Eriu herself had seen Macha disappear into the shapes of wolves or eagles and then lope away into the forest or soar above the earth. All in Metaphor, perfectly sustained.

"You can think of nothing else to say?" Macha asked, the smoky voice pouring from her. "Perhaps that is because you wonder what the Makers called into existence when they created us, when the Raveners emerged from the Braid."

Eriu decided that honesty would serve her best with this trio. She nodded. "I have wondered it often, Morrigu, what the Makers called from the Braid when they called forth the Raveners, for you are as unlike the Danu as are Fomor or Fir Bolg."

Morrigu shrugged as one. "We are what we are," said Macha. "But I do find your honesty . . . fearless and appealing, Eriu. Perhaps they called to some darkness in themselves. Some . . . hunger. For we are always hungry." She smiled. "Surely they amplified some fierceness in themselves, for the Raveners are fierce, and the Danu . . . well." She shrugged again, pitying them their weakness, Eriu supposed. She decided again on directness.

"So how would you deal with these Invaders?"

"Bring the Silver Arms from hiding. Confuse them while they are still at sea. Destroy the Invaders before they reach the shore. Or if they come to shore, destroy them all. Leave the cleanup to the Morrigu." She grinned her wolfish grin. "We have the preservation of the Danu to think of; all others must perish before that need."

"You have not destroyed the Fir Bolg."

She shrugged. "Well, they are like cats or dogs, are they not? Simple but domesticated. We enjoy dallying with them sometimes"—here Nemhain snickered—"but we do not harm them because there would be no point. Of these newcomers we know not. They could be like Fomorians."

"We remember the final battle with the Fomor," said Banbh. Her voice was harsh, deep, almost masculine. She actually licked her lips; the dark almond eyes flared suddenly, as if a fire had been lit deep within them.

"Hush!" Macha commanded. "You go too far as always."

Eriu was startled. It was the first time she had ever realized that Macha was keeping the sisters in check, holding them like the reins on a pair of horses. Something like pity arose in her.

Macha must have sensed it, must have felt it wafting toward her. She stepped toward Eriu.

"Take my hands," she whispered, softly, gently. Eriu put her hands into the long hands of the Macha. "Ravener and Danu," she whispered. "At last! This is how it should have been from the first, our two races linked in the Braid, no separation between us. See what we know."

Suddenly it all came pouring into Eriu's mind, the BraidRising, the smoking weapons, the maimed and the dead, the screams of both Danu and Makers, the long journey, the weeping of the Ancients at their exile, the tumble of the Danu into the sea when the volcano erupted, the Fir Bolg war, the agony of Nuada's severed arm.

She staggered back from the weight of it, held her hands up in the moonlight. They bore the marks of burning.

"This is what we contain," said Macha softly, her voice pitched low.

"It is a terrible burden," said Eriu. She stepped forward suddenly, compelled. She placed her long, slender hand against Macha's cheek. "I am sorry that you bear it."

The Morrigu gasped aloud.

"We revel in it," said Nemhain.

"It feeds us," said Banbh in her strange, masculine voice.

Only Macha said nothing, her eyes fixed on Eriu.

"You are the fulcrum," Eriu whispered. It was so suddenly clear that she wondered that she had never understood it before. Macha kept the other two in balance. She contained the dark; she repelled the dark. She caused sorrow; she kept sorrow at bay. She engendered evil; she kept evil at bay.

Macha blinked, nodded once. "We will assist you with these Invaders," Macha said.

"You will not destroy them."

"Until the time comes that you require their destruction. We will assist."

"Do you know where the arms are hidden?"

Macha made no reply. She touched the triangle at her neck with its spiraled vines. Wolf, eagle, darkness, light, void. Gone.

Eriu dropped to the ground.

"By the Danu!" Fodla rushed to her side.

"What was that? What just happened?" Banba kept batting at the air where they had been, as though she did not understand how they had vanished, had not been vanishing in just that way all of her life.

"That was one of the results our ancient Makers had not counted on. They called upon the Braid; they used its secrets. They did not know that to call upon the Braid is to also call the Antithesis into being."

"Terrifying. And they live among us."

"Usually silently and secretively. How often do you see them?"

"Almost never. Few Councils. No ceremonies or healings. I was shocked to see them at the Great Council."

Eriu nodded. "They are the Shadow."

"Of what?" asked Fodla.

"Of sorrow. Of war. Of darkness and evil. Of our ancestors. Of us. Of our own internal darkness."

"And now they propose to assist us?"

"They propose, I think, that we will need to bring battle against these Invaders. They will be there to simplify that process."

"To provide the darkness," said Fodla.

"And will we?"

"Will we what?"

"Call up darkness against the Invaders?"

"I do not know. Our ancestors surely were forced to war with the Fomor."

"Then we need to know how and why," said Fodla.

"And we need to check on Illyn's journey," said Eriu. The very mention of Illyn's name made her feel better, as though she were grounded in something simple and good.

She faced back out to sea, caught at her sisters' hands. Together, they touched the triangles at their throats.

At sea, off the southern coast of the island, a group of voyagers saw a flash of white light, followed by a blue ovoid.

"Heat lightning," said one of the Greek sailors, though the night was cold.

In the stern, Amergin looked up from the strings of Ceolas.

"Skena?" he whispered, his voice half strangled with sorrow.

19

"Why did the Fir Bolg give away their children?" asked Illyn. She was seated with the Sisters in a garden near a small water fountain, dipping apples into sweet sauces.

Eriu had known that this day would come, that Illyn would need to know why she had been abandoned so long ago. She had practiced her answer for many years.

"Long ago," she said softly, "long, long before you were born, there came a time when no summer came here to the island. The trees did not grow, nor give birth to leaves. No flowers budded forth in spring and no berries grew on the bushes. The animals grew thin; many of them died. There was nothing for the Fir Bolg to eat."

"Just one summer?" asked Illyn.

"No, sweeting; it lasted for eighteen summers. The Fir Bolg starved; it was cold all the time. In some summers, snow fell. So when they could no longer raise their children, the Fir Bolg began to select some to leave on the mountains and in the cold rivers, that the tribe might be thinned and those who were left could survive."

"But if it happened long before my birth, why are they still leaving the children?"

Eriu drew breath, felt her way carefully through the answer.

"The life of the Fir Bolg is hard. Sometimes children are born to them who are special—different from the other children of the tribe. The Fir Bolg have a memory of the cold years and so they leave their children for us so that we can care for them and keep them well."

"And so they save us."

"Yes," said Eriu. "Exactly."

"My mother saved me."

"She did."

Illyn pondered this for a moment. "Eriu, what would cause winter in summer? Did the Fir Bolg do something to anger the Mother?"

"No, child, surely not. The Mother loves her children. She does not punish them. Do you remember the story of the Journey of Exile of our people?"

Illyn nodded.

"Do you remember our first home on the island in the south?"

"Yes, the one that sank into the sea. Oh . . . I see . . . a volcano caused the winter."

"It may be so," said Eriu. "Or it may be that a . . . star . . . fell from the sky and scattered the cold into the air. After our own island was destroyed, the Danu have studied these things. Sometimes there is danger in the Green Orb itself."

"Is that why the Fir Bolg feared the Fomor so? Because they brought another kind of darkness?"

"Oh, you grow wiser by the day, little daughter. But we of the Danu feared them too. The Fomorians were the scourge of the Green Isle for many a year. They brought much grief to both Fir Bolg and Danu."

"How could they have any sway over the Danu?"

"Well, they had help from one of our own," said Banba as she worked a piece of apple.

"A traitor?" asked Illyn with a gasp.

"So we have always been told. But the histories have shown us a different picture," said Eriu. "Perhaps we should know more."

"Why?" asked Illyn.

"To know history is to profit from its lessons in this time. We learned of at least one way to deal with the Invaders just by watching the Fir Bolg war."

"You began the war on my people?" Illyn was on her feet gasping.

Banba shook her head at Eriu. "So I am not the only one with a loose and simple tongue."

Eriu sighed. She held out her hand to the little girl.

"Sweeting, we will watch the histories and we will tell you the truth of them ourselves. Then you can judge for yourself."

"Can I watch with you in the Chamber of Memory?" asked Illyn.

"You cannot," said Eriu, "for there are . . . dangers in the chamber that—"

"You are in danger?"

"Of course not," said Fodla.

"Do not be angry with us, Illyn," said Banba. "Eriu protects you only; she will not keep the truth from you."

"I know that," said Illyn. "Eriu only fears that she will disappoint me." She turned to Eriu. "You could not lose my love; you are my little mother."

All three sisters gaped openmouthed at Illyn. Banba walked to her and took the little face between her hands. "Where did you come from, Little Wisdom Mother?" She turned her around and around, then made a show of patting the air around her. "What doorway did you come through?"

Illyn giggled, a little girl again. "You are always silly, Banba. Call me for the memories when you are finished." She flounced away.

Eriu turned to her sisters. She arched her eyebrows in amazement and surprise. The gesture made her ears go up and down and the feathered tips looked as though they might take flight.

Banba and Fodla burst into laughter.

From the front of the group Illyn spoke again. "Don't make faces behind my back; it isn't nice."

A door opened in the wall and she disappeared up the hall.

"She enters that period in humans when they are most dangerous," said Fodla. "I have seen it before in Hybrid children."

"Nearly as dangerous as Morrigu," said Banba. "I certainly feel small and stupid."

"That is what they do," said Eriu.

"For how long?"

"For years."

"O Danu, spare us," said Banba.

The walls of the room shimmered and became viscous. From the northern sea a fleet of ships moved toward the land, their tall prows carved and dangerous, the rhythmic drop and rise of their oars the only sound on the water.

They drew up on the beaches. From them stepped the Fomor.

"By the Braid. Look at them!" Banba hissed.

From the boats stepped men larger than any of them in the chamber had ever seen, human or otherwise. Most of them were seven feet or taller, broad of shoulder, with thick, muscular legs. Their hair was long, red and gold, and they were bearded and mustached. Together they bore more hair upon their bodies than the Danu owned collectively. They wore worked leather tunics and they carried huge battleaxes in hand. Long broadswords cascaded down their backs, and their belts bristled with dirks and daggers.

"Each man his own army," breathed Banba.

"No wonder Illyn's people feared them," whispered Fodla. "I fear them, even now."

"Our people feared them as well," said Eriu.

"But for Bres the Beautiful," said Banba. "See where he comes."

The Fomorian Invaders had built a small fire on the beach, its flames hidden behind the cliff wall. There they were grilling fish on long skewers. Bres came into their midst.

"So. You return to us, little brother, king of the Danu."

Bres came into view, his face lighted by the flames.

"I do," he said softly. "Not king but Council Leader."

"To us, you are their king."

Bres preened a little in the praise.

"And you have asked your mother for the truth of the story?" one of the Fomor asked.

"I have wrested it from her. She admits that I am of you, just as you said. Danu and Fomor."

"A blind man could see the likeness. Balor himself could see that you are one of us, a handsome Fomor lad."

From the darkness came a huge, rumbling laugh. A shadow detached itself from the deeper darkness and unfolded. Taller and taller it grew. Ponderous and fearsome, it moved from the darkness into the firelight. It was a man, more than nine feet tall. His hair was black, the planes of his face hidden by a massive mustache and beard. One eye was hidden behind a patch. He approached Bres.

Though Bres was the tallest by far of the Danu, this giant was twice his size. He leaned down and down, peered into the face of Bres the Beautiful. Bres did not shrink back.

"I remember you, boy. The spawn of Eri."

"Eri's son."

"And ours, boy. And ours." The giant laughed. "We are proud of that boy. Proud of you. I am told you are king of the Danu."

"Only Council Leader. And I think they plot to take that from me."

"They did not like our Fomor boy?" The giant sounded angry at this, as if he were personally offended.

"I am not Danu. Some say I do not make decisions that befit their people."

"What decisions do you make?"

"I have asked them for chambers, for fine clothing, for some of the jewels of their travels."

"And they begrudge you these? We begrudge our kings nothing!" The giant shook his head. "I remember the Danu well. They came here long ago, built cities on the plains. They were a people full of themselves, truly. All self-importance and wisdom. This was long, long ago, before these boys here were born. When the Nemedians dwelled here. Weak fools those! A puny race of no numbers. We demanded of them their corn and their cattle and their children, and they gave them all. We were rich in both food and slaves. And then one day we came to raid and they were gone. They had a king—Britan, I think his name was. The rumor was that he went east." The giant shrugged. "No matter.

"So we needed more volunteers, and there were your mother's people, ripe for the picking. I did so love Danu slaves. My favorite of all the peoples we have raided. They knew how to do so much and they seemed so healthy. I suppose we overused them some; we were surprised that they died as easily as they did. And oh, those Danu women; so small and light that you could bounce them on your lap. I did it often, boy! I'll wager you do too. And then on one of our raiding parties your little mother escaped us. It was a great loss to us. A great loss." He shook the massive head.

"Danu women do not mate with me," Bres said.

"You are large enough. Simply take them."

"Danu women do not find my looks pleasing."

"How could this be?" said Banba. "I find his looks pleasing. I have said so."

Eriu shrugged. "This was long, long ago. Our ancestors had only just come here. When he was born among them, think how strange he looked. And Eri. Arriving from nowhere with a strange story of having lived among giants. At the very least Bres would have been regarded as suspect. From what he says, it seems that he became greedy soon after the Council Triad chose him."

"Nuada seemed to love him."

"Then why did he betray Nuada?"

"We shall see," said Eriu.

In the firelight, Bres shifted from foot to foot. He lowered his head. "What did you bring?" he asked.

"You liked what we brought you on our first visit?" asked the giant. "The jewels and the daggers?"

"I liked the woman."

"Oh, lad, we bring lavish gifts for those of our own. Lads!" he called. Some of the giant men stepped forward with bags. They spilled jewels and gold before him. One carried forward a sword, richly incised with symbols.

"I thank you," said Bres. "But these are not necessary." He kept looking toward the darkness.

"They are our gifts to the great king of the Danu," the giant said softly; "you will offend us if you do not take them." He jerked his head back toward the shadows. "Don't worry, boy. We have our special gift for you. Well, a pair of special gifts really."

"A pair?" said Bres. His eyes flicked toward the shadows. He licked his lips.

"Better than before, eh? We will provide more each time we come."

"What do you need in return?" So Bres had not lost his senses entirely.

From the darkness came the sound of feminine laughter, followed by a low, sweet moan. Bres closed his eyes.

"We need only the simplest thing, boy. When first we came among your people, they lived in villages on the land. We took slaves and children from them; such are necessary to manage our farms when we are at sea. Now these Danu have disappeared. Where did they go?"

"I will not give you slaves or children!" said Bres. He turned to go.

"Oh no no!" the giant said hastily. "You mistake me. We will find our servants elsewhere. But that requires money. Levy a tax on your people. You can explain to them why you do so; it will keep us from them. Let your mother speak to the assembly. She will tell them well. They will accept the tax, I think." He smiled, a slow baring of his yellow and scraggly teeth.

"And then you will go."

"We have a camp on Tober Mor. From time to time we will return to collect that tax and to bring gifts to you. After all, we are proud of our kinsman, the king of the Danu!"

Bres thought for a time; from the darkness came the soft sound of moans and giggles. At last he nodded. "A tax is fair; it is really all that I myself have asked for," he said.

The one-eyed giant slapped his knee. "Good lad." He signaled with his hand. From the shadows beyond the boats stepped two women, both Fomor, taller than Bres. As they approached they threw off their voluminous cloaks. They were naked but for two golden girdles that rode at their hips. Their breasts were large and pendulous. They wrapped their arms around each other and flicked their tongues as they approached. Then they surrounded Bres, nuzzling and undulating against him.

"The girdles are yours," said the giant, his voice teasing. "And of course what comes with them." He waved off toward the darkness. "Go and enjoy; they have many plans for you, these two. And we will bring more on our next visit. Just you tell us what you want."

"I will," said Bres. His arms were already encircling those of the girls. He was nuzzling at the white breasts.

"Well now we know how he was suborned." Eriu rested her hand on the stone; the picture froze on Bres, his arms around the pale women of the north, the giant looking on. She sighed. "We must blame ourselves, surely. Among the Danu, he was pariah."

"Blame his appetites; obviously they were large," said Banba, her voice caustic.

The door slid open and Illyn entered bearing a tray with steaming mugs of liquid. She gasped at the frozen picture; at her inattention the steaming mugs began to slide to the edge of the tray. Banba launched herself from her chair to catch the tray. She moaned aloud at the motion.

Her cry reminded Illyn of her burden; she righted the tray and lowered it carefully to the table.

"Banba!" said Fodla. "What ails?"

"It is my knees. They actually . . . ached . . . as I stood from the chair. I have never experienced such a thing."

"Time lies upon them like the damp, Sister," Eriu said carefully so that she would not frighten the little girl. "The . . . damp . . . of the room wears at your . . . bones, Banba."

Illyn nodded. "Airmid said that the damp of the chamber might give you aches and pains. She sends this tisane to ease them. She says to drink it all and right away." She handed a mug to each of the Sisters, but her eyes returned to the picture.

"Am I in danger to see it?" asked Illyn. "No, sweeting," said Eriu. "It no longer moves in time."

"Will I have those?" asked Illyn.

"Those . . . breasts?" asked Eriu. She drank the potion, sighed with relief as its warmth spread through her. Among her own people, the indicators of female gender were small and subtle. She had seen larger markings among humans. She looked at Illyn, took the question seriously.

"Stand before me," she said. Illyn complied. Eriu shook her head. "No," she said. "You are slight of bone. Remember your mother."

"She was slender and tall."

"Then so will you be."

"Good," said Illyn. "Those are . . ."

"Overwhelming," said Banba. "Like the mountains of the Green Isle. But obviously an interesting climb for Bres."

Illyn giggled. Mating was no secret among the Danu, nor was it among the Fir Bolg, but Banba made it all seem funny and dry.

"Well, Illyn, are we safe now?" asked Banba, seeking to distract the little girl.

"Safe from the Fomor?" asked Illyn.

The picture faded from the walls, returning the chamber to its stony appearance.

"No, safe from your tart tongue of earlier," Banba replied.

"As safe as we are from yours," Illyn answered innocently.

All three sisters burst into laughter.

"Oh, keep her with us always," Fodla said to Eriu. "She saves us the trouble."

Banba made a face. "Perhaps our little daughter just sees the wisdom of being just like me. She emulates her hero."

"What say you, Illyn?" asked Eriu. "Will your voice be Banba's voice?"

Illyn was quiet for a moment. Then a smile crept across her face. "I will take the sweetness of Fodla's voice and the wisdom of Eriu's voice and the bluntness of Banba's voice and I will speak in a voice all my own."

At this all three sisters applauded.

"By the Danu," said Banba. "I believe that you will!"

"My mother found a voice," said Illyn. "She told me that she wrapped me and placed me among the stones so you would find me."

"So she did," said Eriu, "for you were bundled into wolfskins and laid between the portals of a stone circle. And someone had surrounded you with stones, perhaps so the wolves would not find you."

"And which of you found me?"

"I did," said Eriu. "On the night of a full moon."

"She said that she had arranged it so that the Danu would find me. She called you the Fair Folk."

"Then I'm glad that we could return her gift to her."

"Gift?"

"You are my gift," said Eriu, seriously. "The gift your mother gave to me. The best gift of all my life."

Illyn kissed the tiny woman's cheek gently. "Thank you, Little Mother," she whispered.

Eriu drew her arms around Illyn and hugged her.

"My mother said that she did not wish the Fomorians to find me. What made them so terrible, Sisters?"

"Well, for one thing that they were tall and hairy with long beards, bad teeth, and great bouncing breasts," said Banba.

Illyn laughed aloud. "You make it sound like the beards and the breasts go together."

"Maybe they did; maybe that was what everyone found so scary."

"Banba!" said Eriu. She shook her head, then answered seriously. "From what we have seen of them, they took what they wanted—people, treasure, anything. And they were not above trickery and deceit."

"There is one thing we do not know," said Fodla.

"Why Nuada was rendered king again," said Banba.

"But I am willing to venture that we know one who knows," said Eriu quietly.

20

You restored Nuada's arm."

"My father refashioned the Silver Arm for Nuada. He fit it to the stump of Nuada's arm."

"No. You restored Nuada's arm. His biological arm. You have the knowledge of the Braid."

Airmid lifted her chin. "My brother restored his arm. Miach. I helped him; I hid them and I hid the work. I am proud that I did." Her eyes dropped in shame. "I am only sorry that Miach paid the price." She sighed, a sound full of old sorrows. "And Nuada."

"Nuada died because of the Silver Arm?" Banba shook her head. "I did not remember that from the memories."

"Why must you ask me? These memories are painful," the Ancient woman snapped.

Eriu placed her hand gently on the woman's arm. "We are looking for the way to protect our people from these Invaders. For the past two days we have done nothing but try to study and learn. We are young; forgive us."

"You are more than a thousand years old by human reckoning of time. You are only the third generation born on this world."

"Well for the first three hundred years we were children," said Banba in exasperation. "Then, in our adolescence we were married to the Triad of Brothers that they might . . . train us . . . in the duties of Council of the Braid."

"They did not train you very well, did they?"

"To be fair," said Eriu, "they trained us well in the Journey of Exile and the duties of Council. They paid little attention to the history of this island. By their time, the Danu and the Fir Bolg lived in peace and the Fomor had disappeared. What was to fear on this isle?"

"Well, they had the previous Triad to thank for that, didn't they? Dagda, Nuada, and my father, Dian Cecht."

Banba started to speak, but Eriu held up her hand. "And so we come to you to learn of that, Ancient," Eriu said gently. "Your wisdom and your memory contain it. But if the memories are too difficult for you, we can access them in Lia Fail Chamber."

"Have you begun to experience pain in the chamber?"

"We have," said Banba.

Airmid sighed. "I am a selfish old woman. The Brothers wished to protect you from the price that the Chamber of Memory exacts. Now I am trying to protect myself from the price that my memories exact when my telling will limit your time in the chamber. I will tell you what you want to know. Ask, Eriu."

"We are not sure what to ask, Ancient. We have a new set of Invaders approaching. Should we simply seal the doorways shut between us? Should we bring out the Silver Arms? How should we prepare? We look to history to teach us now. And to you, Ancient. But we do not wish to make you sad."

Airmid sighed, a great wafting of breath. "Oh, Eriu, I have been sad for more than a thousand years. I will tell you what I know; the rest you will have to see in Lia Fail. Perhaps what I know can help you to decide." She shrugged. She pressed a small triangle on her table, and a picture projected on the blank wall of her lab of three tiny men, pale and silver-haired with huge eyes and upspiraled ears.

"There they are: The First Council Triad. They were Braid-Men, a Threeclone. Dagda, the Father of Our Freedom; Nuada, the first chief of Council; Dian Cecht, physician and healer, my father. They called themselves Brothers in the Braid. They were like you three, inseparable and strong. Because of them, Council is always headed now by a triad in each generation."

She shook her head.

"When the Fir Bolg cut off Nuada's arm, my father affixed the Silver Arm to Nuada's stump. I remember well how bravely Nuada bore the pain! The stump was barely healed; even timeshift had not given it enough time, and the arm rubbed the skin until it was raw and bleeding. But back he went among the Fir Bolg. He fought and negotiated as though he were whole and strong. There was a man of the Danu! But when he returned among us, the stump made him ineligible to be Triad chief. That was the way. Physical imperfection was unnecessary and therefore unacceptable. The kingship was given to Bres the Beautiful, whose mother had returned to us after many months as captive of the Fomor."

"Why Bres?" asked Banba. "Why not Dagda or your father?"

"My father was a healer, unsuited to the job. As for Dagda, he bore a weakness that none of our people knew. In the BraidRising on the Homeworld, Dagda had been blinded in one eye. My father replaced the eye with one so realistic that you could not tell, but Dagda was unfit to rule and knew it well. So he . . . provided. Anything the Danu needed, he found it, made it, wheedled it, purchased it. That is why even now the people call him the Great Provider."

"But surely your father had knowledge of the ReBraiding. He was the Great Physician. Why did he not replace the eye with a real eye?"

"That was my father's weakness. Or perhaps his strength," said Airmid. "He believed that no ReBraiding should be permitted by the law. He said that by Braiding, UnBraiding, and ReBraiding, the Homeworld had brought upon itself its own downfall, creating a perfect race and then treating it with fear and loathing. He vowed that he would never UnBraid or ReBraid again."

"And Dagda and Nuada? They agreed?" asked Eriu.

"Dagda agreed. He had been the architect of the BraidRising. He had suffered greatly for being a Braided One."

"And Nuada?"

"We persuaded Nuada."

"We?"

"Miach and I. My brother." She tapped her console. The picture appeared of a handsome man of the Danu. Airmid stared at it for so long that Eriu began to suspect she had forgotten their presence.

"You persuaded him, Ancient?" she said gently.

"We had no choice," Airmid said in a broken voice. "The Fomor came below."

"Below?! Here into our cities?" The sisters were thunderstruck.

Airmid nodded. "Few know it now, and those who know are silent on the subject. Why terrify the Danu? The Fomor are gone."

"Bres showed them the way?"

"He did and more. He began by allowing them to tax us. The tax was not heavy, and he claimed that he had negotiated with them that the tax would be sufficient, that it would keep them from our door."

"This we have seen in the Lia Fail Chamber," said Fodla.

The Ancient shrugged. "Then you know that when the Danu first moved to the Green Isle we lived on the surface. We did not live in fear; the Fir Bolg war was over. We lived in peace with the Bog People. We offered them healing and food and knowledge of provision. They spoke often of the Fomor, but we had never seen them. Then one night, in darkness, the Fomor slipped among us. In the morning, dozens of our people were gone. Just gone. Men, women, and children. At first we suspected the Fir Bolg. We took a war party among them, but when we arrived we found them in chaos and disarray, women screaming for their vanished children, men brandishing spears and shouting vengeance for their missing women. That was when we knew that the Fomorians had come among them as well."

"And so we built our cities beneath the surface?" asked Banba.

"Or so it seems to us; they are on a different petal of time. But we left the doorways between the worlds open. By that time, we had some obligation to the Fir Bolg. We could not abandon them. The years of no summer had come; the Fir Bolg were starving, their children freezing to death. Oh, if only we could have closed the doors! Nuada would be among us still. And my brother Miach."

Eriu lifted her arm across the Ancient's shoulders. "Even we Danu cannot see far into what the future will bring."

"No," said the Ancient softly. "That is how the Mother protects us from sorrow, I suppose."

Banba had been quietly thinking over the story. "And so when Eri returned heavy with child and gave birth to that redheaded boy, you all knew that he was Fomor."

"We knew. But we decided that he was half Fomor, half Danu. We held him in our regard like the race of Penitents and Exiles, the ancestors of you three. We raised him in that way among us."

"And yet no Danu women would mate with him."

"No. Nor marry. Eri herself, his mother, had seen to that. For her stories of her Fomorian captors terrified her listeners, their immense size and the painful ways they had used their Danu women captives." Airmid shook her head. "She doomed her own boy to loneliness among us with the tales. Only Nuada truly loved him; to Nuada he was like a younger brother."

"And he betrayed Nuada."

"He did," the Ancient said softly. "That was when Miach and I decided. After he betrayed us, we knew that we had to do something, that the Fomorians would enslave or kill us all if we did not find a way. So we called Nuada to us. We proposed to ReBraid his arm, to grow for him a true arm. But we would need his cooperation to do that. He declined. But then the Fomor came below. On the next day Nuada came to us; he agreed to our work."

She began to weep in earnest now, her hands clutching her table, but she kept talking through her sobs.

"My brother put all of himself into that work. All of his love for the Danu. And when the arm was ready—I remember it well—he incanted, 'Let this be joined sinew to sinew and nerve to nerve so that there is movement and feeling in every joint.' We worked the arm then, exercising it, submerging it in water. And when it was ready, Nuada stood before the assembly, whole and complete, and the Danu named him as their king."

She was silent.

"And Bres? And your father, Dian Cecht? And Miach?"

"Go and see it, Daughters. Uncolored by my own beliefs or by the tricks of memory. See it as true history. And when you have seen it, tell me if I judged aright. If you say no, I request that I receive the same penalty as my brother. It is, perhaps, what I deserve."

21

Now you come up here," said Bres, drunkenly. He caught at the hair of one of the three Fomor women who were swarming over him and pulled her up. She started to put her lips to his, but he flicked his thumb and forefinger over her nipple and pulled it into his mouth. He licked and swirled at the breast and sighed in satisfaction.

"We've done all right by you then, lad?"

Bres turned lazily toward the side of the room where the giant Balor was bouncing a woman up and down on his lap. His head rested comfortably against the wall; his giant arms supported the woman as she bounced. He had removed the patch from his missing eye; the blue-white orb was grotesque in appearance.

"You have, Balor. The mead, the women, the gifts." Bres sighed lazily as one of the threesome bent to her labors. "I think I could never have enough of women."

"Boy, I say again that it's not right that these Danu women won't mate with you. And head of Council? What is that? You should be king."

He grunted with satisfaction and lifted the woman from his lap, pointed down at Bres. "Take care of our lad there; he needs more of you," he said, and she scurried to join the group.

Balor quaffed a giant tankard of mead. "They've paid their tax, but they've paid you no respect. You are Fomorian; they owe you respect."

"This mating is fine," Bres said. "They will never mate with me."

"It's a shame," said Balor softly. "The little Danu women." He shook his head. "Light as a feather. Bounce on the lap. You could even take one to wife;

she would be smaller than you and half like you. You deserve a Danu wife, lad. Or several Danu women if you wish. You deserve whatever you wish."

"Why should I need a Danu wife when I have all of these?" Bres ran his hands lazily over the flanks of one of the women, bounced the large breasts of another.

"These do my bidding," said Balor. He clapped his hands; the foursome sat up and moved away. Bres raised himself drunkenly on his elbows, his face suffused with lust and anger.

"But a little Danu woman or two," Balor continued, "now they would do your bidding. We would see to that, your brother Fomorians. We could take a selection of Danu, men, women, children. You would have wives, servants, slaves, all Danu. All saying 'Yes, my lord.' It's what they owe you, nothing less."

Bres closed his eyes, the look on his face greedy. "How could this be done?" he asked.

"Can you get us into their cities?"

"Easily," said Bres. "But I wouldn't want them harmed."

"No harm," said Balor. "Just a selection of ten or so. All for you. All yours to command. Consider what women you would want. We would collect them for you. As many as you need. We will build you a great lodge on Tober Mor. There you will rule your household."

"No harm?"

"None."

Bres watched the Fomor women, who had begun to nuzzle each other. He moaned a little.

"Lad, are the cities beautiful?" Balor asked.

"Most beautiful," Bres said distractedly. "Return these to me, Balor: I am full to bursting. Come; you said they were a gift."

"And treasure?"

"Great treasure. Now may I have them?"

Balor smiled. He gestured to the women. They descended on Bres, hands and tongues working busily. They fed him delicacies and poured mead down his throat. He moaned and leaned back on the pillows.

"You!" Bres gestured to the smallest of the girls. "Up on my lap. We will pretend you are one of my Danu women."

"There's my good lad," said Balor. "More Fomorian than Danu by any measure, boy."

*   *   *

"Well, it's an old enough story," said Eriu.

"Mead and meat and women and riches," said Banba dryly. "And slowly, by degrees, suborn the willing to your purpose. And the heart becomes dark. And greed grows. And each time the lost one is willing to give away more of his spirit."

"They also offered him acceptance," said Fodla quietly. "You are one of us. You belong with us. More important than all the rest."

"You are wise as always, Fodla," said Eriu. "I begin to see why Airmid and Miach made the choice they did."

"But the histories tell us that Nuada paid the price of his life. Did he defeat them? And if so, how?"

Eriu rested her hand on the speckled stone. "Sisters, shall we rest or shall we continue?"

"There is no time to waste," said Fodla. "In our hours here, the Invaders approach even closer on the sea."

"We shall see more," Banba said softly. "Now."

At the doorway into the passage, Bres pressed his triangle into the recess in the wall. White light snapped, and then a blue oval coalesced before them. Balor bent low.

Bres held him back. "You will not fit in the passages," he said softly. "The tallest of the Danu only reach five feet; even I have to crouch to reach the city."

With his giant forefinger, Balor pointed at ten men, each under six feet tall. "Will they suit?"

Bres grinned. "Even they are a little large. But they will be fine in the city below."

Balor's voice adopted a wheedling tone. "I should love a piece of treasure, boy. Something I could wear around my neck."

"That is easily done. I owe you that much at least."

Balor grinned, the yellowed teeth half obscured beneath the giant, shaggy mustache. "Good lad," he said. "Now go. And you need not stop at ten. Bring back as many as the group of you can gather. As many as you wish. Or wish to share."

The group disappeared into the passageway, bending low.

In the Chamber of Memory, Eriu spoke softly. "They do not know the price that they will pay, these Fomor. Our price is but small compared to theirs."

"No," said Banba. "They are not Braid or Hybrid. But this is what they deserved. I should laugh to see them tomorrow by their fire, young men gone gray and wrinkled, their eyes rheumy, their pates bald."

"I wonder what he will think," said Fodla, pointing toward Balor.

As if he had heard them, Balor watched the company go and shrugged. "And if he does not bring enough, we can always come back for more," he said. "The boy is mine. Slaves and treasure will follow."

He sat down against the wall; he belched in satisfaction and leaned his head back against the rock.

Deep below the passageway, an alarm began to sound, the deep thrum of bells and drum. The sound of screams echoed up the long walkway.

"Good lad," said Balor. "You'll make a fine Fomor when all of this is over."

The scene shifted.

The Sisters were now observing a surgery.

Under an arc of blue-white light, Nuada was stretched on a table. Around the table a nimbus of electricity crackled and sparked.

Airmid held up an instrument and read it. "The field is sterile, Miach."

From the table Nuada spoke softly. "Beloved Niece and Nephew. I ask you once more. Are you certain of this course of action? I should not wish for you to pay the price for this action. Dagda and most especially Dian Cecht will not approve of this course."

"The Danu have paid the price for our inaction. Even now our city smolders and mothers cry out for their missing children. We have no other choice," said Miach.

"How could he have done this thing?" asked Airmid. She was young, her wide eyes full of sorrow.

"We kept him apart from us. An honored guest. But not a brother."

"You did not."

"No," said Nuada. "I loved him well." His voice broke on the admission.

"We have no choice," said Miach again. "We must find our missing people. We cannot just abandon them. And we must ensure that the Fomor can never come into Tara again."

"The Council has changed the doorway arms," said Airmid softly. "The Fomor can no longer enter."

"They will find a new way," said Nuada. "They have seen our city and our treasures. They have stolen our people. What will stop them now?"

"True," said Miach. "And they cannot change the heart of a traitor. Sister, I say again. You need not remain with us here."

"I remain," she said quietly. "I am proud to defend my people with the Knowledge of the Braid."

"Then you must promise me that you will keep silent in Council, that you will not speak for us and our work here."

Airmid said nothing.

"Promise me or you must go now."

"I promise," she said in a small voice.

"Swear on the Danu," said Nuada from the table. "For I know of your love for us."

"I swear on the Braid, in the name of the Mother." Airmid choked it out.

Miach nodded. "Then with your permission, Uncle, we will remove your awareness of pain so that we can proceed."

Nuada nodded.

Carefully, Airmid affixed small ovoids to Nuada's forehead, behind his ears, and at the back of his neck. She activated a small device in her hand.

After a moment, she took a probe. "Uncle, I will touch the stump now. You must tell me the truth."

She inserted the probe into the uneven layers where Nuada's arm ended.

In the chamber, Fodla turned away and hid her eyes. "Tell me when it is finished," she said softly.

"We need not relive it all," said Eriu. "We know what choice they made." She depressed the stone and gently twisted it to the right. The scene shifted again to the Great Council Hall. Nuada stood before the company, his arm attached. He flexed his fingers before the assembled Danu.

"Restore him as Triad Leader!" cried the Danu.

Dagda stepped to the platform beside Nuada. "Speak to us, Nuada; tell us why this was done."

Nuada nodded. He spoke softly, and the entire company leaned forward to listen.

"It was done that I might save the Danu. Our people must be rescued from the Fomor. We must drive them from the shores of the Green Isle that they will no longer trouble the Danu or the Fir Bolg. The Fomorians are like a ship with a bottomless hold. This even the Fir Bolg told us long ago. No taxes, no slaves, no riches will ever satisfy them. More makes them want more."

Now Dian Cecht stepped forward. "Someone must pay the price for this action. The Braid has been used in defiance of the law. Who has used the Braid Knowledge?"

Miach stepped forward bravely. "I have done this, Father," he said quietly.

Dian Cecht's face blanched and he looked stunned. Miach continued.

"It is not just that the Danu should always hide from their enemies. Nor is it just that the best and brightest among us should be unable to serve as a result of physical imperfection. Hear me, People of the Danu. The laws of the Old World should not be the laws for this world. We are a different race. Our circumstances here are different. The laws of Braiding must change. Of course we should not do what the Homeworld did. The power of Creation belongs to the Braid, not to any of her children. But those who have been created by the Braid should be healed and made whole! This the Mother would expect of us, that we would heal her children."

Among the Danu there was murmuring and shouts of agreement.

"Still, the law is the law!" cried Dian Cecht. "The law must be obeyed. There is a price affixed to this transgression."

"No, brother," said Dagda. "Such a price is too high."

"I will pay whatever price the law requires," Miach shouted. "I have done what I believe is right and just."

Dian Cecht turned toward his son, his eyes wide and sorrowful. "My son," he said softly. "The penalty is death."

"No!" Airmid screamed. "No! Do not kill my brother."

Both Nuada and Miach whipped in her direction, their eyes fixing on her.

"Sister!" Miach cried. "By the Braid."

Airmid pressed her lips together. Slowly, as though her legs had turned watery beneath her, she crumpled to the floor. The people of the Danu rushed to assist her.

"It is too much," they cried.

"The penalty goes too far!"

"He has restored Nuada to us."

"We will defeat the Fomor and rescue our lost children."

On the platform Nuada and Dagda stared out over the crowd. Dian Cecht began to weep like a child in great gulping sobs until at last Miach enfolded his father in his arms.

"And so he was executed?" Eriu asked softly.

"He was," said Airmid.

"And you never spoke?" Banba addressed the Ancient quietly, with none of her usual blunt attack.

"Never," said Airmid softly. "I begged them to let me speak and they would not. 'Live,' they said. 'Work to change the law. Heal the Danu.' And that is what I did."

"It is because of you, then, that we can save the Hybrid children of the Fir Bolg," said Eriu softly.

"It is because the people of the Danu changed the law," Airmid said softly. "It is because of the courage of Miach and Nuada."

"You asked me to tell you if we thought you had done aright," said Eriu softly. "We believe that you and your brother chose well. We believe that the fear of the Braided Ones against the use of the Braid was overdone, based on their own experiences on the Homeworld. We believe that the change in the law was wise. Had you not restored Nuada, the Danu might well today be the slaves of the Fomor, and the abandoned children of the Fir Bolg would be freezing on the hillsides."

Airmid nodded quietly. "I thank you." She kept her head bent above her table, her hands clutching the edge.

"But our acknowledgment does not ease the pain, does it?"

"No." Airmid whispered the word, forced it from her. "I thought that it might, but it does not."

"Because you did not speak."

"I should have died with my brother. I should have spoken that day before the Council."

Banba brought a chair and placed it behind Airmid. The Ancient collapsed into it, her little frame shaken by weeping.

Eriu knelt before her. "You gave them your sacred vow."

Airmid nodded.

"Your brother was wise. Do you not see? He knew that the law must change and he knew that the First Triad could not change it. You were the only hope for change."

Airmid looked up. "You are saying what you truly believe?"

"I am. Did not Nuada defeat them in battle?"

"So I am told."

"You were not there?"

Airmid shook her head. "I buried my brother high in the hills overlooking the sea and then I ran away. I went far to the north, alone. I lived in a cave in a hillside, nor did I speak to anyone. I studied the herbs of this planet and the healing medicaments and I stayed alone for many months. Once my father journeyed to find me. He pleaded with me to return, but I turned my back to him and would not speak. In his rage and anger, he tore my herbs from the ceiling, scattered the contents of my medicine jars, tore through my gardens and ripped my plants out at the roots. This from the gentlest of fathers that ever a child had known. But still I would not look at him or speak. He returned to Tara; later he died, his heart broken by grief and guilt, but I did not know then. I think that I would never have returned among the Danu. Never."

"But you did. What changed?"

"Lugh," she said softly, and her face folded into a smile that looked almost like a girl's. "I met Lugh."

22

I remember Lugh!" said Banba. "I was a young girl—long before they married us to the Brothers. By Danu, he was a handsome man!"

"He was indeed," said Eriu.

"You too?" said Fodla. "Are you catching her disease?" She gestured at Banba.

"Do you think he was her beloved?" said Banba.

"By the look on her face, what else should we conclude?" said Fodla.

"It would have been rude to ask," said Eriu.

"If only we had not been betrothed to the Brothers," said Banba with a sigh.

"Banba!" said Fodla. "Those were happy days. The Fomor had departed and the Fir Bolg were in our care. There was no danger for the Danu. The six of us wandered the Green Isle, always laughing. They were to us as elder brothers."

"We did seem to be always laughing, didn't we?" said Eriu.

"Well, they were such great friends, to us and to each other," Fodla said softly. "How much longer do you think they might have lived, had it not been for the Lia Fail?"

"Do not think on it," said Eriu. "We do what we must."

Fodla nodded. "I think of them often. Mac Cuill, Mac Cecht, and Mac Grene. Handsome men and good."

Banba sighed. "But oh, Lugh. There was a man!"

"He was not Danu, you know," said Fodla.

"Surely he was," said Banba. "He possessed our light and our eyes."

"But not our hair or our height."

"Don't you mean our lack of height?" said Eriu.

The door slid open. The Sisters were surprised to see Airmid silhou-etted in the passage, her tiny, bent frame leaning on the arm of Illyn.

"Ancient!" said Eriu. She leaped to her feet. "How may we assist you?" Illyn bowed from the room, and Eriu conducted Airmid to her own chair.

"The Invaders will make landfall on the morrow."

"How do you know this?"

"I have had a watch posted for these three days; at dusk they saw the lights in their top rigging. Our spear warriors have heard music from their ships."

"We have heard it too. It is most sorrowful."

Airmid nodded. "So they have said. Only I hope that they do not blame their sorrows on us."

Banba snorted. "Well, the Fomor always did. And the Fir Bolg as well, at least for a time. Why should these newcomers be any differ-ent?"

"What shall we do?" Eriu asked the Ancient. "Should we abandon our studies here and prepare?"

"In the past is the answer to the present, Sisters. You have very little time left for this work . . . and that is probably well." She regarded Banba, squinted her eyes. "It seems to take a toll on you."

Eriu turned to look at Banba. Banba looked weary; soft circles curved beneath her eyes.

Airmid seated herself and closed her eyes, resting her head on the back of the chair. "As for me, I know what I will do."

"Ancient, you cannot stay here with us," Eriu said, alarm in her tone.

"Have you seen him yet?"

"Seen who? Where?" asked Banba. She made a face at her Sisters as if the Ancient were crazy or mindless.

"I see that," said the Ancient, her long finger admonishing. "One day you will be as I am now and the youngsters will gesture behind your back and call you mindless."

"Or mean-tongued," said Fodla.

"It is likely that they already call her that," said Airmid, and all three sisters burst into laughter.

"True enough," said Banba. "I apologize, Ancient."

"Lugh Lamfhada," said Airmid. "Have you seen him yet? Here in the Chamber of Memory?"

"No."

"But you will return to the final battle, will you not?"

"We will," said Eriu. "But memory is difficult, Ancient, just as you warned us. Sights, smells, sounds, fears and joys. It is as if we were there among them. Even the immediate effects . . ." She glanced again at Banba.

"What should I fear, Eriu?" said Airmid, the infant smile creasing her face. "Old age? I have lived for three millennia. Weariness? I have been weary in my spirit since Miach died. Death? There is no death, as well you know. We return to the Braid who wove us, she who will weave us again. Only you three know my secret and you have forgiven my choices. With you I feel myself again. As I have not felt since . . . well, for a long time."

Banba snorted. "Since Lugh. You wish to see Lugh again."

"I wish to see Lugh again," said Airmid. And her voice was the voice of a young girl.

The Plain of Mag Tuiread shimmered into view, morning sunlight pouring down among the stones.

"So we come to battle here again," said Eriu. She was curled on the floor at Airmid's feet, resting on a pillow, her back against the chair in which the Ancient sat.

The Ancient tousled her curls. "Always here, girl. You know that history repeats; it is as true for us as for every culture we have ever known."

The Fomorian horde was gathered at the far side of the field, among them ten ancient, shrunken men dressed in the garb of much younger warriors. None of the other Fomor stood near them, as if they bore a disease that all could catch.

"So," said Airmid. "They paid the price for entering Tara."

"Rather for departing from it," said Eriu softly.

The giant Balor stood at the head of the Fomorian army. He bristled with war armor, a huge two-horned helmet on his head, a giant war ax in his right hand. He was all hair and beard, black like some ancient animal. He had removed the patch from his eye and the cloudy blue-gray orb appeared luminous and large, terrifying in the morning light.

Beside him was Bres, dressed in the war garb of the Fomorians.

"False king," he called out now, taunting Nuada. "A damaged man of the Danu. Ask to see his arm, Balor."

Nuada said nothing. Slowly, almost gently, he removed the silver gauntlet from his hand. He held up his arm, whole in the light. He clenched and unclenched his fingers.

"You betrayed us," he said. "I treated you ever as a brother." Though his voice was soft, it carried across the field. He replaced the silver gauntlet, pulling it on like a glove.

"No brother to those who did not want me."

"Bres is ours!" cried Balor.

"Bought and paid for!" cried Dagda. "What did it take, little halfling? Wine, women, treasure?"

Bres had the good grace to lower his eyes.

Dagda stepped from behind Nuada, his own arm clad in silver. The Danu ranged up beside the two, holding their Light Spears. "Know this, men of the north!" Dagda cried. "This day we will defeat you. This day you will sail to the north from whence you came. For a thousand years hence, you will whisper of the little people of the Danu. You will fear to return among us. This day you will return our people to us!"

"Do you mean these?" cried Balor. More than a dozen Fomorian warriors stepped forward. Each held a leash in his hand, dragging at its end a Danu captive. Men, women, children, some of them so small that they did not reach even to the knees of their Fomorian captors. The Fomor held the little people before them, using them as human shields.

An uneasy shifting moved through the Danu.

"Come, Nuada Argetlamh!" called Bres. "Unleash your weapons now."

"We will hit them," Nuada whispered to Bres. "What course now, Brother?"

Suddenly there was a blast of sound and light from the rear of the Fomor company, followed by an unearthly scream of pain. Fomorians began to run for the front of the line, pelting in front of Bres and Balor and their Danu captives.

"What has happened?" Dagda shouted at Nuada.

"I know not. But take the tide that turns for us. Let us rescue our people!"

Lightning began to stream from the thrown Light Spears, which hissed as they arced toward the enemy. The Silver Arms began to spit blue light, flame, concussions of noise. Fomor stiffened and fell, great clods of dirt exploding around their tumbling forms.

While the Sisters watched, the little Danu sped among the Fomor, appearing and disappearing, unleashing confusion and terror.

Balor came at a run toward Nuada and Dagda.

"Obscure the field!" screamed Nuada.

Suddenly, Balor swung his great club. It connected hard with Nuada's shoulder. The Danu gave out a cry of pain.

Dagda held forth his own Silver Arm. He pulsed it once toward the sky, once toward the earth. A high wind began to wail in the trees. Fog began to creep along the ground, threading through the great stone portals of the plain. In moments the battlefield was obscured by fog.

Suddenly, into the midst of the company rode a man on a great horse. He was tall and strong-limbed. His curly golden hair and wide eyes proclaimed him Danu, but he was a man of over six feet. He thundered in, straight at Nuada and Balor, who had raised his club for the death strike. Balor staggered back before the thundering hooves of the horse. The huge man leaned down and stretched out his arm to Nuada.

"Clasp it, brother!" he cried. "I will not play you false." Nuada reached up; the great man hauled him into the saddle and they thundered across the battlefield.

The big man deposited him at the edge of the field.

"Physician," he cried. Airmid came running from the edge of the field toward Nuada, her belt with its healing instruments and medicines bouncing at her waist.

"This is Nuada?" the big man asked.

"It is," she said. "Our captives, mo ghra. Save them." He turned and rode hard for the field.

Nuada looked up at her. "Welcome back, Airmid."

"Uncle," she said softly.

"It has been nearly seven years," said Nuada.

"I have been in the north."

"Your father has passed."

She nodded. "He could not bear that he was author of Miach's execution."

Nuada nodded toward the horseman. "And the rider?"

"Lugh."

"He is one of us?"

She nodded once.

"And who else? He is not Penitent."

"He knows not. He is Danu."

The big man rode back on his horse, a captive before him and two behind him. "Take them below," he called. He rode away.

"They will not readily accept him," said Nuada. He winced as she pressed a pulsing instrument into the shoulder. "Not after Bres."

She shrugged. "He is what he is. He does not need our acceptance. Nor theirs."

Nuada smiled. "And he has yours."

Airmid smiled. "You can return to battle, Uncle."

"So that was Lugh," Banba said softly.

Airmid was leaning back against the cushions, her eyes closed. She said nothing.

"Ancient," said Eriu. "You are well?"

"I am well, child. It has brought him back to me again in all his beauty."

"Did they accept him?"

"No. Not at first. Between Lugh and Nuada and Dagda, they rescued all the hostages. When the battle had ended, Lugh returned with us here to Tara. The people shunned him."

"Despite what he had done?"

"Perhaps because of it. They feared his purpose; they feared that he would be as false as Bres. None of it bothered Lugh. He simply laughed and said, 'They will come to know me.' And eventually they did."

"How did you come to know him?" Banba asked.

"When I was in the north. One day, there he was in the forest, hunting on foot, silent as wind." She shrugged. "Obviously Danu. Obviously something else as well."

"What did he say of that?"

"He did not know. Rumors swirled about him here at Tara. Some of the Danu said they had heard that Dagda had a son by a Fir Bolg woman. Others said that he was the son of Cian of the Danu, who had taken to wife Ethlim of the Fomor. For many years there had been a story, that Balor of the Fomor had a daughter, that he kept her locked in a tower that she might never be troubled by a man. Among the Danu, it was whispered that Cian had seen her and been smitten, that he had used Metaphor to transform himself into a woman. In that guise, he had visited her in her tower. Nine months later she gave birth to triplets."

"Triplets?" said Eriu.

"It does lend weight to the story, does it not?"

"It does. Where were his brothers, then?"

"Among the Fomor there was a legend that Balor of the One Eye would be killed by his own grandson."

"So there is the truth of why he walled his daughter up," said Banba. "He was not protecting her virtue."

"Well, when he saw the triplets, he knew that the tower had failed. The story was that he tried to drown them all. He succeeded with all but Lugh."

"Who raised him?"

"He was raised in the deep northern forest by a woman named Birog. She was a wise woman. Druii, he called her. She told him that he was Danu and that he should learn well, so that the Danu would know him as a wisdom keeper when at last they met. When he was seven, he was fostered to a blacksmith. It was the first of many apprenticeships."

"Did our people come to accept him?"

"At length," she said. "He simply worked his way into their hearts. I say this literally, daughters. He was a carpenter and a smith, a warrior, a poet and a harper, a physician . . ."

"That last thanks to you, I suppose," said Banba.

Airmid nodded. "He did whatever he was asked. Whenever. Without complaint and always in good spirits. He even taught the Danu to be horsemen. The Danu came to call him Lugh Ildanach, Lugh All-Craftsman. It was not possible not to love him."

"You called him Lugh Lamfhada," said Eriu.

Airmid nodded. "He earned that name in the battle."

"How?" asked Eriu.

"Why did Nuada not speak for him among the Danu?" asked Banba.

"So it was Lugh who began the battle from behind the lines?" asked Fodla.

"Too many questions, daughters," she said softly. "And the answers are troubling and sad. You must see them for yourselves."

She pointed to the speckled stone.

Nuada returned to the field, dashing in and out of the Danu, appearing and disappearing in the battlefield fog. Bolts of lightning emerged from the spears of the Danu, and Lugh on his white horse pounded across the field.

Suddenly there was a huge roar.

Balor had sighted Nuada. He heaved back his spear arm. The spear flew true, piercing Nuada through the heart.

In the chamber Airmid let out a sob.

Nuada fell to the ground lifeless, the Silver Arm falling hard across his chest. The people of the Danu began to scream.

"Nuada Argetlamh."

"Nuada! No! Nuada!"

Balor began to move inexorably toward the dead man, his huge frame leaning forward at a heavy run, his eye focused on the Silver Arm.

Suddenly Lugh rode toward the fallen Nuada. Without ever leaving his horse, he swept his arm down and snatched the Silver Arm, pulling it from Nuada's own. Holding it out in front of him like a spear, Lugh called out, "For Nuada."

He shifted the arm and it gave out a bolt of great light and noise. It pierced Balor, directly through the blind and rheumy eye. Balor fell.

A great cry arose from the Fomorians. The began to scatter, to flee between the lintels of the great stone circle and run for the forest below. It was not long before they fled for their sea boats, leaving the rest of the Danu captives behind.

The fog began to lift at the edge of the battlefield. In the trees at the far side of the circle, where once they would have been behind the Fomor lines, a shadow moved. The Morrigu stepped onto the Plain of Mag Tuiread. Macha wore a Silver Arm.

"Well begun, Sisters," said Macha softly.

"And well ended," said Banbh in her scratchy, masculine voice. "Let the Danu take our wounded and our dead. I will take the rest." She touched the triangle at her neck. Ravens began to circle the field, to dip to the grisly work below; Banbh flew among them.

In the chamber, Airmid wept softly.

"And so we lost Nuada?" said Eriu.

"And Lugh became known as Lugh Lamfhada, for the way he used the Silver Arm, as if it were a spear," said Fodla.

"And if the legend is true, Balor was indeed killed by his own grandson." Airmid nodded.

"And the Morrigu?" asked Banba.

"They are sowers of chaos," said Airmid quietly. "They make war very well indeed; they are the necessary evil."

"There is one thing I do not understand," said Eriu. "The fog that covered the field. It was not raining. Was it created by the Light Spears?"

Airmid smiled. "That is the beauty of the Silver Arms, child. They are not weapons only. Each finger of each arm is articulated to a specific purpose. Wind, fog, noise, lightning, images of warriors, even sweet music."

Eriu tried to stand from the floor, but her legs would not come up with her. She hissed in pain, pressed her palms to the floor to lift her own weight. When she was standing, she shifted gingerly from one leg to the other. Airmid watched from her chair.

"It will pass," Airmid said. "These are temporary effects only. The long-term costs will be assessed later, five hundred, a thousand years from now. And you are finished now with Lia Fail. Eriu has learned the answer from the history, have you not?"

Eriu nodded excitedly. "I have. Sisters, the answer was before us always. The Silver Arms. You must teach us, Airmid. All three arms."

"You will destroy the Invaders with them?" asked Banba.

"No. We will use them on their minds, not their bodies. We will make them wary of us and wise."

"Until now, our memory had shown me only three ways: we could hide from the Invaders, seal the doors to Tara—"

"Which would abandon the Fir Bolg," said Airmid.

"Precisely. No Danu wishes such a thing. Or we could destroy the Invaders."

Airmid sighed and shook her head. "We have seen what price our history paid for that choice."

"We have," said Eriu. "If these Invaders were enough like Fir Bolg, we might frighten them into submission."

"But they are far more sophisticated than Fir Bolg," said Banba. "Superstition will not keep them from the doors."

"We know not yet if they are more like Fir Bolg or Fomor," said Fodla.

"Oh, they are more like Fomor," said Banba.

"What makes you say so, child?" asked Airmid.

"Airioch Feabhruadh and the way he was eyeing the jewels we wore in Metaphor," Banba replied.

"When he was not eyeing the jewels your Metaphor created elsewhere," said Fodla.

"And Eber Donn, that great hairy beast who kept muttering about cattle pasturage." Banba shook her head. "Stupid but dogged. Small-minded but determined."

"So they are greedy," said Airmid quietly. "As Bres was. You could feed their greed with treasure."

"No," said Eriu. "Greed feeds on itself and grows larger. Think of Bres. He became all greed, all wanting. It destroyed him and nearly destroyed us."

"And so the arms?"

"Do you see?" she said. "If the arms are not destroyers alone, if they are many-purposed . . ."

"We could make a show of strength; we could seem to be more in numbers and to be more skilled and dangerous than we are," said Fodla.

"Yes," said Banba. "Now have we learned from our memory. We can appear to be as Lugh Lamfhada was—so skilled in all things . . ."

"That the Invaders will respect us," said Fodla, "and so let us be, or work with us in truce."

"Airmid," said Eriu, "will you take us to the hiding place of the Silver Arms?"

Airmid stood and held out her hand. "Come," she said. "This is a wise plan. It honors them all. Nuada, Lugh, Miach, all who protected the Danu.

"Braid hands," Airmid commanded. "I will stand in your midst. Encircle me; braid me into your Triad. I will press upon my triangle. You will see it pulse and grow warm. Do not touch me or stop me. Promise this."

"We promise, Ancient," said Eriu softly. "Begin the chant of vision."

Banba and Fodla issued the deep sounds, reed and chanter. Eriu began the chant. She watched as Airmid pressed her palm to her own triangle. She could smell the flesh of the Ancient's palm burning, burning. But she remembered her promise and did not break hands or cease chant.

All around them, the room grew viscous; lights pulsed within her frame of vision, then darkness. Complete darkness.

"Sisters, you may unbraid."

It was Airmid's voice.

"Ancient," Fodla whispered. "Are you well?"

"You need not whisper," said Airmid. "No one knows of this place. No one can hear you. We hid the arms here, Lugh and I. Not even Council knows where they are. Nor can they be discovered by any but a triad. After the battle was done and the Fomor departed for the cold north. This is how we hid them, that they could not be reached by one person alone. The Danu have not needed them since."

Eriu could hear her moving in the darkness. Suddenly the room began to illuminate with an eerie blue light. Airmid was standing to the side, her triangle pressed into a depression in the wall.

"How did you find it?" asked Banba.

"I can see it," said Airmid. "Have you not wondered why we of the Braided Ancients wear the dark lenses over our eyes? Our eyes are more sensitive than yours by a thousandfold. I see in darkness." She took small blue torches from a niche in the wall, each seeming to contain its own source of light. She handed one to each of the Sisters. Eriu stepped toward Airmid and looked at the Ancient's palm. It was burned and blistered. Airmid shook her off.

"A little salve will heal me. It is nothing."

"Where are we?" asked Eriu.

The light began to illuminate the walls, which seemed crystalline, almost opalescent. Clear crystal towers grew from the ceiling and the floor.

"Deep beneath the earth and sea," said Airmid. "Where these three would remain safe and untouched forever."

She turned her torch toward a depression in the wall. Before it shimmered a waterfall, softly descending, seeming to chime, small lights flickering within the viscous cascade. Airmid gestured to a triangular recess at each side of the waterfall. Eriu stepped up to one side of the cascade while Airmid pressed her triangle into the recess at the opposite side. The water ceased to fall. Behind the cascade, illuminated in soft light, were the clear tubular chambers that should have held the Silver Arms of the Danu.

The tubes gleamed in the ambient blue light.

They were empty.

23

By the Danu!" The Sisters rushed to catch Airmid, who swayed in place, her eyes riveted to the wall in horror. "Just so we left them, Lugh and I. I do swear it."

Banba nodded. "There is no mystery here, Ancient. You said they could be accessed only by a Triad. Who were the only ones who knew to use them in the battle other than Nuada and Dagda and Lugh?"

"The Morrigu." Airmid wailed it out into the cold cave. "But how did she find them here? We hid them well."

"Like darkness, she slips into the hollows of the world," said Eriu softly. "Oh, I fear the work that she will do. Does she know all of their powers?"

"I know not. Nuada knew, and Dagda. When Nuada had passed, Dagda taught their uses to Lugh. He became chief after the death of Dagda."

Eriu patted the shoulder of the Ancient. "It will be well. We will speak to the Morrigu."

"What leverage do we have? How can we bargain with her from a position of strength? We do not have the arms and we know nothing," said Banba.

"We will act as though we know. Airmid will teach us," Eriu replied.

"Except that I do not know their uses," said Airmid softly.

"How can that be?"

"Council Triad knew the weapons. My father, Nuada, Dagda. And after Dagda died, Lugh. No others."

"And Lugh is dead."

"There is no death," Airmid said.

Eriu sighed. "So I have heard the Ancients say. If only that could help us now."

"Then hear me," said Airmid. Her tone was urgent. The Sisters sat before her in Triangle.

"Speak, Ancient," said Eriu. "We are listening."

"What do we say of death?"

Eriu replied. "We say that the departed has gone into the west, that he dwells on Mag Mell, the Isle of the Ever Young. We say that when his time is right, he will return. We celebrate his departure, for that country is beautiful and devoid of sorrow. And when a child returns to us, we toll the bells and thank him for his sacrifice, his return to this world."

"And the Isle of the Ever Young? It is a place to which we can sail?" asked Banba.

"It is . . . an idea?" asked Eriu.

"A state of being in the Braid?" asked Fodla.

"Perhaps a leaf," Airmid responded.

For a moment the Sisters were still. Then they all answered at once.

"We see," said Fodla.

"Like the leaves of time," said Eriu.

"If only we could speak to them there," said Banba. "Then such knowledge would be useful."

"But you cannot. That is not your gift. Yet, among the Danu are those who do see and hear what is not there. We call them second-sighted." Airmid was silent.

"And you are one of those?"

She nodded simply. "It has always been a useful skill for a physician, a deeper way of knowing. I am very old and most of those I love have crossed to Mag Mell. There are places in this world which serve as doorways between this world and the next. At such a doorway I have spoken once to Miach. In the Chamber of Memory, when I said that you had returned Lugh to me?"

Eriu nodded.

"Now I will speak to Lugh again."

Eriu tilted her head and regarded the Ancient. "Why have you not done so before now, Ancient? Why not more often, for surely we can see how he resides in your heart."

"Like accessing memory, it takes much to do it," she said softly. "We ask much when we ask for this world and the next to intersect, for they are much different from each other. The . . . space . . . between this world and the next vibrates with voices, with presence, with all that comes and goes. It is more difficult than the Lia Fail because the Chamber of Memory shows us only selected . . . episodes. But to speak to those who have passed is to hear all of the voices who have crossed and then try to select from them. It is like standing in a forest in a great wind and listening for the sound of a single tree. And some of those voices come bearing a darkness."

"Then you shall not do it," said Eriu.

"But I shall," Airmid said softly. "How shall I do less than you have done, in immersing yourself in Lia Fail? I have told you that I have nothing to fear."

"It is we who fear," said Fodla.

"You are one of the last of our Ancients, one of so few remaining to us who were born on the Homeworld," said Banba. "If you die in trying to speak to Lugh, we will lose you."

"You will not lose me; I will always be here in memory for you. The very walls around me will remember me for you. But let me show you something." Carefully, she placed her memory triangle in the wall, pressed the stick language incised below it. Onto the walls came an image of a Danu of the Braid, a young woman, diminutive and pale, her huge dark eyes wide with wonder. She was laughing at the man beside her as they ran side by side along a windy beach.

"Come, Brother," she cried. "Just because this world is rainier and cold does not mean that I should beat you every time."

He put on a burst of speed and passed her at a run, a tiny pale man with a large childlike mouth.

"You let me win!" he cried.

She shrugged. "You are my brother Miach. We can run races together forever."

A silence prevailed in the room for a long time.

Then Eriu spoke softly. "Tell us what we must do to help you prepare."

*   *   *

In the deep forest at the top of a little rise, a huge flat rock rode unevenly across two great upright stones incised with whorls and spirals. Moonlight spilled across the surface of the rock, inched down its sides, making it looked like a giant ill-pitched table covered with a patchy tablecloth of white. Ivy had twined and curved around the uprights, hiding much of their carved surface in a moon-silvered profusion of leafy green triangles.

"It is a dolmen," said Airmid softly. "It is not like the doorways to our cities. Rather, it is a place of concentration; forces gather here. You must not enter it with me; stand here and wait. You will know when you can come for me."

The Sisters stopped at the foot of the hill, peering upward into the darkness. Airmid climbed carefully upward, leaning on her medical staff, her tiny body and her great age making her seem fragile and vulnerable in the darkness. She stepped beneath the great stone.

The space beneath the dolmen shimmered and wavered. In the sky beyond, the stars seemed to lengthen, the moon to stretch its shape from round to oval. A long time passed. An hour, perhaps two, by the reckoning of this world. And then he was there. Lugh Lamfhada, his huge frame silhouetted in the doorway.

"By the Danu," Banba whispered. "Surely we are seeing him there."

"Or so it would seem," Eriu whispered. "This is a fearsome thing; I am joyful and afraid at once. Oh, Sisters, we have learned much in these last days."

"And still we know but a single leaf on the vine of Airmid's knowledge," whispered Fodla.

In the dolmen, Airmid and Lugh stood apart, the air between them shimmering and thick. Once he turned his head toward the Sisters, who stood awestruck and still at the base of the hill. Collectively, they drew in their breath at his gaze.

A soft wind moved high in the trees above them; small animals skittered on the floor of the forest, as though a meeting between the living and the dead were ordinary, as though they should go about their business as they always did. Time seemed to slow, almost to still. Eriu felt heavy; her limbs, weighted and watery. And then Lugh was gone.

Airmid stepped from the dolmen and crumpled to the ground; the Sisters rushed to assist her. Eriu lifted her into her arms, gently poured drops of cool libation between her lips. For her part, Airmid smiled and smiled, though she was weak as a newborn Danaan.

"I did not see him leave," said Banba, "though I was watching him well."

"He did not leave," said Airmid. "He simply closed the door. But he is here still. The Braid contains us all at all times. We are sustained inside the Braid."

"Why do we weep their absence, Ancient? When all the while their presence is right here next to ours?"

"We weep their absence from their bodies in this time and in this place. We weep their incarnation. We see from a single leaf, Daughter. But do you see the vines that twine around these lintels?"

Eriu nodded.

"The Braid knows all of that; the beginnings and the endings, the intertwinings, the new and the old, the death and the reblossoming. She tries to show us; she weaves the worlds in Metaphor. Over and over again. But we are singled-minded and blind. We see a single leaf, we cannot see the pattern."

"It is all too much for me," said Banba, her reaction to the strange and the new being irritation, as always.

"You are young," said Airmid. "You will come to see it clearly. Lugh has told me what we need to know. You have much to learn, Daughters. Return me to Tara, for I have little time."

"This also Lugh has told you?" asked Eriu.

Airmid nodded. She kept smiling and smiling, touching her long fingers to her lips as though she held some wondrous secret.

"Hurry now. We have much to do."

Far out at sea, Amergin stood on the deck of the ship and looked toward the land, silhouetted in the moonlight. Airioch Feabhruadh slipped up beside him in the darkness.

"What do you see, Brother?"

"I see only the outline of the island in the moonlight. But the wind seems full of voices."

"And they all speak of treasure," said Airioch Feabhruadh. He clapped Amergin on the shoulder. "On the morrow, you will see. The treasure is bottomless." His face was flushed with excitement. Amergin regarded him in silence. Airioch returned across the deck and descended below.

Amergin remained on the deck.

"My treasure has vanished into the sea," he whispered. "Skena, do you hear me? Is our child within you still? And Ir? Do you care for them both? Oh, forgive me, love, that I did not reach the railing first."

Around him the wind twisted and grew, snapping at the sails, howling in the rigging. He leaned far forward over the railing.

"It would take so little, love, a shift forward, that is all. But then I would betray my father and Uncle Ith. My duty to the tribe. Always duty."

Amergin dropped his head to the railing and wept.

24

"Sisters, I would speak to her alone!"

"You do not wish our presence?" Fodla's voice sounded at once wounded and surprised.

"And with, of all people, Morrigu?" Banba was incredulous and angry.

Eriu shook her head. "It has naught to do with you. It has to do with her sisters. I would meet with Macha alone, separate from Nemhain and Banbh."

"That I understand well enough," said Banba. "Those two make my very skin crawl."

Eriu nodded. "Precisely. We know now what we need to know of the functions of the arms. I stand a better chance of learning what the Morrigu knows and of negotiating a reasonable position if I meet with Macha alone. What she sows, she does with intelligence; the other two are all instinct, all base. But Macha will never meet with us in triad if she is alone. Her position would be too weak without her sisters."

"Well reasoned," said Banba.

"But still I like it not," said Fodla.

"And yet you see its wisdom?"

The Sisters nodded.

"But promise us that you will stay near the doorway."

"And that you will have your triangle at the ready should you need to return to Tara."

"I promise."

Yet now, sitting on the spring ground, her back against a sarsen stone, she felt no fear. A soft breeze blew up from the forest, and the stars, which had been spread across the sky like a veil, blurred and lightened as the soft gray of predawn paled their fire.

Eriu sighed. What she wished, just once, was to see what Airmid had seen in the dolmen, to see on the face of a beloved absolute recognition, a look of complete belonging.

The Brothers had been good men, funny and wise in the ways of the Danu. They had been good companions and gentle elder teachers for the mating. They had been friends. But they were interchangeable; the Sisters had been bonded to them because that was the way of the people—triad to triad, that the learning might be passed on, the duties of triad. And of course, there had been the hope that one of the matings would itself produce a triad.

But none had; the Brothers had passed from the world leaving no off-spring at all. Briefly, Eriu wondered again if that too had to do with the Brothers' long immersion in Lia Fail. She was filled suddenly with a terrible sorrow at the thought that neither she nor her sisters might bring children into the world.

Eriu wondered if her sisters sometimes felt lonely, if they too wished for a companion of the soul. Even when they were bonded to the Brothers, the Sisters had been bonded first to each other and to their duty to the Danu.

Eriu thought of Illyn, and a small smile crossed her face. In Illyn she had a daughter of the heart, but Banba and Fodla did not even have that. Her heart ached for all of them.

She began to feel panic rising in her. They would produce no triad, none of them. There would be no Council to serve the Danu. Chaos would reign; the Invaders would defeat them, would kill the Danu. Those who remained would be trapped below world, never to see the sun. . . . Eriu gasped. She stood.

"Nemhain, show yourself!"

Nemhain stepped into view from behind the stone, her face sulky, her black eyes beginning to lose their luster.

"You were causing my panic!"

"And I was feeding on it too." Nemhain smiled, her look almost ecstatic, the white teeth gleaming in the moonlight. "You are not as good a subject as the Invaders, but you were doing well, racing down some path

of self-destruction in much the same fashion that they do. The only difference is that they do not know me as the cause and I can feed on the mount-
ing panic for hours, days, sometimes years." She actually ran her small,
dark tongue over her lips.

"How do you know about the Invaders?"

"I have been on their ship. One of them I infected with such sorrow
that he weeps on the railing and thinks of drowning himself in the sea.
The other is so hard with his lust for treasure that he has to relieve himself
whenever I am near."

"You disgust me," Eriu said bluntly. "I asked to meet with your sister."

"We did not approve of your meeting with her alone. So we came. But
now I fear I have given myself away. Macha will be furious." She smiled
again. "I can feed on fury, too."

Eriu felt a shiver run up her arms, drew her cloak closer around herself. "What are you?"

"We are that part of you that you do not acknowledge. We are the Antithesis. We dwell everywhere in all times. We plant ourselves and feed
and wait for growth."

"Banbh is with you."

"She has shifted. There are dead in the water. She awaits them."

"What dead are in the water?"

"The Invaders have lost some of their own to drowning. Banbh will
feed."

"Banbh!" Eriu called it out. A huge raven came spinning up from the
direction of the sea and landed at the top of the sarsen stone. A moment
later Banbh stepped from behind the stone. She was brushing her cloak
into shape, dark iridescent feathers drifting from it. She turned on
Nemhain immediately.

"So. You could not keep your presence hidden for a little hour, Chaos.
I am hungry."

"I never keep my presence hidden, Feather. It is only that Eriu recog-
nized my presence. Most do not recognize chaos or panic. They take it
into themselves and let it grow." She smiled. "And then I feed. Have you
fed tonight?"

"The dead have not washed to shore. Soon enough they will. I would
be sated soon had you stayed hidden."

"Then I am somewhat sated and you are empty."

Banbh stepped toward her sister, her masculine, nasal voice low and threatening. "I can feed from you, Sister. Never forget that." In a flash, she raised a single finger with its long curved nail and swept it across her sister's throat. A thin trail of blood appeared.

"I will share," said Nemhain, softly, seductively. She tilted her head back in the moonlight.

Eriu backed against the stone; her hand went reflexively to the triangle at her neck. Her sisters had been right to tell her not to come alone.

Banbh looked at Eriu, her eyes glittering. She turned back to Nemhain.

"You will share because you know that our little ritual will repulse her and throw her sweet vision of the world into chaos and then you can feed again."

Nemhain chuckled. Blood was trickling now down into the neck of her gown.

"But then," said Banbh, "we both win, do we not, Sister? I feed and you feed."

"We do," said Nemhain. "Come, Sister."

Banbh bent her head toward Nemhain's neck, her long black tongue flicking. Eriu turned toward the stone, raised her triangle.

"Stop!" The word was so commanding, the sound thundering across the clearing, that Eriu turned back around at the same moment that Banbh raised her bloodied lips from Nemhain's throat. Macha had appeared suddenly beside the stone, her face contorted with anger.

"Get you gone from here!" she commanded. "Return to the rook and go nowhere else. You have not obeyed me; you will answer for this transgression."

In a flash the two sisters were gone. Eriu could hear a raven flapping and winging toward the sea at the same moment that a cold wind passed across her face.

She leaned back against the rock, her knees gone wobbly, trying hard not to let Macha see the weakness.

"They will be severely punished," said Macha.

"They will enjoy that, I am sure."

Macha tilted her head and a curious expression came into her eyes. "What do you mean?"

"When you punish Banbh, Nemhain will feed on her rage and indignity. When you punish Nemhain, Banbh will feed on her . . ." Eriu trailed away, her mind picturing the carrion sister at the neck of her own sister.

"Her blood," finished Macha. "Aren't you the wise one, Little Triad Sister? One would think you were as old as we. But you should know me better. I have found ways to punish that do not feed either of them, that leave them hungry and void. How do you punish your sisters?"

"Punish? I love my sisters; they love me. We care for each other and bear each other up."

Macha seemed completely taken aback by the admission. "You have never had to punish them? Not even once?"

"Of course not," Eriu said angrily. "They are not mine to punish. They are the Danu's children, as am I, as are . . ."

"Ah," said Macha. "Now you see. Whose children are we?"

The sea breeze wafted Macha's gown, and her scent drifted toward Eriu—musk and spices, exotic and dark. Quite beautiful really. Eriu closed her eyes, inhaled. When she opened her eyes, Macha was inches from her face, the dark inquisitive eyes taking her in, the long black hair drifting against Eriu's wrist and hand.

"But you have asked to meet with me. Privately. I too like you best of your threesome."

Eriu laughed. "Do not play your games with me, Ravener. You know why I have asked you to come."

Macha sighed. She folded down onto the ground in a sitting position and gestured to Eriu. Eriu slid down the rock, glad for its support for her quavering legs.

"I know why you have asked," said Macha. "You have asked because my sisters are beasts. They function on instinct alone, and all their instinct drives toward sating their endless desires for chaos and carrion. And you see in me something else."

"I see in you a tree that thrashes in the storm, throwing branches first this way, then that. I see lightning, jumping cloud to cloud, then striking at some poor soul skittering along the ground. I see a wind that can shift direction in a moment, here leave destruction, here spare another. You are the bringer of battle, Macha, but you fight a war within yourself, always. And yes, I see intelligence. And loneliness. Vast as these stars."

Macha's mouth had formed into a wide circle of surprise; her dark eyes had gone soft. "It is the loneliness, Eriu," she whispered. "The loneliness drives it all."

As if she had admitted too much, her whole face closed up.

"And the fact that I am tethered to those two fools for all of time. How would that do for you, Triad Leader? To be a woman of mind, linked forever to two giant, dark, hungry mouths? Never mind; time will come, I will find a way to destroy them . . . or to swallow them; I will find a way to move in the world alone."

"And when you do that, will you be worse or better for the action?"

Macha shrugged. "I neither know nor care."

"Do you not fear that they are listening, that they will hear you say these things to me?"

"It is a relief to say them to you. And no, I do not fear it. I have told them the selfsame thing many times. 'Beware of me. Obey me. I am coming for you and I will destroy you.' They fear me well."

"Ah," said Eriu, the dynamic becoming suddenly clear to her. "And this is how you feed. When you cannot feed your battle lust with Danu war or human war, you cause a war within your triad, and so you feed on Morrigu itself."

"Aren't you the clever girl," said Macha admiringly, "to see through us so clearly? You have a good mind, Eriu. But you did not call me here to unwarp and unweft Morrigu."

"You have the arms," said Eriu bluntly.

Macha nodded. "This time we have all three. In the war against the Fomor, we had but one."

"And it would do no good to ask you to return them to us?"

"None whatever."

"And you know how to use them?"

"We know enough. We used them once before. In human wars, it is enough to cause chaos. They do the rest themselves. But . . . you do not know their uses, do you? Would you like us to teach you? Morrigu will be happy to provide such a service to the Sisters."

Eriu felt her arms and neck prick up again at the very thought of spending time in the company of Macha's sisters. "I thank you, no," she said formally, as if she were declining an invitation to share a feast.

Macha chuckled. "Well, I cannot say I blame you. We are not a pleasant threesome. But you can trust us. What we want from those who come will not harm the Danu; that will not be necessary."

"I ask you not to harm these humans until we know their character. I think that they will be again unlike either Fir Bolg or Fomor."

"Why should I do this for you?"

Eriu took a deep breath. "I know uses for the arms that you cannot imagine."

Macha regarded her silently. "This is not possible," she said. "All those who knew the arms have passed."

Eriu said nothing. She had promised herself that she would make no one but herself vulnerable. Not her sisters, not Airmid. She waited quietly. Already she knew that Macha would ask for knowledge; already she knew which function of the arms she would trade. It was almost funny to imagine the Morrigu unleashing music against the coming invaders.

Macha closed her eyes as if she were thinking. At last she opened them. "Well, I will promise you this. If you give me just one gift, we will kill none of them unless they come for us in battle."

"What gift?" She prepared herself to explain the steps which would result in music.

"I ask you to take my hand again."

Surprise welled up in Eriu. This was not what she had expected. "I took your hand once before; your darkness poured into me like rain," she said.

Macha nodded. "That is why I ask. For that one moment, I will not be lonely."

"And for this you will kill none of them?"

"None until they come for us in battle."

"And if they do not?"

"They will, Eriu. They are human. Generation after generation, they make war on each other. Morrigu has depended upon it for thousands of years."

Eriu held her hand forward. She leaned back hard against the rocks. "Take it," she whispered.

"I will remember this," said Macha. "For you and for yours I will remember."

And she closed her hand around Eriu's own small hand.

25

What did they do to her?"

"I know not. Her eyes are bruised and swollen and she cries out as though she is asleep."

"All our time in Lia Fail did not weaken her like this. Only Airmid looks closer to death!"

"Banba! Hold your tongue!"

"I am afraid, Fodla. What should we do without her?"

"I fear to wake her with the sorrowful news."

"We must."

Eriu opened her eyes to find her two sisters bent above her bed and whispering. She smiled softly. "I do love you both."

"We know that," said Fodla.

"It was awful, wasn't it?" asked Banba. "You should have let us go with you."

"She asked to hold my hand. For that she promised not to kill the In-vaders unless they come against us in battle."

"For holding your hand?"

"That cannot be all; you look like a ship that has washed against the rocks."

"I tell you now that was all. But it was enough. What she contains is terrible beyond belief. All of the darkness, all of the evil of all of the worlds."

"You pity her?"

"No. And yes. She chooses for darkness. But I pity anyone who dwells in those choices. At the same time that they fill me with loathing."

"Are you well enough to rise, Sister? We bring news."

"Airmid has passed? Her work in the dolmen took too much of a toll upon her?"

"No, she is at the shore," said Banba.

"At the shore? When the Invaders are nearly upon us!" Eriu sat up. "Is she maintained in Metaphor?"

"Something has washed up on the beach," said Banba.

"Someone," said Fodla. "A woman and a little boy."

Eriu leaped to her feet.

"The Banbh said that there would be dead in the water."

"The Banbh?" asked Banba, her tone cross.

Eriu waved her hand. "They tried to join us. The Macha sent them away. Now come, we must go to the sea."

For a moment they stood silent at the headland. Below them Airmid worked feverishly, waving her arms at the Light Spear warriors who ran for the portal.

"At first the people thought a porpoise had beached," Fodla whispered softly. "Or perhaps one of the seal folk. When they realized what they were seeing, they posted a guard."

"Against the Banbh?"

Fodla nodded; she pointed skyward. Ravens and gulls swooped and circled.

Eriu moved to the shore with a heavy heart. She stepped to the first figure on the sand.

It was a woman, pale and heavy with child, her long hair matted against her head like seaweed. Airmid had lifted her gown to expose her pale skin. Over her swollen belly she had placed a long transparent strip. Near the woman on the beach was a small boy, now pale as the moon, his sightless eyes wide.

Eriu knelt beside Airmid. "Is there any hope for them, Ancient?"

"Not for the woman or the boy," she said, shaking her head sadly. "They were too long without breathsong." Suddenly she pointed, trembling, to the long clear strip, which had begun to pulse with faint red rhythms. "But look you now! The womb-child lives. It lives! Hurry, daughters. Send for bier bearers. We have much work to do."

"Surely the Danu watches over both of us with this blessing."

Airmid nodded. "Then pray that she continues to watch. She is not out of danger, this little one; look how tiny she is, nearly as small as a Danu babe. Too early; we have been forced to bring her into the world too early."

The baby was suspended in fluid in a tube which hung from the ceiling in Airmid's Healing Chambers. Lights of various warmth and colors shifted position on the infant.

"What is this chamber?" asked Eriu softly.

Airmid sighed. "It is my father's womb cradle; this is the way the Homeworld made him; remember that the Braided Ancients were not born of women, but of science." She shook her head. "You see now why such practices were banned, and yet, with this tiny child, my father's womb cradle will sustain her and allow her to grow. She dwells in her mother's own fluids. How sometimes we receive gifts from sorrows." She smiled. "The Mother never wearies of finding ways to care for us."

"Why did the child live?"

"Because her mother was so cold; because inside her mother she was so cold. Because she did not need breathsong to live. The boy and his mother were too long without breathsong under the cold sea. Had they been there less time they too might have survived. The cold slows all of the processes of the body, it . . . suspends. It holds functions in a kind of stasis."

"Imagine the joy of a man of the Invaders who finds that his child lives, that something of his love for his woman has survived," said Fodla.

"You cannot tell him!" Airmid shook her head. "No. You must not!"

"But, Ancient," said Eriu. "We must. She is not our child."

"Her survival is not yet guaranteed, Sisters. You look into the womb cradle and you see a little child. I see a child that has been too cold for too long. Will all of her functions return? And what of her mind? I see a child who cannot yet draw breathsong. She cannot be removed from this cradle."

"For how long?" asked Eriu.

"These humans carry their infants for nine full turnings of the moon. This wee one I judge to be at six turnings."

"We must keep her a secret for three months?" asked Fodla.

"Well, what else would you do? Would you bring him here to see her, this Invader father?"

"If we do, he will return to his people a withered Ancient," said Banba. "He is not one of us."

"No, nor Hybrid," said Eriu softly. She looked at the tiny child. "Nor is she."

"No," said Airmid. "We have brought her here among us and we can raise her here among us, but she is neither Danu nor Hybrid."

"So she cannot return to them. By Danu, what have we done?"

"Now you see our dilemma," said Airmid softly. "And why our ancestors so struggled with this knowledge. And why they outlawed Braid Creation. And why my father chose for Miach as he did. And why it took so long to change our laws even to allow ReBraiding. It slips away from us like water, the answer to this question; soon it becomes a raging cascade." Airmid sighed. "Should we have let her die, Eriu, her little heart beating away inside the womb cradle of her drowned mother?"

"No!" said Eriu in horror. "To abandon a child of the Mother that way! Never."

"And yet," said Airmid, "we must now answer a great question. If she were a child who could not breathe, or a child with a missing limb, or a child whose mind was trapped inside itself, I could alter her braiding, rebind the sequence with our own braid, correct the problem. The laws that we have revised permit us to do that; to return a child to normalcy. Then, like Illyn and like we of the Danu, this little girl would be so long-lived that she could come and go in both worlds as she pleased; the added age for moving in their world would not even show upon her, as it does not show on Illyn.

"But she is a perfect human child. They age much more rapidly than ours. Their leaf of time progresses much more swiftly than ours. She will have to remain in the womb cradle for three more turnings of the moon. And then what do we do? Do we take her back among them, she appearing suddenly as a woman of bearing years, but with no speech and no experience of one that age? Would they believe she was one of them, or would they think her bewitched, a creature of their superstitions fit only for burning or drowning or exile? Or do we wait until she is of bearing years and then take her among them, a woman in her late years, past her bearing, a woman raised by Danu, speaking Danaan, possessed of Danaan knowledge, thrown suddenly among humans?"

"So we must raise her here," said Fodla quietly. "The only one of all of us who can never leave the confines of Tara."

"Or braid her," said Banba quietly. "This you could do, Ancient. A healthy human braids well with Danu. This we know from those who have been born of both. Lugh. Bres."

"But those were births of mating between a Danu and a human. The law does not permit me to alter that which the Braid has made whole. The law provides that I can repair and mend and heal. I cannot wholly alter that which is already whole."

"What should we do, Ancient?" asked Eriu softly.

Airmid walked over to the womb cradle where the infant was sucking on its thumb. "I don't know," she said softly. "I did what a healer does; I saved the life of a child of the Mother. Now I do not know what to do. My life seems to have been composed of these choices." She shook her head. "I will do the only thing I know to do. I will prepare her mother and her brother for burial with all the love and care of the Danu. I will hide the fact that the womb-child is no longer within the mother. I will bring this child healthy into the world. I will love her as if she were my own child, but I will give her no name until I know their tongue. The language of the Invaders. And then I will give her one of their names. That will be her braid. Beyond that, I cannot say. She is here among us; it is done."

For a long moment the Sisters stood in silence; then Eriu moved to Airmid and put her arm gently around the tiny woman's shoulders.

"Come," she said. "We will help you prepare their dead for the journey."

PART THREE

Á ILIU
ÍATH NÉIREANN

I CALL YOU FORTH,
O IRELAND

I SING THE LAND OF ERIU,
MUCH TRAVELED ON THE FERTILE SEA.
FERTILE THE FRUITED MOUNTAIN,
FERTILE THE ABUNDANT WOOD,
SHOWERED THE RIVER OF WATERFALLS,
WATERFALLS TO LAKE OF DEEP POOLS,
POOLING DEEP THE HILLTOP WELL.
A WELL OF TRIBES BE GATHERED,
A GATHERING OF KINGS AT TARA;
TARA BE THE HILL OF THE CLANS,
THE CLANS BE THE SONS OF MIL;
MIL OF THE SHIPS, OF THE GREAT BARKS.
THE HIGHEST BARK TO ERIU,
LOFTY ERIU, WIND-SUNG
A CHANT OF DEEP WISDOM . . .
I SING THE LAND OF ERIU.

THE INVOCATION OF AMERGIN

26

I came to shore a broken man carrying a broken child on my shoulders. Skena and Ir were waiting for us.

The were laid out on a bier of some kind of transparent crystal, their heads raised as if they gazed out to the west.

I have seen the drowned before; many have perished in the Internum Mare. Someone had ministered to them with love and care. Skena's auburn hair had been washed and braided with flowers, and her face looked in repose as it had in life, gentle and full of love. She was dressed in a white gown of some iridescent material. Ir was curled into her arm, his little body seeming to sleep with his head on her shoulder. Someone had positioned their hands so that both the hand of Skena and the hand of Ir rested gently across our unborn child. Between her feet was the cup of Ith, the gift that he had carried with him across the water. It had been filled with iridescent stones of blue and gold.

Somehow the kindness of it, the beauty, opened the wide doors of my sorrow. I dropped to my knees on the sand and wept in great, gulping sobs, much to the embarrassment of my brothers, who made signs against the bier and would come nowhere near me or it. Though I knew that my behavior was unseemly for a warrior, I am not one of them. I could no more have stopped my tears than I could have stopped the wind. I could not even let Ceolas sing our gratitude for this kindness, so shaken with sobs was my body.

Bile, on seeing his two beloved ones so carefully adorned, could not stop vocalizing, circling the bier, throwing his one arm into the air over and over and crying out "Ah, ah, ah" like a wounded, lopsided seabird. Pity for him moved me to further weeping.

At last, my mother came up behind me and rested her hands on my shoulders. "See where they watch us," she whispered, inclining her chin toward the top of the cliffs. "Consider your duty to the tribe."

There on the headland were three women, dazzling, beautiful, obviously Greek from their white gowns to their elaborate cascades of curling hair. The wind caught at their gowns and swept them out to the side so that collectively they looked like a sail. It was that image which brought me from my sorrow; I looked back at our own ships, at our people unloading goods and gear. I sighed and stood.

I gathered Bile into my arms and half carried, half dragged him away from the bier. He leaned into me as he had when he was first injured, but his body, now at twelve years, was much larger and harder to carry.

It struck me that all the work that Skena had done, all the wonders that Ir had wrought, were lost to Bile now; he was as inarticulate and uncoordinated as he had been when he was first injured. In the short three days since Skena and Ir had disappeared into the sea, Bile had retreated into the body of that child who had been broken on the wagon wheel. I did not know if we would ever bring him back.

An Scail had been standing a little way behind me, silent and still, her white-clad body in an attitude of waiting. I came to stand beside her, deposited Bile on the sand. He curled into himself, shaking and vocalizing.

"Bile is most troubled," I said softly.

"Skena and Ir are here?" she asked quietly.

"They are, Wise One. I apologize for my grief; when I saw them I could not contain my sorrow."

"Never apologize for love or sorrow," she said softly. "Your weeping will help to cleanse your heart and make it ready for what must be done here. Describe to me what you see."

For a moment I felt startled—it was the first time that An Scail had ever asked me to describe our surroundings. And then the strangeness of all of it washed over me. She needed my descriptions because, for the first time in her life, she had departed from Galicia. No longer did the tower and the oaks, or even the roots of trees, dwell in her memory. I came out of myself then, forced myself up from my own sorrow.

"You would not have come if Ith had not died," I said to her softly.

"No. But I must now take on the burden that he would have carried. I must be eyes and ears and wise choices for you and for our people. That is what Ith would have wished of me; I give it gladly."

The greatness of her sacrifice strengthened me for my own; I bent myself to the task of describing for her what I saw. "Three women watch us from the headland."

"How do they appear?"

"As Greeks in both clothing and mien."

"Describe Skena and Ir to me."

"Skena and Ir have been cared for; they are washed and dressed and flowered, laid on a crystal bier."

"So they do not burn their dead."

I was startled at the conclusion, saw its correctness immediately. "On such a bier they could not. Their faces are raised as if they face the west."

"And in their care of our dead, they show themselves to be a civilized people. People who know that the soul continues."

"Yes, I can see that conclusion."

She nodded, gestured for me to continue.

"We have anchored in a great, round bay at the mouth of a wide river that winds in toward the land. Here, the hills slope upward toward the headland. The sea is richly blue, the land green and forested."

An Scail nodded. "That is all well. Describe for me the women on the headland."

I did so, observing their blowing white gowns, the long, ringleted hair.

"Red hair, black hair, and golden hair, you say?"

"Yes, all long and perfectly coiffed."

"Hmm. We will speak to these three, I think. Let me walk on your arm."

Bile, who had been sitting on the ground beside us vocalizing, suddenly stood and raced around to An Scail's other side, threading her hand through his one good arm.

"Bile," I said gently, but she raised her hand at me.

"I thank you, young man," she said in a dignified voice. "In this new country I am blind. You must be my eyes and ears."

He seemed to draw himself up, ceased vocalizing. Once again the wisdom of An Scail penetrated my grief.

I offered her my other arm, and together we made our way up toward the headland, surely the three most broken members of the Galaeci to make a first impression on those who dwelled here.

When we were halfway up, Airioch dashed up behind us, his heels kicking up sand.

"Wait until you see them," he said, excitement threading through his voice. "So beautiful. And the gold and jewels."

"You shall not accompany us," said An Scail. Her voice brooked no disagreement.

"But I have met them before. They are the Sisters, Banba, Fodla, Eriu."

"Yes, and you must tell us later of all that you learned of them, but for now we must form a new and first impression of our own. Return to the work of the ships."

I did not tell her that he had been doing none of that work; in truth I myself had been doing none myself, though not for lingering.

Airioch returned to the beach and began to give orders to Greeks and Galaeci alike.

When we reached the Sisters, I could see that in person they were more beautiful still, tiny women who just crested five feet, perfectly shaped in their billowing white gowns, their exquisite hair. Only their eyes seemed a little off, not quite the size or shape or color that I remembered the dancing eyes of the Greeks. They wore no jewels, no gold or silver, but for odd triangular shapes at their throat, crystalline, each incised with three spiraling and intertwined vines.

They were standing in a sort of triangular shape, the sister with the curling red hair at their head. I mimicked their formation, placing An Scail before me and stepping slightly back and to her left. Bile, in perfect silence, his eyes wide, did the same on the right.

I said nothing at all, assuming that there could be no way that any of their people could know the language of the Galaeci, so I was startled when the threesome inclined their heads toward An Scail and spoke in perfect Gaeilge.

"Elder woman, we welcome your wisdom among us. We are surprised at the return of the sons of Mil. Where is Ith among you?"

"Ith's spirit has departed from among us. I am An Scail, the Shadow. He sends me as his voice, his eyes and ears."

I was surprised again to see an expression of real sorrow shift over the faces of the Sisters.

"We sorrow to hear that he is not with you. We valued his wisdom. It was the decision of Ith that the sons of Mil would not return to this place. May we ask what it was that made him change that decision?"

I spoke for the first time. "Ith returned to us wounded and unable to speak. He was not able to tell us of a decision."

The lead sister turned her face up toward me; her eyes seemed to take me in and swallow me. "How was he wounded, Amergin?"

"How do you know my name?"

"You were beloved of Ith. He spoke of you often and in detail, as he did also of An Scail and Bile and of Mil, your father. We thought that the chief of the sons of Mil would attend this first meeting."

"Our father has also died," I said.

The little woman looked down at the bier on the stony beach below, looked back at me. "And these?"

"My wife, our unborn child, and my brother." I could feel my eyes filling again with tears. I blinked them back.

She sighed, a sound so reflective of our own sorrow that I nodded my head and raised a shoulder at the obvious overabundance of our sorrows. There was nothing more to say on the subject and I could not speak.

"What names do you bear?" I asked when I could speak, hoping to move away the awkwardness of the moment.

The lead sister looked flustered. "Forgive my rudeness," she said quietly. "We have forgotten the courtesies. It has been long since strangers came among us. I am Eriu. These are my sisters Banba and Fodla." She gestured first to one side and then the other. The sisters inclined their heads in acknowledgment, but still they said nothing. I began to wonder if, like Bile, they were mute.

"Is it you who have cared for . . . our dead?" I asked quietly.

"We have," she said softly.

"Then I thank you for your kindness." My voice broke on this last and I lowered my eyes from her gaze.

"Tell me their names that we may honor their journey with our chant."

"She was my wife, Skena. The boy is our brother, Ir."

Bile raised his eyes skyward but he made no sound.

"And you are his beloved brother?" Eriu said. She had turned her whole attention to Bile, her eyes fastened upon him. He nodded once. "And you loved Skena as though she were your mother?" He looked startled, vocalized once, a long "Ahhh." Eriu smiled gently. "I understand. I saw you weep them, child; your very bearing spoke of love."

She turned back to me. "She was bearing with you a child of the Braid?" she asked this softly.

"The Braid?" I shook my head. "I do not know the term; Skena was bearing our first child."

A look of such sadness passed over her face that for a moment I thought she might also weep.

"What does this mean? The Braid?"

"The cup," she said. She gestured with her slender hand. "The gift of Ith. It is chased and incised with braidwork. We assumed that it was important, thought perhaps that it might refer to your god."

"It is the pattern of life," said An Scail quietly. "Life is braided into life, ever and eternal."

"And there is no death," said the woman quietly.

"Ith has told you this?"

"It is what we believe, as well."

Eriu seemed to think for a moment, then raised her hands skyward. Without a word, her sisters stepped forward and caught at the upraised hands. A deep chanting sound began to issue from them that reminded me of the sound of our gaita.

"From this moment," said Eriu, "this place shall be known in your tongue and in ours as Inver Skena, the river of Skena."

Bile could not help himself after this pronouncement. He threw back his head and cried out, "Ah, ah, ah."

"It is our honor to do this," said Eriu, inclining her head toward Bile as though he had said something she understood perfectly.

He nodded and then suddenly stepped forward and extended his good hand toward her. She put hers into his instantly with no hesitation. He lifted it gently to his lips. It was an old Galaeci custom, courtly, an expression of appreciation, but I feared that she might not understand it that way. I stepped toward him; she turned her face toward me and shook her head once. Her eyes shimmered with water.

And that was the moment when I knew that at least she had not wounded Ith.

I interrupted them. "Speak to us of how Ith was wounded."

She looked perplexed. "This is what we asked of you, Amergin."

"We have been told that it occurred on the night before his return voyage, which he spent with you in his dwelling."

For the first time, the dark-haired sister spoke. "And was that piece of intelligence given to you by Airioch Feabhruadh?" Her voice was caustic, intelligent. I looked at her in surprise.

"It was," I said.

"He is your brother, is he not?"

"He is."

She said nothing more.

Now the golden-haired sister spoke.

"Know that Ith was safe among the Danu. He was an elder of great wisdom, and so we treated him."

"The Danu? That is the name of this place?"

"No . . . No . . . This place has no name." The tone of her voice was surprised, as if it were something she had not considered before. "We call it as we found it—the Green Isle."

I looked around and nodded; it was green in shades and gradations, richly emerald.

"We are the Danu," said Eriu. "That is what our . . . tribe . . . is called. The Children of the Danu."

"And you have come here from Greece?"

"A very long time ago, yes."

"I have traveled much in Greece."

She nodded and smiled. "Then we must speak of it further. We have not returned for many years. It has undoubtedly changed behind us."

"I knew of no Danu in Greece," I said softly. I changed my language to Greek, asked softly, "Where did you dwell in your time there?"

For a moment Eriu was quiet. She lowered her head, touched the triangular shape at her throat. I was reminded suddenly of the shape that had appeared in Uncle Ith's ogham curve.

In perfect Greek, Eriu answered me. "We lived on the isle of . . . Thrace."

"My mother gave birth to my brother—he that you have cared for—on Irena." I felt suddenly ashamed for the trick, remembering their gentle care of Ir and Skena.

Still in perfect Greek she continued. "And for that she named him Ir? Ah, our neighbor then. So you too have seen the exquisite blue of the waters?"

I could not fault her answers, yet all the while that we were conversing, the Sisters seemed to tighten their formation, to move closer to each other in their odd triangular shape.

Suddenly, An Scail spoke. "But surely these are all things of which we will speak further, Sisters, as time does not hurry us to know all things at once. Will you join us for the Feast and Spirit Fire tonight?"

"Spirit Fire?"

"We release the spirits of our dead in fire."

"Release them to where?"

"To the Western Isle of Feasting."

Suddenly Eriu smiled full on and her face lighted with the look. "We have much in common, An Scail," she said. "We would be honored to join you."

27

That did not go well at all," said Banba. She tapped her triangle, releasing Metaphor, and folded back into her tiny, wide-eyed self.

"Banba!" said Fodla. "The Ancients have asked us to remain in Metaphor at all times."

"I don't care; it wearies me. We are safe here in Tara."

"Remember the Fomor," said Fodla. "They penetrated the cities. These Galaeci strike me as very intelligent indeed; they do not miss much in conversation. What would happen if they saw us as we are?"

"Fodla speaks wisely," said Eriu. "They did seem especially skilled at nuances of conversation, winding back to the things they wished to know when we least expected it, picking up on every slip in our story. Always with great courtesy." She shook her head. "Of course there were no Danu among the Greeks. No city-state with such a name. What a fool I am. Amergin lulled me into a feeling that I was safe; how was this done?"

"Do not berate yourself overmuch, Sister. It is the same story we told to Fir Bolg and Fomor alike, and they never questioned our journey," said Fodla.

"But they had never been in Greece," said Banba. "These sons of Mil have journeyed there and farther. And Ith. Wanting to know how he was wounded and when and by whom. As if we, with our little hands, would knock an elder to the ground. And Ith one of their priests!"

"Evidently Airioch has hinted so," said Fodla.

"Oh, do you think so?"

"Banba!" said Eriu. "You take out your worry on our sister with your stinging tongue."

"I do," said Banba. "I am sorry. But Eriu is right; even the eyes of Amergin are intelligent . . . questing. We must be careful."

"We are all worried," said Fodla with a shrug.

Banba nodded. "He is beautiful though, is he not, their Amergin?"

Fodla shook her head. "Do you never stop?"

"Well, so tall. Taller than a Greek. And all that dark hair and those eyes. So large a man."

"He is a man in grief for his beloved and his child," said Eriu. "A child he believes that he has lost."

"That, in effect, he has lost," said Banba.

Eriu nodded. "These are the things that we must remember when we speak to him. His sorrow may make him overquick and oversensitive for quite some while. He may be too quick to draw conclusions; he will think with his anger and his loss. He may wish to place the blame for their loss on this journey, and hence on the Green Island or on us, who dwell here. Or his own grief may cause him to miss things among his own people, to make decisions based in haste and sorrow. Such a man is dangerous."

"Less dangerous, I think, than Airioch, who thinks with his greed and his lust, or Eber Donn, who thinks with his anger," said Fodla.

"Not so," said Eriu. "You are right, Banba. Amergin is intelligent. Dangerously, deeply intelligent. Know it, Sisters; I see it clearly in his eyes. He is a seeker of truth; he does not rest until he knows the truth. The Children of the Danu are in much danger there." She sighed. "Well, I am glad for our care of his lost ones. Such kindness will mean much to such a man. And he is, I think, a voice of wisdom for his tribe. I do so wish that we could tell him . . ."

"We cannot," said Banba. "And we must not speak of her except among ourselves. Ever."

"Come," said Fodla. "Think not on it. When the time comes for the child to be born we may all be surprised. The Mother works in the world in ways that none of us understands."

"True enough," said Eriu. She sighed. "We will prepare for their feast."

*   *   *

Sparks rose skyward at the edge of the water, in preparation for the funeral pyre. In the quiet bay, the Greek ships rode at anchor, their sails furled. The cargo ships, hired for the trip only and returning empty of plunder, had made for the sea at first light.

Already, the Galaeci had begun to make themselves a permanent place at the edge of the river. Dwellings had hastily been erected near elaborate tents of silk. Horses were penned at one edge of the beach, cattle at the other. Though there were not many, they looked like good breeding stock. With each group were giant dogs with curly hair. They seemed to patrol the stock both within and without; they were themselves the size of ponies.

At the very edge of the tide, the Galaeci had built a great bonfire. They had placed Skena and the child together on a wooden bier at the edge of the water. Beside the bier were two urns.

From the headland above, Banba whispered to her sisters. "These must be the vessels for their dead."

"There are so many of these Galaeci," said Fodla softly. "They number more than two hundred surely."

"And they have not even begun to reproduce," said Banba dryly. "From the look of them they can do that very well indeed."

"Banba!" said Eriu sharply. "And they do not know how few our numbers are." She sighed. "Let us go among them and try to behave as Greeks."

"How do Greeks behave at Galaeci funerals?" asked Banba.

"How should we know that?" asked Fodla, her tone exactly like that of her more caustic sister.

The funeral feast that followed the fire was held at hastily assembled trestle tables under the open sky. The Sisters were given a place of honor between Bile and An Scail although most of the Galaeci avoided them completely, not even meeting their eyes.

To the Sisters it seemed a raucous celebration for a funeral feast. The Galaeci danced wildly under the stars while they beat on drums and whistled on bone flutes. From time to time, their pipers would play haunting and eerie tunes on the pipes. At those times the Sisters saw several couples slip away into the darkness.

"I told you that they would mate well and often," hissed Banba to Eriu, who sat at the center.

"Hush," Eriu said softly.

Only Amergin and Bile sat silent at the table, eating nothing and speaking not at all.

In a lull in the merriment, An Scail leaned toward the Sisters. "You wonder why we celebrate with such gusto at such a time."

"It seems a most joyful occasion," said Eriu cautiously.

"We keep vigil with the dead. We wake with them and celebrate the journey they begin. Our couples mate that we celebrate the force of creation and life, which will eventually return them to us. There will be time for grief on the morrow."

"We too celebrate the passage of our Ancients, Wise One. We are only sorry that these two have left you so young."

"Three," said An Scail. "For among us, a child is a returning spirit."

Eriu drew in her breath, closed her eyes briefly.

An Scail continued. "Among you, few die young?"

"Few until this time," said Eriu. "We have lived without war for a very long time."

An Scail nodded. "We too. Galicia was far removed from Rome and Greece, from Carthage and Persia. We mined our metals and herded our cattle. We made our wines. We traded, but we had precious little contact with the outside world."

"And you were happy?"

"We were."

"So why did you come here? What impelled this journey?"

"Mil, the father of Amergin, was ever a wanderer. A restless warrior and a dreamer. Inisfail was his dream."

"Inisfail?"

"That was his name for this place. Isle of Destiny."

"And how did he hear of this place?"

An Scail closed the rheumy silver eyes. "I know not," she said softly. "Sailors speak of it; they say it is a place of magic. They have seen lights emanating from the place, even far out to sea. Perhaps Mil heard of it from them. Ith told me that Mil had dreamed of the place from childhood, saying that here the clan of Mil would meet its destiny."

"And you wish that he had not."

An Scail smiled, a small, sad smile. "In the pursuit of this place we have lost Ith and Mil, Skena and Ir, and Amergin's unborn child. Scota, the mother of Amergin, has lost her beloved husband and her child. She continues on fury. Eber Donn, eldest of Mil, vows revenge. I suspect that we are not yet done with losses."

"Why do you tell us this?" asked Eriu, astonished.

"We have come among you with our purposes and our sorrow. I hear in your voices that you are . . . older . . . than we, and perhaps wiser. I tell you so that perhaps wisdom will prevail."

"And Amergin?"

"He is our Bard; his word carries much weight with our people."

"And yet he does not seem to be of your people."

"A bard stands apart. He trains with druii. He captures the history of the tribe. He sings our history. He directs its behavior when it is most required."

"Druii?"

"What I am. Perhaps what you are to your people."

"His wife was also druii?"

"Skena was that rarest of healers, a weaver."

"A weaver?" Eriu felt excitement coursing through her. "Speak to me of this."

"A weaver binds people together. Skena wove Amergin and Bile into the tribe. She wove the tribe together with her presence and her calm. She wove the sick into the care of the healthy. She saw us as one people, and so she behaved. Among us, as among all people, are those who weave and those who sunder. We will miss her great skills here in this new place."

"We have among us a healer of great wisdom. I should like for you to meet her."

Eriu turned toward Amergin, spoke softly. "When you were at sea, we thought that we heard the sounds of music. It was . . . most sorrowful. Was it you?"

"It was Ceolas."

"Ceolas? Who is he?"

Suddenly Bile stood and loped away from the table.

"Have I said something to trouble him?" Eriu half stood, as if she would follow the child.

Amergin halted her, his hand on her wrist. Eriu stared down. The great hand covered and encircled her slender bones, seemed to cover half her forearm. Would he feel the true bones beneath the skin of Metaphor?

Fear beat suddenly in her throat. Then just as suddenly he released his hold. "See where he returns bearing Ceolas."

Bile came loping across the beach, a small harp in his arms. It was shaped almost like a triangle, small enough to sit on the lap of the singer.

"Ceolas is a harp."

"She is a clarsach, a bardic harp for traveling. She is my singer."

"Will you sing for us?"

Amergin shook his head, but Bile thrust the harp at him repeatedly. "Ah, ah, ah!" he cried, pointing toward the wooden biers at the edge of the water.

Eriu spoke softly. "Bile says that they would wish to hear your song for their journey."

Amergin turned toward her. He looked directly into her eyes. The expression that moved across his face moved from anger through surprise and then to something else. He leaned in, as if he would regard her more closely. Eriu turned toward Bile, held out her hand. He took it immediately.

"What song would they hear?" she asked him, as if he could answer perfectly.

For answer Bile began to hum.

Amergin nodded. He ran his fingers gently along the strings and began to sing.

"Green is my longing, Inisfail,
Isle of Destiny, northern diadem.
Why do you call to me?
How shall I sing them,
sloe-eyed creatures at your shore?
Do you await me, Inisfail?
Country of my dreams;
I am Amergin, son of Mil,
warrior, wanderer.
Dream of the father now become
the harpsong of the son.
Inisfail, land of mystery,
Sing to me."

"It is beautiful."

"It is the song which began our journey. Long long ago."

"And now you wish that it had not."

"I do."

"I cannot blame you, Amergin. You have sustained too many losses. The heart is hard-pressed to bear them."

He nodded, silently, his mouth working.

"What sloe-eyed creatures do you speak of? The deer of the Green Isle? They are large indeed."

He faced her directly, looked full at her eyes. "I speak of you. Of your people. Of your eyes. I think that I saw them once on the journey."

Eriu could think of nothing to say, found that she could not look away. Her heart thundered in fear. What did he see? Did Metaphor waver? O Mother, do not let him see us beneath this guise!

From across the beach Airioch danced with a woman of the tribe, moving through the elaborate squares, his handsome face lit with laughter. He leaned down over the woman, his golden hair falling across his face. He said something into her ear. She laughed and pushed him away. He turned away from her, began to weave his way toward their table, calling aloud, "Banba! Fodla! Eriu!"

"Trouble approaches," Banba said aloud.

The whole table burst into laughter, Amergin with them. He broke his gaze with Eriu.

Airioch stumbled toward them. When at last he reached the table, he bowed low before the Sisters. "I fear that we have not made you a part of our feasting," he said. "Allow me to correct that. Come and dance with me." He stared directly at Banba. Eriu turned toward her sister, her eyes dancing mischief. Banba raised a hand.

"I dare not," she said. "I do not know the dances of the Galaeci. I will damage your feet for trying."

He laughed aloud. "One so small and light as you? Come then, we will dance a Greek dance." He grabbed a square of linen, held it up from the table, shook it in the air.

An almost palpable stillness fell over the table. Banba gently fingered the triangular necklace that she wore around her throat. The Sisters turned and looked at each other as if they would ask or answer a question.

"He means no offense," said Amergin. "It is our custom to sing and dance for the dead."

"Well said, Brother," said Airioch. "Well?"

Banba stood suddenly and smiled. "Prepare yourself," she said. "I can dance forever, son of Mil."

28

W ho invited them?" Scota moved angrily across the tent, pacing before her assembled sons.

"This An Scail has done," I said quietly. "Will you question her druid
wisdom, Maither?"

Scota was fairly spitting. "These who have wounded Ith? These who
have killed your father? Why would she invite these among us?"

"Father died in Galicia, Maither; these three had naught to do with
him. And as for Ith, I do not think that they are responsible for his death."

"How can you say that?" shouted Eber Donn. "Airioch has told us that
he was wounded in their company."

I felt so weary that it was an effort even to speak in the company. I
wanted to lie down and sleep. Perhaps forever. I sighed. "Airioch is at the
mating," I said softly.

"With the Danu woman?" Scota sounded horrified.

"Of course not," I said. "He mates with one of our own and he is not
here to defend his position. Only I tell you that I do not think these Sisters
wounded Ith. They seem to me small and gentle."

"Do not equate gentle with small," said Scota, a warning in her voice.

"In your case, Mother, none would dare equate the two." I spoke
wearily but I smiled nonetheless; it was hard not to smile at the power in
her little frame.

"Good then," she said, rapping me on the forehead with a flick of her
finger. "Now consider this, my sons. Are there more of them than these
three? Surely there must be, but where are they? Have we seen any but

the Sisters? Why do they hide their numbers from us? We must find their dwelling places. This is what your father taught us; know the enemy's position."

"Why must you think of them as the enemy?"

"Why do you not think of them so?"

"I would rather wait to know them. They have been most kind to Skena and Ir in preparing them for the crossing."

"They have killed Uncle Ith!"

"And Mil," said Eber Donn.

I sighed again. It was like reasoning in a circle; they came back to their original argument like dogs to bones. "Do you look for reasons to war?" I asked aloud.

"You reason with your grief," said Eber Donn. "You do not think like a warrior."

"Well, if it means thinking like you, then I am glad that I do not."

Before Eber Donn could turn his wrath upon me, our brother Eremon stood among the company. "We should begin investigating the land," he said. "There may be good cattle pasturage, good running land for the horses. We should decide how to divide up the land."

Eber Finn nodded. "Eremon speaks wisely," he said. "What do we care for these Danu? At dawn we should leave this beach to begin our mapping."

"It is not ours to map!" I snapped. "Has it escaped you that there are others living here?"

"Three Greek women," said Eber Donn, shrugging. "Between Airioch and me we can mate with those or marry them."

A burst of laughter spread throughout the tent.

"They are the representatives of their people," I said softly, trying hard to be reasonable. "Surely there are others. We are on the beachhead here; we have not yet seen the interior. There may be vast cities of the Danu."

"Danu?"

"This is what they call themselves."

"But you have just made my argument for me. And Scota's as well," said Eber Donn. "We must know what we face; we must be ready to work from a position of strength."

Scota nodded. "You speak well, eldest of Mil. You speak as your father would speak. We will go among them and investigate."

"This should be done in darkness," said Eber Donn. "And quickly, while they are still surprised by our arrival."

"They did not seem surprised," I said.

"What do you mean?" asked Scota.

"They seemed to be expecting us. Although they said that Uncle Ith had told them that he had decided to recommend to father that we not re-turn." I sighed at the complexity of that chain of logic; my brothers would reject it, I knew.

"So you see?" said Eber Donn. "The very fact that they expected us puts what they say about Ith to the lie. They would not have been awaiting our arrival if Ith had not told them we would come. So much more does that put to the lie their claim that they did not wound him."

His argument was actually logical, and I nodded as I thought it over. "Only that they seemed to hold him in such respect."

"Seemed," said my mother. "I care not for seemed. I will avenge the deaths of Mil and Ith."

"Here, here, Scota," shouted Eber Donn. "Most worthy wife for Mil."

My mother basked for a moment in his admiration, then made a deci-sion. "I claim the right of a chieftain's wife," she said. "We will go among them this night with a party of exploration. We will scout and we will map. We will search out their weaknesses."

She chose for the party Eber Donn, Eremon, Eber Finn, and, for bal-ance, two warriors of the Galaeci who were not of our clan. They all scrambled for their shortswords and daggers, their cloaks and sandals. I removed to my tent and began to assemble my equipment. Bile was sleep-ing soundly on his little cot; I envied him the deep oblivion of sleep, but my preparations awoke him. He did not vocalize, but watched me with his huge dark eyes, now so full of sorrow.

"They go to explore the Danu territory," I whispered. "I must go with them."

Bile shook his head violently. He jumped from his cot and scrambled among his chalks and papers. From the pile he drew up a portrait. It was of the Three Sisters of the Danu, standing in perfect triangle. They were surrounded by a nimbus of warm light.

I nodded. "I see what you see, little brother. I will do my best to keep them from mischief. They think with their grief and their anger."

He came to me suddenly and wrapped his arm around my waist. This he had not done in more than a year, Skena being the recipient of all his hugs, his incipient manhood keeping him from such displays with his brother, but I could feel in this hug all his grief and loss, all his love for me.

"I will return to you," I whispered. "Then we will have time to mourn for Skena and Ir. All will be well."

His eyes met mine and I could see that it was too late for such a statement, that Bile would never fully believe such a thing again. Nor, I knew, would I.

CEOLAS CAUTIONS WISDOM
Do not think with your anger
Do not act on your grief
Do not reason with sorrow
Sorrow does not reason well.
Oh, think and be still, Mother,
Reason, Brothers, do not act in haste
Haste is the father of regret,
Haste will increase our sorrow.

"I did not choose you for this party, Amergin," said my mother.

I silenced Ceolas, set her beside me. "I am a poet," I said softly. "You know that we choose for ourselves. You know, too, that the clan should heed the wisdom of the poets, for we are the voice of the past, the whisper of caution, the hint of what will be."

My mother simply waved her hand at this, dismissive. "And what is your purpose here?"

"It is the same purpose as always with poets, Maither. Wisdom."

She tossed her head and set off toward the headland. I reflected that wisdom was in very small supply in this company, nor would any chant of mine increase its supply.

We moved through the dark forest at the crest of the hill. Here, the trees were towering and ancient, their trunks thicker than the arms of several druids linked. I reflected on how much Uncle Ith would have loved them, anticipated showing them to An Scail, letting her place her hands against their contained wisdom. We had gone less than an hour's time from the sea when we came upon a doorway of stone, two huge white pillars, carved entirely in braidwork and standing thirty feet tall. Stretched across them was a lintel of almost transparent crystal. All around this doorway the forest stretched in profusion; it was a doorway to nowhere.

Eber Donn signaled.

The company stopped. He circled around the structure, examining the pillars, peering up at the capstone. He did not walk through it as one might a door, nor lay his hands upon the intricate carvings. He circled back to us. For a time we stood silent in the forest. Eber Donn shrugged. "I know not," he whispered softly. "Perhaps it is the doorway of a fallen temple. I think we should continue on."

Suddenly, with no warning, our little mother simply stepped between the pillars.

Brave and foolish Scota.

"Mother," I hissed. "Come out from there."

She stood staring at us, then stepped through the other side. She looked at us through the portal and shrugged. She stepped back between the pillars again. Still nothing happened. She looked to either side. Something caught her eye; I saw her peer toward it, concentrating on something in the pattern of carvings on the pillar.

"Touch nothing, Maither," I whispered, but it was already too late.

She had pressed her hand to some shape in the pattern.

There was a sudden flash of light, white and pure. For a moment it seemed to me that I could see through my mother, could see her bones and her beating heart, could see her held in the white light like the rabbit who dwells in the moon.

Behind me I could feel the scouting party moving back away from Scota, and I knew that they too had seen the same thing.

And then just as suddenly the light went out.

My mother fell forward, crumpled to the forest floor.

I knelt over her, pulled her from between the pillars. I cradled her against me, my brave and foolish warrior mother.

"You were right, Amergin," she whispered. "Their city is vast. It is . . . I have seen it. Do not let them stay here; take them home." Her breathing stilled; she closed her eyes.

I closed mine with her. I knew it was too late for that. We might have learned the truth of Uncle Ith, given time. But now Scota was dead, mother of the clan. The sons of Mil had just declared war on the Danu, and there would be no going home.

29

You gave me your word!" Eriu spat the accusation at Macha.

"Nor did I break it. I understand honor even if it is not our practice."

"They have laid out another of their dead, the little woman warrior."

"Really?" asked Macha. "Her death was not of our doing. But then why should this trouble you? If they lose enough of their company, surely they will return to their homeland with tales of the terrors of the place. That in turn will keep others from our shores. Is this not what you wish?"

Eriu was leaning back against the stone, its face warmed in the May sunshine.

Macha stretched out an arm, leaned it against the stone above Eriu's head.

For her aspect of Metaphor she had chosen a man, tall with thick golden hair and green eyes, his body rangy and muscular.

"Do you like him?"

"Who?"

"Him that I have adopted?"

"Did you wish to look like a Fomor?"

Macha laughed aloud. "You know as well as I that I imitate these new-comers with their height and their warrior bodies. I like them well; I would be just as happy if they did remain. My sisters enjoy the simple Fir Bolg, but these seem much more sophisticated folk. I like my . . . chal-lenges . . . sophisticated. I have begun to imagine all of the ways that I could . . . interact . . . with these Invaders. I could trouble them for years, for centuries."

Eriu shook her head. "You weary me."

Macha shrugged. "That's as may be, but I tell you this so that you will understand. I did not kill their woman. I would prefer for them to stay. Why do you not ask them how she died?"

Suddenly and without warning, Amergin appeared over the crest of the hill. He looked weary, old, his steps heavy, his head lowered. He did not raise his head until he was nearly upon them.

Eriu watched as he took in the huge man leaning over her, his arm on the rock, her back against the stones, her face tipped up toward Macha's Metaphor. Amergin's face changed like the sea: sorrow to anger, confusion to certainty. His pace changed, lengthened into long, deliberate strides.

Eriu had the sudden wild urge to duck from beneath the arm, to run, to press her triangle to the stone and vanish into the city below, to scream for her sisters. He must have read the emotions in her face; she saw him nod, as if he had reached a decision. He moved toward them.

Eriu lifted her chin, stepped forward. "We see that another of your company has died. We extend our sorrow."

"You see it? You did not cause it?" Amergin leaned toward her as he spoke.

Macha drew an arm around Eriu's shoulders, protectively. Eriu shot her a look of contempt. Amergin looked between them, confused.

"Your . . . mate . . . need not fear me, Eriu. I will not harm you. I seek to know what caused the harm to Scota."

Macha laughed aloud, a rich, masculine sound, ripe with promise. "You could not harm her as long as I am here. So this is the one you have spoken of, Eriu, sweet. Amergin, is it not?"

"It is." Eriu straightened, ducked out from beneath the arm.

"And you are?" Amergin addressed Macha directly, a challenge in his voice. Macha strode forward, clasped his arm at the elbow.

"Macha," she said. "I welcome you among us. You and all your clan." She bared her teeth in a blinding smile. "The Sisters speak well of you; Eriu knows how much I value her opinion."

Eriu wanted to slap the grinning face, to warn Macha not to toy with Amergin, to warn Amergin not to trust Macha, but she could say nothing.

"Have you come looking for us?" Eriu asked.

"I have," said Amergin. "It is my clan I come to speak of."

"Ah, certainly," said Macha. "Eriu has told me; one of your company has died. A pity. How did it occur?"

"It is Scota," he said. "My mother." He closed his eyes, inhaled a deep, shaking breath.

"Oh no!" Eriu pressed her hands over her mouth. "Your mother. Oh, Amergin, the weight of your sorrow."

He nodded, but before he could speak again, Macha broke in.

"How did it occur, for we do not know." She gave a strange sidelong smile to Eriu.

"We were hiking in the forest last night when we came upon a door."

"Why?" said Macha. Eriu saw with a start that even in Metaphor Macha was not as tall as Amergin.

"Why . . ." Amergin seemed confused by the question, but he did not retreat before Macha. He seemed untroubled by her approach, though he shook his head.

"Why were you hiking in the forest? The forests of the Green Island are most dangerous, especially in darkness." Macha turned toward Eriu. "Did you not tell him, sweeting?"

Eriu ignored the gambit, looked directly into Amergin's eyes. "She was struck by a bolt of white lightning?"

"More than struck," said Amergin. "She was immersed in it, bathed. She held her hand to the stone and seemed to be caught in the light. It killed her."

Eriu closed her eyes. She nodded. "These are ancient doorways, Amergin. They are . . . harnessed with lightning for the protection of my people. Had you asked me before you wandered, I would have warned you from them. No one has tried to enter them for . . . many years."

Amergin let out a long breath, shook his head as if he searched for something to say. A long silence prevailed.

"Doorways to where?" he asked at last.

It was not what Eriu had expected. She thought for a moment, then answered honestly. "Into our city."

"I saw no city, though Scota said that she had seen it."

"It is there; you will not see it. Nor can any of your people pass through the doorway into the city."

Amergin thought about this in silence.

"So much for Greece," he said at last, softly. He met Eriu's eyes.

"We came here from Thrace as we told you," she said. She could hear the defensiveness, the panic in her own voice.

Macha spoke. "Any who try to pass through the doorway will be wounded or die. We are quite skilled at weapons, Amergin. Would you like to see more?" She grinned, easy in her superiority and enjoying her masculine Metaphor.

"Do you threaten the sons of Mil?" Anger moved across Amergin as suddenly as a thundercloud and he stepped toward Macha. She actually stepped back, so sudden was his movement. It struck Eriu that it would be most unwise to underestimate these Galaeci. Both their intelligence and their anger seemed swift.

"She does not threaten," said Eriu, holding up her hands.

"She?"

"Macha. He. You frighten me! Both of you." She leaned against the rock and pressed her hands over her face, her knees weak with terror, with the certainty of trouble. Suddenly she heard familiar voices from the other side of the hill.

"She said that she would be here."

"Eriu, where are you, dear? We bring the morning repast."

Fodla and Banba came up over the hill. Each maintained her original Metaphor, but they were dressed as Greek peasants might be and swinging between them a woven basket full of bread and skins of wine.

Eriu nearly collapsed with relief. She ran to them, embracing them both. "I am glad to see you," she said loudly. "The men are threatening war."

"The men?" said Banba.

"Amergin and Macha. They posture with each other like stags."

She saw Banba's eyes widen, saw Fodla turn a white face in the direction of Macha. Suddenly, Banba ran toward Macha, raising up high on tiptoe to kiss his cheek.

"Macha," she said. "How wonderful you look; we haven't seen you looking this good for so long."

Macha burst into laughter, rich and masculine. "You Sisters never cease to surprise me," she said.

"Well good, for we bring the morning feast. Will you join us, Amergin?"

"I cannot." He shook his head. "My mother stepped into one of your doorways. She was . . . wounded unto death."

Banba ran to him and took both of his hands in hers. "No. Oh, the doorways. Your mother. Oh, Amergin, we should have warned you about the lightning. Sister, we must speak to the Ancients. Surely we must change the doorways. We would not wish for any more of the sons of Mil to be injured."

"I shall do that," said Eriu. She was working hard to keep a straight face, her true sorrow for Amergin's loss at war with her sister's overdone performance. Still, the arrival of Banba and Fodla had broken the tension of the moment.

"Can you change the doors?" asked Amergin.

"We can," said Eriu, "though we have not done it for many . . . years. There was no need until you came. Certainly we will try."

"Will you come before our Council? Will you say so?"

"Does their anger move them toward war?" Eriu asked. She met his eyes directly, saw the answering response. He nodded.

"Will they be in any danger if they come among you?" asked Macha. "I would not want the Sisters put at risk."

"Come with them then," said Amergin. "And bring as many warriors as you like. Come armed if you like."

Eriu understood. Amergin too was worried, thought that perhaps a show of strength might calm—or frighten—the warlike Galaeci. Before she could speak, Macha responded.

"So we shall," said Macha. "We will be among you at the noon hour."

Amergin turned and walked down the hill, his shoulders bowed.

Eriu turned angrily on Macha. "You make a mockery of his sorrow!"

"I care not for his sorrow. I am playing a game. I am sorry that you did not enjoy it. Banba did."

Banba shook her head. "One does not enjoy you, Dark One. One plays with you, like a fidchell board, moving the pieces, vying for position."

Macha inclined her head. "You play well. Next time you should kiss me here." She tapped her lips and grinned.

"There will be no next time."

"But there will. For we will accompany you at noon. My sisters and I. Warriors to protect the beloved Sisters from the sons of Mil. He's a thick one, this Amergin, though surely not as thick as the Fir Bolg. Although he saw through none of us, I did think the question about the city was well chosen and well timed. And he will not be accepting Greece as our origin place. He might prove an enjoyable player. Still, if he is the best of his lot, they are ripe for the picking."

Eriu closed her eyes. "This becomes too tangled," she said softly. "O Danu, if only they had not come."

30

I saw them assemble at the crest of the hill, a huge company of them this time.

I alone climbed the hill to meet them, our people gathered below on the beach in a tight semicircle, weapons at the ready.

The Sisters stood to the forefront; Eriu's eyes seemed overwide and fearful. With them was an ancient little woman with gray hair and gray eyes who looked remarkably like An Scail. Behind that quartet was a phalanx of warriors, among them the man Macha whom I had already met. Flanking him were two dark-haired warriors who looked as tall and fierce as any I had encountered in my travels and had in their bearing and their blank facial expressions the look of professional soldiers. Macha and his companions each wore on his arm an elaborate silver gauntlet, a mark, I supposed, of their military rank within the company.

To either side of that cluster were dozens of warriors, men and women, all surpassingly beautiful, all carrying slender spears which looked to be made of some kind of crystal. I wondered at the efficacy of such weapons.

I took in a deep breath and steadied my hand, then raised it to the company. "I am Amergin, poet of the Milesians. I give you greeting and guarantee of peace."

"How will you guarantee that, poet?" asked Macha.

"I will," I said simply. "I have spoken to my people. If any of them moves against you, you may have my life."

Behind Macha, the two dark soldiers exchanged a glance.

I heard Eriu inhale sharply.

"No such penalty will be necessary, poet," she said. "We will take our safety at your word."

"Nor are we without recourse of our own," said Macha.

"Hush!" said Eriu.

Macha shifted his stance, met my eyes. His eyes seemed to hold some dark amusement in their depths.

"Come among us and we will talk as civilized peoples do," I said.

Eriu nodded.

I moved to the head of this great parade and led the people of the Danu down among my own people, feeling somehow as though I were leading wolves into the fold, although my own people were larger and better armed than these.

When we had everyone seated on opposite sides of the circle, I stood. I drew my longsword from over my back and drove it upright into a bale of hay that Bile had covered with fabric for the occasion.

"Here I draw erbe ndruad," I intoned, "the fence of battle. None shall cross it."

My people raised their hands, palms out, to indicate their agreement. I saw Eriu watch the gesture, raise her own hand. Her people followed, though Macha and his warriors seemed reluctant and he looked at me with insolence as he complied.

"I invoke the right of Poet. All will hear!" I called out. The company came to immediate silence. "People of the Danu, people of the Galaeci." I nodded at the assembled tribes. "I will speak truth before you. Teangu do dhia, teanges mo thuath. This I swear by the god by whom my people swear. Hear me.

"We need not come together as enemies if we will reason with wisdom. The Galaeci have come here to Inisfail as journeyers. Yes, we have seen this place ever as our destiny, but we know now that these, the people of the Danu, have preceded us. Surely that gives them first rights on the land."

Eber Finn and Eremon bristled and twisted in their seats, but I raised my hand. They remained silent.

"Although we do not know your numbers, the land and sea seem vast to us. If there be an empty space upon this isle, send us there. There we will raise our cattle and ride our horses. There our women will give birth to our children. We have sustained many sorrows in recent days."

I drew in a deep breath to steady my voice; for a moment I felt over-whelmed by the thought of our dead—Skena and Ir, Ith, my father and mother. Surely this was a fool's journey, a journey of sorrows. But what should we do now; turn around and go back upon the sea from whence we came? I shook my head.

"We wish only for pasturage and a green hill on which to build our vil-lages. We wish to bind our wounds and increase our clans. We will not trouble the people of the Danu, nor will we attempt to enter your door-ways." Behind me Airioch cleared his throat. I gestured at the upraised sword; he remained silent. I continued.

"Eriu of the Danu, what response do you make?"

Eriu stood among the company. She closed her eyes and raised her hands. Her sisters stood suddenly and took them. They issued forth the deep, throaty chant that sounded so like the bass note of the pipes. Though I had heard it before, none of my people had heard it. I saw them move restlessly in their places; one or two made the signs against enchantment.

Eriu spoke. "People of the Galaeci. The Children of the Danu have lived here on the Green Isle for hundreds of years. When your heralds came among us, we explained our ways to Ith, your druid. Ith decided that it was best for the sons of Mil to remain in Galicia, where their ways were known and loved. Yet now you tell us Ith has died. Here you are among us with your goods and your gear, and on your first night among us one of your number is wounded unto death by the doorway to our city. This brings us great sorrow. It seems but a poor welcome to ask you to return to the sea, but this is what we ask."

A wave of angry murmuring swept over the Milesians.

Eber Donn jumped to his feet. "We will not return to the sea! Here we are and here we will remain!" Some of our people cheered him; I saw others turn and look longingly for the water.

Eriu raised her hand.

I put my hand on the hilt of my longsword. "She has not finished her argument!" I thundered it out. "I have commanded silence. Silence will prevail."

A complete silence fell over the company; Eber Donn dropped to his seat. Eriu met my eyes, and I saw something that resembled surprise move across her face. She nodded, continued.

"Sons of Mil. We do not ask you to return to the sea forever. Nor do we ask you to sail back from whence you came. We ask you for three days. Three little days. Retreat to the ninth wave of the sea; give us time. In those three days we will change our doorways that none will wound you anymore; this we have not done for many years, and it requires time. There will be some danger while we work.

"We will select from the great fields and forests of the Green Isle pasturage and fortified hills where you may build your cities."

"Our cargo ships have departed," shouted Eber Donn.

Eriu nodded. "Leave your cattle and your horses here on shore; none of the Danu will trouble them. We do not herd cattle, nor do we own horses. You need not reload your ships. Only take yourselves to sea that our . . . lightning . . . will not trouble you. When you return, we will retreat into our cities. Perhaps in time, our peoples can learn of each other's ways. Perhaps in time we will encounter each other without fear. But until that day comes, Danu will keep to Danu cities, Galaeci to Galaeci."

I looked at my brothers and at our assembled clan. Eber Donn was shaking his head. Eber Finn and Eremon, having heard of pasturage and hillsides, were debating with each other whether or not it was safe to leave the cattle and horses with the Danu. Airioch was doing his best to catch the eye of Banba, the dark-haired sister. I noted with surprise that our youngest brother, Colpa, was seated beside him, his hand clasped firmly in Airioch's. I felt a sudden wash of shame for not considering him, suddenly motherless and fatherless at not quite ten years. Too many sorrows.

I took a deep breath. I spoke for the company.

"It is decided. We will retreat to the ninth wave of the sea. At sunset, we will send Scota's spirit to join our father's. When we have waked the dead, we will depart. We will return at dawn in three days' time."

Across the circle, Eriu nodded at me, her face a mixture of relief and sorrow. Behind her, Macha was shaking his head.

CEOLAS SINGS FAREWELL
Proud spirit, Scota,
mother of many sons,
go into the West,
seek there our father, Mil;
say that his sons remember.

Seek there our uncle Ith;
say that we will try
to bear wisdom in a new place.
Seek out our brother Ir,
say that Bile misses his laughter.
Seek out Skena my beloved,
who will bear our child in the West;
say only that I love her,
say only that my song is for her.

From the darkness at the far edge of the beach, I watched quietly as the sparks carried the last of my mother's spirit skyward, as the drums began the waking that would last throughout the night. In the quiet bay, our Greek companions began the process that would allow us to go to sea on the remaining three biremes. They muttered among themselves, perhaps worried at being in the employ of the crazy Galaeci, who could not decide whether to go or stay. I sat down heavily against a sea rock. I dropped my head down on my knees and let the tears spill.

"Amergin?"

I leaped to my feet and wheeled around, the tears still making rivers on my cheeks. Eriu was standing right behind me, the sea wind moving her long gown. I could not imagine that I had not heard her approach. I realized suddenly that I towered over her, saw her sudden fear of my size flare up in her eyes. She waved me back to a sitting position; I dropped to the sand so as not to frighten her further. I motioned for her to sit beside me; to my surprise she did so unhesitatingly.

"I have heard your song. I grieve your many losses. We of the Danu are sorry for the loss of your mother," she said softly. "We did not anticipate the . . . curiosity . . . of your people. The Fir Bolg are not a curious folk."

I smiled sadly. "It is our strongest trait. We roam the world and we learn the world. We question and we voyage. It brings us always to trouble and to grief, but that is the way of the sons of Mil." I shrugged. "But speak to me of these Fir Bolg."

She smiled suddenly, and I knew that her smile made reference to my curiosity even in the midst of my grief. I smiled back through the glistening water in my eyes, nodded my head, shrugged.

"They are the others who dwell on this island, in the far, stony north. They are a simple people; they hunt and gather, farm a little. I would ask that you not mention them to your clan. They are under our protection and I would not want them harmed."

"And you trust me not to do this?"

She nodded. "You are a man of honor; this I know."

I met her eyes. "I have thought that same thing of you. Yesterday when you spoke to Bile. I do not know who injured our uncle Ith, but I know that it was not you or your sisters."

"I thank you for this trust. I will give you something in return. I also do not know who injured Ith, but I give you warning; do not trust the Macha in any of her guises."

"Her? This is the second time you have referred to this warrior as a woman."

She shrugged. "Like my sisters and me, Macha comes always in her . . . threesome. I tend to think of her . . . that way. As I think of my sisters," she amended.

"The threesome with the silver gauntlets! They are companions."

"They are . . . a warrior triad. Be wary."

"Macha seems to favor you. Is he your . . . beloved?"

"No! Never! Macha plays games with everyone; even I am not immune to them."

"Ah. I have a brother cut from that cloth."

"Yes, Airioch Feabhruadh. We see that as well."

"Do you think it was Macha who injured my uncle Ith?"

"I do not know. There are some among you who also move with dark, specific purpose."

I leaned back against the rock and sighed deeply.

"You are troubled, Amergin," she said. "You have good reason. Your griefs crowd around you like gulls, and your clan will be hard to control."

I nodded. "My clan is impossible to control as always. We should not have come. Ith had died and my father . . . So many of them wished to come, some for vengeance, some for gain."

"And you?"

"Where Skena was, I was home. It would not have mattered where. You must understand that, Eriu."

"No."

I turned to look at her, surprised by her answer. "You are beautiful, gentle, and wise. I cannot believe no man has spoken for you."

"We were bonded once, my sisters and I, but those to whom we were wed have died. They were good men and kind."

"It was arranged for you?"

"Yes."

"We do not arrange among the Galaeci. We choose, each for the other and both must agree."

"And the tribe as well?"

"Not so much agree as see what is before them and recognize it."

"And if they do not agree?"

I shrugged. "I have not seen it happen. We are . . . a strong-willed people."

"I envy you so great a love. Even in her leaving, your Skena remains with you in the chamber of your memory."

"Yes." I drew in a raggedy breath; Eriu touched my hand lightly with her own.

"Our ancient, Airmid, whom you saw tonight?"

I nodded. "She who resembles An Scail."

Eriu laughed aloud. "She does, doesn't she?"

"Your Ancient has told An Scail that she can restore her sight. Can you imagine?"

"If she says that she can do so, then it is so. Airmid is a healer of great skill."

"Why do you bring up her name?"

Eriu smiled. "Because once she had so great a love as yours." She was silent for a while, and then she spoke softly beside me. "So surely you are thinking that if you had not come here, you would still have your great love to you. And your uncle, your father, your brother."

"And my child."

She turned suddenly and looked up the hill toward the headland. Her face, which had been open, suddenly shuttered.

"Do they watch us?"

"No, we are alone."

"What do you fear?"

"Fear?"

"Something has made you suddenly afraid."

She shook her head and stood.

"Wait," I said.

She turned back toward me. I was struck again by the fact that her eyes did not quite fit her face, that even here in the shadows they looked overlarge. I found that I wanted her to remain, that the thought of being alone again with my sorrows gaped before me like the vast cold sea. I composed a hasty question.

"What will you do while we are at sea?"

"We will destroy all of the doors between our . . . cities and yours. They will vanish from this place; you will not see them again. We will depart and leave the land to you."

"Depart? Forever?" I felt suddenly bereft. "I shall miss you. And I am deeply sorry for the grief my clan has caused you with our arrival."

She looked surprised and then nodded. "I shall miss you too, Amergin. We are a strange pair, are we not, two outsiders who bear the weight of their peoples? Here in the shadows we have unburdened to each other. I thank you for bearing my troubles."

"And you for bearing mine."

"We shall try, Amergin, that our people do no more harm to each other, but I think that is a battle that we two will fight alone."

She turned and walked into the darkness.

31

ow shall this be done?" Eriu spoke to the assembled company of the Danu.

"It should not be done at all! We have had the run of the Green Isle for nearly a thousand years. Ever since we vanquished those disgusting Fomor." Macha had resumed for the occasion her true aspect; the huge dark almonds of her eyes snapped, the cloudy nimbus of her darkness crackled with electricity. To either side, Banbh and Nemhain regarded the assemblage with their unblinking predatory eyes.

"This we know," said Eriu. "But change has come among us; they do not know that our numbers are barely double theirs, nor do they know that we are not a warlike people. They are; I see it clearly. We cannot vanquish them, so we must change to accommodate them. That is wisdom, Ravener."

"No! Wisdom says that we should go among them now, before they set foot on their ships. Of course we can vanquish them. We should use the arms, destroy them all, but for a few souls who can race back to Galicia with the terrible news and frighten the rest of their company away forever."

Eriu could hear some agreement among the Raveners, but most of her people would, she knew, seal up the cities and vanish like the mist before they would destroy the Invaders. She faced Macha.

"You have given me your word."

"I have. I wish that I had not. But I have said that I will not injure them until they come against us in battle. And they will, people of the Danu. Believe me on this; they will!"

She stormed from the chamber, Nemhain and Banbh hissing along in her wake.

Eriu sighed. "Can any speak to us of how we might seal our cities and hide our doorways?"

Airmid stood. "I can," she said softly. "But oh, my people, you will not like what I will say. The doorways must be destroyed. All the dolmens and the sarsen circles. All the passageways. They must be razed so that stone no longer stands on stone. All the triangle portals must be ground to dust, for it is in touching those that the woman was killed. Then we will dwell in complete safety here on our leaf of time. None will see us."

"Speak to us of the benefits and of the sacrifice," Eriu said quietly.

"None on the Green Isle dwell on our leaf of time; we will be able to frolic in the fields and the forests alone. None will molest us or trouble our children. These are the benefits. But we will be alone. We are fewer than a thousand people. We who are Ancients among you will die soon. We will have to abandon the Fir Bolg because to remove them with us would be too terrifying and too lonely for them. We will no longer be able to heal their children; those who are abandoned will die. Should the Invader come against them, we cannot defend them. We will also have to make a difficult decision for our own Hybrid children. Will they seal themselves into this time with us? If so, they will never see their parents again. Or will they go alone into their own time on the Green Island, a tribe at once neither Fir Bolg nor Milesian, brilliant and long-lived, but few in number and vulnerable, in danger from both their own clan and from the sons of Mil, fitting in nowhere." Airmid sighed.

"Speak the worst, Ancient."

Airmid nodded. "We were many, many more when first we came to this world. For our safety, our company divided. In our own part of the world, we have lost all who came here before us. Of our own number, we lost many when the volcano sent our island into the sea. We no longer have the numbers to rebuild great cities beneath the sea or elaborate cities in their world. Our race is depleted. The Danu create few children and those slowly. Our numbers will begin to diminish. Even when our numbers were larger, the Danu have depended, since we arrived on this world, on our contact with humans, on the blending of their Braid with ours and also on their knowledge and their need for our knowledge. Without them, our line will die out, little by little, but as surely as the trees grow ancient and then die. We will be alone, unheard of and unseen, a diminished race of people on an empty leaf of time. And then we will vanish entirely."

One of the historians stood. "Can we raise the Light Ships, go else-where?"

Airmid replied. "Surely we can go. The question is where would we go? We are familiar with the world of the Internum Mare, but it is too crowded for our return. When first we came to this world, we chose three directions. Some of our company traveled here before us; they are gone. Some traveled to the far west; are they also gone? Are there Danu elsewhere in this world? We know not."

Eriu held her hands out. "What say you, people of the Danu? I am but young in wisdom. Shall we journey? Shall we depart from the Green Isle? Or shall we seal our cities shut?"

"Perhaps a delegation," said the historian. "Those who have no children here, who are not healers for the Fir Bolg. We could take one or two of the small Light Ships, look for our lost brothers and sisters."

General agreement moved across the company. A dozen volunteers assembled themselves before the Danu.

"Go now," said Eriu. "While the sons of Mil put out to sea. While they stand no chance of seeing either our ships or their hiding places."

The group departed from the chamber.

Soft weeping moved across the room, and Eriu felt like joining them, like dropping into sorrow for their lost companions.

"How will they return to us if all the doorways are sealed?" Eriu asked softly, turning to Airmid.

Airmid just shook her head. "They will not," she said softly. "Once the doorways are destroyed, there can be no return. These twelve will be alone in the great world unless they find our lost companions."

"Perhaps Macha is right," said Eriu softly. "Perhaps the time has come to use Nuada's Silver Arms."

Airmid regarded her quietly. "Many will die, both Danu and Milesian."

Banba whispered softly. "It is our duty to protect the Danu, Ancient. Help us to choose."

Airmid smiled sadly. "I cannot. Only that I tell you that each choice has consequences; this I well know."

"Come, Sisters," said Fodla softly. "Together, we must decide."

Eriu stood before the company, raised her hands. Behind her, Banba and Fodla stepped up, linked with her arms.

"People of the Danu!" she said. "We have examined all of the choices. We have heard all of the arguments. Now, the Council Triad will decide the course of the Danu. Prepare yourselves to enter the Braid." Behind her, Banba and Fodla began the deep, nasal chant. In the room the people began to chant with them, to counterpoint the sound. They linked hands over and under, their eyes closed. In a high sweet voice, Eriu began Braidsong.

"Mother of the World,
All-Maker, hear us.
Bringer of Fire,
Singer of Song,
Keeper of Creation's Forge,
Womb Cradle of the World,
Cradle are you,
Comfort are you,
Hear our cry.
We call upon you,
Children of the Mother.
Sing wisdom to the Danu,
O Weaver of the Braid."

Eriu could feel her people entering the deep state of awe, the reverence in which they would wait upon the wisdom of the Braid. Eriu closed her eyes, tipped her head back. She felt herself begin to slip from her body, to enter the stream of the Braid, where wisdom dwelled.

Suddenly, the chamber door slid open.

Illyn rushed into the room. "People of the Danu," she cried. "Forgive me for interrupting Braidsong. We Hybrids have been watching from the headland; the Morrigu is there, pointing her Silver Arms at the water. There is a great storm at sea; the Milesian ships are in danger of the rocks; they will drown in the sea!"

32

"Y ou trusted them! See what a fool you are." Eber Donn shrieked it over the wind.

"It is a storm!" I cried. "Do you assume that these Danu control the wind and the sea?"

"Perhaps they do not control it, but perhaps they knew that it would come. Why else send us out to sea, vulnerable to wind and weather? It was a strange request, and you assented to it."

I could not deny his point, turned from him to hasten our company belowdecks, where at least they would not be washed overboard. I was glad that An Scail had refused to accompany us, had insisted that she would remain on shore. I looked out at the roiling water.

"I will prove it to you, Amergin!" shouted Eber Donn. "This is a Danu trick. And when I have shown you, we will attack them. We will kill every Danu on the island. That you will owe me, you great fool."

He began to clamber up the rigging toward the crow's nest.

"Eber Donn," I called into the wind. "The ship pitches. Do not go aloft."

But he scrambled higher. The fog was so thick that in a moment I could barely see him.

"Come down, Brother!" I called into the tearing wind. Suddenly and without warning, all went still. The ship ceased its pitching, the fog began to clear away from the rigging. I could see Eber Donn dangling high above me though I could not yet see our other two ships on the sea around us. Eber Donn looked down from his perch.

"Now do you see?" he called.

I nodded. How could I help but see? The very suddenness of the change was proof enough. No storm ceased in midrage, sudden as a cry. The Danu had sent us to the waters and they had stirred the waters, hoping that we would drown. Just as suddenly they had stopped them. We were nine waves from shore and completely at their mercy; at any moment they could stir the tempest again. And I had trusted them. I had led the whole of our tribe out to sea on that trust.

Rage coursed through me then, hot as fire. I felt it shake my very core.

"I see!" I called up to my brother. "We will kill them all! Come down, Brother. Before they set the sea to raging once again."

Eber Donn screamed in toward the shore, shaking his fist, clinging with one hand to the rigging. "We will destroy you, Children of the Danu. Prepare yourselves for the sons of Mil! Prepare yourselves for the thunder of battle!"

Airioch Feabhruadh came up from below, Colpa by his side, as he had been since the death of our mother. They stood looking up at Eber Donn.

"He believes that they brought the storm?" he asked softly.

I nodded. "What else could he believe?"

Suddenly and without warning, the storm came howling down upon us again, a huge wind catching at our sails. Our ship tilted on its keel.

Colpa was thrown to the deck, began to slide toward the water.

"No! No!"

I heard Airioch scream, saw him throw himself across the deck, reaching for Colpa. At the same time I saw Eber Donn, clinging with a single arm to the mast. I saw him swing out over the sea, hanging by a thread over the surging water. I saw precisely the moment when his great arm would no longer hold. He plunged into the sea, looking for all the world like a child's doll of rags.

"No!" Rage coursed through me, stronger than the storm.

"Beware, O Danu!" I cried. "Beware the vengeance of the sons of Mil."

As suddenly as it had begun, the storm ceased again. The sea was quiet. At first I could see nothing, but slowly the fog began to lift. Against the wall of the ship I saw Airioch, his body curled around a thick rope. I ran to where he lay. Curled in his arm was Colpa, coughing seawater and looking anxiously at Airioch. I knelt and held my hand to his neck.

"He lives," I said to Colpa; "he has banged his head."

Airioch moaned and opened his eyes.

"You'll be all right in a moment," I said softly. "But Eber Donn is gone from us."

Airioch dragged himself to his feet and stared up at the mast. "My brother," he whispered. "Oh, my brother. O you gods, what have I done?"

The wives of Eber Donn surged up from below the deck, looking around for his presence, their many children clinging to them.

I told them what had happened; the deck was filled with their high keening wails.

I stood; one of our ships, its sails broken, limped toward us across the water.

"Where is our third bireme?" I called across the water to the Greek captain.

"We do not know; we could see nothing."

"Make for shore!" I cried. "We will anchor in the bay."

An Scail came to meet us on the shore, her hand shading her eyes.

"You were wise to elect to remain on shore, Wise One. See what they have wrought with their false promises. We arm for war!"

"Are you certain they have done this?"

"Who else could raise a storm and make it cease, all in but three hours' time?"

"What of the three days the Danu requested?"

"It is they who began this storm," I said, my fists clenched in fury. "They no longer deserve our trust or our promise."

An Scail shook her head. She turned and walked toward the headland, her hand still shading her eyes.

"Do not go among them," I shouted, but she continued, raising the back of her hand against me.

"Someone must make wisdom if you will not," she called. Her voice carried out over the sea, above the watery grave of the Milesian dead.

By nightfall, our Greek sailors began to ready themselves for departure in the remaining two biremes. The sons of Mil would now be residents of Inisfail, like it or no.

33

On the headland, Eriu ran at Macha, pushed her hard from behind. Macha staggered under the blow, dropped to her knees. The Silver Arm pointed downward at the rocky beach and carved a long trench into the sand. For a moment Nemhain and Banbh ceased their work with the arms, turned in their sister's direction.

At sea, the storm suddenly abated.

"You gave me your word!" Eriu screamed. "What will you bring upon the people of the Danu?"

"I said that I would not harm them and I did not; I stirred the sea and that is all."

"What, will you dance words with me? Cease now!"

She screamed it at Nemhain and Banbh, who had begun to direct their streams of light at the sea once again, roiling the water and thickening the fog. Nemhain's lips curled in a smile. Suddenly a burst of light struck Nemhain's arm. Another grazed the shoulder of her sister Banbh. Banbh screamed. Simultaneously, the two sisters shook their arms free; the silver gauntlets crashed to the ground.

Banba and Fodla swept in from either side, Light Spears in their hands. Lightning swift, they gathered the abandoned Silver Arms into their hands and ran toward Airmid, who stood silhouetted in a doorway.

Airmid held out both arms; the Sisters slotted the gauntlets down over her hands.

"Go, Ancient!" screamed Banba. "Hide them where none will find them."

In a flash of blue light Airmid vanished.

With a scream of frustration, Nemhain and Banbh began to transform, Banbh's cloak spinning into iridescent black feathers, Nemhain's hair beginning to sweep outward in a wind of chaos.

"Cease!" cried Eriu. On Eriu's right arm gleamed Nuada's Silver Arm. Macha lay on the ground, a bolt of lightning seared onto her right shoulder. "Stand before me, Raveners, as you are, or before Danu I swear that Macha shall die."

Slowly, reluctantly, Nemhain and Banbh ceased transformation, stood beside Macha. Macha raised herself up on her elbow, used her good hand to feel at the scar on her shoulder. "It will be permanent," she said, her eyes flashing angrily at Eriu.

"Good, then all will know you at your coming and your going for what you are, a force of destruction, a faithless, lying . . ."

Macha stood. "Your decision for the Danu was unwise. You chose to close the doors. And that is wrong."

At that moment, three triangular Light Ships rose up into the sky, one from the sea, two from the deep interior. Like winged birds of light, they rose and hovered, then vanished toward the west.

"Do you see?" cried Macha. "You would divide the Danu, each from the other. And for what? A race of uninvited Invaders who would destroy us on a whim, were not the poet reining them in. How long do you think they will be controlled by a poet, a maker of words?"

Eriu shook her head.

"You would wall us up in isolation. The Morrigu cannot survive in isolation. We heard your arguments in Council; their conclusion would spell our death. How would we feed in a world that contained only our own kind? Or would we remain in this world forever isolated from our own kind? But did your conclusions take the Raveners into account? They did not; I have my own people to defend. How much better for us to destroy the Invaders, to drown them in the sea, to continue here as we have always done, Danu and Ravener, with the wide human world available for us to explore. We did what we always do—that which must be done. If you had not stopped us, your problem would now be solved." She faced Eriu. "See it, Sister, for it is true." She met Eriu's eyes, waited quietly.

"I cannot deny the truth of what you say," said Eriu. "But you have made the Three Sisters liars all; the sons of Mil will never again trust our word."

"As you should never trust theirs."

"There are other ways; yours is not the only way."

"It was the best way," said Macha. "The best and the most necessary. And now you have caused it to fail. We will pay a price for that failure."

She gestured toward the bay. Two Greek ships limped into harbor, their masts broken, their sails in tatters.

"Where is the third?" asked Eriu.

"Perhaps it was our only success," said Macha. "We shall see."

She made a flicking motion with her hand; suddenly Banbh was a raven. Just as suddenly, she dug her claws into Eriu's shoulder, twisted her beak to pluck at her eyes. Eriu raised her hands to defend her eyes. She felt Macha wrench the Silver Arm from her hand, saw her transform as swiftly as her sister.

An eagle lifted north, dangling a Silver Arm from its talons; a flock of ravens followed, borne on a sudden wind.

By afternoon, the third ship had still not returned to harbor. Eriu and her sisters stood at the headland, watching as the remaining Milesians moved from the ships to the shore, disappeared into their dwellings, some bearing wounded. Beside the Sisters now, a contingent of Danu Light Spear Warriors stood uneasily by, Light Spears at the ready.

Toward evening there was sudden movement in the tents below. Suddenly and without warning, the Milesians burst from their dwellings in full war garb. Beside them were the huge curly-haired dogs. The dogs bolted for the headland, moving faster than the Milesians on their long slender legs. They were howling in unearthly discord. Behind them, the sons of Mil let out a huge, visceral yell and ran straight for the headland, brandishing their shortswords high in the air as they ran. At the back of the company came Milesians on horseback, among them Amergin. Eriu could see his black hair streaming out over his cloak. Fear clutched at her heart.

"Mag Tuiread!" cried Eriu. "There at least we stand a chance. There at least there will be enough portals. And tell Airmid to have the physicians at the ready."

Some of the Danu made for the portals, for the swift transport to Mag Tuiread. But there were not enough portals to accommodate them all.

Eriu began to run beside the Light Spear carriers.

"No!" cried Banba. "You must transport to Mag Tuiread."

"And what of these?" Eriu screamed, gesturing to the runners.

"We run, Sister! We have trained for it well!" cried the chief of the spear carriers. "To the portals. Meet us at Mag Tuiread."

Swift as wind, the Danu veered into three columns, began the run toward the Plain of Mag Tuiread, the furious Milesian dogs hard upon their heels.

34

I watched as they ran from us, dividing at the headlands, their spear bearers seeming to vanish before us in the green forest. From beyond them,
I saw the white flashes of light from their doorways.

"They vanish into their cities!" I called. "Avoid their doorways! They
harness their lightning against us!"

I am not a man much given to anger, but it felt good, thrusting
through me, hot as lightning, carrying my losses with it—all rising, raging, in my internal fire. Gone was all my wisdom, my knowledge of the
Danu as dwellers here before us, my feeling that we should not have journeyed here at all.

And now we would be trapped here, for our Greek sailors would sail
away from us, even while we were fighting these Danu. And some of our
remaining number would surely be among them.

I could not blame them. We had returned from the sea with only two
of our ships. A third of our company was gone into the sea. At our return,
there was no sign of An Scail. Had they killed her as well?

Then consign her as well to the fires of my vengeance.

They had played us false, the Sisters. They had brought the sea
against us. I did not stop to consider how they had done this deed. It did
not matter now. I would avenge them all with the white-hot fire of my
rage. Ith and Mil, Skena and Ir, Scota, An Scail. My child, my unborn
child.

I ran in the forest, heedless of branches, heedless of direction, following the swift retreating forms of their Light Spear bearers, following the baying of our own great wolfhounds. My only prayer was that they would lead me to the Sisters. To Eriu. Let her feel the weight of all our losses. Most damnable of liars.

In a hot, white heat I ran.

It was not until I reached the forest at the base of the Plain of Many Towers that I thought I heard the voice of Skena, calling me.

"Amergin!" it cried. "Husband! Hear me!"

I stopped and drew in a ragged breath, my heart thundering against my chest wall. I looked around me. At the crest of this hill were stone doorways, a dozen of them in a great circle.

Skena's voice seemed to come from between the standing stones. I looked up the hill toward them.

"Amergin!"

Was there a figure there? Standing between the stones?

"Skena?" It came out as a half-strangled gasp.

I saw a shadowy form between the stones. This I swear. It spoke.

"Anger is a hot healer. This you know. Anger heals a wound with scars." I saw the form shift, begin to coalesce.

Eber Finn came up beside me then, Airioch behind him. He followed my eyes.

"What is it?"

"Who is there between the stones?"

"I see nothing. Wait . . . no. It is the shadow of a great tree."

I looked again. Eber Finn was right. A shadow moved between the stones. I closed my eyes, took in a deep breath.

Eber Finn clasped me hard at the elbow. "They have not reached the place. Victory is ours. We will avenge our dead."

Whatever I had seen or thought that I had heard was gone. I nodded, clasped him back in the warrior grip. Behind us Airioch Feabhruadh regarded us both in silence. He lowered his eyes, would not clasp arms with either of us.

Before I could address him, our warriors came into the forest behind us. They had some of the Danu spear bearers in their possession, wounded and struggling, their huge eyes shifting and widening.

Blue light snapped between the doorways.

"The Sisters come," I whispered to my brothers. "Gather the dogs. Vanish into the forest. I will circle behind the stones; await my command."

I slipped into the darkness, a man in whom the god of war was raging.

35

Dusk was falling on the Plain of Mag Tuiread.

In doorways between the standing stones, the Three Sisters waited. Opposite her, in separate doorways, Eriu could see Banba and Fodla. She had hoped to find Airmid in the city below, to supply each of her sisters with an arm, but the Ancient was nowhere to be found, applying herself to their own command to hide the arms, Eriu thought, securing them from Macha.

In each doorway of the circle, she could see Danu spear carriers, one facing inward toward the circle, two facing outward toward the forest at the base of the hill.

They scanned the forest anxiously for their companions.

Suddenly from a distance, Eriu heard the baying of the Milesian dogs. "They come," she whispered. "Danu, guide my hand."

No sooner had she spoken the words than the first dogs burst into the circle, running wildly in across the open space, crisscrossing each other. Eriu saw the outward-facing spear carriers turn inward toward the dogs momentarily, then return to their post.

The inward carriers pointed their spears; arcs of blue light flashed across the open space. There was a high squealing sound from some of the dogs.

Now Danu spear carriers began to run in among their companions; they were flanked by the horses of the Galaeci. Eriu did not see Amergin among them but she cringed as one of the horses trampled over one of the Danu spear carriers. She saw him tumble beneath the horse's hooves, saw Metaphor slip from him as he fell.

"Physicians!" she called into the gathering dusk.

A flash of blue light sparked in an empty doorway. Two physicians swept onto the field and spirited the little Danu back between the uprights, only to vanish below.

"By the gods!" cried the Milesian on horseback, the look on his face reflecting terror.

Then suddenly the whole company was upon them, scrambling up the hill, dogs and horses, spear carriers and riders, Milesian runners, their swords clanging metal on metal. Flashes of blue light echoed crazily around the circle. Eriu heard screams, but she could not tell if those screaming were Danu or Milesian. It crossed her mind that creatures in pain screamed alike regardless of their origins.

Now flash after flash began to appear between the doorways as physicians came and went with the wounded.

Eriu heard the sound of hooves behind her; a horseman swept past. She stayed still and silent in her doorway, waiting for the signal to use the portals, to unleash upon the Milesians the full fury of the time portals.

Suddenly, she felt a huge hand at her throat and the cold horror of a thin, metal blade against the soft flesh.

The voice of Amergin boomed out over the chaos. "I have as prisoner Eriu of the Danu. Cease or I will kill her as she stands."

Slowly and by degrees, the field died to silence.

"Assemble!" cried Amergin.

From behind the stone doorways, torches flared to light. Eriu saw Fodla held tight in the grip of two Milesians.

"Portals!" she called aloud, and she saw the flashes of blue as some of the spear bearers escaped below. She heaved a sigh of gratitude; at least the Danu would continue.

"Bring the prisoners to the center of the circle," called Amergin.

As the Milesians led the spear bearers into the circle, Eriu began to weep, the tears streaming silently down her cheeks. Some of her people were bleeding from the face and arms. At least two dangled limbs that would be difficult to save, even if she could get them to the physicians. A few of the wounded were slipping in and out of Metaphor. She could see their eyes go large and ovoid, their height drop and then return to human size as they struggled to hold to their human aspect. She could hear the

Milesians cursing as they held them, probably wishing that they could run away, held past their fear only by their military training.

In violation of everything the Council had decided, Eriu called aloud in Danaan. "Have we lost any of our company?"

"Five have fallen in the forest," one of the spear bearers answered. He received a cuff for his trouble, but Eriu knew that physicians would be running even now for the fallen. They would be taken below, restored to health. More of the Danu to safety.

"You will speak no more!" said Amergin low into the back of her head.

She nodded once. How had this happened? The Danu had the advantage of weapons, of age, of wisdom, of technology, of knowledge of the place. Even for all her saying, she had underestimated the sons of Mil.

As if he had read her thoughts, Amergin leaned close to her ear. "Did you think us fools?" he whispered. "We have fought with Greeks and Romans, Carthaginians and Egyptians. We know how to track and how to fight in darkness. We know how to circle the enemy and come in from behind. I should never have trusted you; I should have fought you and your sisters this way from the first."

So. The Danu had become the enemy. Eriu wished that she had destroyed the doorways, that she had let the Morrigu drown all of their ships in the sea.

"Take me before my people," she said softly, in defiance of his edict.

The circle was now lit by torchlight, the flames flickering eerily against the huge stone uprights, throwing the elaborate braided carvings into relief.

Eriu closed her eyes. Years from now, when the remainder of the Danu had died, humans would come here among the stones. They would stare at the carvings and wonder at those who carved them. They would never know of the little people of the Danu, the Children of the Braid. She stifled a sob.

Amergin led her into the center of the circle. He had lowered the knife from her throat, maneuvered her gently into the ring of flickering light.

Opposite her, Eriu could see Fodla, her eyes wide. Where was Banba? Eriu prayed that she had opened portal, vanished into the city below.

Amergin released her. Eriu started to turn, to face him, but he placed his hands on her shoulders.

"Face those you have betrayed," he said.

She looked at the assembled company. "Will you allow our physicians to care for the wounded?" she called to the assemblage. "We will care for yours as well."

"Why should we allow that?" called Eremon. "Today we have lost an entire ship of our comrades in the sea. We have lost our mother and our father, our beloved brothers Eber Donn and Ir, our uncle Ith, Skena our healer, wife of our bard. For these deaths you and yours must pay the price."

"I invoke the right of Poet!" Eriu called into their midst. "All will hear."

She heard Amergin's intake of breath. The Milesians began to call out in anger. Behind her, Amergin spoke.

"She invokes the right. She is their Poet. Even among these who have betrayed us, we can obey our own law."

The company fell to silence.

Eriu closed her eyes.

"It is true that those of our company have called up a storm at sea," she said. Even the Raveners were of the Danu; she would not give them away. "For the loss of your comrades we are most sorry. But hear me, sons of Mil. This island has been our place. We have lived here for a thousand years. We did not ask you to come among us. What would you do if your own country were invaded by such as you?"

"You gave us your word," said Amergin from behind her back. "We expected to battle you, but you promised our safety for three days' time. You broke your word."

"And the penalty for breaking such a vow is death!" called Eber Finn.

Eriu drew in a deep breath. "Then take my life. But spare my people. They will return to their cities. They will never trouble you again."

"We have lost fifty of our company on such a promise; even now their souls cry out from the sea," shouted Eremon. "Why should we believe a further promise from one who looks at us and lies?"

"She did not lie." The voice was nasal, soft. "She never lies."

In one of the empty doorways Macha stood, bathed in blue light. She was garbed in her male warrior Metaphor, wearing one of the Silver Arms. Eriu blinked and closed her eyes. What damage would Macha do among them now?

Slowly, Macha lowered the arm and pointed it directly at Amergin. Suddenly Eriu felt his body close around hers, felt his arms encircle her Metaphor.

Macha hesitated.

"Do what you must," Eriu cried. "Save the Danu."

"I will lose you," said Macha quietly. "You took my hand; I gave you my vow."

"Your beloved keeps his word," said Amergin, low against her ear.

"Where did you come from?" The voice belonged to Airioch Feabhruadh, who called from the crowd.

"From wherever I wish," Macha said softly. "Do you see this Silver Arm upon my own? With it I control the wind and sea. With it I have drowned your ships."

"That is not possible," called Eremon.

Macha flexed a finger of the arm and pointed it toward the canopy of trees. They began to whisper, then to thrash and sway, heaving above the forest floor. Branches crashed down into the center of the circle. Macha withdrew the arm; the forest quieted.

"It was I who brought the storm to your vessels. Eriu knew nothing of it; she and her sisters forced me to stop, else I would have rid our isle of all of you. When you experienced the lull in the storm, it was because this little one"—she gestured at Eriu—"had knocked me flat on the ground to stop me."

"Why?" asked Amergin quietly. "Why would you do these things in violation of the word of the Sisters?"

"Because Eriu and her sisters would have closed the doors to Tara. They would have sealed the Danu away from the sons of Mil. We Raveners cannot live apart from humans."

"Raveners?" asked Amergin.

"Will you see me as I am?" asked Macha. The voice was mocking, dangerous. The company shifted and murmured, obvious fear now threading through the Milesians.

"Sisters!" Macha called. A high wind sped over the tops of the sarsen circle; the flames danced and whirled. A huge flock of crows suddenly wheeled in the sky above the torchlight. One huge raven descended among them, landed on Macha's shoulders.

"We are Morrigu!" Macha cried. Suddenly the threesome began to shift and vary, now three women with dark hair and robes, then wolves and ravens, wind and fire, suddenly three small, pale creatures with dark ovoid eyes, surrounded by clouds of darkness, then just as swiftly the three warriors of the headland, then three beautiful women of Greek bearing. A few Milesians ran screaming in fear for the forest; the warriors stood their ground, their eyes wide, their hands making signs in the air.

"You should not be among us," said Macha, her tone offhand. "Now you see why."

"Return to the ships!" called one of the wives of Eber Donn.

"We will return to Galicia!" shouted several of the Milesians.

"Hear me!" cried Amergin. The crowd fell silent. "Our return is not possible. Even while we followed these Danu into the forest, the Greeks departed from us. We have no choice but to remain on Inisfail."

"Then we must exact a penalty from these Danu," cried Eremon, his voice echoing in the circle.

"Exile!" cried Eber Finn. "Exile. Make them pay the price that they would have exacted from us. Put them on rafts and set them adrift on the sea."

The murmur spread through the Milesians like a fire. "Exile," they cried. "Send the Danu away from the isle."

"If that is what you wish, we will go," said Eriu. "We will depart the isle tonight."

She did not say that they would depart in their own great Spear Ships.

"Morrigu will not depart," said Macha, her voice echoing from the doorway.

With a sudden snap of light, she and her sisters were gone.

Suddenly there was a thunder of hooves from the outside of the circle. Between the sarsen stones rode a great horse of the Milesians. Clinging to Banba front and back were two tiny white-haired women, An Scail and Airmid. Each wore a silver gauntlet on her arm.

"Cease!" the two ancient women cried at once. "Hear the wisdom of your elders."

Banba swung from the saddle, her diadem askew, her Greek gown twisted. "Bloody, vicious animals," she spat. She swatted at the flank of a great horse three times her size. "Stupider than the dirt." This brought a laugh from the company of Milesians. Some of the tension dissipated.

"However do you big fellows ride them?" Banba asked, straightening her gown and looking around the circle in admiration. "Really, one of you must teach me."

"I would be happy to . . . ride." The voice of Airioch Feabhruadh drifted from the darkness.

Again the company laughed.

The two Ancients stood side by side, their hands linked. As one, they pointed their weapons at the assembled companies.

"Will you use the arms, Ancient?" asked Eriu, her voice filled with terror.

"First we will call physicians," said An Scail.

Airmid nodded. She tapped her triangle; blue light snapped at the portal. Physicians appeared and began to minister to Danu and Galaeci alike.

"Now we will use the arms," said Airmid softly. A gasp arose from the assembled company, both Danu and Milesian. Airmid and An Scail pointed the arms skyward. Gently, each flexed a finger. Sweet music began to weave itself through the portals and around the company, joyful and light. Tiny firework stars arced over the assembly in blues and greens and reds, then fell upon them, cool as snowflakes.

"Like people, such weapons can be turned to good or ill," said Airmid.

"It is time that we both turn to the good," said An Scail.

"I call forth the Triad Sisters of the Danu," said Airmid. Eriu stepped next to Banba. Fodla's captor released her and she stepped into triangle.

"Sons of Mil." An Scail turned and pointed into the darkness. "Eremon, Eber Finn, Airioch, come forward." The three oldest sons of Mil stepped uneasily into the circle.

"Hear me, sons of Mil," said An Scail. "These, the people of the Danu, did not ask for us to come among them. We have. They defend themselves. That is their right."

"Hear me, Children of the Danu," said Airmid. "These sons of Mil are a learned and well-traveled race. They are deeply spiritual and their love of learning carries them around the world. The vision of their leader compelled them here and they cannot now return; we must accept them here among us."

"True enough," said Eber Finn. "Though we would not be here had the Danu not wounded Uncle Ith and rendered him unable to warn us from their shores. For that alone, the Danu must suffer exile. Or one of them must die."

He lunged forward suddenly and caught Banba by her hair, raising his shortsword as he did so. He hacked at the hair, then put the blade to the point of her throat.

"No!" Airioch stepped beside Eber Finn. He moved the blade gently so that it rested just beneath his own chin. "None should die for that transgression but I. The people of the Danu did not wound Ith. I was responsible for that."

A wild babble erupted on both sides.

Amergin drew his longsword from his back, stepped among them, and stabbed it into the dirt. "Silence."

The crowd grew silent.

"Speak, Airioch," Amergin commanded.

"It was our last night here. Ith had spent it in the company of the Sisters. He told me of his decision not to return. I had seen their jewels, their diadems. I had seen the rich fields and the deep forests. I wanted to return. I argued with Ith, but he would hear none. He insisted that the place belonged to the Danu. He said—I remember it well—'They dwell in beauty and in magic, Nephew. Our presence would take that from them.' I said that I would not leave without treasure. I had seen you come through one of your doorways in the forest." Here he pointed at the Sisters. "I thought that if I could cross that portal I could return with gold and silver. I knew then that I could convince my father and my brothers to return, even against Ith's wishes.

"Ith followed me. He knew me well, our uncle. I stepped into the portal. I began to feel along the wall. Suddenly a bolt of hot light seared me. And then there was Ith. He simply stepped between me and the lightning. It knocked him flat to the ground. I carried him back to the hut, left him there until morning. He returned with us to Galicia as you saw him, unable to speak. And I blamed the Sisters."

"How do we know that this is true?" asked Eber Finn. "You have the eye for this dark one." He gestured at Banba. "Perhaps she has promised you riches if you will speak this tale."

For answer, Airioch rolled back the sleeve of his tunic, pushed it up above his elbow. A puckered scar streaked all the way to his elbow.

"That night at the shore," said Amergin suddenly. "You tried to tell me."

Airioch nodded. "And I could not. I know how much you loved him."

"Why now?"

"Colpa. He has no one now. He deserves a man like Father, like Ith. A man who speaks the truth."

Airioch turned to face the Milesians. "I will take responsibility. I will pay the price. Exile or death."

"It is too heavy a price, Brother," said Amergin. "For any to pay, Danu or Milesian. An Scail is right; we came here with our vision and our greed. All of us bear responsibility. We owe you our apology, Sisters; we judged you unfairly. We were wrong."

"Hear our brother!" Eremon called out.

An Scail smiled suddenly. "Look at you, Eremon. How strongly you resemble your father. He would want you to learn to dwell with these of the Danu. Did he not dwell with Greeks and Egyptians, Scythians and Persians?"

Suddenly from behind Eriu, Amergin drew breath. "An Scail," he said softly. "Wise One. How do you know that Eremon resembles our father?"

"I can see him," she said. "As I can see you, dark Amergin. And you, beautiful Eriu. And these stars that fall upon us cool as snow. And the beach and the sea. This is the gift that Airmid has given me," said An Scail. "A gift that would bring joy to Ith. Return the gift, Amergin. As bard of the Milesians, rule on the fate of both of our peoples."

Amergin stepped forward. He looked long into her eyes.

"How handsome you are, my dark-eyed boy," she whispered.

He turned to Airmid. "For this I thank you, wise one of the Danu." He looked long at her eyes as well, but she met his with perfect Metaphor.

He closed his eyes, stood silent at the center of the circle. Both the Milesians and the people of the Danu were silent.

At last he spoke. "I will rule. I give to the people of the Danu their cities beneath the ground and sea. I give to them their doorways. We of the Milesians will not enter their cities or cross their doorways. We will take nothing that belongs to them and trouble none of their kind. We will build our own great rath on a hill." He paused. He looked at Eriu. "What do you call your city?"

"Tara," she answered.

"Just so we will call our rath. We have begun ill, all of us. We will require time to think things through. There will be no contact between our people for one year. We will each mourn our dead and consider these events. At the end of that time we will meet in Council. We will decide then whether we will seal the doorways between us forever or open them wide. For that year, the Silver Arms will be kept, one each by Airmid and An Scail. Hide them well, elders. Let none know of their whereabouts."

Eriu spoke. "We have no control of Morrigu, as you have seen. But with the exception of this last, we of the Danu will abide by your ruling. Remember that Morrigu too possesses one of the Silver Arms. She will not relinquish it to either side," said Eriu.

Amergin nodded. "Airioch Feabhruadh, in accordance with our law, you will be responsible for those to whom you have brought much sorrow for the period of one year. You are the companion of An Scail; you will do as she bids in all things. You are both husband and father to the wives of Eber Donn and to their children. Into your care we place also our brother Colpa, who has neither mother nor father. You are father to the children and grandchildren of Mil."

Airioch nodded solemnly, then suddenly broke into a huge smile.

"You punish him by making him part of the family," An Scail whispered softly. "This is wise, Poet."

Amergin looked now at the assembled company of the Danu, many still held at the swordpoints of the sons of Mil.

"Release them," he commanded.

The Danu moved silently and immediately between the stones. Flashes of blue light moved stone to stone around the circle, illuminating the circle with bright blue light, brighter than the light of day. In moments, all but the Sisters and Airmid were gone.

Airmid stepped into a portal, the Silver Arm gleaming on her hand.

"Good work this night, friend," she said to An Scail.

"How beautiful the torches are," said An Scail in return. "With each day of this year, I shall think of you. With each sight that I see." She raised the Silver Arm in salute.

"I will take this horse," she said to Amergin. "Lift me to his back."

Eremon and Airioch rushed to comply.

"You can ride, Ancient?" asked Eremon.

"I have lived long. I can do many things." She saluted them with the arm, which gleamed in the torchlight, turned the horse, and rode through the portal.

Eriu stepped into a portal with her sisters. She lifted her triangle.

"Eriu! Wait!" Amergin called. She hesitated.

"We owe you reparation and apology," said Amergin to Eriu.

"You owe us nothing but peace," said Eriu. "Please, I beg you to leave us alone."

In a snap of blue light she was gone.

36

CEOLAS SINGS OF PASSING TIME
A year of peace is like a thousand,
A year of peace is like a sea,
A year of peace unfolds slowly
like a blossom in the light,
like the promise of the spring.
Bloom and heal in a year of peace,
Bloom and heal, my people.

For me, it has been the most difficult year of my life." Airioch Fe-abhruadh leaned back against the rock, his golden hair ruffled by the wind. He grinned at me. "This child needs a new cloak and the cows are calving and this wife of Eber Donn wants mating. . . ."

"How sad for you, Brother," I said, grinning back at him. "Three wives requiring mating."

"Sometimes all at once!" said Airioch. "They wear me down to the bone. And Colpa! He grows taller than your Bile."

"So the punishment was too much."

"Too much, too much, too much entirely." He laughed aloud.

I looked at him and shook my head.

His face grew serious. "You are thinking that you would never have thought it possible that we could sit here side by side in friendship, as we do."

"I am thinking exactly that."

"I wish that Ith could see it," Airioch said softly. "And Mil."

"Ith knew that the heart could change, Brother. He knew."

Airioch nodded. "I think much on what my selfishness cost us."

"Do not carry all the burden, Brother. Scota was herself a force of nature, full of loss and determined to avenge it on someone, anyone. And Eber Donn was ever angry, always putting action before thought. And me. I am Poet of the clan and yet I did not trust their word. I nearly took us all to death."

"I think much on your losses, Brother."

I nodded. "I think on them too. Skena would have made me wise. I would not have gone to war against them had she been by my side. I know this now and I am ashamed."

"Well, shame sits upon us both then, Brother."

I nodded. "And I wish that I had known my child."

"I wish that for you," Airioch said solemnly. I shrugged, sighed. He punched me lightly on the shoulder. I smiled at him.

"Thank you, friend."

"Thank you for your gifts to me, Brother."

We sat side by side in companionable silence. I fingered Ceolas lightly, dreamed the poem that I had been composing, telling the tale of the Battle of Mag Tuiread. I sang a bar or two.

> "They have vanished from among us
> In a sudden flash of light,
> The Danu with their large eyes;
> In my dreams I see them,
> Always I remember their eyes."

Airioch turned toward me. "Do you think that they will ever emerge from the portals?"

I shrugged. "It has been three days more than a year and we have seen no signs. Bile stands vigil at the portal on the headland."

"Why?"

"I know not. He dresses himself each morning and rolls his pictures beneath his arms. He marches up the headland and stands at the portal in the forest. He has thirteen years upon him. Who knows what they think at that age? And Bile cannot tell us, but for drawings. Those we must puzzle at for meaning; when the meaning will not come, he grows angry and shouts aloud." I shrugged. "I trouble for him, but I know not what to do."

"What does An Scail say?"

"She says only that she and Airmid have discussed the problem."

"I thought that I had seen them together once near midwinter, the two of them seated side by side in the leafless forest. But when I approached, An Scail was there alone. So she admits freely that they have both broken the year of exile?"

"She does. She says that she and the ancient Danu have left to them but little time, and there is much that they must learn, each from the other. What should I do, Airioch? Call our most ancient druid before the Council for violating the ruling of her own pupil?"

He laughed. "She has you trapped there, does she not?"

"She does."

For a moment, he looked out to sea; then Airioch faced me. "What do you hope, Brother, that they do or do not return among us?"

"I do not know what to hope. Eber Finn has gone north and built his rath. Eremon constructs the rath of Tara on his hill. Those who have remained here in Inver Skena have made a quiet life, dwellings and cattle, mating and babies." He gestured at the village that straggled up the headland from the sea. "It is quiet; I like it quiet. And if I never saw their Morrigu again, never would be soon enough."

Airioch shivered. "True enough, though I would like to see that darkhaired Banba once more."

"Is Banba what you see when you see her?"

"That was far too druidic for me, Brother."

"It is just something that I wonder, something about Eriu's eyes."

"Well, never mind," said Airioch. "I do not know that I would have anything left to give her if she did arrive. Look where they come for the mating." Two of Eber Donn's wives approached, hand in hand, their hair coiffed, wrapped in their finest shawls.

"Airioch," they called, "we find ourselves with a free hour."

"Go have your sport," I said. "You and I both know that you enjoy it."

"They have offered to share with you, Brother. The wives of Eber Donn like you well; this you know. You need not remain without a woman forever. I know that you are lonely." Here he paused. "I have been lonely in the tribe, Amergin."

"Well, perhaps lonely is the proper way for the poet. We keep the history of the clan; should we prefer one over another? We rule for the clan; in any ruling, half are satisfied and half are not."

"I cannot solve those problems for you, but women, ah, women I know and love. I can solve that problem for you, Brother. I do not want your loneliness to dwell on you forever."

But I shook my head; Airioch's idea of the mating was as unlike mine as the moon is unlike the sun.

"Hurry, Airioch," called the wives of Eber Donn. "We have but little time."

Airioch groaned but he stood and dusted off his braichs.

I grinned up at him. "You know that you were released from your promise to Eber Donn's family three days ago. The period of punishment was one year. You need not oblige any longer."

Airioch grinned. "Well, I owe them at least this much, now don't I?" He rubbed his hands together. "Ladies, what is your wish today?" He wrapped an arm around each waist, looked back over his shoulder at me, and winked.

I shook my head. Still laughing, I stood and dusted off my braichs. I chose a flat stone from the beach and skipped it across the still bay. I could not fault Airioch his pleasures. For the past year, Airioch had been husband and father to a host of women and children, had built dwellings and walked his brother's children along the shore and discharged all of his responsibilities like a man on a mission.

I glanced up toward the headland. Perhaps Airioch would have done better with Bile this year. But I owed him at least my attempt to be a father.

In a little while I would climb to the headland and sit beside Bile, give him my brotherly duty. I leaned back against the rock and sighed. In just a little while.

CEOLAS DREAMS OF LONGING
What am I but a man?
A strange and lonely man,
a man composed of words and dreams.
What am I but a dreamer
in a world where no one dreams.
I am as lonely as the wind,

I am as vast as the sea.
Oh, my beloved,
sing to me as wind and sea,
say that I will not be lonely forever.

"Bile, I do not think that they will return among us. We frightened them terribly. As they did us. Perhaps we are better apart from each other."

He shook his head stubbornly.

He had grown tall, this baby brother. At thirteen years, he approached six feet tall. His hair was a sweep of thick darkness, his eyes an expressive gray. His one good arm was well muscled and strong and his legs were thick with muscle. His stump he hid well behind tunics and cloaks. When he did not vocalize, one might think him a strong and well-made man of the Galaeci.

We had long since run out of paper and chalks; Bile had exhausted what supply we had brought on our journey. Those that he carried so carefully rolled under his arm were the record of his life, the Internum Mare, the wild reaches of Spain, the towers of Galicia, our mother and father and Uncle Ith. Now he carved on rock and metal, imitating the spiraling patterns of the Danu, linking them with our own braidwork, incising ogham and spirals onto stones and cups and cauldrons. Our people much prized him for his craftsmanship.

Now I walked around the portal, stood at the opposite side, facing him through the uprights.

"Come back to the village, Brother. I do not think they will come."

He shook his head. He waved his arm at me and began to vocalize, "Ah, ah, ah." His roll of drawings dropped to the ground.

Suddenly there was a flash of blue light. Airmid stood in the doorway. Because I was behind the doorway, her back was to me.

Bile went silent; his face turned crimson that she had seen him vocalizing. He stooped and gathered up his drawings. He shot a baleful look in my direction.

Airmid followed the look, turned around to see me.

"Well hello, Amergin. Have I startled you?" She sounded as though she had seen me only yesterday and not a year ago.

"It is most difficult to accustom to the comings and goings of the Danu."

"I suppose that's true," she said brightly. "You have decided to accompany your brother, then? Are we ready?"

"Ready for what?"

An Scail appeared suddenly, moving through the forest, leaning hard on a beautifully carved cane covered with Danu braidwork. She was puffing with the effort.

"You should have waited for me," she said quietly to Bile when she reached us.

He lowered his gaze. "We are ready," she said to Airmid.

"For what?" I asked again.

"Bile has asked Airmid to evaluate his speech, to see if aught can be done. She has waited for three days past the year mark to accord you their respect of our law."

"It was nothing," said Airmid, waving her hand. "What is three days more or less? Or three years for that matter? Except to this young man."

Bile regarded her solemnly, held his drawings forward.

"I like it not," I said.

"It is not yours to like," said An Scail. "Come then, Bile. Airmid and I have prepared a place to work." And the twosome led Bile away through the woods. I made to follow, but An Scail held up her hand. "Bile will let you know when you may join us," she said.

I was dismissed.

I sat down heavily and leaned my back against the stone.

"Now I am the outsider with my tribe, my teacher, and my brother," I muttered.

Suddenly, there was a crack of blue and Eriu stepped forward into the forest. She was exactly as I remembered her, the long, curling red hair, the sweeping white dress. She looked away into the forest.

"Are you following them?"

She started back when I spoke, turned quickly to face me.

"I did not see you there," she said.

"Well, I never see you or yours coming or going," I replied.

"Where did they go?" she asked.

I gestured toward the forest. "Out there, and I was not invited to accompany them."

"Nor was I."

"I feel much better knowing that."

"A year has not improved your disposition," she said tartly.

"Nor yours it would seem," I said.

"I advised against this plan."

"I do not even know what this plan is."

"Our physicians have some skill with the . . . brain, with the . . . pathways of speech and movement."

"You need not speak as though you speak to a child. Mehmet explained all of this to me when both Bile and Ith became wounded. Pathways become blocked. Sometimes new pathways develop; sometimes they do not."

"Very well; we have techniques to allow new pathways to develop. Airmid told An Scail so and An Scail told Bile. Evidently Bile has petitioned An Scail, and An Scail and Airmid have decided that it would be a fine idea to see what they could do. These two Ancients are harder to control than . . . Morrigu!"

At this I laughed aloud. "I doubt that, but I will say that they are very . . . strong willed, the pair of them. And my little brother becomes just like them, silent and stubborn."

"Airmid came through the portals, in defiance of the ruling. I was so afraid for her."

"Afraid for her? What? Do you think us barbarians that we would molest an Ancient wisdom keeper, wandering in the woods, accompanied by one of our own druids?"

"I do not know," she said, waving her hands at me. "What I have seen of you is dangerous and . . . ill-disposed. Hard to predict. We love Airmid; we have a responsibility to protect her. And off she goes, wandering around your world."

"And what if they damage Bile?"

"They will not damage him! They are physicians of great skill! How could you think that of us?" Her eyes had actually begun to fill with tears.

I stared hard at them; they seemed to me once again overlarge.

"What do you stare at?"

"Your eyes; when you are frightened or sad, they seem to shift shape within their orbs, changeable as the sea and nearly as large."

Now her eyes grew measurably larger; terror flitted across her face.

"Do your people know?"

"Know . . . what?"

She glanced around at the forest as if she expected an answer suddenly to appear. "Do they know that Airmid has been on the Green Isle in defiance of the year ruling?"

"Only Airioch, and he will say nothing."

"Airioch will say nothing?"

"Human beings have immense capacity for change, Eriu. Do not underestimate that capacity; it is larger than any of our other traits."

"For good and for ill, I am supposing."

I inclined my head. "But if we speak of ill, surely we must speak of Morrigu. Does she bear that same capacity?"

"No. She is a constant, is Morrigu. Constant as darkness. Do your people . . . talk of her, talk of the Danu? What do they say in the year that has passed?"

"At first they spoke of nothing else. What they had seen at the Plain of Mag Tuiread terrified them. They wanted to swim after the ships. They wanted to leave the cattle and the horses and the dogs behind and return home on rafts with sails made of their tents. Some of them wanted to run into the sea, preferring drowning to remaining here where the portals could open at any moment."

"She terrifies us as well."

"They were afraid of more than Morrigu, Eriu."

"What do they think they saw?"

"Not think. Saw. I saw it too. Your wounded warriors, those golden-haired Greeks. Our people saw them grow small and tall again, saw their eyes shift shape and return, as yours have just done."

"O you gods!"

I stood, though that may not have improved anything, as I towered over her little frame. She cringed back into the doorway.

"I will not harm you, Eriu," I said softly. "Only tell me the truth. I do not fear the truth."

"The truth is that you very well might hurt me. When last we met, you held me as a shield."

"When last we met, I thought you responsible for all of our troubles on the sea. I was a fool."

"I was no wiser," she said, though she did not leave the doorway. "It might have ended badly were it not for these two Ancients who so frustrate us."

I laughed aloud. "When I think of those two heaving into the circle on that horse."

She began to laugh too; her laughter tinkled like the soft bells that Galaeci women braid into their hair. Our laughter together seemed to make her less fearful. She stepped back out from the doorway and tipped her head up; her eyes were laughing.

"And fearless Banba, asking someone to teach her to ride."

I shook my head. "And she got offers!"

"O Danu, what fools we are, Amergin."

"We were afraid. We did not trust each other. We were strangers. People who act on their fear and their lack of wisdom often make foolish choices."

"A year was wise."

"It was? What do they say of us in your cities?"

"That some of you are worthy of . . . consideration. Of course, Airmid has helped that opinion to prevail."

"What do you say, Eriu?"

"What I say does not matter. It matters what the Danu say."

"It matters to me." I actually put my hand up to my own lips, surprised. Having spoken the words, I knew them to be true.

"I . . . think our life was simpler before you came."

I shrugged. "True enough. Ours was certainly simpler before we came." I felt dismissed, turned to walk away.

"Amergin," she said quietly.

I turned back.

"Given time, I think that it might be more interesting now that you have come."

Her face was tipped up again.

"Your eyes," I said softly; "they are like the sea. They change color and mood and shape. They are . . . quite beautiful, Eriu. I do not fear them."

I watched as her face began to suffuse with color. She stepped back into the doorway.

"I did not mean to offend you. Did I frighten you? I simply spoke the truth. You need not fear the truth with me."

She lifted her triangle.

"Wait!" I commanded. She stopped, her hand held aloft.

"Will you return?" I asked. She stood as if frozen. "Please?" I said it softly, so as not to frighten her.

She smiled. "I will return, Amergin."

She nodded once, then slotted her triangle into the portal and was gone.

I took to waiting at the portal, dressed in my finest tunic. I felt stupid and hopeful all at once, like a boy new with sap. Oh, I made pretense that I was accompanying Bile and An Scail to the doorway, awaiting the arrival of Airmid, but they were not fooled.

Worse, Eriu did not come. For three days I stood there, dressed in my finery, Ceolas by my side, feeling like a great fool as Airmid came through the portal, as she and Bile and An Scail made their lopsided way through the forest, as content and as odd a threesome as ever had lived. On the third day Airmid took pity on me.

"You await Eriu."

"She . . . indicated . . . that she would accompany you. I thought it only . . . courteous . . . that the bard should be here to greet the chief of the Sisters."

"Courteous."

I nodded, but I could feel the hot blood moving under my cheeks. I longed suddenly for Skena, for the sweet familiarity of her touch, for our easy movements together, for the long life that we had planned.

What was I doing here?

"Well." I smiled brightly. "If she will not accompany you, then surely I am not obligated to appear. I have much work of the tribe to do."

"Obligated," said An Scail, nodding. She met the eyes of her Ancient friend. Some message seemed to pass between them.

"Eriu comes with me tomorrow," said An Scail. "For these past days, she has had much work of the Danu to do."

I knew that they were laughing at me, two Ancient women with all the experience of love and change in their past. I hung my head like a stripling boy. Bile slid his hand into mine. I looked down at his face. He smiled, radiant, encouraging. He nodded. Something in his eyes made me feel less stupid, brave.

"You are so brave," I said to him suddenly.

I saw the surprise flare up in his eyes, but I knew it to be the truth. He had moved through his life with determination, learning to walk, drawing with his weak hand. Now whatever work he did with An Scail and Airmid was brave as well. How could I do less than my broken brother? And suddenly I knew that Skena would want me to be here, would want me to heal, to change, to be brave in the world without her. I turned to Airmid.

"Tell her that I will await her tomorrow," I said. "Tell her that I request her presence."

A tiny smile played at the edges of An Scail's lips. Never mind, Skena would say.

Airmid met my eyes. "I will surely tell her, Amergin."

And so she came, her gown a soft sky blue, a vessel for the breeze, the spiraling red hair caught up at the sides, cascading down her back in glorious ringlets that lifted and curled in the wind, all of her seeming to me light as a breeze, vast as the sky. We sat by the portals when the Ancients had departed with Bile. I played Ceolas for her and she tilted her head back and regarded me as I sang. I swam into her eyes, into the secrets there, and I trusted that she would tell them to me when she knew that she could trust me as well. For the first time since Skena had died, I felt hope lift in me, a birdling, a breeze, but singing, singing.

37

CEOLAS SINGS OF AWAKENING DESIRE
I did not think I would love again.
Joy rises in me, trembling.
I am the green force in the leaves,
I am the turn of the tide.
I have been winter, cold and still.
My fires have been banked.
Today, the earth smells green;
the wind is full of promise and the sea.

From behind the portal, from behind the doorway of time that separated them, Eriu could hear the harpsong of Amergin. She sighed
deeply. She was, she knew, the source of the song. Had she skill with the
harp, she too would have been singing. She closed her eyes to the soft
sound of the song, muffled by the temporal distance between them. She
hummed softly in accompaniment. Her heart lifted. She would see him
again! In a moment, in a little moment of time, her tiny hand would rest
inside his, like a ship coming safe into port. Today, she would tell him the
truth. All of the truth. Today he would know who she was, know that she
kept his child safe and well. Today she would trust the great soul of
Amergin with the complicated truth. He would understand it; she knew
this now.

In that sudden knowledge another truth came suddenly to Eriu.

She loved him. Eriu of the Three Sisters, ancient herself and stranger to the place as well, loved Amergin, son of Mil, poet of the Milesians. What would come of that love she knew not, but it moved through her with certainty, with joy. Surely Danu herself rejoiced at this, at the love that bloomed between the people of Mil and the people of the Danu.

"Mother," Eriu whispered. "Make my voice fearless; bless the truth that I will tell."

She stepped toward the portal, raised her triangle toward the key.

"Eriu!" She turned. Banba stood behind her. "Where are you going?"

"I . . ."

Banba stepped up to the doorway, heard the harpsong on the other side of the portal. "Did you not hear it? He is there, the poet."

"Yes . . . I know."

Banba regarded her sister for a long moment. Eriu watched as disbelief flitted across her face, then knowledge, fear, disappointment.

"Were you going to tell us, your Triad Sisters?"

"You meet with him . . . every day?" Fodla's tone was disbelieving.

"For these past weeks, yes. I . . . escort Airmid to the portal, and he brings Bile and An Scail. And when they go off for their work, we sit at the portal and talk until they return."

"Every day? For weeks?"

"I have said so, Banba; why do you taunt me?"

"What do you talk of?" asked Fodla.

"We talk of everything. The world. He tells me of Greece and Egypt. He has told me how Bile was injured so long ago and of how his people traveled in their wagons. I have told him of the earthquake and of how it destroyed our ancient city."

"And did you tell him that you were alive when that happened? That you were a babe on that isle off the coast of Greece?" Banba's tone was caustic.

"No. Here, give me the baby."

Eriu lifted little nine-month-old Skena from Banba's arms and dandled her against her knee, bouncing her up and down. Skena giggled aloud and threw her chubby hands into the air.

"And did you tell him," asked Banba, "that you care for his nine-month-old daughter that he believes to be dead and gone?" Her voice was slow and soft, as though she spoke to a lunatic or an idiot.

"No."

"And do you remain in Metaphor all the while, or are you Danu and just so he thinks you beautiful, with your vast eyes and your fluted, feathered ears, your many long fingers twined in his, in your true form with a thousand years upon you?"

"Enough, Banba," said Fodla. "She talks with him; she does not Braid him or bond with him."

"Thank you, Fodla," said Eriu.

"Not yet," said Banba.

"It is just that you do not talk to him honestly," said Fodla.

"Sisters! Will you allow me no peace, no moment of joy in my existence? I do my duty by the Danu as I always have."

"No one faults your duty," said Fodla quietly. "We worry for your heart."

"My heart is fine."

"At least in those 'moments of joy' with Amergin," said Banba.

"Perhaps I should not say joy. Perhaps I should say pleasantry," said Eriu. She twirled little Skena around and laughed aloud as the baby giggled.

"Have you noticed how pleasantly this baby looks like its mother?" said Banba, her voice caustic.

Eriu dropped down onto a curved chair. She held the baby on her lap. Tears welled up in her eyes. "Oh, Sisters, what should I do? We cannot keep this child from him forever; he is so lonely. Nor can we forever hide our true selves from the Milesians."

"We must do both," said Fodla.

"Precisely," said Banba. "We have no choice. What good would it do him to know of his child? He cannot come into our world to see her; she cannot go into his. The knowledge would lodge in him like a seed; it would grow and give fruit to a bitter and frustrated tree. It would make his loneliness worse, and you would be its cause. His heart would turn against you and then against the Danu, and our tribe would be in danger. We have seen how quick these Milesians are to go to war."

"And as for our appearance," said Fodla. "We have seen that the Milesians are quick to act and slow to think. Already, there are rumors about us from the night of the Battle of Mag Tuiread. They call us 'little people' and 'shape-shifters,' and whisper about our eyes. Were they to see us as we are . . . I believe that they would kill us all simply from the fear of it."

"It would be better," said Banba, "if you did not see him anymore, unless we two are with you."

"But I—"

Banba held up her hand. "We speak from our love of you. You know this. But more, we speak from our love of the Danu. From our duty to our people."

The tears spilled freely from Eriu's eyes then. Banba lifted the baby from her. Fodla enfolded Eriu, holding, hushing. At last her weeping subsided. Eriu sighed, a great gusting of wind. Suddenly she looked old in her tiny body, a vessel for centuries of sorrow. She nodded.

"I have heard you, Sisters, and I know that you are right. I will do as you have said."

He was standing at the portal, on his face a look of anticipation, when the blue light snapped and all three sisters stepped into view.

"Banba," he said courteously, "Fodla. I am glad to see you again." But his eyes did not leave Eriu's face. "Eriu, I have been waiting. I feared that you might not come today. It is almost time for Airmid and An Scail to return with Bile."

"Amergin," she began. "My sisters and I . . ."

"Wait," he said, holding up his hand, his face all smiles. "It is good that you are all here! Today I bring an invitation. The festival of Lughnasa approaches, the feast of samhradh, the warm months. We will celebrate our first planting season here on the Green Isle. There will be a feast and dancing, Banba, just for you, and music and song, poetry, horse races. We will hold a naming ceremony for the Green Isle. We would like for the people of the Danu to be our guests. All who wish to come!"

Eriu stood quietly between her sisters. She shook her head.

Banba tilted her head sideways, regarding him. "Is this the Amergin that once we knew?"

He laughed aloud and shrugged. "I have reason for joy," he said softly, his eyes on Eriu.

"Human beings have a great capacity for change, Banba," said Eriu. She smiled at Amergin sadly. "But I am sorry to say that—"

"Hello, children!"

From the forest Airmid and An Scail came wandering along the path, deep in conversation. Behind them Bile walked side by side with a girl of his own age. Their two dark heads were bent together. The girl was chattering to him of something, and Bile nodded solemnly and then broke into a huge smile. He seemed unaware that anyone else moved in the forest at all. They joined the little group by the dolmen.

"How lovely," said Airmid, "for all of us to be together."

"Who is this?" asked Amergin, gesturing at the young woman.

"This is my . . . foster daughter, Illyn," said Eriu. "She was born of the Fir Bolg." She turned toward Banba and Fodla. "Sisters, did you know of this?"

Banba and Fodla shook their heads, eyes wide.

Illyn came forward and held out both of her hands to Amergin. Amergin extended his to her almost automatically.

"You are Amergin!" she said with delight. "I would know you anywhere. Bile speaks of you constantly."

"He . . . speaks . . . of me?"

"Oh yes," she said. She turned to Bile and in his finger language said rapidly, "He is very handsome, your brother the bard."

"And you are quite the charmer," said Amergin.

"Oh my," said Illyn. "I forgot that you also spoke the finger language."

"Of course you did," said Amergin, but he grinned nonetheless. "She has had some training from you, Banba, I see."

Banba laughed aloud, her tone surprised. Amergin turned to An Scail and Airmid.

"Ancients"—Amergin inclined his head—"I was just asking the Sisters to the Lughnasa Feis," said Amergin. "And all of the people of the Danu who wish to come."

"Of course we will come," said Airmid.

"Ancient," Banba began. "We of the Council Triad—"

"We will be there," said Airmid. "Give notice to the Danu."

*   *   *

"You come to me without your sisters, Eriu; you must be troubled."

Airmid was bent above her instruments, incising notes on leaves of silver.

"I am . . . I do not know . . . oh, Ancient, help me," she said. Tears began to stream from Eriu's eyes.

Airmid stood and regarded her quietly. "I will assume that this sudden shower has to do with Amergin."

"Only that we care for his child and cannot tell him."

"Only that? Then do not worry. Care for the child with all your love and let me worry. If that is all, I will return to work."

But she did not return to work and stood watching Eriu, her head tilted to the side.

"And he thinks me a tall Greek woman with copper hair."

"Why should it matter if he thinks you that? The Milesians seem to think our aspect pleasant enough."

"What does An Scail think of you? In your chosen Metaphor you look so much like her."

"An Scail has seen me as I am; she does not fear it. She came to know me when I was but a voice and she was sightless; she trusted that person in any aspect."

Eriu regarded the Ancient in stunned silence. "You have let her see you?"

"We have worked hard with Bile these past months. First medical work, then therapeutic work. There came a day when Metaphor slipped."

"And what did she say?"

"She said, 'I knew there could not be two in the world who looked as much alike as we.' "

"And that was all?"

"No. She said, 'Choose carefully among the Galaeci those who see you truly.' "

"Wise advice surely. Would you choose Amergin?"

"Ah, so we come to the heart of the matter. It does not matter if I would choose Amergin."

"My sisters say that I must not see him unless they accompany me."

"And what do you say?"

"I am one of the Council Triad."

"What does Eriu say?"

"Ancient, my hours with Amergin at the portal . . . they fill me with . . . joy. And when I am not there beside him, I anticipate the next time that I will be there. And yet, how could he feel that way for me? He knows me not at all. He sees a Greek woman; it is his visits with her that he anticipates."

"And you want him to anticipate his hours with Eriu?"

Eriu nodded. "But I fear that once he sees me as I am, he will not anticipate. He will feel . . . revulsion, fear. He will cease to come to the portal. And I fear that I will put the Danu in danger if he knows. Perhaps my sisters are right; perhaps I should not see him at all."

Airmid nodded. "You think through it well, Daughter. All of these things are possible. But something else is possible too."

"What have I overlooked?"

"It is possible that Amergin loves the soul of Eriu, that his soul is braided to her soul. And that spirit would be the same in any body, would it not?"

"O Danu," Eriu whispered. "I am afraid."

They attended Lughnasa Feis by the hundreds, the Danu garbed in their finest Greek raiment, their diadems and armlets. Banba wore deep red, Fodla soft gold, Eriu a shifted gown of beautiful emerald green, the color of the Green Isle.

For the Children of Mil, the Danu brought gifts, hammered gold torques for the men, spiraling armlets for the women. The Galaeci, who loved fine raiment, put their gifts on with delight and exclaimed their thanks again and again.

Eber Finn had returned from the north with his wife and his clan, Eremon from his rath, and the Milesians were joyful with reunion.

The feasting tables were prepared and spread with abundance; fish steamed in seaweed, deer and boar roasted in deep pits in the ground. For the occasion, a cow had been slaughtered and beef roasted over a turning spit. Honey cakes and loaves of bread, mead and precious wine still remaining from the journey burdened the trestles. While the people were preparing the food, the Galaeci raced horses up and down the beach. The Danu looked on in admiration.

"Come, Banba," cried Airioch. "Try it once again. We all saw you ride before; you were . . . most natural at the horses."

Banba laughed aloud. "Do not taunt me, Airioch Feabhruadh; as I recall I nearly wore you out with dancing!"

She approached a beautiful white horse with trepidation. She walked from one side to the other and stroked his neck gently. At last she placed her hands on either side of his face and blew gently into his nostrils.

She turned. "He has agreed to take me," she said. "But I will need a lift."

The Milesians burst into laughter and Airioch rushed forward to assist her onto his back.

"Use your legs," he whispered softly as he was boosting her up. "He will understand your directions that way."

Banba looked at him. "You do not toy with me?"

"You are far too beautiful for injury," said Airioch, and he grinned. "Now go!" and he smacked the rump of the horse.

At first Banba wobbled from side to side, clinging hard to the horse's mane.

"Hold on!" cried Fodla. "Oh, Eriu, I fear she will be injured!"

"She is Banba," said Eriu. "Watch her."

Halfway down the beach, suddenly Banba shifted position. She sat up straight and then released her arms from the mane. Then, in a single, graceful gesture, she lifted her arms up and out and backward, like the wings of a bird. Her red dress floated out behind her and her black hair streamed backward in the wind. She and the horse seemed to drift gently together, as the sea itself, as wind.

"Ohhhhh," said the people of the Galaeci and the Danu on one great sigh of admiration.

Before Banba had returned to them, Danu were standing in line for their turn to ride, and the Spear Carriers were already bargaining for breeding stock.

"How will we get those great beasts through the portals?" Fodla whispered to Eriu.

"I know not," Eriu replied, "but we will have to think of something. I doubt that the Danu will ever be without such creatures again."

"Call to feast!" shouted Amergin, and there was a rush to the tables followed by silence as the entire company fell to eating. When the tables had been cleared, Amergin stood before the company. He tuned Ceolas and began to sing. Colpa came to one side of him with his little bone whistle; the haunting notes floated out across the company; they were matched by Bile, humming the accompaniment, as always. Amergin drew a deep breath, looked toward Eriu where she sat between her sisters.

"This is our gift to the Danu," he called aloud. "You have let us share your Green Isle; we name her for one of your own: I invoke the land of Eriu," he sang.

> *"Much traveled the abundant sea,*
> *Eire of the wild fruited mountains*
> *Eire of the tumbling waterfalls,*
> *I invoke the land of Eriu."*

On and on he sang, weaving in the rivers and the green forests, the great trees and the fish who swam the waters, returning again and again to his verse, "I invoke the land of Eriu." On the fourth time that he sang the verse, he heard a voice accompany him, male, clear, though the words were slurred and slightly round.

"I . . . voke the wand of Airuu."

He turned. Over his shoulder Bile was singing, his eyes closed, his head tipped back, the speech childlike, but nonetheless speech.

Amergin stopped playing. He stared. Bile opened his eyes and smiled full into the eyes of his brother.

"I um 'ere, Broher," he whispered, "no diffent than fore, but now my voi can sing my 'eart."

Amergin handed Ceolas to Colpa. He stepped to Bile. He pressed his fingers against his brother's lips. He turned toward where An Scail and Airmid were sitting; suddenly he came at them at a run, dropping to his knees before them. Gently he lifted first one ancient hand and then the other, and pressed his lips to the withered fingers.

"This day," he whispered, "in Tir Nan Og, Skena herself is singing."

38

Why joy cannot remain joy always I do not know. Surely it is one of the most sorrowful mysteries.

Our feast was a moment of joy; it was a joy that was not to last.

Bile was the first to see them; he was walking by the sea with his enchanting Illyn when he pointed up toward the headland. I almost expected to hear him vocalize again, his "Ah, ah" sounds puncturing the evening, so unaccustomed was I to his speech.

"Bro'her," he cried. " 'Ere dey come!"

I looked up at the headland. Macha stood silhouetted in the torchlight, his handsome warrior face angry. He was flanked by his two dark warrior companions. Behind them was a company of some two dozen or so. They descended the headland in procession and chaos began again.

Our warriors ran for their weapons, swearing aloud as they strapped on broadswords and bucklers. Eriu and her sisters stood quietly and formed themselves into a triangle, facing the approaching Morrigu. That threesome stopped and did the same.

"We see that there has been a feast among the Danu and the Milesians and we were not invited. We and our companions are deeply offended."

Suddenly, among the Milesians, women began to scream and run for their children. One or two ran into the sea, their infants in their arms.

"Nemhain!" Eriu shouted. "Cease, or this day we will contend, Danu to Morrigu."

"Nemhain," said Macha quietly. "Now is not the time."

The screaming stopped. Women who stood in the sea looked around them, surprised to find themselves there, their babes in their arms.

"What is happening?" I asked softly.

"Her sister curses your women with fear; she has ceased now."

In the triad of Morrigu, one of the threesome turned his head to me and smiled. He tipped his head in a gentle, female gesture and put a slender finger to his lips.

"It was not the intention of the Children of Mil to offend you," I said to the threesome. "We have not seen you in more than a year; we did not know how to find you to invite you."

"Your attentions are for naught now. The feasting is over and my little company is hungry. How shall they feed?" Macha made a little sweeping motion with her arm.

She waved her hand, and those who had accompanied Macha and her sisters straggled into the firelight. They were as terrifying a lot of creatures as ever I have seen in all my travels. Some were ancient stick-men with long, bony arms and huge eyes, their mouths a round and toothless O. Others looked as though they had cobbled themselves of parts, horns of beasts and hooves of goats, their dark eyes flickering with firelight. Women with long, eerie faces of alabaster white were dressed in unrelenting black from their hair to their sweeping gowns.

Our warriors flanked me on all sides now, weapons at the ready, all of them making signs against the evil. My own hand itched to come up and do the same.

"People of the Galaeci, hear me," Eriu called into the darkness. "What you see is not the true appearance of these creatures. They . . . bewitch . . . your minds to see what is not there."

"Yes," said Macha softly. "Eriu knows well how we . . . bewitch . . . your minds."

Airmid stepped forward. "This will cease. You bait them with your repertoire. You delight in their fear. I command you to cease."

Macha tipped her head. "Very well, Ancient," she said. "We shall obey." She tapped the triangle at her neck; her company followed suit.

Suddenly the entire company shrank before our eyes. They appeared to us then as folk of half our size. The heads were huge, their dark hair crackling with some kind of electricity. Their eyes were black as night, huge and ovoid, devoid of any color or expression, their skin a pale and dusty gray. Their ears winged up and back in folded layers tipped with dark feathering. Their arms were extremely long and their hands possessed of long, slender fingers. Macha pointed one of these fingers at me.

"Is this better, Poet of the Milesians?"

I could say nothing. I stood riveted to the spot, speechless, our warriors around me, our women sobbing in the darkness. I have traveled the wide world, but never in my travels had I seen creatures such as these.

Macha tapped her triangle again and her sisters imitated the gesture. Now before us stood three women, all beautiful. Macha had long dark hair, and dark eyes. Her figure was slender and feminine. Her sisters too were dark and compelling. Behind me in the darkness, I heard my brother Eber Finn call out.

"By the gods, oh, by the gods." I heard him fall to the ground, his swords and armor clanging on the stones.

Macha turned toward Eriu. "How easy it is then, is it not, Little Sister? It requires so little to make such a change."

Suddenly Eremon ran forward, his sword outstretched. Macha simply gestured toward him. Lightning traveled up the sword and into his arm. He was lifted off his feet and landed hard on the ground near Eber Finn.

"Almost too easy," said Macha. She heaved a great sigh, then simply turned and walked toward the headland.

Eriu stepped into our silent midst. "Hear me, sons of Mil," she said. All of the faces of the crowd turned toward her, including those of her own people. Banba and Fodla stepped up behind her.

"Among you, have there been those who carried a darkness within them? Who worked not for the good of the tribe, but for other, darker purposes?"

No one made response. The dark power we had seen this night far surpassed anything our people had ever seen.

Suddenly from the crowd Airioch Feabhruadh called aloud. "We must admit to our own darkness. Though such dark creatures as we are look the same on every given day."

His caustic self-criticism broke the mood of terror.

A wave of uneasy laughter moved among us.

"These are our dark ones," said Eriu. "We call them the Raveners. They are ours; we claim them so. They journeyed here with us from . . . Greece. But we of the Danu bear no such dark magic. Our magic is of science, our portals and our spears. You have come here among us, unaware of what awaited you. We tell you this now. We, the Children of the Braid, do here declare that you are under our protection. Call upon us and we will come to your side. We will meet you at the doorways between our worlds. For all of time, I do declare that we will be your friends and your companions."

Behind her suddenly her warriors began to range up with their Light Spears; her physicians encircled her. I saw the look of gratitude flood across her face.

"We will defend you with our knowledge and presence, with our Light Spears and our Silver Arms. When you are ill, our physicians will heal you. We ask that we do not return to our ways of a year ago. Here at the feasting table, we have known joy together. We offer you our friendship; we ask you to return it in kind."

Some of our people backed away. I could see others shaking their heads in the negative. But Eremon and Airioch stepped forward.

"Eriu of the Danu, we have heard you," said Eremon. "I and my clan accept your offer of friendship."

"As do I and mine," said Airioch.

Eber Finn said nothing, but I felt gratitude for the courage of my brothers wash over me.

An Scail came up beside me. She whispered softly. "I think this night that our people begin what will be a long and troubled relationship with the Children of the Danu."

"Troubled defines it well," I whispered back.

Eriu spoke again. "We thank you for the hospitality of this wondrous night. Accept our apology that these of ours have sundered the celebration. We will depart from you to give you time to contemplate these things."

She met my eyes; hers were brimming with sadness, and as usual, they were overlarge.

When the Danu had left us, I helped Eber Finn to his feet. He lay where he had fallen, still as a log but for the look of terror on his face.

"We have seen these before," said Eremon. "At the Plain of Mag Tuiread. Granted not as horrible as what we have seen tonight. But, Brother, you are a warrior. You set a bad example for your clan."

Eber Finn hissed under his breath. "Brothers, I must speak with you." He glanced around, saw his wife with a group of women by the fire, their heads bent low in whispered conversation. "Alone," said Eber Finn.

We settled in my dwelling, Airioch, Eber Finn, Eremon, and I. At the last moment, Colpa and Bile ducked beneath the door of the dwelling.

"We are brothers too," said Colpa.

"You have but fourteen years upon you," Eremon began, but Airioch held up his hand.

"There is much wisdom in these little brothers. They should stay."

Eber Finn cleared his throat, looked at the assembled company.

"My wife does not like the north."

"Then return back to us here at Inver Skena," said Airioch. "We have missed you; how easy it is."

"It is not easy," said Eber Finn quietly. "It . . . there is a woman in the north. I have been . . . bedding her for quite some time. She . . . was most beautiful. And she knew . . ." He glanced at our two youngest brothers. "She knew of new and pleasurable ways to mate that my wife did not know."

Airioch shrugged. "So what of this? It is the way of the Galaeci to like the mating."

"The woman," said Eber Finn. "It is she that you saw tonight."

"Who?" said Eremon. "One of the sisters?"

"Not Banba I hope," said Airioch, grinning. "I would still have designs there had I not so many wives wearing me out."

But I was watching Eber Finn's face; it was white as the sea foam, his eyes large and unfocused.

"O you gods," I said softly. "You have been mating with Macha."

"I have," he said. "In this last visage you have seen. I had not seen her as a man. Nor had I seen her as . . . whatever those dark-eyed little folk were. I have all along been mating with . . . that . . . and I did not know. My wife." Here he looked again at our youngest brothers. He swallowed and closed his eyes. "She came upon us once in a wooded glade. She flew into a fury and cast herself upon us. She tried to scratch at the eyes of Macha—she did not call herself that, Brothers—and Macha simply stood, naked in the clearing, lifted her arm, and threw my wife to the ground."

He shook his head. "I scrambled to help my wife. I voiced my anger at . . . Macha, but my wife stopped speaking to me entirely. And when

Macha came again for me, with her raven hair and her pendulous breasts, I went."

Airioch put up his hand. "You will move back among us; you will never see her again. You will be an attentive husband and father. Your wife will come to forgive you."

"No," said Eber Finn. "There is more. My wife has made a friend among the people of the north. She is a woman, a warrior. She has taught my wife the ways of war, to swing a broadsword and wield a dagger, to move in the forest silent as the deer. She has whispered to her that Eremon got the better piece of land, that he builds a better rath, that he is safer and happier where he is. My wife stirs our people to come against Eremon."

Eremon shook his head. "But why should they do so? Clan is clan."

"Because the woman is Banbh," I said softly.

"Banbh?" said Eremon.

"Sister of Macha, Brothers. She is the bringer of war."

"Still," said Eremon, "your clan will not come against me. I am your brother."

"Our cattle fail, our crops wither in the ground. Our children are thin and the darkness around us moves with strange lights and odd noises."

"Because the Morrigu causes such things to happen; those sisters feed upon destruction and rage, confusion and greed," I said. "Think clearly, Eber Finn."

"I think that my clan will come against you, Eremon. And my wife will be at their head."

"And where will you be?" asked Eremon.

"They are my clan; I am their chief. I wish to remain as chief; I wish to return my wife to me."

"But you need not do that with war," said Airioch. "Hear me, Brother."

"You are not really my brother, are you?" said Eber Finn. He stood and left the dwelling.

"I am sorry for that last, Airioch," I said softly.

"My broher," said Bile. He held forth his good arm and Airioch clasped it.

Eremon followed suit.

Colpa looked thoughtful. He turned toward Airioch. "Each day before us there are choices. For good or evil. For strength or weakness. For care of the tribe or care of the self. Is this not what you have taught me, Brother?"

Airioch nodded.

"You have taught him this?" I regarded Airioch.

"I had to learn it the hard way," said Airioch.

"But that is what Eber Finn is doing," said Colpa. "Do you see? We cannot blame the Morrigu entirely. They put choices before Eber Finn, before his wife. They are choosing badly."

"Very wise indeed," I said.

"What shall we do?" asked Eremon.

"I do not know," I said. "We shall try to keep him here with us. We shall hope that his thinking clears. We shall pray that brother will not come against brother."

CEOLAS SINGS OF DARKNESS
Why must you move in the world,
Sower of evil, bringer of sorrows?
And why do we turn toward you,
Licking our lips for desire,
Losing ourselves to sate a hunger?
Who are you, darkness?
Why are you always among us?

39

"he has been waiting at the portal for more than a fortnight." Banba shook her head. "Ever since the night of the feast."

"He waits at the rising of the sun and he returns after sunset. It makes my heart ache to see it," said Fodla.

"What would you have me do? You were the two who told me not to see him. I have done as you asked."

"Well, we were wrong," said Banba. "It has been known to happen before. And we have made you both miserable."

"Well, I happen to think that you were right after all," said Eriu.

"If you let Morrigu change your mind," said Fodla, "then she has won."

"It is not Morrigu," said Eriu. "It is what they saw inside Morrigu. They saw Morrigu without her Metaphor and they were repulsed, terrified."

"But we look nothing like the Raveners."

"Of course not," said Banba. "Not to us. But Eriu fears that perhaps to them we would. Perhaps they would see us and see our common ancestry. Perhaps they would think that we are all evil, as Morrigu is. Perhaps this poet of Eriu's would take one look at her without her Greek Metaphor and run screaming for the sea, having lost his mind, a gibbering idiot, reduced to drooling in terror for all of time."

"Banba!" said Fodla. "You go too far."

"She does it to make me see my foolishness," said Eriu softly. "And she is right. But there is more than just my fear that a human man cannot love a Danu woman. We have his child and she is trapped with us and he is trapped in his world."

"But neither of them knows that," said Banba softly. "Skena is the happiest of babies, and Amergin has put aside his grief for his lost wife. He loves a woman of the Danu. It shines from his eyes. Did you hear his song? He calls the place Eire—the land of Eriu."

"And if he sees me as I am?"

"Why is that necessary? Let him see you as your Metaphor. If I were to succumb to Airioch's invitations, as I just might one of these days, I would surely encounter him as that Greek woman he seems so smitten by. Why not do the same?"

"Because I do not want Amergin to be smitten by a Greek woman. It will be more than just mating, Banba. I love him; I love his eyes and his hair and his big human frame and his soul and his song. I will not cease to love him. I will love him when we both have left these bodies and have gone into the Braid."

"And you want him to love you as you are," said Fodla softly.

"Is that too much to want?" asked Eriu.

"There is only one way to know that," said Banba.

Moonlight was streaming over the clearing when she came through the portal, the blue light snapping shut behind her.

He was seated with his back against the rock, Ceolas on his lap, but he leaped to his feet as she stepped into the clearing.

"I thought that you would never come again."

"I considered never coming again."

"But why?"

"We terrified your people and wreaked havoc on your Lughnasa feast. Is that not enough?"

"Eriu, we Galaeci can wreak havoc all by ourselves. Even now, my brother Eber Finn threatens to make war against my brother Eremon."

"Why?"

"Because his wife wants Eremon's land. Because Eber Finn has been mating with . . ." Amergin paused.

"Macha! In one of her guises." Eriu waited for his answering nod. "You see, it all comes back to her, doesn't it? She likes you; she finds the Galaeci complex and troublesome. You are her favorite new target. I am ashamed of that, ashamed that she is related to the Danu. And I fear all the trouble that she will cause you."

"As my brother Colpa says, Eber Finn had to choose for her as well. But that is not all, is it? I have waited for you for almost one full waxing of the moon."

Eriu sighed. "I know. I have stood on the other side of the portal and listened to Ceolas."

"Why did you not come to me?"

"Because you are right. Macha is not all that troubles me. Is there somewhere we can go, Amergin? Somewhere where your kinsmen cannot happen upon us."

"There is the dwelling where An Scail and Airmid taught Bile to speak. It is that way"—he pointed—"through the forest."

"Take me there," she said softly. "There is something I would show you."

He built up the fire, shook out the pelts and skins. When the little conical hut was warm and bright, he took her hands. "Show me," he said quietly.

She withdrew her hands, took a long, deep breath. "O Danu, I am afraid."

"Of me? I would never harm you, Eriu."

"This I know," she said softly. "I am afraid of me."

She raised a trembling hand to the triangle at her neck. She closed her eyes and tapped it once. She remained quite still, her eyes closed.

"Open your eyes, love," he whispered softly.

She opened them.

"Can I . . . touch you?" he asked softly.

"Yes," she said, her voice broken and small.

He ran his hands gently along her cheeks, then traced a finger gently along the multiple curves of the ear, threading up along the fine feathering there.

"Like shells of the sea," he whispered softly.

He slipped his fingers into her curls and watched as they slipped back into place with sparks of electricity. He leaned back.

"I remember these eyes," he said softly. "I have been watching for them ever since I first saw the magic of them hidden inside the . . . Other. How beautiful they are, how like a sea, turquoise and blue and gray. I feel as though I could drift away inside them."

She sat very still, her long fingers pressed together. He lifted them quietly, pressed his lips to each hand.

"You are not still afraid, are you?"

"I am," she said softly. "You can see that I am not . . . human."

"I have known that something else was underneath your guise from the night that I held you on the Plain of Mag Tuiread. I could feel the tiny fragility of your bones beneath my arms. And I have seen your eyes and the eyes of your companions."

"I do not repulse you?"

"You are like quicksilver, like moonlight on water, like the water itself. I would think that I might frighten you, all of us Galaeci, great hairy beasts that we are."

"You have never seen the Fomor," said Eriu. A small smile played at the edges of her lips.

"They must be hairy beasts indeed, then."

A little laugh escaped her; it sounded half like a sob. "Oh, they are." She shook her head. "I thought that you would find me . . . frightening, that you would see in me the Morrigu."

"How could I see her at all? She seemed to me a wizened lump of darkness, a void where there should be color and light. But you; you are all color and light. It is like looking at the sun upon the water. Oh, Eriu, for months we have sat side by side against the portals and we have talked of all the world. I hear the same voice that I heard beside me. It is the voice that I love. Beyond that . . . how magical you are, how delicate and beautiful to me. I am almost afraid to touch you."

"Touch me here," she said softly, putting her hand against his lips. "Touch your lips to my lips. I have been longing for it, Amergin."

"Ah, sweeting," he said softly. "So have I."

And the kiss, when it came, was like a feather, like a breeze, oh, like a promise.

CEOLAS SINGS OF LOVE REBORN
My heart, oh my resilient heart,
My joy, oh you my joy.

I am laughter once again
I am sweet desire
I am a man made whole in you.
How shall I bless you, love
For this gift of yourself
Perfect as you are?

40

"Two go 'mong them, Amer'in."

"But why, Bile? Are you not happy here among the clan?"

At fifteen he had become a giant of a boy, long and lean, with a quick smile. He turned to look at Illyn, and I saw the shining black braid that cascaded down his back. I knew that she must have braided it for him. His good hand held tight to Illyn's hand. He inhaled.

"'Ear me, Amer'in," he said. "Once when I 'as 'oung," he struggled.

"Young," I said.

He nodded. "We 'ere live ina t . . . tower by the sea. I woke dark."

"You woke in the dark?"

He nodded. "You 'ere stand window, arms round Skena. I watch." He took a deep breath. It was still difficult for him to string together multiple sentences. I had to hold myself back from saying it for him.

He continued. "I 'oped one day I love someun 'ike 'at."

"And you have found that with Illyn?"

He nodded. "More. I wish two"—he held up his fingers, falling automatically into his old finger language—"arms, two wrap round Illyn I love."

"That is not possible," I said. "And surely that does not matter to Illyn; she loves you as you are."

"I do," she said softly, smiling up at Bile.

"Is," said Bile. "Possbe."

"What do you mean?" I looked at An Scail and Airmid.

Airmed took a deep breath. "You know that we have physicians of great skill among us."

I waved my hand. "I know who you are and where you are from. I know how old you are."

She smiled and her whole mien relaxed. "Good," she said. "She has told you everything." She nodded. "We can restore his arm," she said.

"With a Silver Arm?"

"No. A real arm with nerves and sinews and bones. It is a technique that my brother and I perfected . . . long, long ago."

"But we have been among you now for three years. Why did you not restore it before?"

"In the beginning, to have done so would have frightened your people too much. But they have grown . . . accustomed to our oddities now, although they still see us in Metaphor. A new arm, more or less, will no longer frighten them."

I thought about this for a while and realized that it was true. I smiled, and shook my head. "True enough," I said. "Will Bile be in danger or in pain?"

"No."

"Then I say that it should be done."

"There is one other thing," she said softly.

Bile spoke then. "Go 'mong."

"To go through the portal?"

He nodded.

I looked at Airmid. "Will he be able to return?"

"Yes."

"But I too have asked Eriu if I can travel through the portal; she has denied me."

Illyn smiled at me. "What do you see when you see me, Poet?"

"I see a bright and beautiful girl of the Fir Bolg. I see my brother's beloved. Why?"

"Would it surprise you to know that when the Danu took me in I had a harelip and a clubfoot?"

"They . . . repaired these, as they will Bile's arm?"

"They did."

"I am less fearful, then, seeing you here whole and well."

"Would it surprise you also to know that I was . . . slow and stunted, unable to speak?"

"That would surprise me greatly. I see no trace of that young woman before me now."

"To repair those damages, it was necessary for the Danu to blend some of their braid with mine. I am Fir Bolg and Danu. This is why I can come and go through the portals as the Danu do."

"You are . . . as old as the Danu?"

"No. Nor will I live to their age. But I will live much longer than you will live, Amergin. I am a Hybrid of the Braid."

I turned to Bile. "And this is what it will take to repair the arm? You too will be a Hybrid?"

Airmid answered. "We will repair the arm and the pathways in the brain to make it work and we will clear the pathways of his thought and speech. . . . And yes, he will be a Hybrid of the Braid. He will be as Illyn is. He will live as long as she lives. He will have two good arms and perfect speech and he and Illyn will be together for a long life."

"I fear this," I said softly. "And at the same time I wish it."

"Good," said Airmid. "Because I am very old and have little time."

"You have been saying that for as long as I have known you," said An Scail.

"It has been true for at least that long. You are no blushing maiden yourself, Ancient." The two burst into laughter.

"For myself," I said softly. The idea formed completely as soon as I spoke it. "I wish it for myself as well."

Airmid shook her head. "I cannot give you that gift," she said softly. "We cannot tamper with what the Braid has made whole. You are well and strong. Our law permits us to repair that which is damaged; we do that in the name of the Braid, that all of her children be made whole. But I cannot tamper with what is not damaged. It is Danu law."

"What would happen if I went through the portal with Bile?"

"You would never be able to come back again," she said softly. "If you did, all that you knew and loved would be gone. You would instantly age into a withered and ancient old man and you would die among strangers. That is why Eriu denies you; it is her love for you that makes her say you nay."

"Then it must be my love for Bile that lets him go," I said softly.
The light in his face tore at my heart as he threw his arms around me.

CEOLAS SINGS OF BELONGING
When you go among them, Brother,
Take my soul for keeping
For I cannot go with you,
I cannot be of them.
Journey with my spirit
To the children of the Light,
Carry me into belonging.

"Brother, awaken." It was Colpa, his frame bending low to move through the doorway.

"I am awake," I said softly into the darkness. I had been lying awake for hours staring at the ceiling of my dwelling, my heart hammering with fear for Bile. I had stood with him as he stepped into the portal, lifted his good hand to me. Then he had raised the triangle that the Danu had given him, pressed it into the slot in the portal, and disappeared into an eclipse of blue light.

Eriu had stood beside me, silent, her hand on my arm.

"I am afraid," I said softly. "And I am . . . envious. He goes where you go. And if all goes well he will be able to come and go, while I wait here, forever at a portal, waiting for your return, stealing little moments with you until I die."

"I will always come to you, love. Forever."

I bent my frame and closed my arms gently around her; even in Metaphor I was always aware of her delicate fragility. It was one, only one, of the reasons I loved her.

"And all will go well. Bile will be back among you soon, with two good arms and a tongue as glib as that of his brother."

But it had been six weeks and Bile had not yet returned. Each time Eriu came through the portal I looked anxiously for Bile, for Airmid, but they did not accompany her. Though she protested that all was well, I wished to see my brother with my own eyes.

"Amergin!"

I bolted upright. "I am sorry, Colpa. I worry for our brother. Why do you keep such late hours?"

"Eremon approaches at the headland. He is gravely wounded. He brings with him the wounded of his tribe and those of Eber Finn's who have survived. He needs you to send for the Danu physicians."

"Oh no. O you gods! Eber Finn has gone against Eremon then. I will punish him dearly for this."

"I think not," said Colpa quietly. "Eber Finn is dead."

"No. Oh no."

I threw on my braichs and ran from the dwelling. My bare feet drove against the stones as I ran. Eremon was staggering down the hillside, leading a horse on which one of his own warriors was draped. Blood ran down Eremon's face and leg, down the side of the great beast.

"He came in darkness," he said softly. "Against his brother he came in darkness."

"Where is he?"

He gestured back. I ran along the line of horses, of men supporting their wounded brothers. Eber Finn was dangling over the back of a great black horse. His eyes were wide and white, his mouth surprised. His head was nearly severed from his neck. Perched on the flank of the horse was a large black raven.

"Get you gone!" I screamed. I swatted at the bird, which rose into the darkness, cawing out.

"Keep away from us, bringers of darkness," I cried.

"Amergin." Colpa was beside me, Airioch straggling up the headland behind him. "You must find the Danu physicians or we will lose many more."

I turned. I began to run toward the portal, my bare feet cut and bleeding now with trampling over stones.

I saw a figure running toward me in the darkness. I reached for my sword and remembered that I had come away swordless.

"Halt!" I cried. "Or I will cut you where you run."

The voice that came from the darkness was familiar, strong and whole.

"It is I, Brother. Bile. We have heard of this tragedy. I bring the Danu physicians."

He emerged from the shadows and embraced me, his two strong arms closing around me.

"Light!" he cried, and the Danu physicians lit their ice-blue torches as they followed us down the path.

Bile was gathering his drawings and some of the tools that he used to etch in metal and stone. We had sent Eremon, healed and much saddened, back to his rath, which he had called Tara. The wounded of Eber Finn's tribe had remained here among us at Inver Skena. Now that several days had passed, they seemed to be shaking off some horrible malaise, to be themselves shocked that the sons of Mil had turned against each other. I had seen great warriors standing by the sea, their arms around each other's shoulders locked in shame and weeping. I shook my head.

"It will be well," said Bile.

"Will it? Sometimes I think it will never be well, that the smallest time of joy will always be followed by sorrow or crisis."

He smiled at me. "This is not the Amergin who raised me," he said softly.

"I know," I said. "I suppose that I am lonely."

He knelt before me and clasped my upper arms.

"Do you think I would ever abandon you, Brother? You who have loved me from the start, and in all my imperfections?"

I shook my head at the beauty of him, at the completeness of his arms and his speech. "I cannot believe it is you," I said softly.

"Nor I," he replied. "I dwell in this body with such joy and gratitude." He jammed a few more tools into his leather pack.

"You will dwell among them now?"

Bile smiled. "No, Brother. Do not fear. I will go back and forth with my goods and my gear. The portal will be snapping so often that you will forget that there is any other kind of doorway."

"What are their cities like?" I asked. I knew I sounded like a lost and plaintive child, but Bile seemed to understand.

"How you would love it," he said softly. "This world is . . . the same world, but . . . different. It is so hard to explain. The cities are beautiful, Brother, crystal and soft fabrics billowing and music as soft as wind and chambers where memory is stored like the stories of Ceolas." He shook his head. "I cannot describe it; I will bring you a sketch when next I come."

"I will miss you," I said softly. It was not that he seemed different, so much, but that he seemed so much himself, so much the young man that I had thought he would grow to be before we left Egypt, before the wagon. And that he would now become different. And that the new man would come to prefer the country of the Danu. How strange and simplistic our journey must seem to him now, our wagons and our ships. He had gone beyond us, beyond our knowledge.

"How Skena would delight for you. For your recovery. How she would love to see you this way, restored."

"She would delight for you too, Brother. For your love for Eriu."

"It seems a long, long time ago, does it not?"

"To you too?" Bile said softly. "How often I wished to talk to you about it, Amergin. All of it. Egypt and the isles. Uncle Ith. Our tower by the sea. And Skena . . . oh, I . . . brought you something, Brother, while I remember." He rummaged around in his bag and brought up a roll of fresh parchment. "They have supplies for me to draw again. Although I'm still drawing with my left hand, that being the hand I'm accustomed to. Maybe soon I'll draw with both hands," he said, grinning.

He spread out his roll of sketches and began to page through them. "There is a child among them. Perhaps two years old or a little more . . . Ah, here she is."

He drew forth a sketch and laid it before me.

I stared at the little face, the thick, curling hair. "O you gods!"

"So you do see what I see? Does she not look like Skena?"

"She is the portrait of Skena. Who is she?"

"Illyn did not know. She said she thought she was a Fir Bolg child, a new Hybrid of the Braid. She said the Three Sisters themselves care for the child as they did for Illyn. I would have asked Airmid, but then Eber Finn went against our brother." He shrugged. "Illyn and I will ask her when I return."

I looked long at the little sketch.

"May I keep it?" I asked quietly. "Perhaps Eriu will know."

41

Eriu came through the portal in Metaphor. She looked around her, as she always did, for any of the sons of Mil who might have accompanied Amergin. When she saw none, she tapped her triangle and folded down into herself, the tiny wide-eyed woman of the Danu.

Amergin looked into her eyes. "You are troubled, love."

"Have I become that easy to read?"

"Yes; your eyes are their own story. Is Bile unwell?"

"No. Bile is well and happy and sends you greetings. He and Illyn will come through the portal at the new moon."

"Then what? Speak quickly or my mind will anticipate the worst."

"It is Airmid. She has taken to her chamber. She says that soon she will return to the Braid. She wishes to see An Scail."

"I will tell our An Scail."

"No! You cannot! Airmid is not well enough to come through the portal, and if An Scail were to go to her . . ."

"She too would die?"

"She would, Amergin. She could never return through the portal. The minute she returned, she would die."

"Then Airmid will die without her. They are as twin daughters of two different worlds. An Scail will never forgive me if Airmid departs this world without her, and yet, I cannot put An Scail in danger. I don't know what to do. What is the right thing to do?" He stood and began to pace around the tiny hut, rapping a rolled scroll of papers on his hand.

"What do you carry, love?"

He looked down, surprised. "Oh, I forgot that I carried it. It is some sketches that Bile made for me among your people."

"Let me see."

Amergin opened the sketches out onto the little table in the hut. The first was of a city, all spires and intricate scrollwork, all crystalline light and color.

"Tara," said Eriu softly. "How beautifully he captures its magic. But you must hide these, Amergin. Your people would be frightened to see so vast and complex a city in a place where they could not 'see' it at all."

He folded out the next one.

"O Danu," said Eriu softly.

"Who is she?"

Eriu drew a deep breath. She closed her eyes. "I have feared this day for so long, and now that it has come, I find that I am glad."

"Speak clearly; you frighten me."

"Clearly then. She is Skena's child. We call her Skena. Skena's child and yours."

"This is not possible. I saw Skena and Ir. I burned their bodies on the seashore. What have you done? Have your people worked some dark magic?"

"No magic, love. Their bodies washed up on the shore. Skena and Ir were gone; their bodies had been too long without breathsong. But the child in the womb; she lived, Amergin! Her heart beat. But she was too small to yet live outside the womb, so . . . Airmid took her from the womb and took her into our cities and kept her alive there until she was ready to come into the world."

"Kept her alive?"

"Yes, love, in a Danu womb cradle."

"She was born of a Danu woman?"

"No. No. It is a womb cradle, a cradle of life fluid. Airmid used Skena's life fluid. She is a beautiful child, Amergin. Happy and sweet and loving. She is as Skena must have been."

He stood staring down at her, his expression horrified. Suddenly, he leaned forward and lifted her into the air with his great hands, until her eyes were level with his.

"Are you telling me that I have a child of almost three years? That she lives and is well? And that you never told me?"

Eriu spoke very softly. "Yes," she said. "That is what I am telling you."

"O you gods!" He released her, staggered backward, away from her. "I see now that you are like Morrigu after all. All deception. All subterfuge. All this time that you have proclaimed your love for me. And instead you have been keeping this secret. This terrible secret. You have been keeping me from my child. You knew how much I loved Skena. You knew. Oh, my child!"

The sound wrenched from him like a cry thrown to the heavens.

Eriu began to weep, the huge tears falling from her eyes. She tapped her triangle and folded into Metaphor, the tall red-haired woman of old.

"I am sorry, Amergin," she whispered. "Please forgive me."

"How can I forgive this? Oh, my child. I would see my child."

Suddenly his hand flashed forward; he closed it around Eriu's triangle and yanked with all his might. Her head jerked forward, but the pendant did not come loose.

"Please, love," she whispered. "Please do not make me hurt you further. You cannot go into our world."

Amergin yanked again hard, the triangle in his palm.

Eriu reached into his palm. She touched the triangle once. A bolt of lightning shot up Amergin's arm. He was knocked back onto the ground; the cloth of his tunic smelled of burning.

Eriu was weeping, her tiny body shaken with sobs. She stepped into the portal, leaned against it weeping.

"Think, love," she whispered. "Please. I know that you will understand."

He gathered himself to his feet and launched toward her with a roar, his face a mask of rage. She pressed her triangle into the portal. In a flash of blue light, she was gone.

42

I ran. Away from the portal. Away from the hut in the forest where I had loved her. Away from the village of our people. I ran like a man possessed by demons. It seemed to me that I ran forever. At last I came to the shores of a small lake, and there I collapsed onto the shore. I wept for a while, like a child. Then, for a time, I raged, heaving rocks into the water, screaming my rage at the sky.

When I had exhausted myself at last, I leaned against some boulders there by the water and closed my eyes. I must have slept. When I awoke, a soft dusk was beginning to fall over the water. I saw a woman walking toward me along the shore of the lake.

She was a woman of the Galaeci, tall with dark auburn hair, her plaid cloak undulating with her as she walked. She moved closer and I was able to see her clearly.

It was Skena.

I stood, unthinking, and ran to her, drew her into my embrace.

I ran my hands through the thickness of her hair, lifted her face to mine. She returned my ardor, lifted on tiptoe and pressed her lips against mine.

"Oh, love," I whispered. "Oh, how I have missed you."

I unpinned the cloak and watched it drop to the beach. Underneath she wore her finest silk tunic, and I watched as she shrugged it from her and stood before me. Her belly was flat and white. I ran my hand over it.

"They took our child," I whispered. "They took her from us."

She said nothing at all, just lifted her arms around my shoulders and pressed into me, her long white nakedness gleaming in the evening light. She smiled. "Come," she said softly, seductively. "Remove your cloak."

I tilted my head sideways. It was not Skena's voice. Not the voice that I remembered.

"How is it that you have come to me?" I said.

"That was easy, love. Now come to me." The voice was throaty, deep, seductive.

"Macha!" I pushed her from me. "What have you done? Where is my Skena?"

Macha laughed aloud; she folded down into the male warrior form that I knew best, stood before me naked on the beach.

"Your Skena is dead, of course."

"This is cruel."

She shrugged, nodded. "Well, cruel, I suppose, from your point of view. From mine, it is a game."

She shifted again. Before me on the beach was a black wolf with gleaming yellow eyes. It bared its fangs at me and growled.

I arched my head backward and exposed my neck.

"Here," I said, "I offer it to you."

She folded back up again, a tiny gray Danu with dark ovoid eyes.

"You do not find it cruel that the great poet of the Galaeci would be found dead by the shores of a lake, his throat torn out by a wolf, all his golden words ripped away from him?"

"More ironic than cruel, Macha."

She burst into laughter. "Very good, Poet. This parsing of the language, the subtle shades of meaning."

I shrugged. "Is this what you did to my brother?"

"Eber Finn? There was almost no challenge there. It wasn't quite as easy as terrifying the Fir Bolg in the forest, but it came close." She shifted again, a beautiful woman with large breasts and long hair. She lifted the breasts in her hands, ran her tongue over her lips. "As easy as this. Eber Finn was captivated by human breasts and a human tongue. His wife was captivated by her own rage; my sisters and I do no more than feed what is there."

"What did you hope to feed in me?"

"Betrayal. Betrayal is always a good doorway," she said.

"Why?"

"Why do we do it?"

I nodded.

"It is . . . what we do. What we are. Always. Many forms. Many worlds." She smiled, shifted again as Skena. "Some find us . . . comforting."

"I do not," I said. "Skena was real and I loved her. We had a child."

She shifted, the tall woman with dark flowing hair. "Well, that is a child that you will never see."

"No," I said softly.

"But I can help you there," she said softly. She reached behind her neck and withdrew the triangular pendant. She put it into my hand. "Now go and get her," she said softly. "Just press the triangle into the recess in the portal. Go and get her and bring her back into your world where she belongs, among your people."

I looked down at the pendant in my hand. "Why would you do this for me?" I asked softly.

"She is your child. You deserve to have her. The Sisters should never have kept her from you." She pointed at the far side of the lake. "Do you see the dolmen?"

I nodded.

"It is a doorway, just as the portals are. You may enter there."

I turned toward the dolmen, the triangle in my hand. I thought of my child, Skena's and mine. Something that Eriu had said stopped me in my tracks. I turned back toward the Macha.

"And if I find my child and I bring her among our people . . . she will die. Of course. That is why you have offered me this key. My child will die. She has lived among the Danu for many years."

"Not right away," said Macha with a shrug. "For a time she would look like this." She folded back into her metaphor of Skena again. "That would be a comfort to you, would it not?"

"Yes," I said softly.

"Well, there you are." She pointed again at the dolmen. "Go and get her."

"But my comfort would cost her life. Oh, Eriu. Oh, love. Now I see. My comfort would cost my child her life."

I looked up at Macha, where she stood before me. "Dark one," I said. "You have helped me to see Light."

"I have?" She looked nonplussed, angry. She folded out of Skena and into the form of a Ravener, the dark-eyed Danu.

"Skena would be very proud of you," I said. "And Eriu."

I held the pendant with its triangle out to her.

"Keep it!" she snapped. "I do not enjoy you, Amergin. I do not like the way you play the game."

"Thank you," I said. "I am gratified to hear it."

CEOLAS SINGS OF SACRIFICE
I will keep you safe,
Child of my heart,
Child of my first love,
As Eriu has kept you safe
Within the walls of Tara.
Now do I see clearly;
More worlds than ours,
More loves than one,
More sacrifices asked of us
that love must give.

I knelt before An Scail and put the pendant gently into her hand. "Airmid is dying," I said softly. "This pendant will take you to her. But if you use it, know that you will not be able to return to us. To return would be death."

"Why do you give me this?"

"Airmid is your friend. And they have my child among them."

"Eriu bore you a child?" She shook her head, confused.

"Skena bore me a child. They have kept that child alive. She dwells among the Danu. She cannot come into this world or she will die. I cannot go into that world, for if I do I can never return."

"And yet you give me this knowing that I would have to remain with them or return and die."

"All of our life you have given to our tribe. You endured years of separation from Ith and came here with us when I knew that you would rather have remained among the Wise Ones in Galaeci. You trained me in the druid ways and now you train Colpa. Yet I know well enough that Airmid is your sister in spirit. The choice should be yours."

"And why do you not use the triangle to go among them? Bile is there and Eriu and now your child."

"I am Poet of the tribe; I cannot leave the tribe."

She regarded me for a long time, then placed an ancient hand against my face. "I love you my sweet, sad boy."

I nodded my head. I could say nothing.

"Take me to the portal," she said softly.

At the doorway, I raised my hand to her.

"Live well among them, Ancient," I said.

She smiled. "I have lived well, Amergin. I have lived well indeed." And then she was gone.

I do not know how long I sat in that forest. Day passed into night and then into day again. Eriu did not come to the portal. I knew that she would never come again. I had seen to that with my anger and my lack of understanding. Beyond that door were those I loved. Eriu and Bile. An Scail and my child, unknown to me. And I would never see them again. And I would never be able to go among them.

At last I stood and dusted off my braichs. I turned back toward our village. I had moved only a few steps toward the path when I heard the distinctive crack of the portal. I turned, expecting to see Eriu, hope rising in my heart. An Scail stood in the doorway.

"No!" I screamed. "No! Why did you return?"

I could see that she was folding down into herself; her ancient face looked withered, her body frail and brittle. I rushed to the portal and gathered her into my arms.

"Why, An Scail? Why?"

She smiled softly. "Airmid has passed," she said. "Wake us together; that is our wish." She pressed the pendant with its shimmering triangle into my hand.

"Oh, why?" I said. The tears streamed down my face.

"Because the choice should also be yours," she said softly.

43

The door slid back on its silent track and Illyn entered. It was clear she had been weeping. Eriu held out her arms.

"Do not weep for the Ancient, sweeting. She goes into the West."

Illyn nodded, gulping. "An Scail returned through the portal."

Eriu jumped to her feet. "Why? O Danu, she went to her death."

"For Amergin," Illyn said softly. "She and Airmid . . . They wish to be woken together. In the world of the Galaeci."

At dusk the Danu emerged from their doorways, shimmer after shimmer of blue light. Down to the sea they moved, hundreds of them, devoid of Metaphor, the small bodies and long limbs like so many wide-eyed children on the sea paths.

Airmid was borne on a bier of light, moving through the air with a soft humming sound. At her head and feet and at her sides, the bearers were chanting, the sound like whalesong, asking and answering, calling the name of the Braid again and yet again.

At the shore, the Galaeci were ranged up around the bier of An Scail with its attendant fire. The Danu moved beside them.

When they came among the Galaeci of Inver Skena, the people did not shy away. They simply bowed to the Danu.

"They knew!" whispered Eriu to Banba.

"Maybe it's just that we are so much an improvement over Morrigu," Banba whispered back.

Together they placed the two Ancients side by side facing away over the water.

"By the wish of Airmid," Eriu called, "Illyn, Hybrid of the Braid, is called to the foot of the bier."

Illyn moved into place.

Amergin stepped forward. "At the wish of An Scail, Bile, Hybrid of the Braid, is called to the foot of the bier."

Bile stepped to the foot.

Eriu and Amergin each moved to the head of the bier. Amergin turned his head toward Eriu, but she looked far out over the sea and did not meet his eyes.

Now Banba and Fodla and the Spear Bearers of the Danu moved to each of the platforms. Into the sand, they staked spiraling, twisting, braided poles of light in blue and gold, streaming arcs of electricity around them in winding spirals that looked like strips of sparkling cloth.

In ancient Danaan Eriu chanted, "Comes our beloved to the shore; oh, bear her into the West."

In Gaeilge, Amergin followed suit: "Comes our beloved to the shore; oh, bear her into the West."

The Danu and the Galaeci ranged around the biers, still chanting, Danaan in counterpoint to Gaeilge.

The tall Galaeci in their plaid cloaks flanked the tiny Danu, their iridescent garments blowing and shifting in the sea wind, their collective presence giving off such a nimbus of blue and gold light that the beach seemed to contain its own crescent moon.

From within the bier of Airmid, Eriu lifted a long braided rope of diaphanous fabric. In its depths tiny lights sparked and glittered. Carefully, she placed Airmid's arms together before her and then gently tied one end of the rope around Airmid's wrists in a braided knot. She passed the rope to Banba, who looped it around one of her wrists and turned to Airioch, who wound the braided rope around his own right wrist.

Danu by Milesian, Milesian by Danu, the braided rope made its way among the people, knotting and twisting, weaving itself throughout all of the company.

At last it made its way back to Eriu. She looped it around the wrists of An Scail and wove it into a gentle, braided knot.

She returned to the base of the bier and nodded at Illyn and Bile. Together they reached for the torches that stood at either end of the bier. To-gether they locked them together high above the reclining figures of Airmid and An Scail so that they were overarched by a braid of pulsing, streaming knotwork.

"Lift our sisters into the Braid," called Eriu. "Oh, bear them into the West, Danu, Weaver of Worlds."

As one the people of the Danu and the people of the Galaeci lifted their braided arms. The looped and braided fabric that moved among them began to pulse and spin, to discharge streams of light into the air.

The Danu began to sing and the song was wondrous with joy. It wove itself again and again into the night sky, a canticle of joy, arcing out over the waves and up toward the stars.

Suddenly Banba gave out a cry. "See where they come, the messengers of the Danu!"

From far to the west in the water, lights began to stream toward shore, triangular phalanxes of light in blue and gold that broke above the Danu and the Galaeci and showered down upon them, raining light over the braidwork on the beach.

Now Eriu called aloud in prayer. "Danu, our mother, Weaver of Worlds, we return to you two of your children. The Children of the Braid and the sons of Mil have borne them to you with joy. We thank you for sharing them with us. We will embrace them again in the Braid."

Amergin lifted Ceolas. He began to sing.

"I am the wind on the Water
I am the wave of the Sea
I am the light of the Sun
I am the hawk on the Cliff
I am the fire in the Mind
I am the salmon of Wisdom
I am the hill of the Poem
I am the noise of the Wind
I am the wave of the Sea.
Who sets fire to the Mind?
Who throws light onto the Mountain?
Who sings the ages of the Moon?
Who teaches the pathway of the Sun?

Who carves the pathways on the Sea?
It is I.
It is I."

Silence and darkness fell over the beach.

The people began to disperse, to return to the village for the Feast of Waking. Eriu turned toward Amergin, her eyes full of sorrow.

"I am sorry that An Scail came back through the portal," she said softly. She turned to go.

"This is why she came," he said to her retreating back.

She turned. He had lifted the triangular pendant from beneath his tunic. It glistened against the rough wool of his cloak.

Eriu's eyes grew wide.

"You understand? Why we have kept her from you?"

"I understand. Forgive me, love. Is she beautiful?"

"Beautiful and good and kind. As her mother must have been. As her father is." Eriu held out her hand. "Give me the pendant. You must not come among us. You would never be able to return."

"An Scail said that the choice should be mine."

Eriu shook her head. "You belong to your people."

"Are you not now my people as well? For among you are those I love—Eriu of the Danu; Bile, Hybrid of the Braid; and my child, whom I love sight unseen."

Eriu shook her head. "You must think upon this carefully, for what is done cannot be undone."

She turned and walked into the darkness, Bile and Illyn beside her.

He sat for a long time on the beach, watching the stars throw their gauzy veil across the sky, watching the sky lighten toward dawn.

Airioch appeared suddenly beside him, Colpa by his side.

"Why did you not come to the feast?" Airioch asked. He saw the triangle at Amergin's neck. His eyes widened. "She returned to give you this?"

Amergin nodded.

"You will go among them then?"

Amergin smiled sadly. "Skena's child lives. My child. My little girl. There among the Danu."

Tears welled up in Airioch's eyes. "She lives? And you cannot see her?"

"Do not weep for me, Brother," said Amergin.

"I do not weep for you," Airioch said softly. "As always, I weep for myself. I shall miss you. Remember always, Amergin, that I am a man because of you. Because you remained my brother. Because you knew what to do that I would become a true son of Mil."

"I have not said that I would go."

"Your heart has said so. Your child has said so. You have given your life to the clan. Now go to them. Be joyful."

"What of my duties to the tribe?"

Gently, Airioch lifted Ceolas from Amergin's lap; gently he placed it in Colpa's hands. Colpa strummed the strings softly.

"I invoke the land of Eire," he sang,

"Much traveled the abundant sea."

Amergin laughed aloud. "You know them?"

Colpa nodded. "All of them, Brother. I will sing them just as you wrote them. I will pass them down from bard to bard."

Dawn light was pearling up in the sky.

"Come," said Airioch. "We will walk you to the portal."

In the doorway, Amergin raised his hand to them, his heart thundering in his chest. "I am afraid and I am joyful!" he called.

"Send word with Bile!" Airioch cried. "And tell Banba to come and see me!"

Amergin laughed aloud. "Remember me!" he called.

"Ceolas will remember," said Colpa, lifting the harp into his arms.

With a shaking hand, Amergin pressed his triangle to the depression in the stone. There was a flash of blue light and he felt himself shrink and expand suddenly.

Then he was standing in the archway, exactly where he had been a moment before. Airioch and Colpa were nowhere to be seen.

He stepped from beneath the portal. The forest was the same forest. He ran down the path to the headland. Below him, the hills stretched gently to the sea. No village of Inver Skena scattered itself along the river and down toward the waiting sea. Amergin turned around, confused. He walked back to the portal, walked through it, walked around.

A soft pathway seemed to weave itself away from the portal toward the forest, and he began to follow it. He came through a patch of trees; glistening in the distance was a city of crystal towers and buildings of rich turquoise and coral hue. He began to run.

And then he saw them.

Bile and Illyn were coming over the hill on horseback, their white garments shimmering in the light. Behind them were Banba, Fodla, Eriu; before Eriu on the saddle was a tiny child with curling auburn hair. And behind her, hundreds of the Danu.

They were singing. The Children of the Danu were singing him home.

Amergin ran then. He ran toward his child. He ran toward his beloved. He ran toward the people of the Danu. He ran, at last, toward belonging.

epilogue

CEOLAS REMEMBERS
Among us once was a Poet
Beloved of his people
Bard of the Galaeci
Amergin the Voyager
Who has gone among the Other.
In Harpsong we remember,
Poet of the Braid.

"Tell us again, Skena," said the three boys.

The beautiful woman with the flowing auburn hair laughed aloud. "They are Da's people and they are your people. And when you go among them for the first time, you must say, 'We are the children of Amergin, Poet of the Galaeci, and of Eriu, mother of the land of Eire.'"

"And they will know us?"

The door slid back softly and a tiny woman entered.

"They will know of you, Airioch," Eriu said softly. "All who knew your father in that time are gone now. But those who dwell beyond the portals are their children. And their children's children. They will know of you. They will remember your father in their stories and their songs."

"So some of them are older than Skena?" asked the dark-haired boy called Airioch. He blinked his huge grey eyes at his sister Skena.

"Oh, ancient. Older than I if that is possible," said Skena. She ruffled his hair. "Now listen, you three."

JUILENE OSBORNE-MCKNIGHT

The three boys looked up attentively.

"Airioch, Ith, Colpa."

"No," said Ith. "I am Ith and he is Colpa. You would think that you could tell us apart; you are our sister, after all."

"It's not so easy," said Skena to the three dark-haired boys. "Even for your mother." She pointed at Eriu. "And she gave birth to your triad!"

"Aither could tell us apart," said Colpa.

"Aither could do everything well," said Skena softly. "And besides, you look like Amergin, except that your eyes are Eriu's."

Eriu crossed to the woman; although Skena was almost double her height, Eriu hugged her hard at the waist. "I miss him too," she whispered.

"I know, Little Mother," Skena said softly.

The door slid open again.

"Uncle Bile!"

The tall dark-haired man swung into the room. "Are we ready for our first visit then? Illyn awaits us at the portal. You are seven years of age; you are to be on your best behavior."

"That is what we say? That we are seven?"

"That is how you will look to the villagers of Inver Skena."

"And how do we call ourselves?" asked Airioch. "Do we say that we are the people of the Danu? Or do we say that we are the sons of Mil?"

Eriu blinked. "You are neither. You are both. You go into the land of Eire, the land your father named."

Skena smiled. "You are the Eireann," she said softly. "That is what you say. Wherever you go in the world. Wherever you carry Amergin's songs. Wherever you carry Eriu's magic. You are the people of song and magic. You are the Children of the Braid.

"You are Eireann."

HISTORICAL AND
MYTHOLOGICAL BACKGROUND

The next time you are at the movies, munching on a huge tub of buttery popcorn, consider myths, legends, folklore. Why? Because mythology is popcorn; inside each fluffy, buttery, rich, and multifaceted puff of corn is a hard kernel. You know this; you have bitten down on those hard nuggets, and you know that they do not yield. The puffs are stories, i.e., myth and legend; the kernels are history, i.e., verifiable truth.

An incident in history becomes a myth or a legend because something happened, something awesome, something memorable, something which carried deep significance for those people in that time, deep significance on the journey toward understanding. That incident is captured in story, elaborated and decorated, passed down through generations.

Myth and legend embellish upon history because human beings seem to need patterns—archetypes, if you will. The archetype of the wisdom keepers, the archetype of the hero, the archetype of the villain, the archetype of the journey, the archetype of the grailquest. Story seems to be one of the essential, even necessary, ways for human beings to learn the world and our purpose in it. You might say that we come "hardwired" for story.

This book weaves together a complex myth and an ancient legend over a repeating thread of real history.

The myth of the Tuatha de Danaan, the tribe of the Danu, is, as all myths should be, large and metaphysical, incomprehensible and strange. It is one of the oldest and most pervasive of the Irish myths, so much so that the perception of the "little people" or "An Sidhe"—the Other—of Ireland continues even in our day. What is its kernel? We do not know, but we have numerous clues.

Let us begin, however, in "real" history. The legend of the sons of Mil and their journey to Ireland comes to us from an ancient Irish text, the *Lebhor Gabhala,* the *Book of Invasions.*

Written by the early Christian monks, possibly in the eleventh century, the *Lebhor Gabhala* posits five "races" of creatures—not all human—who inhabited Ireland: the Partholon, the Nemedians, the Fir Bolg, the Fomorians, and the Tuatha de Danaan. By the time of our story, the Partholon and Nemedians had vanished from the Irish landscape and the Tuatha de Danaan had negotiated a peace with the Fir Bolg and banished the Fomor. Sometime around 500 BC, this chain of residence was capped by the arrival of a huge (more than sixty-five ships and forty chieftains, according to the legend) invasion force of ships from Spain bearing the Celts of the sons of Mil (descendants, according to the *Book of Invasions,* of Japheth, the son of Noah of flood fame; this is most likely an attempt by the monks to give Mil and his lineage a Judeo-Christian ancestry). This force landed in Kerry on Beltaine, the first of May, in the Bay of Kenmare, at the place called Inber Scene, named after the drowned wife of Amergin the bard.

However, the *Lebhor Gabhala* is currently the source of major controversy in the archaeological branch of Celtic studies (the other branches being anthropology and mythology, anthropology containing language and culture, mythology containing folklore, legends, myths, stories, and songs). So in those fields of study, how can we "know" exactly what happened in or around 500 BC in a culture that kept no written records? Evidence. Thus, archaeology. Currently, the archaeological evidence does not fit the legend. At least not precisely.

Archaeology deals with artifacts, the sifted detritus of a past culture. And nowhere in Ireland can anyone find evidence of a massive invasion from Spain. There is, however, evidence of a rather advanced culture moving into Ireland at this time and taking up residence next to an already existing group. At the Hill of Tara, the seat of Ireland's high kings, archaeologists have found Roman artifacts such as wine goblets, lead seals, and glass vessels. This would indicate a well-traveled trading culture.

Anthropologically speaking, there is no question that the Celtic language and culture came to dominate Ireland. Linguists tell us that a language can come to dominate only if large groups of people predominate in a certain area over a long period of time.

While archaeologists are the "crime scene investigators" of historical study, folklorists and mythologists work from a basic premise: that inside each story is a core element of the "real"—real people, real events, real history.

For the storyteller, finding that "core" in the Milesian "invasion" becomes one of degree. All stories are embellished. Scale back the embellishment; remove the embroidery. What if the original "invasion" force was basically a single clan and its circle? Their language and culture would come to dominate as the clan grew, if the clan was sophisticated, if the news of the new location filtered throughout the Celtic world. Successive waves of immigrants would further increase that cultural dominance.

So who were these Milesians of legend? Well, we know that Goidelic-speaking Celts began to migrate and settle across the Iberian Peninsula of Spain during the Bronze Age. (Goidelic is the form of Gaelic which includes the Irish, Scots, and Manx languages.) By the seventh century BC, Greek mariners had established numerous trading harbors with these Celtiberians, and these Spanish Celts also traded with Phoenicians and Etruscans. There was, for example, a thriving silver trade among the Greeks and the Celtic tribes of a king named Arganthonios and his tribe of silver miners near the Tartessus River in southern Iberia.

Near the Douro River in Spain, Celts of the Arevaci tribe built the city of Numantia, which covered twenty hectares and boasted houses of stone, huge multistory stone *brochs* or towers, and a planned city street system. Evidently the prosperity of these people arose from their mining of copper, tin, gold, and silver and their production and trade of fine jewelry and weaponry throughout the civilized world.

Nowhere was the Celtic influence more predominant than in the northwest corner of Spain. According to Galician travel guides, the first city founded by the Celts in this region was Saefes in the tenth century BC. In the region that is today called Galicia, an ancient Celt named Breogan or Breogam built a lighthouse tower by the sea and founded the ancient Celtic city of Brigantia. The weather and topography of Galicia are much like those of Ireland, and even today that region of the world retains its Celtic identity.

These Celts spread their culture throughout the region, building *castroes* or circular stone hill fortifications with multiple ditches (similar *raths* or ring-forts were built for hundreds of years afterward in Ireland). Likewise dolmens, two upright stones with a slanted capstone, or lintel, are similar in both Spain and Ireland. The Galaeci worshipped creation in forest cathedrals with their druids; had a fluid but general concept of numerous tripartite gods throughout the Celtic world; understood the idea of an eternal soul; cremated their dead; played a special bagpipe called the *gaita* (listen to Carlos Nunez—his music is so eerie and beautiful that it will raise the hairs on your arms); rode domesticated horses; herded cattle; made rye bread; and were generally known for their unique combination of delicate artistry and advanced warrior skills (as were all the Celts on the European continent). In fact, the Celtiberians were so renowned for their warrior skills that they served as mercenaries in the Carthaginian army and as cavalry in the Roman army.

Eventually their settlements were abandoned around 400 BC. This may have been because of war, or it may have been because of a plague that traveled through Greece in 430 BC. Even if the plague had not reached Galicia, it would surely have curtailed or ruined the trade lanes. Perhaps more Galicians traveled to Ireland on the heels of these catastrophes; we do not know.

In Irish history, the most famous son of the Spanish Celts was Milesius or Mil (whose original Celtic name was Golamh). According to the legends, he served as a mercenary chieftain for the king of Scythia and married his daughter. One theory says that the Milesians were originally Scythians, whose tribes stretched from the Carpathian Mountains to the Don River. The Scythians were known as stunning horsemen and nomadic wagon travelers. Scythians and Celts may indeed be ancestrally related.

Later, Milesius served the pharaoh of Egypt (who at this time was actually Cambysis of Persia, this worthy having overthrown the last native Egyptian pharaoh, Psamtek III); married the pharaoh's daughter Scota; and by his two wives fathered numerous sons, some versions of the legend saying seven, some nine.

This period in history was a sophisticated one in the countries surrounding the Mediterranean Sea (the Romans' Internum Mare, later Mare Nostrum, "Our Sea"). The democratic Greek city-states were well known for their learning, advanced philosophies, and high culture, for their ships and trade, complex architecture, beautiful physical adornment, and sexual sophistication (or decadence, depending upon the period and your particular cultural viewpoint).

Nearby Rome had declared itself a republic in 509 BC and continued to practice that form of government until 44 BC, when the age of emperors (and Rome's eventual decline) began.

The clan of Mil, then, would have been very sophisticated indeed, well traveled, probably fairly fluent in four or five languages, accustomed to sophisticated thought and government patterns, and certainly familiar with advanced fashion and architecture—full dwellers in the highly civilized Aegean culture of the time.

Why then did the Milesians decide to return to wild Galicia? Did Mil tire of war? Did he run into trouble in Egypt? And when they had returned to Spain, why journey from there to even more remote and less civilized Ireland, at that time an unnamed dot in the Atlantic Ocean? There, of course, lies mystery, for we can know the food and clothing and vessels of the ancients, we can know their wars and migrations, but their "quest" motivations, the reasoning of their hearts and minds, was known only to them and is lost to us forever. There, of course, is the doorway for the storyteller.

Practically speaking, although the Celtiberians themselves possessed boats, both coracles (round wickerwork vessels covered with hide and often navigated with a pole) and curraghs (longer and wider fishing vessels), it is unlikely that they would have used either of these vessels to travel the open sea to Ireland, or even to hug the coasts. We are told that the Veneti of western France were actually Celtic sailors who manned very large boats, but the Galicians did not. Such boats as theirs were not equipped for sea travel and would have had to hug the coastline and try to cross the channel with the weather. Too, their little vessels could never have carried the Galaeci horses, which were precious. It is much more likely that the sons of Mil would have used the services of people who regularly plied the sea and knew its vagaries, hence the Greeks.

It is when the Milesians reached Ireland that legend begins to intersect with myth. For there, in Ireland, the Milesians would first encounter the Tuatha de Danaan, the Children of Danu, whose mythical leaders would become the adopted gods of the early Irish Celts and whose tribe would dwell with the Irish, even unto this day, as their "little people" or "other people."

Who were they?

All cultures have myths of the little people. For the Welsh they were the Fair Folk; to my Seneca Indian friends, the *jo-ge-oh;* to the Ojibwe friends of my childhood, the *manitou;* to the Hawaiians, the *menahune.* In most cultures these little people share some traits. Sometimes they function as "tricksters," causing travelers to become lost, stealing items or even babies, rearranging households. Oftentimes, they are agents of great good, repaying kindness with good luck, by doing household chores, or even by bestowing wealth. In many of the myths, time does not pass normally among these others; Americans will recognize that concept in the Rip Van Winkle tale of little men who dwell in the Catskill Mountains of New York.

This timeshift is, in fact, one of the most difficult aspects in the myths of the Irish little people, the De Danaan, because we are told that some humans could pass back and forth between the real world and the "time-stretched" world of the Danaans and return unscathed, while others would return to real time only to age suddenly, turning from youth to old age in a matter of moments. How to solve or explain this timeshift in the myth and its uneven application to travelers in that realm?

How also to explain that the ancient myths abound with stories of "fairy children," humans who are stolen from their own families to be raised among the little people, sometimes replaced in their cradles by fairy babies or "changelings"? Why would the little people do such a thing, and what purpose would it serve?

It is important to realize that "little people" need not literally mean little. "Other" people can range in size from the diminutive through human size to giants. We are probably more accurate to call them "other" as opposed to "little" because whatever their size or appearance, they are other than human. Very few cultures exist that do not have some sense of the presence—and interference—of the "other." At the most basic psychological level, such stories indicate the deep-seated human need for the "other," the wish to not be alone in the world. Such a need might serve to explain the bug-eyed alien abduction stories that abound in modern times.

Or are they just stories?

The myth of the Irish Danu is a complex and multifaceted story. They came to Ireland: (1) perhaps from Greece, (2) perhaps from a city beneath the sea, (3) on cloud ships that simply appeared over Ireland, much to the consternation of the hunter-gatherer people who dwelled there.

One permutation of the myth indicates that they were an ancient race who settled at various places around the world, serving as architects and designers, inspiring or assisting with the construction of pyramids and sarsen circles, palaces and temples, and serving as wisdom-keeper figures in various religious myths. One group (our own for the purposes of this story) first settled on an island off the coast of Greece, but when that island sank into the sea, these people migrated to Ireland. Historically, a volcanic eruption and earthquake of massive proportions did occur around 1500 BC in the Mediterranean Sea in the vicinity of Thrace and the island of Santorini, taking a large portion of the latter to the bottom of the sea. This may be the Atlantis of legend. In mythological time, it caused the Danu to flee north.

We do know that the pyramids of Egypt and Stonehenge are actually contemporaneous, both being under construction around 3000 BC. This is actually one of the interesting sources of controversy in the current debates. For many years, scholars claimed that the stone circles of Ireland and the British Isles could not have been erected by the Celts, who came to those areas later. Previous scholars had claimed that they were Celtic structures serving druidic religious and calendrical purposes. Current scholarly argument goes back and forth between claims for the people who dwelled in those areas prior to Celtic arrival and the Celts themselves, the idea being that their arrival was not much later after all.

Then who did erect them? It was great fun to speculate on an entirely new set of architects for all ancient structures, though such speculation falls, of course, into the realm of fantasy.

The obvious complexity of such structures has also led both scholars and mythologists to contemplate their possible metaphysical significance. Certainly such structures do possess a sense of transition, of cathedral, of gathered awe. We may never know their specific original purposes.

However, the Danaans themselves were deeply metaphysical according to the mythology. They considered themselves Children of Danu, a mother goddess who presided over all of the creative forces of life— childbirth, fire, poetry, spring lambs, song, women, language. Danu had a tripartite aspect: she is referred to in the myths as Brid/Anu/Dana and is beautiful, loving, protective of her children. So powerful and enduring a figure is she that in later times in Ireland she was permuted into Brigid and then in Christian times into Saint Brigid, known in Ireland as the Mary of the Gaels and reputed to have been the midwife at the birth of Christ.

Evidently the Milesians of Spain arrived in Ireland without knowledge of her and later adopted her as their primary female deity. They also adopted as deities characters in the Danaan pantheon who were chieftains or skilled warriors: Dagda, a provider who became known as the "good god"; Ogma, an orator who became known as the "honey-mouthed god"; Lugh, the all-craftsman who came to be known as the son of the Sun; and so on.

Perhaps it was the attributes of these De Danaan that caused the Milesians to elevate them to godly status, for the Danu themselves seemed to hold their mother creator in her three aspects as the only god of the universe.

However, like human beings, the Danu were not immune to either evil or bad behavior. According to the myths, Dian Cecht the physician did have his son executed for re-creating the arm of Nuada, though some of the versions say that it was jealousy that caused his anger, that he killed his son with four blows to the head and subsequently destroyed his daughter's pharmaceutical gardens.

More terrifying than bad "human" behavior is the presence among the Danu of a tripartite goddess called Morrigu. Her three aspects—Macha, Banbh, and Nemhain—live for the purposes of bringing hatred and war, death and carnage, panic and chaos into the world. Morrigu is pervasive and long-lived in Irish mythology, a shape-shifter who appears variously as a wolf, a raven, a fog, a heifer, an eel, an old hag, and a beautiful woman. She shows up in the first myths, is still wreaking havoc in the Cuchulainn legends in the first century AD, and is still sowing chaos in the Fionn legends of the third century AD. So powerful is Morrigu that by the time of the Arthurian legends she has conflated into a single person—Morgan le Fay, the dark sorceress who is responsible for the downfall of Camelot.

Other than Morrigu, however, the Danu are reputed to have been quite beautiful. In physical appearance, they are described as being slender and tall, with golden or strawberry hair and compelling eyes. They are almost always surrounded by a nimbus of eerie blue or white light. They never grow old or sick, and although they can die, it is usually through warfare or attack, not sickness, and not until extreme old age.

They dwell in huge cities below the ground and the sea, and their culture is reputed to be highly sophisticated. Moreover, the ancient story of Nuada indicates that these were people who not only knew how to create sophisticated and terrifying weapons, but had also mastered the art of limb regeneration, indicating at least a mastery of the processes of cell regeneration, DNA, etc.

The legends tell us of three battles on the Plain of Mag Tuiread. The exact location of these battles is unclear, and several places in Ireland lay claim to the distinction. Some say that Cong in county Mayo is the proper location; it is a place riddled with dolmens, sarsen stones, and circles. Others claim that the battles took place in Sligo. Whatever the location, the Danu seemed to find it the only "safe" place for their battles, as they were not a warlike race, but rather a race who relied on subterfuge and illusion as the strongest weapons in their arsenal. There are, of course, hundreds of dolmens, passage graves, sarsen circles, and standing stones throughout Ireland. The pre-Christian people of Ireland believed that these were entrances to the otherworld, the country of the Danu. What would cause such a legend to arise? Even today in Ireland, numerous of these locations are reputed to be haunted; there are reports of fires and strange lights on the hillsides.

The legends also speak widely of the fact that these people were often led by tripartite sister and brother groups. Mac Cuill, Mac Cecht, and Mac Grene as well as Banba, Fodla, and Eriu are specifically named in the tales. Ireland is named, of course, for Eriu.

Eventually in Ireland, these "others" became an accepted presence, from the banshee (from *bain sidhe* or "woman of the other") who attaches herself to human families and sings the impending death of a family member, to the widespread idea that eventually there were generations of intermarriage between the Irish and the Danu, creating a race of people who could travel in and out of their world and our world and who possessed, at the very least, some special psychic or healing abilities.

Certainly the Danu's truce with, care for, and adoption of the Fir Bolg has some historical status; the people of Connacht claimed to trace their history to the Fir Bolg all the way up until the eighteenth century. Too, the story of years without summer is also historically accurate. Beginning around 1159 BC there was no summer growth of trees for a period of eighteen years; a long cold nuclear winter may have been caused by a volcanic eruption in Iceland, or by comet debris. Modern movies which posit such a catastrophe do not seem to be far off the mark. People and animals starved; crops would not grow. In mythological time, this is when the Danu began rescuing and rebraiding the Hybrid Fir Bolg children of our story.

Of course, the Tuatha de Danaan, the tribe of the Danu, dwell in Ireland still.

The Milesians were, in all likelihood, a real and historical clan; much specific detail accrues to their travels. We also have three poems that are purportedly by Amergin, generally called the "Invocation," the "Song," and the "Challenge." The "Song" and the "Challenge" contain many similar lines, so the two may actually be one poem that has been separated for content or theme. The "Invocation" is a celebration of Ireland. There are literally dozens of translations of these three poems. However, all three poems meditate on the interconnectedness of all life, on joy and sorrow. All three are written in a first-person voice in broken lines characteristic of ancient verse. Are they really Amergin's words? Conventional wisdom would have it that they were written down by monks sometime after the eighth century, largely because the Celtic world did not permit writing. However, the Milesians were members of Aegean civilization, which highly valued written records and kept vast libraries of history and literature. Perhaps Amergin himself wrote the poems; perhaps not. If they are Amergin's poems, they indicate a large soul, a man aware of the Braid that binds the universe. I would like to have known him.

Can we also believe in the Danu—the Tuatha de Danaan—as a "real" people? Some say impossible; others hope that they did—or do—indeed exist. And you? More things under heaven and earth, friends.

As for me, I have loved my time with all of them, braided as I have been into the fictional complexities of both worlds. I hope that this story affords you the same journey.

Bail O Dhia ar an obair
Bless, O God, the work

Juilene Osborne-McKnight